The Story of King Arthur

TOM CRAWFORD

Illustrated by John Green

DOVER PUBLICATIONS, INC.
New York

DOVER CHILDREN'S THRIFT CLASSICS

EDITOR OF THIS VOLUME: THOMAS CROFTS

For James and Jennifer

Published in Canada by General Publishing Company, Ltd., 30 Lesmill Road, Don Mills, Toronto, Ontario.

Bibliographical Note

The Story of King Arthur is a new work, first published by Dover Publications, Inc., in 1994.

Library of Congress Cataloging-in-Publication Data

Crawford, Tom, 1941–
    The story of King Arthur / Tom Crawford ; illustrated by John Green.
        p.   cm.—(Dover children's thrift classics)
    Summary: Recounts Arthur's chief adventures including his becoming King, his marriage to Guenevere, and his benevolent but troubled reign over England.
    ISBN 0-486-28347-X (pbk.)
    1. Arthurian romances—Adaptations. [1. Arthur, King.   2. Knights and knighthood—Folklore.   3. Folklore—England.]   I. Green, John, 1948–   ill.   II. Title.   III. Series.
PZ8.1.C863St   1994
398.2—dc20   94-3363
                                                                                    CIP
                                                                                    AC

Manufactured in the United States of America
Dover Publications, Inc., 31 East 2nd Street, Mineola, N.Y. 11501

Note

Tales of the legendary British monarch Arthur and his companions Merlin, Lancelot, Gawaine and others, come to us through poems, novels and ancient (often doubtful) historical accounts. Historians do speculate that a king of some military distinction, whose name was Arthur, was active in Wales in about the 6th century, but the threads of historical fact are impossible to separate totally from the great tapestry of legend and poetry in which most of these marvelous tales exist.

In this book, which is based upon Sir Thomas Malory's famous *Morte D'Arthur* (written in 1469), Arthur's chief adventures are recounted, including his becoming King, acquiring the magic sword Excalibur, his marriage to Guenevere and his benevolent but troubled reign over England. Recounted also are many of the exploits of Arthur's greatest knight, Sir Lancelot.

Contents

List of Illustrations

I
The Sword in the Stone

IT WAS a clear, cold December day, perhaps a thousand years ago or more, as Sir Ector and his two sons, Sir Kay and Arthur, made their way to London. The kingdom was in terrible turmoil, for King Uther Pendragon had died and a new king had not yet been chosen. Indeed, the knights and barons of the realm were fighting bitterly among themselves over who should have that honor. Finally, the Archbishop of Canterbury summoned all the knights and lords to London at Christmas in hopes that some sign would be given as to who should be king. It was for that reason that Sir Ector and his two sons were on their way to the great city.

Before long, the walls and towers of London appeared in the distance and the little party passed through one of the city's great gates. Within a short time, all the lords, including Sir Ector, gathered in one of the great churches of London to attend services

1

and pray for guidance in choosing a new monarch. As they left the church that morning, the nobles noticed a great square stone in the churchyard. It had not been there before. And protruding from the middle of the stone was a splendid sword, its jeweled hilt gleaming in the sun. Surrounding the sword were these words written in gold: "Whoever pulls this sword from the stone is the true king of all England." The knights gasped in wonder. What could it mean?

In no time, several men had tried to pull the sword out of the stone, but no one could budge it. "He is not yet here who can move the sword," said the Archbishop, "but surely he will soon come." With that, it was decided to hold a great tournament on New Year's Day. There would be jousting and feasting, games and much merriment, and at that time, anyone who wished could try to pull the sword from the stone.

Time passed quickly and before long, the day of the tournament had arrived. As Sir Ector, Sir Kay and Arthur rode toward the tournament grounds, Sir Kay realized he had forgotten his sword. He asked Arthur to go back and get it. But when Arthur returned to their lodgings, there was no one about, and he was unable to find Kay's sword. On his way back to the tournament, Arthur remembered the sword in the stone. Determined that Sir Kay should have a sword that day, Arthur quickly rode to the churchyard. He swung down from his horse and walked over to the stone. Quickly and easily he pulled the sword from its place. Then he remounted and rode to the tournament. There he gave Sir Kay the sword.

As soon as Kay and his father saw the sword, they knew it was the one from the stone. "How did you get this sword?" Sir Ector asked Arthur. Arthur explained how he had been unable to find Sir Kay's sword and had taken the one from the stone instead. Sir Ector bowed his head. "Now I realize that you are the true king," he said to Arthur. Arthur's mouth fell open in surprise. "But father," he said, "surely there is some mistake. How can I be king?"

Then Sir Ector explained everything, how Arthur was actually of royal blood, the son of King Uther who had died several years before. The wise old magician, Merlin, in exchange for arranging the wedding of King Uther and Arthur's mother, had demanded that King Uther give him their first-born child. When Arthur was born, the King gave him to Merlin according to the agreement. In turn, Merlin had turned the baby over to Sir Ector, commanding him to raise the child as if it were his own.

Arthur, of course, was greatly saddened to learn that Sir Ector was not his real father. He rode along in silence as they went to the Archbishop to tell him what had occurred. After his initial surprise, the Archbishop decided that the sword must be put back in the stone and Arthur be allowed to show what he had done in front of all the assembled lords. Soon the nobles were once again gathered in the churchyard. The sword was replaced in the stone. One by one the lords stepped up and tried to extract the gleaming weapon from its place. One by one they failed. No one could move it even an inch. Then it was Arthur's turn. The lords whispered among themselves as the boy stepped forward. "How could a youngster like that withdraw the sword when the strongest men in the kingdom have failed?" they asked. Then everyone grew quiet as Arthur stepped up to the stone. He grasped the sword and, with one quick pull, withdrew it easily from the stone. The lords shook their heads in astonishment. Then they became angry. They said it wasn't right for the kingdom to be ruled by a boy who was not of noble blood.

He grasped the sword and, with one quick pull,
withdrew it easily from the stone.

But, as Merlin now explained to them, Arthur *was* of noble blood, and the common people who were there said it was God's will and they would accept no one but Arthur as their king. After much argument and debate, the nobles gave in, and in due time, Arthur was crowned king of all England. Even after he had become King, however, some of the lords challenged Arthur and tried to overthrow him, but the King was fast becoming a great warrior and with skill and determination he put down the revolts that threatened his realm.

II
The Round Table

ONE DAY while out hunting in the forest with Merlin, King Arthur came upon a fierce knight who insisted on jousting with every knight who came his way. Sure enough, the knight challenged King Arthur to do battle, not knowing he was the King. Arthur agreed and the two men fought a fierce battle. In the course of the fight, Arthur's sword broke in two. Seeing his opponent had no weapon, the knight prepared to strike off King Arthur's head. Before he could do so, Merlin quickly cast a spell on the knight, causing him to fall deeply asleep. Arthur scolded Merlin for killing the knight, but Merlin assured him the fallen knight was only asleep and would soon awaken. "You are wounded, though," he told Arthur. "There is a hermit's hut nearby. He will heal your wounds."

After a few days in the hermit's care, the King felt well again. It was time to leave. As the King and Merlin rode along, the King realized he had no sword. It had been broken in the fight with the knight. Merlin said, "Follow me and you shall have a sword." Before long, they came to a beautiful lake deep in the forest. In the middle of the lake, an arm, clad all in white, held a sword aloft above the water. King Arthur stared in amazement. He had never seen anything like it before.

At the water's edge stood a beautiful young woman. "Who is that?" asked Arthur. "That is the Lady of the Lake," replied Merlin. "Go and speak kindly with her. Perhaps she will give you the sword." Arthur did as Merlin suggested and told the Lady of the Lake that his sword had been destroyed in battle and he was greatly in need of a new one. "The sword in the lake is mine but you may have it if you promise to give me a gift when I ask for it," said the Lady. "It is a strange request," said King Arthur, "but I will do as you wish." "Then take the boat you see yonder and row out to the sword. It is yours," said the Lady of the Lake. King Arthur quickly made his way across the water to the sword. It was soon in his hands—Excalibur, the finest sword he had ever seen. Its blade shone brighter than a hundred suns and it seemed to Arthur that this sword had been made just for him. As they rode off, Merlin told him to be sure and always keep the scabbard of the sword with him, for as long as he possessed it, he would never shed his blood in battle.

Several years passed. King Arthur was now a strong and handsome young man. His kingdom was at peace. He began to think about getting married, especially since the knights of the realm had been urging him to find himself a wife. "Every kingdom should have a queen," they said. King Arthur decided to talk to Merlin about it. "My barons want me to get married," Arthur told Merlin, "but I wanted to ask your advice first." "I agree with the knights," said Merlin, "a man of your rank and power should have a wife. Now is there any woman you especially love?"

"Yes," said King Arthur, "I love Guenevere, the daughter of King Leodegrance of Cameliard. He is the king who possesses the Round Table you told me he got from my father, King Uther."

"She is certainly one of the most beautiful women in the world," said Merlin, "and I can see you will have no other but her."

"It is true," replied King Arthur.

"Then I will go and see King Leodegrance and tell him of your wishes," said Merlin.

When Merlin told King Leodegrance that

King Arthur wanted to wed his daughter, King Leodegrance was overjoyed. "That is wonderful news—that a king so renowned for strength and nobility wishes to marry Guenevere. As a wedding present, I would give him land, but he already has enough land. Instead, I will give him something he will like even more—the Round Table that King Uther Pendragon gave me. Not only that," continued the King, "I will give him a hundred knights to go with it. The table is big enough to seat a hundred and fifty, but I have lost many knights in battle lately."

And so it happened that Guenevere, Merlin and the hundred knights set out for London, transporting the Round Table with them. When at last they arrived at King Arthur's court, the King was overjoyed. "I have loved this beautiful lady for a long time," he said, smiling at Guenevere, "and I am very glad she is to become my wife. What's more, I would rather have this Round Table and these noble knights as a wedding present than anything else I can think of."

With that, the King gave orders to plan the royal wedding and coronation. Then he said to Merlin, "Go and find me fifty of the finest, most noble knights in the kingdom to fill the rest of the seats at the Round Table." Within a short time, Merlin had returned with twenty-eight knights but could find no more. Then the Archbishop of Canterbury was sent for and he blessed each seat at the Round Table. After the blessing, Merlin told the assembled knights that they must arise and do homage to King Arthur, that is, they must pay the King their respects and assure him of their loyalty and devotion. After paying homage, the knights departed. And at each seat, the name of the knight was written in gold.

Shortly after, the King married Guenevere in a solemn ceremony at Saint Stephen's Church in Camelot. The wedding was followed by much feasting and merriment. Then the King called all his knights together. It was time to take their vows of allegiance to the Round Table. Glancing around the table at the assembled knights, the King told them quietly but firmly what he expected of them: that they were never to be guilty of murder or treason; that they must always grant mercy to those who asked for it; that they must always help ladies in need; and that they must stay out of quarrels and fights over goods and property. When the King had finished, a hush fell over the table. Then all the knights arose: "We swear," said the knights solemnly, "to abide by and uphold the rules and ideals of the Round Table."

It was not long after this that Merlin fell in

love with Nimue, one of the beautiful young
Ladies of the Lake. He followed her around
like a puppy dog and seldom let her out of his
sight. For her part, Nimue put up with him
while she learned many secrets from the old
magician. One day, Merlin told King Arthur
that, in spite of all his magic powers, he, Merlin, would not live much longer. He then predicted many things that would happen in the
future. He especially warned King Arthur to
keep his sword, Excalibur, and its scabbard
always with him, for if he did not, Excalibur
would be stolen by a woman he trusted
completely.

"But, Merlin," said King Arthur, who was
greatly saddened by the prospect of the old
man's death, "if you know in advance how
you will die, why don't you use your magic
powers to escape?"

"No," said Merlin, "it cannot be." And with
that he departed.

After leaving King Arthur, Merlin rejoined
Nimue and the two of them traveled over the
sea to the land of Benwick. At the time, the
King of Benwick was fighting a fierce war
against King Claudas. At the court, Merlin
spoke to the King's wife, a good woman
named Elaine, and saw her young son, a boy
named Lancelot. Elaine told Merlin how much

she was worried about the war King Claudas was waging against her husband and the kingdom.

"Don't be afraid," Merlin told her, pointing to Lancelot, "for the time will come when this boy will defeat King Claudas, and the whole world will know him as the greatest knight of all."

"O Merlin," said the Queen, "shall I live to see my son become such a great knight?"

"Indeed you will, my lady, and for many years afterward," replied Merlin.

A short time later, Merlin and Nimue left the castle and resumed their journey, arriving after a while in Cornwall. By now, Nimue was heartily sick of the old man and wanted to be rid of him, but she was afraid of his magical powers. Then one day Merlin showed her a great rock, under which he said there was a marvelous sight, placed there by magic. "You go under and tell me what is there," said Nimue. Merlin agreed and managed to wriggle under the rock. As soon as he was out of sight, Nimue cast an enchanted spell over the rock and, in spite of all his magic, Merlin was unable to escape. That was the end of the old sorcerer, just as he had foretold.

III
Morgan le Fay

BACK AT court, King Arthur was preparing for a hunting expedition with King Uriens and Sir Accolon of Gaul. When all was ready, the three men rode deep into the forest. Spotting a great red stag ahead of them in the woods, they quickly gave chase. Mile after mile they pursued the magnificent deer until their horses could go no further. The poor animals were nearly dead with exhaustion. "What will we do now?" asked King Arthur. "Let's continue on foot," replied King Uriens, "until we find someplace to refresh ourselves." So they walked on through the forest for many hours, until, finally, they came to a strange body of water. There, to their astonishment, they saw a little ship, all draped in silk, floating near the shore. King Arthur beckoned his companions. "Come, let us see what's inside," he said.

So all three boarded the mysterious vessel to have a look around. By this time it was get-

ting dark. They had no sooner entered the little ship, than a hundred torches suddenly
blazed up, lighting the walls, which were also
richly hung with silk. King Arthur, Sir Accolon
and King Uriens stood there speechless with
wonder as twelve beautiful young maidens
appeared as if from nowhere and made them
welcome.

Then the maidens led them into a dining
room where they were served the most delicious meats and wines. They ate until they
couldn't eat another mouthful. King Arthur
could not remember when he had enjoyed
such a wonderful meal. When dinner was
over, the maidens took each man to his own
bedroom. The rooms were furnished with the
most beautiful furniture and luxurious rugs
and draperies. In no time, the three exhausted
men fell fast asleep.

The next morning, to his great surprise,
King Uriens found himself back in Camelot,
with his wife, King Arthur's sister, Morgan le
Fay. He had no idea how he had gotten there.
King Arthur, on the other hand, awoke to find
himself in a dark prison. All around him,
knights were moaning and complaining. "Why
are you so unhappy?" asked King Arthur. The
knights explained that they had been imprisoned by an evil knight, Sir Damas, the owner

of the castle. This Sir Damas had a younger brother, Sir Ontzlake, who was rightfully entitled to a share of the castle and its lands, but Sir Damas would not share. Sir Ontzlake had offered to fight his brother for his rightful share, but Sir Damas was a coward and afraid he would lose the battle. Instead he tried to get other knights to fight for him. But knowing Sir Damas to be evil and false, no knight would agree to it.

When Sir Damas realized none of his own knights would fight for him, he decided to capture knights traveling near the castle and imprison them until he found one who would. But even though Sir Damas promised to free the other knights if one would agree to fight Sir Ontzlake, the knights still refused. They preferred to die in prison than to do battle for such a false and treacherous man as Sir Damas.

As King Arthur pondered this unhappy situation, a young woman suddenly appeared out of nowhere. "Sir," she said, "if you will fight for Sir Damas, you will be set free; if not, you will never escape!"

"That is a hard choice," replied King Arthur, "but I will fight on one condition: that if I do, all these prisoners will be set free."

"It shall be as you wish," said the young lady, preparing to leave. "But wait," cried King

Arthur, jumping to his feet, "I have no horse and no armor!"

"You shall have whatever you need," she replied, mysteriously.

The more he looked at the young woman, the more King Arthur thought he had seen her somewhere before. "Have you ever been at the court of King Arthur?" he asked. "No, I was never there," she responded. "I am the daughter of the lord of this castle." But that was not so, for in truth, she was one of the ladies who waited on Morgan le Fay.

After leaving the prison, she went straight to Sir Damas and told him that Arthur had agreed to fight for him. "Wonderful," replied Sir Damas, "have him brought here immediately." When Arthur came, he and Sir Damas agreed that Arthur should do battle for him and that the other knights were to be released. "Set the knights free," said Sir Damas to a servant, "so they can watch this noble knight take up arms against Sir Ontzlake."

In the meantime, Sir Accolon of Gaul had awakened from his sleep aboard the ship to find himself in a strange place, dangerously close to the edge of a well. "God help me!" he exclaimed, "those women on the ship were not women, they were devils!"

As Accolon thought angrily about how he,

King Arthur and King Uriens had been tricked, a dwarf suddenly appeared at his side. The dwarf brought greetings from Morgan le Fay and told Sir Accolon that she wished him to fight a certain knight early next morning. And to help him in the fight, she had sent King Arthur's sword, Excalibur, and its scabbard. "Return to Morgan le Fay and tell her I will do as she asks or die trying," Accolon told the dwarf. "I assume she will use her sorcery to help me win this battle." "You may count on it," said the dwarf, and vanished as suddenly as he had come. A few moments later, a knight and a lady, with six squires, appeared and whisked Accolon off to a manor to rest and enjoy himself.

Back at his castle, Sir Damas was in a fine mood. He sent for his brother, Sir Ontzlake, and told him that he had found a knight to fight with him the next morning. Unfortunately, Sir Ontzlake was in no condition to fight; his legs had been wounded in a jousting competition and he could not possibly do battle. Deeply disappointed, he returned to his room. To his great surprise, he found Sir Accolon there. Morgan le Fay had been working her magic again. Accolon told him that he knew Sir Ontzlake was wounded and offered to fight in his place. Sir Ontzlake could not believe his good fortune. He accepted Accolon's offer immediately and told him that if the opportunity ever arose, he would do the same for him. With that, Sir Ontzlake sent word to Sir Damas that he had a knight who would fight for him the following day.

Bright and early the next morning, King Arthur put on his armor and mounted his horse. As he prepared to make his way to the jousting field, a young woman suddenly appeared in the courtyard. "I come from Morgan le Fay," said the woman; "she asked me to bring you your sword, Excalibur." Arthur was a little surprised at this, but he took the sword, thanked her for her trouble and rode off. Little did he know that the treacherous Morgan le Fay had deceived him a second time.

When King Arthur arrived at the battlefield, the other knight was already there. When all was ready, each man rode to the opposite end of the field. A shrill trumpet blast sounded and the two knights charged toward each other, their spears lowered. Crash! King Arthur and Accolon hit each other in the shields with their spears so hard that both men were knocked from their horses. Still dizzy from the force of the blows, they slowly staggered to their feet and drew their swords.

King Arthur and Accolon hit each other so
hard that both men fell from their horses.

Again they charged toward each other, thrusting and slashing with all their might. As they fought, a beautiful woman appeared along the sidelines. It was Nimue, the Lady of the Lake, who had put Merlin under the stone. She knew that Morgan le Fay had arranged it so that Arthur would be killed that day and she had come to save him if she could.

Meanwhile, Arthur and Accolon were fighting like furies, dealing each other mighty blows, each trying to gain the upper hand. But something was terribly wrong! It seemed to Arthur that his sword was dull and heavy. Even when he hit Accolon as hard as he could, it had little effect. Accolon's sword, on the other hand, was having a great deal of effect. Dancing in Accolon's hand, its gleaming razor-sharp blade blinded Arthur with its bright light and before he knew it, Arthur had been wounded many times.

A feeling of dread came over the King. The ground was sprinkled everywhere with his blood. If the fight continued this way, he was sure to die. Still, he fought back as hard as he could. He was a brave and strong man and he would not give up. Gathering all the strength he had left, he struck Accolon a mighty blow on the helmet. Accolon staggered backward, struggling to keep his feet. But his heart leapt with joy at what he saw then: Arthur's sword had split in two from the force of the blow. The blade dropped useless into the grass.

"Knight," cried Accolon, "you are at my mercy. You have no weapon and you have lost much blood. You must surrender to me or die!"

"Never," replied King Arthur coldly and calmly. "I have sworn on my honor to fight to the death. And even though I have no weapon, I would rather die a hundred deaths with honor than surrender in shame."

"Very well," said Accolon, advancing with his sword upraised, "if that is what you wish, then prepare to die right now!" But the Lady of the Lake could not bear to see Arthur killed, for she loved the noble king. So, just as Accolon was about to strike off King Arthur's head, she cast a spell on him, causing him to drop his sword. Quick as a cat, Arthur leaped on it. "Knight," he cried, "you have cost me much pain and blood with this sword. Now you must die by it." With that he rushed upon Accolon and felled him with one mighty blow. Pulling off Accolon's helmet, Arthur made ready to cut off his head. "Kill me if you wish," said the fallen knight, "for you are the finest warrior I have ever fought. But I, too, promised to battle to the death. I can never surrender!"

As he gazed at the man, Arthur thought he recognized his face. "Who are you and where are you from?" he asked. "I am of King Arthur's court and my name is Accolon of Gaul," the knight replied. Arthur shook his head in amazement, beginning to connect his sister Morgan le Fay with the enchanted ship. "O knight," he said, "I beg of you to tell me where you got this sword and from whom."

"I am deeply ashamed that I used this sword, for I think it will mean my death," said Accolon softly. "It was sent to me by Morgan le Fay, King Uriens' wife. She wanted me to kill her brother, King Arthur."

"But why should she want to kill him?" asked King Arthur, shocked by these words. "She hates her brother more than any man in the world," replied Accolon, "because she is jealous of his great power and influence."

"Continue," said King Arthur, eager to know more about this strange plot. "Morgan le Fay loves me and I love her," declared Accolon defiantly. "Through her magic powers she has arranged for me to kill King Arthur. When Arthur is dead, she will kill her husband, King Uriens, and make me king in his place. Then Morgan le Fay will be queen.

"But now all is lost," cried Accolon, burying his face in his hands. After a moment, Accolon raised his head. "I have told you everything," he said to King Arthur, still unaware of his foe's identity, "now I would like to know who *you* are."

King Arthur raised the visor on his helmet. He spoke sternly: "Accolon, I am Arthur, your King, and you have severely wounded me."

Accolon gasped in astonishment. "My lord, I beg you for mercy. I did not know it was you!" Then he hung his head in shame.

"You shall have mercy," replied King Arthur, "for I honestly believe you did not know who you were fighting just now. But you *did* plan to kill me, which makes you a traitor. You deserve to be put to death, but I forgive you because I know you fell under the evil spell of my sister, Morgan le Fay."

With that, King Arthur swore to avenge himself on his traitorous sister, whom he had always honored and trusted above anyone else.

Then, turning to Sir Damas, King Arthur told him he was an evil, brutal man who had tortured and imprisoned innocent knights. As a punishment, King Arthur awarded the castle and the entire estate to Sir Ontzlake. After commanding that all prisoners be freed, King Arthur invited Sir Ontzlake to come to Camelot and be one of the Knights of the Round Table.

"God bless you," replied Sir Ontzlake. "I shall always be at your service."

At last, it was time to go. Unfortunately, King Arthur and Accolon were still suffering from their wounds. They needed a place to rest before they returned to Camelot.

Sir Ontzlake directed them to a nearby abbey where the nuns would let them stay while their wounds healed. But Accolon had lost too much blood. After four days at the abbey, he died. King Arthur was luckier. He recovered from his wounds and became stronger every day. After Accolon's death, he directed that the body be sent back to Camelot.

"Take him to my sister, Morgan le Fay," said King Arthur. "Tell her that I send her a present, and that I have recovered my sword Excalibur and the scabbard."

When Morgan le Fay discovered that Accolon was dead, she was broken-hearted, but she kept her grief to herself so that no one else knew how much it hurt. At the same time, she knew she had to leave Camelot. If she was still there when King Arthur returned, her life would be in great danger.

Early the next morning, Morgan le Fay mounted her horse and rode all day until she reached the abbey where King Arthur was staying. Morgan le Fay asked the nuns in charge where he was. They told her he was sleeping and should not be awakened. Morgan le Fay promised not to disturb him and silently stole into his bedchamber. She hoped to steal the sword Excalibur while the King slept. To her dismay, Morgan le Fay saw that King Arthur's hand grasped his sword, even in his sleep. She knew she could not get Excalibur without waking him. Then she spied the scabbard standing in the corner. Quickly and silently, she snatched it up and slipped from the room.

When King Arthur awoke, he immediately realized the scabbard was gone. "Who has been in my room?" cried the furious King. The nuns told him his sister, Morgan le Fay, had been there but she was gone. "Ah, she has tricked me again," moaned Arthur. "We must catch her!" With that, the King summoned Sir Ontzlake, who had remained at the abbey with him. The two men hastily donned their armor, mounted their horses, and galloped furiously away in pursuit of Arthur's treacherous sister.

It was not long before they caught sight of Morgan le Fay and a group of knights far in the distance across a wide plain. "There she is!" cried Arthur, "after her!" But as they thundered across the plain, the sound of their horses' hooves caused Morgan le Fay to look back. She knew instantly who it was. "It is my brother!" exclaimed the Queen. "If he catches me, he will kill me! We must hurry!"

Morgan le Fay and her followers spurred their horses and galloped off in a great cloud of dust. After passing through a forest, they came to a small, gloomy lake. Morgan le Fay stopped her horse and jumped down. "Whatever happens to me, King Arthur shall not have this scabbard!" she cried, and hurled it into the deep, murky water. Heavy with gold and precious jewels, the scabbard immediately sank out of sight. The Queen then remounted and rode on.

But soon she again heard the hoofbeats of pursuing horses. This time they seemed closer than ever. She must do something quickly! Morgan le Fay, of course, was a sorceress who possessed many magic powers. She called on those powers now to save her life. In a twinkling, she changed herself, her horse and her followers into a cluster of large rocks, just like the others in the valley around them. When King Arthur and Sir Ontzlake arrived, still in hot pursuit, Morgan le Fay was nowhere to be found. "Tricked again," grumbled King Arthur, knowing his sister had once more outwitted him. "We won't find her now. Let's return to the abbey."

As soon as they had gone, Morgan le Fay reversed the magic spell. When everything was back to normal, she said, with a contented little smile on her lips, "Now we may travel wherever we wish. Let us go to the land of Gore." When they arrived in that country, Morgan le Fay was greeted with cheers and shouts by the people, who did not know of her evil ways. While she was there, she took special care to strengthen her castles for she feared that sooner or later King Arthur would attack.

Meanwhile, King Arthur had left the abbey and returned to Camelot. Queen Guenevere and the Knights of the Round Table welcomed him back with great joy. When they heard about the evil deeds of Morgan le Fay, they marveled at her treachery and many wished her burned at the stake. But, of course, Morgan le Fay had escaped and no one knew where she was.

Not long after, a young woman arrived at Camelot. She brought with her the most beautiful cloak ever seen in that kingdom. It was made of rich, luxurious fabrics and studded with diamonds, rubies and emeralds. The young woman presented the cloak to King Arthur. "Your sister sends this cloak as a gift.

She is deeply sorry for any trouble she has
caused and she wants you to have the cloak
with her apologies," said the maiden, a mysterious smile playing about her mouth. King
Arthur was speechless with astonishment. It
was the most magnificent garment he had
ever seen. He longed to try it on.

But just as he reached for the cloak, a
golden mist swirled before his eyes and the
Lady of the Lake appeared out of nowhere.
"Sir," she whispered, "whatever you do, do not
wear that cloak until the maiden that brought
it puts it on first. I beg of you!" The King
stared at her in amazement. What possible
harm could there be in trying on a cloak? Nevertheless, she had saved his life before and it
might be a good idea to do as she said.

Turning to the maiden, King Arthur told her
to put on the cloak. A look of dread stole
across her face. "Oh no, Sir," she cried, "I
could not possibly wear a cloak meant for a
king!" But King Arthur would not be denied.
"You must wear it first or no one will wear it!"
thundered the King. Finally, after many protests, the trembling girl pulled on the cloak.
No sooner had she wrapped it about herself
than she fell dead to the floor. In an instant,
nothing remained of her body but a small
heap of glowing coals.

With a cry of rage and pain, King Arthur

turned to King Uriens. "Your wife, my sister, is always trying to have me killed. I would suspect you of being involved, too, except that I know she planned to kill you as well!" With that, the angry King stormed out of the hall.

IV

Sir Lancelot's First Adventures

SOME TIME after his close call with the deadly cloak, King Arthur held a great tournament at Camelot. Knights from all over the realm came to take part in the jousting and feasting. It was a warm spring day and the air rang with the sound of clashing spears and swords as armored knights rode against each other in furious combat. As the day wore on, one knight stood out above all others. He not only defeated every knight he fought, he was modest in victory and kindly toward his fallen foes. Before long, his name was on everyone's lips.

The name of the noble knight was Lancelot, the very same young boy Merlin had seen so many years before in the land of Benwick. Now grown tall and strong, he had been at court several years. Everyone agreed he was the greatest Knight of the Round Table. He was especially favored by Queen Guenevere. She loved him more than any other knight and Sir Lancelot loved and respected her in turn.

After the tournament was over, Sir Lancelot rested and enjoyed himself at court for a time. But soon he grew restless. Perhaps it would be a good idea to go in search of adventures beyond the walls of Camelot. He invited his nephew, Sir Lionel, to join him. Soon the two knights had ridden their horses through the city gates and left the towers and spires of Camelot far behind.

It was a beautiful sunny morning. Birds sang in the trees all about them and the road wound away toward the misty blue hills in the distance. After riding for several hours, they stopped to rest. The heat had made Sir Lancelot very sleepy. He lay down under an apple tree with his helmet for a pillow and was soon fast asleep. Sir Lionel kept watch. Before long, three mounted knights came into view, hotly pursued by one of the biggest, strongest knights Sir Lionel had ever seen. As he watched in amazement, the great knight caught up with the other three knights and knocked them off their horses one by one. Then he tied them up with their own bridles.

After seeing those knights so badly beaten, Sir Lionel could not sit still. He decided to challenge the great knight himself. Quietly, so as not to wake Sir Lancelot, he picked up his spear and mounted his horse. Once out of earshot, Sir Lionel challenged the other knight in a loud voice. Instantly, his powerful foe wheeled around and charged forward. Almost before he knew what had happened, Sir Lionel found himself lying dazed on the ground, knocked from his saddle with one mighty blow of the knight's spear. Before he could move, the knight leaped on him and quickly tied Sir Lionel up just like the others. Then the great knight threw his four captives over their saddles and led them all off to his castle. There, they were soundly beaten and thrown into prison. All around him in the dark and dirty dungeon, Sir Lionel heard other knights moaning in pain and despair.

In the meantime, Sir Lancelot was still sound asleep under the apple tree, unaware that Sir Lionel had been captured and taken away. As he slept, four great queens approached, riding on white mules. Four knights rode with them, holding a green silk cloth aloft with their spears to shade the queens from the hot sun. When they got a little closer, the queens recognized Sir Lancelot stretched out under the tree. Immediately they began squabbling over who should have him. "Let us not argue now," said one of the queens, who happened to be Morgan le Fay, King Arthur's evil sister. "I will put a spell on

The queens recognized Sir Lancelot stretched out
under the tree.

him and take him back to my castle. Once he is my prisoner, I will remove the spell and he can then choose which of us he wants."

The other queens agreed, and in no time Morgan le Fay had cast a spell over the sleeping knight. Two of her knights laid Sir Lancelot on his shield and carried him back to her castle. There he was locked alone in a damp and cold stone chamber. Sir Lancelot could hear rats scurrying in the dark corners. That evening, a young maiden brought his supper. By this time, the enchantment had worn off and Sir Lancelot was very curious about where he was and how he had gotten there. "I can't tell you anything now," whispered the girl, "but I will explain everything tomorrow." Then she left, leaving Sir Lancelot to puzzle over his fate.

Early the next morning, the four queens came to his room. "Sir knight," one began, "we know you are Lancelot, the greatest knight in the realm, and that you love only Queen Guenevere. But you are our prisoner and you cannot have her. Therefore, you must choose one of us." His eyes wide with disbelief, Lancelot was too shocked to reply. The Queen continued: "I am Morgan le Fay, Queen of the land of Gore; over there are the Queen of Northgalis, the Queen of Eastland and the

Queen of the Out Isles. Now you must choose one of us or die in this prison."

"This is a hard choice," replied Sir Lancelot, "but I would rather die in prison than to choose a woman I do not love."

"Then you are refusing us?" asked Morgan le Fay, unable to believe her ears.

"Yes," replied Sir Lancelot quietly but firmly. And with that, the four angry and disappointed queens swept out of the room, leaving Sir Lancelot thinking sadly about spending the rest of his life in that lonely cell.

At noon, the same young woman came to deliver his meal. When she asked how he was, Sir Lancelot admitted he had never felt so bad. The young woman smiled. "Sir, if you will promise me one thing, I will help you escape." "Gladly," replied Lancelot, "for I am afraid of these witch-queens. They have destroyed many a good knight."

"If you promise to help my father, King Bagdemagus, at a tournament next Tuesday, I will get you out of here," said the girl.

"I know your father well as a noble king and a good knight," replied Sir Lancelot. "I would be proud to help him."

The young woman then told Lancelot to be ready early next morning, when she would come with his armor, a spear and a horse. He was then to ride to an abbey ten miles away and wait until she and her father arrived.

True to her promise, the young girl appeared the following morning and unlocked the door. Lancelot was free! Outside, his horse and armor were all ready, just as promised. As quietly as possible, he donned his armor and rode swiftly away from the castle.

He rode all day until he reached the abbey. He had no sooner arrived than the girl and her father, King Bagdemagus, rode up to the entrance. Sir Lancelot and the king exchanged warm greetings. Then King Bagdemagus explained how his knights had been badly beaten at the last tournament by three Knights of the Round Table.

"Who were they?" asked Lancelot.

"Sir Mador de la Porte, Sir Mordred and Sir Galahantine," replied the King. "Against them my knights and I could do nothing. It was humiliating. Will you help us at the next tournament?"

Remembering his promise, Sir Lancelot then agreed to fight for the King—but in disguise. "Send me three knights that you trust," said Lancelot, "and give us all white shields with no identifying marks on them. When the tournament is well underway, we will appear and fight on your side." The King was well pleased with this arrangement, and after a hearty meal, they all retired to bed.

On the day of the tournament, the battle was not going well for King Bagdemagus. A number of his knights had already been knocked from their horses and badly injured. Watching from a hiding place, Sir Lancelot decided it was time to enter the battle. Riding into the midst of the fighting, he struck down the King of Northgalis, who broke his thigh in the fall. Then Sir Mador de la Porte challenged Lancelot. The two knights rode together, their strong spears fixed in place. Crash! Sir Mador fell to the earth and lay still. Now it was Sir Mordred's turn. He armed himself with a great spear and rode directly at Sir Lancelot. When they came together, Sir Mordred's spear splintered to pieces against Lancelot's shield. Then Lancelot gave him such a blow that he flew backwards off his horse and fell to the ground unconscious.

Having watched his two companions go down to defeat, Sir Galahantine took the field. Once again Sir Lancelot prepared for battle. Their spears in place, the two knights galloped directly toward one another. This time, both their spears shattered from the force of the blows. Drawing their swords, they swung at each other with many slashing strokes. Finally, Sir Lancelot landed a great blow on

Sir Galahantine's helmet. Dazed and bloody in his saddle, Sir Galahantine lost control of his horse. The frightened animal reared up and threw Sir Galahantine from his back. He hit the ground with a great thud and did not move.

Now the tide began to turn in favor of King Bagdemagus. Sir Lancelot went on to defeat many more knights that day, and by the end of the tournament, the forces of the King of Northgalis had been thoroughly defeated. Thanks to Sir Lancelot, King Bagdemagus and his knights were declared winners of the tournament.

Back at the castle, Sir Lancelot was showered with gifts and heartfelt thanks from the king and his daughter. But in all that time, he had not forgotten Sir Lionel, who had been kidnapped while Lancelot slept. Now it was time to try and find him. Bidding his hosts a last farewell, Lancelot rode away from the castle.

It was not long before he found himself in the same forest in which Sir Lionel had disappeared. Suddenly a beautiful young maiden on a snowy white horse came into view. After greeting her, Sir Lancelot asked if she knew of any adventures in that part of the country. The maiden said she did, and that if he would tell her his name, she would take him to meet one of the strongest, most skilled knights in the realm. Lancelot told her his name.

"Sir," she replied, "you have come to the right place to find adventure, for this man is one of the strongest knights in the world. His name is Sir Turquine and he holds in his prison sixty-four knights from Arthur's court. He defeated them all himself.

"I only ask one thing," she continued. "When you are finished here, I beg you to come and help me and other maidens who are attacked every day by a treacherous knight."

Sir Lancelot agreed to do as she asked if she would first take him to Sir Turquine. "All right," she replied. Leading the way, she soon brought Lancelot to a shallow stream. Nearby, a basin hung from a tree. Sir Lancelot banged on the basin with the end of his spear to summon Sir Turquine, but there was no response. They continued on, passing by the wall of a great manor. Then, in the distance, Sir Lancelot saw a knight coming toward him. The knight was leading a horse and across the saddle an armed knight lay bound hand and foot. When they had come closer, Sir Lancelot recognized the bound knight. It was Sir Gaheris, brother of Sir Gawaine, and a Knight of the Round Table.

Sir Lancelot then addressed Sir Turquine, for it was indeed he who led the captive knight: "Take that wounded knight off the horse and let him rest. I am told you have done great harm to the Knights of the Round Table. Prepare to defend yourself!"

"If you are a Knight of the Round Table, I defy you and all your kind," sneered Sir Turquine.

"Then, you had better be ready to fight," answered Lancelot, barely controlling his anger.

The two knights then put their spears in place and galloped toward each other as fast as they could. They struck each other so hard in the midst of their shields that both horses were knocked off their feet. As the horses fell, the two knights leaped down and drew their swords.

For almost an hour, the sounds of sword on sword echoed through the forest as Sir Lancelot and Sir Turquine fought ferociously. Finally, they stopped to rest, panting and heaving. Neither had been able to get the upper hand. When he had finally caught his breath, Sir Turquine spoke with admiration: "You are the strongest knight I have ever fought, and you remind me of the one knight I hate above all others. As long as you are not he, I will agree to stop the fight now and release all the prisoners I hold."

"That is a generous offer," responded Sir

Lancelot. "But tell me, which knight is it that you hate above all others?"

"Sir Lancelot," replied Turquine, "for he killed my brother, Sir Carados, one of the best knights who ever lived. I have sworn to avenge my brother's death, and if I ever come across Sir Lancelot, I will fight him to the death. If you are not he, then we can be friends and I will let all the captive knights go free."

"Then you must know," responded Sir Lancelot, "that I am indeed the knight you seek. I am Sir Lancelot of the Round Table."

Roaring in rage, Sir Turquine raised his sword and fell upon Lancelot, determined to put an end to his sworn foe. They fought like two wild bulls, dealing each other many fearful blows, until blood sprinkled the forest floor. At last, Sir Turquine stumbled backwards a bit, lowering his shield from fatigue. Seizing his opportunity, Sir Lancelot leaped on the exhausted knight and hurled him to the ground. Ripping off Turquine's helmet, Lancelot severed his head with one mighty blow of his sword.

After Lancelot had rested a while and recovered himself from this exhausting battle, he told the young maiden he was ready to accompany her, but his horse had been injured in the fight. She suggested he take Sir Gaheris' horse. That knight was only too happy to lend Lancelot his horse, for Lancelot had saved his life. Sir Lancelot then told Sir Gaheris to go to the manor and free the knights imprisoned there, among whom were many Knights of the Round Table. "Greet them for me," Lancelot commanded Sir Gaheris, "and tell them I hope to be back at the Round Table soon, after I have helped this maiden." Waving farewell to Sir Gaheris, Lancelot and the girl on the white horse set off on a new adventure.

At the manor, Gaheris soon released all the knights and told them of everything Sir Lancelot had done. They all cheered Lancelot in his absence. Delighted to be free after many days and hours in the dark prison of Sir Turquine, the men joyfully gathered up their belongings and prepared to return to Camelot. Of all the knights, three chose not to return right away. Sir Lionel, Sir Ector and Sir Kay decided to try and find Sir Lancelot if they could.

As they rode side by side through the green forest, the maiden told Sir Lancelot about the knight who haunted these woods and robbed women passing by. "What!" cried Lancelot in disbelief, "he claims to be a knight and yet he attacks and robs women traveling on this road! He has dishonored the oath of knighthood. He must be punished."

Then Sir Lancelot had an idea. "Ride on ahead," he told the maiden, "if he troubles you, I will come to your rescue and teach him a lesson." The young woman did as she was told, and sure enough, a short way down the road, the evil knight came riding out of the bushes. Grabbing her by the cloak, he pulled the maiden off her horse. Terrified, she cried out. Sir Lancelot, who had been staying out of sight, now came at a gallop.

"O false knight," cried Sir Lancelot, "who taught you to attack women? You are a disgrace to knighthood!"

The other knight did not respond but drew his sword instead. But he was no match for the greatest knight of the Round Table. With one shattering blow, Sir Lancelot drove his sword through the knight's helmet and deep into his brain. No more would that evil knight attack and rob innocent women on the highway.

V

The Chapel Perilous and Other Adventures of Sir Lancelot

AFTER RECEIVING the grateful thanks of the maiden and saying goodbye, Sir Lancelot rode on in search of new adventures. He passed through many strange and wild places, until at last, as night was coming on, he found a cottage where he could stay for the night. The old woman who lived there served him a delicious meal and later showed him to his room on the second floor, overlooking the gate. Weary from his long ride, Sir Lancelot fell into a deep sleep. In the middle of the night he was awakened by a great commotion in the courtyard below.

Looking out the window, he saw one knight fighting for his life against three others who were attacking him with swords. "I must help that knight," said Sir Lancelot to himself, "three against one is not a fair fight." Quickly fashioning a rope from the bedsheets, Lancelot lowered himself to the ground. To his great surprise he recognized the lone knight as Sir Kay of the Round Table.

"Leave that knight alone, you villains!" he shouted, "I dare you to fight with me!" As soon as he had uttered those words, the three knights immediately dismounted their horses and attacked Sir Lancelot. But his great strength and skill with the sword proved too much for them. One after the other he struck them down. When all three had surrendered, Sir Lancelot commanded them to report to Queen Guenevere at Camelot and to throw themselves on her mercy. Having sworn on their swords that they would, the three knights quickly left the scene of their defeat. Sir Lancelot and Sir Kay then went into the cottage and spent the rest of the night in undisturbed slumber.

Early in the morning, Lancelot slipped out of bed and quietly dressed himself in Sir Kay's armor. He took his shield as well. He then went to the stable, mounted Sir Kay's horse and rode off. When Sir Kay arose, he discovered that Sir Lancelot had taken his armor and horse and left his own in its place. At first Sir Kay was puzzled. Then he realized that, dressed in Lancelot's armor, no one would bother him. No other knight would dare attack Sir Lancelot. That meant Sir Kay would have a nice peaceful ride back to court.

Meanwhile, as Sir Lancelot was passing through a deep forest, he noticed four knights gathered in the shade of a great oak tree. They were four Knights of the Round Table: Sir Sagramour, Sir Ector, Sir Gawaine and Sir Uwaine. When they saw Lancelot approaching, they thought it was Sir Kay. Sir Sagramour decided to have some sport with Sir Kay, little realizing it was Sir Lancelot in disguise. When Sir Sagramour rode toward him, his spear at the ready, Sir Lancelot struck him so hard both man and horse fell to earth. "Did you see that?" asked Sir Ector. "He looks like a much stronger knight than Sir Kay. Watch what I do to him." But Sir Ector fared no better. Sir Lancelot felled him, too, with one powerful thrust of his spear. Next, Sir Uwaine challenged Sir Lancelot. One minute he was on his horse; the next, he was sitting in the dust, his ears ringing. For a long time Sir Uwaine did not even know where he was.

Finally, Sir Gawaine took his turn. He and Sir Lancelot gripped their spears and raced toward each other as fast as their horses could run. Crash! Sir Gawaine's spear splintered in pieces against Sir Lancelot's shield. At the same time, Sir Lancelot's spear hit Sir Gawaine such a blow that his horse fell from under him, and Gawaine barely managed to leap off to avoid being crushed.

Sir Lancelot then rode on aways, concealing a little smile, for he well knew those fellow Knights of the Round Table, but they did not know him.

The four knights were astonished. Sir Lancelot had soundly thrashed them all with one spear! That was practically unheard-of. "Whoever it is, he is a man of great might," said one of the knights. "You are certainly right about that," replied Sir Gawaine, gazing at the retreating figure of the victorious knight. "I am almost sure it is Sir Lancelot. I recognize his riding style." Still wondering, the four knights went in search of their horses, which had wandered off, and prepared for the journey back to Camelot.

Sir Lancelot, meanwhile, rode on for a long time through a dark forest. After a time, he noticed a small black dog up ahead. It seemed to be following a trail of blood through the woods. As Sir Lancelot followed along, the dog kept looking back over her shoulder, as if to make sure he was still there. Finally, they came to a great old house, surrounded by a moat. The dog ran over a bridge and into the house. Sir Lancelot followed. Inside he found himself in a great hall, and in the middle of the hall lay a dead knight. The black dog was there, licking his master's wounds.

Sir Lancelot was just wondering what to make of all this, when a woman came into the hall weeping and wringing her hands. "O knight," she moaned, "it's terrible!"

"Why, what has happened?" asked Sir Lancelot. "What befell this knight? I simply followed the dog who was following a trail of blood."

"Oh, I did not think it was you that killed my husband," said the woman sadly, "for the one who did it is severely wounded and is not likely to recover."

"What is your husband's name?" asked Lancelot.

"His name was Sir Gilbert," replied the widow, "one of the best knights of the world. I don't know the name of the man who killed him."

Seeing nothing more to do there, Sir Lancelot comforted the woman as best he could and departed. He had not gone far before he met a young woman who appeared to know him. "Thank goodness I have found you," she cried, "for I need your help badly. I know that, as a knight, you are bound to help those in need."

When Sir Lancelot asked what the trouble was, she told him that her brother had been badly wounded in a fight with Sir Gilbert. Her brother had killed Sir Gilbert in the fight, but now he was in danger of bleeding to death.

"What can I do to help?" asked Sir Lancelot.

"There is a witch who lives nearby, who told me that my brother's wounds would never heal until I found a knight who would go into the Chapel Perilous. Inside there is a sword and a dead knight wrapped in a bloody cloth. My brother will only be cured when a piece of the cloth and the sword are applied to his wounds."

"That is truly amazing," replied Sir Lancelot. "What is your brother's name?"

"His name is Sir Meliot," answered the woman.

"I am very sorry," said Sir Lancelot, "for I know him well. He is a Knight of the Round Table. I will do whatever I can to help."

"Then follow this highway. It will bring you to the Chapel Perilous," said the woman. "But please hurry! I fear for my brother's life!"

With no further ado, Sir Lancelot remounted his horse and rode off. In no time he was at the gate of the Chapel Perilous. He dismounted and tied his horse in the little churchyard. Then he saw something that made his blood run cold. On the front of the chapel were thirty knights' shields, each turned upside down. Many of the shields belonged to knights Sir Lancelot knew. What terrible fate had they met?

He didn't have time to wonder long, for suddenly before him were thirty huge knights, very much alive, and all dressed in black armor. They all had their swords drawn and their shields ready. Gnashing their teeth, they grinned hideously at Sir Lancelot, as if daring him to try to enter the chapel.

His heart pounding, Sir Lancelot drew his own sword and prepared to fight his way through the dreadful swarm of knights that stood in his way. But to his utter surprise, as he advanced, they stepped back, and he entered the chapel unharmed.

Inside, a single candle lit the bare stone room. Sir Lancelot could just make out a corpse covered with a silk cloth. He bent down and snipped away a piece of the cloth. As he did, it seemed to him the earth shook. Fear gripped his heart but he tried to ignore it. Then he noticed a sword on the ground near the body. He snatched it up and got out of there as fast as he could.

Outside, the same horrible knights were

waiting. They all spoke as one: "Sir Lancelot, put that sword down or you will die."

This time, Sir Lancelot was less afraid. "If you want the sword, you must fight me for it," he said. Then he walked right through them and no one raised a hand against him.

Outside the churchyard, he met a young woman. "Sir Lancelot," said she, "leave that sword behind or you must die."

"I will not leave it behind for any reason," replied Lancelot.

"You are right," said the strange young woman. "If you had left the sword behind, you would never have seen Queen Guenevere again."

"Then I would be a fool to leave it," answered the knight.

"Now," said the maiden, "I demand that you give me a kiss."

"That I cannot do," replied Lancelot.

"You are right again," she answered. "If you had kissed me your life would have ended. Then I would have kept your body with me always and cherished and preserved it. I have loved you for seven years, even though I know you love Queen Guenevere."

"God save me from your witchery," cried Sir Lancelot, "I must depart from here!" Leaping into the saddle, he rode away from the churchyard, leaving the mysterious young woman gazing after him sadly. Indeed, her unhappiness was so great that it was said she died of a broken heart shortly after.

Sir Lancelot now returned to Sir Meliot's sister, who greeted him with great joy. They went immediately to where her brother lay pale and faint from loss of blood. Sir Lancelot could see he was nearly dead.

When he saw Lancelot come into the room, Sir Meliot raised himself weakly from his bed and gasped with his last ounce of strength: "O lord, Sir Lancelot, help me!" With that, he sank back down on the pillow, his eyes closed. Sir Lancelot rushed to the bed. First, he touched the wounds with the sword from the chapel. Then he wiped the wounds with the piece of bloody cloth.

To his utter astonishment, the wounds suddenly disappeared! Sir Meliot opened his eyes and sat up. A big smile spread across his face. First he hugged his sister. Then he hugged Sir Lancelot. "It's a miracle!" he cried. "I'm well again!" Then they all three celebrated far into the night.

In the morning, Sir Lancelot departed for Camelot and the court of King Arthur. When he arrived, everyone at court turned out to greet him. When Sir Gawaine, Sir Sagramour,

Sir Ector and Sir Uwaine saw Lancelot in Sir Kay's armor, they knew it was Sir Lancelot who had beaten them all with one spear. There was much laughing and joking about it. Also present were many of the knights Sir Lancelot had freed from Sir Turquine's prison. They could not thank him enough.

Then Sir Kay told how Lancelot had rescued him from the three knights who would have killed him, and how Sir Lancelot had switched armor so that Sir Kay would not be attacked on the way home. Finally, Sir Meliot came in and told how Sir Lancelot had just recently saved him from death. After hearing about these great deeds, everyone there cheered and applauded Sir Lancelot till the rafters rang. And all agreed that he was, without doubt, the greatest knight of all.

VI

Sir Lancelot and Dame Elaine

ONE DAY, some time later, as King Arthur and the knights sat at the Round Table, a hermit came in. When the hermit saw that one of the seats at the Round Table, a seat called the Siege Perilous, was empty, he asked about it. The King and the knights told him that only one man could sit in that seat without being destroyed. "Do you know who that man is?" asked the hermit. The King and the knights admitted they did not know. "Well," said the hermit, "I know, and I tell you that he will be born this year. And there will come a time when he will sit in the Siege Perilous and he will win the Holy Grail." Having made his mysterious prediction, the hermit vanished before the King and the knights could ask him anything more.

The following day, Sir Lancelot departed from the court once again in search of adventure. Eventually, he came to a city called Corbin. In the middle of the city stood a beautiful stone tower. As he approached the tower, the people of the city began to crowd around him, for they well knew that he was Sir Lancelot, the greatest knight of the kingdom. "Sir Lancelot," they cried, "you must help us! Something terrible is happening here!"

"Why, what is wrong?" replied the noble knight.

Then the people told him about a beautiful young woman imprisoned in the tower. She had been there for five years suffering terrible torment and no one could seem to help her. Even Sir Gawaine had been there a few days before, and he could do nothing. Sir Lancelot told them that if Sir Gawaine had been unable to help, it was quite possible that he, Sir Lancelot, could not assist the lady either.

But the people would not take no for an answer and they insisted that he at least try to help the poor suffering woman. Finally, Lancelot agreed. Then they brought him to the tower, and when he came to the chamber where the lady was, the door locks unbolted as if by magic. Sir Lancelot entered and stopped in his tracks. The cell was boiling hot. Through clouds of steam he caught sight of one of the most beautiful women he had ever seen. It turned out that she had been put under a spell and imprisoned in the tower by

Morgan le Fay and the Queen of Northgalis, who were jealous of her great beauty. But astonishingly, as soon as Sir Lancelot took her by the hand, the spell was broken. Quickly he led her out of that horrible chamber.

After she had recovered a little from the shock of being rescued after all those years of torment, the lady put on new clothes. Sir Lancelot thought he had never seen anyone as pretty, unless it was Queen Guenevere.

When the people of Corbin saw that Sir Lancelot had rescued the lady in distress, they showered him with thanks. Then they told him about another problem they were having. There was a terrible dragon living in a tomb nearby. Could he slay the dragon? Sir Lancelot told them to take him there and he would do his best. When they arrived, Sir Lancelot saw these words written in gold on the tomb: "Here shall come a leopard of king's blood, and he shall slay this serpent, and this leopard shall father a lion in this country, and that lion shall excel all other knights."

Wondering what those strange words could mean, Sir Lancelot lifted the lid of the tomb. Out sprang a horrible dragon, roaring with anger and breathing fire from its mouth. Dodging the monster's searing breath, Lancelot stepped back and drew his sword. He had

Out sprang a horrible dragon, roaring with
anger and breathing fire from its mouth.

only a moment before the dragon, screech-
ing with fury, charged forward, trying to
catch Lancelot in its razor-sharp claws. But
the knight was too quick for the lumber-
ing creature, and darting in, he plunged his
sword deep into the dragon's breast. With a
final bloodcurdling shriek, the hideous creature fell to the ground with a great thud.
Writhing in convulsions, the monster breathed
its last.

While Sir Lancelot was resting from his
labors, a king named Pelles approached and
introduced himself. He congratulated Lancelot on killing the dragon and invited him back
to his castle. Sir Lancelot accepted, for by
that time he was quite tired, and hungry as
well.

Soon Lancelot and King Pelles were seated
at the dinner table in a great hall. A fire crack-
led in the great fireplace at one end of the
room, which was ablaze with candles. On the
table were huge platters of meat and vegeta-
bles and many other good things to eat and
drink. Just as they were about to eat, a pretty
young woman came in carrying a golden cup
in her hands. Suddenly King Pelles and everyone else in the hall bowed their heads in
prayer. "What does this mean?" asked Sir
Lancelot, gazing about as a sudden hush fell

over the room. Then the king told him that the cup was the holiest thing on earth. "Be well aware," the King told Sir Lancelot, "that today you have seen the Holy Grail." Everyone in the hall then turned back to their plates piled high with food and enjoyed themselves mightily.

As King Pelles sat with Sir Lancelot, he found himself wishing that the noble knight would fall in love with his daughter, Elaine. Somehow he knew that if that were to happen, Lancelot and Elaine would have a son named Galahad, a great knight who would free all captured lands and would secure the Holy Grail forever.

But the question was how to bring it about. While King Pelles wondered about this, an enchantress named Dame Brisen stole to his side and whispered in his ear. "Sir Lancelot loves only Queen Guenevere," she informed the King, "but leave it to me. I will use my magic powers to make Sir Lancelot think your daughter is Guenevere." "Do you really think you can do that?" asked the King. "Wait and see," replied the sorceress.

Later that night, Dame Brisen arranged to have a messenger come to Sir Lancelot with a ring from Queen Guenevere. "Why, where is my lady?" asked Lancelot. "At the Castle of Case," replied the messenger. "It is only five miles from here." "Well, I will go and see her there," said Lancelot, and made preparations to leave. In the meantime, Dame Brisen arranged to have the King's daughter, Elaine, go to the same castle that night.

When Sir Lancelot arrived, Dame Brisen was already there. She led him into the castle and brought him a cup of wine. No sooner had he drunk the wine than Lancelot began to feel quite strange. Little did he know that Dame Brisen had put a magic potion into the wine. Sure enough, when Elaine came into the room, Sir Lancelot imagined it was Queen Guenevere, his true love. After spending a pleasant evening together, they retired for the night.

But in the morning, when the spell had worn off, Sir Lancelot found himself with Elaine. He was very angry. He knew he had been tricked. "What kind of treachery is this?" he shouted, drawing his sword. "Who has deceived me like this?"

Frightened and ashamed, Elaine threw herself at his feet. "Oh noble knight," she cried, "take pity on me. I know I have played a trick on you but it means that I am going to have your son, who will be the noblest knight in the world." Sir Lancelot was still angry. "Why have you done this?" he cried. "Who are you?"

"I am Elaine, the daughter of King Pelles,"

replied the young woman in a trembling voice. Suddenly, Sir Lancelot realized what had happened. Feeling ashamed over his anger, he apologized. "I forgive you," he said, taking her in his arms and kissing her. "We have both been tricked by Dame Brisen. And if I ever catch her, she will lose her head by my sword."

After bidding a tender farewell to Elaine, Sir Lancelot then departed and returned to the castle at Corbin. And in due time, just as King Pelles had foreseen, his daughter Elaine gave birth to a fine young son, who was named Galahad.

Some months later, after Sir Lancelot had returned to Camelot, a rumor went around that Lancelot had a son by Elaine, the daughter of King Pelles. When Queen Guenevere heard this she was furious. She called Lancelot many names and accused him of being false to her. Then Sir Lancelot told her how he had been tricked by Dame Brisen into thinking that Elaine was Queen Guenevere. After a while, the Queen saw that he was telling the truth and she forgave him. Meanwhile, King Arthur had just returned from France where he had defeated King Claudas in a great battle. To celebrate, King Arthur announced a splendid victory feast at Camelot.

When Dame Elaine, daughter of King Pelles, heard about the feast, she asked her father's permission to go. King Pelles gave her his blessing, but insisted that she dress for the occasion in the finest clothes money could buy. When she arrived at Camelot, accompanied by a magnificent procession of twenty knights and ten ladies, King Arthur and Queen Guenevere thought she was the most beautiful and richly dressed woman who had ever come to Camelot.

But when Sir Lancelot saw her, he would not speak to her because he was still so embarrassed about threatening her with his sword that morning at the castle. Even so, he thought she was the loveliest woman he had ever seen.

When Dame Elaine realized that Lancelot was not going to speak to her, she was heartbroken, for she loved him dearly. Seeing her mistress so sad, Dame Brisen promised that she would fix everything.

That night, Queen Guenevere insisted that Dame Elaine sleep in the bedroom next to hers. Then she summoned Sir Lancelot and told him to be ready to come and see her when she called him. Sir Lancelot promised that he would. But Dame Brisen overheard their conversation and decided to play a trick on them. First, she went to Dame Elaine and told her that she would bring Sir Lancelot for a visit later that night. Dame Elaine was delighted to think that Sir Lancelot would soon be coming to see her. Then Dame Brisen, disguised as a maid, went to Sir Lancelot and told him that Queen Guenevere wanted to see him. "Please take me to her," said Lancelot. "I will gladly," replied Dame Brisen. But instead of taking him to Queen Guenevere, the crafty sorceress took him to Dame Elaine's chamber. Just before they arrived, Dame Brisen cast a magic spell over Sir Lancelot that once again made him think Dame Elaine was Queen Guenevere.

As you might guess, Queen Guenevere sent for Sir Lancelot later that evening. But, of course, Sir Lancelot was not there. At this, the Queen grew furious, for she suspected he was with Dame Elaine. "Where is that false knight?" she cried, "he has betrayed me!" No one could calm her down. Finally, when her anger had subsided, she went to bed and cried herself to sleep.

The first thing next morning, she summoned Sir Lancelot. "False knight!" she cried out as soon as she saw him, "you are a traitor. Leave my court at once and never come back!" Sir Lancelot was so taken aback by these harsh words that he felt dizzy. He had never been so unjustly accused before. He didn't know what to do. Confused and shocked, Sir Lancelot leaped out a nearby window into a garden. Then, maddened with grief, he ran toward the woods at the end of the garden and disappeared. It was the last anyone saw of him for two long years.

VII

Sir Lancelot's Exile and Return

WHEN DAME Elaine heard what had happened, she accused Queen Guenevere of chasing Sir Lancelot away. In turn, Queen Guenevere commanded Dame Elaine to leave her court immediately. In truth, both women loved Sir Lancelot very deeply and now neither one of them had him.

Queen Guenevere began to think that maybe she had acted too hastily in chasing Sir Lancelot away. She summoned three knights—Sir Bors, Sir Ector and Sir Lionel— and commanded them to search for the missing knight. Eager to find their beloved friend, the three men searched far and wide. They rode through villages and towns. They looked for him in the forest. They asked everyone they saw. But after three months, they gave up. Sir Lancelot was nowhere to be found.

Although the three knights had been unable to locate Sir Lancelot, he was indeed in the forest. Month after month he had wandered through the wild woods, living on fruit and nuts, and speaking to no one. Dressed only in shirt and trousers, he had little protection from the rain and wind. But he hardly noticed. He was out of his mind with grief and sadness over the loss of Queen Guenevere.

Then one day, purely by chance, he happened to wander into the city of Corbin. Sir Lancelot did not know it then, but Dame Elaine lived there now with their son, Galahad. But when people saw him in the street, all dirty and ragged from his time in the woods, they laughed and made fun of him. Dogs barked at this strange-looking man who had suddenly appeared in town, and small boys threw stones at him. To escape his pursuers, Lancelot climbed over a wall into the garden of a nearby castle. There he lay down beside a well and fell sound asleep.

A little while later, Dame Elaine and a few friends came into the garden to play a game. They soon noticed the sleeping man. Approaching more closely, Dame Elaine gasped. In spite of his dirty clothes and ragged appearance, she knew at once it was Sir Lancelot. Weeping with happiness, she ran to tell her father, King Pelles. The King ordered that Sir Lancelot be brought into the castle and treated with the greatest kindness.

Anyone could see that Sir Lancelot was not in his right mind and there was no telling what he might do when he awoke. They then carried him into a room in a tower that contained the cup of the Holy Grail. Sir Lancelot was laid gently down near the holy object. And because of the miraculous powers of the Grail, Sir Lancelot was cured of his madness. When he awoke, he groaned and sighed and told everyone about how sore he was.

As soon as he recognized Dame Elaine and King Pelles, Sir Lancelot begged them to tell him how he had gotten there. Then Dame Elaine explained that he had come into the city like a madman and that she and her friends had discovered him asleep by the well. Sir Lancelot marveled at this, because he remembered none of it.

After a few weeks of rest and good food, Sir Lancelot felt much better. It was time to leave the castle, but he could not go back to King Arthur's court; Queen Guenevere had forbidden that. Instead he asked Dame Elaine if her father might have a place he could use. Dame Elaine told Sir Lancelot she would ask. As luck would have it, King Pelles owned a small castle that was empty at the time. He gladly offered it to Sir Lancelot.

Soon after, Sir Lancelot, Dame Elaine and a

group of knights and ladies moved into the castle. Sir Lancelot called it Joyous Gard, or Happy Island, for the castle was surrounded on all sides by water. And although Sir Lancelot was delighted to have this beautiful place to live in, he often gazed in the direction of Camelot and a look of sadness and longing came into his eyes.

Some months later, two knights arrived outside Joyous Gard. One was Sir Percivale and the other was Sir Ector. They had both been looking for Sir Lancelot for many months, but they did not know he lived there now. Sir Percivale decided to approach the castle. Perhaps the people inside might know something of Sir Lancelot's whereabouts. Sir Ector decided to stay behind until Sir Percivale returned. So Percivale took a small boat across the moat and entered the castle. There he told a guard to tell the knight in charge that Sir Percivale wished to joust with him. When Sir Lancelot received this message, he put on his armor and prepared for battle. At a jousting place within the castle, the two knights set their spears in place and galloped towards one another. When they met, neither missed. The force of the blows knocked both knights off their horses, with a clatter. Getting to their feet, they pulled out their swords and hurtled together like two wild boars. The clanging of their great swords echoed off the great stone walls.

After fighting for almost two hours, both knights were exhausted and bleeding from their wounds. Panting for breath, Sir Percivale said, "Fair knight, I ask you to tell me your name, for I have never fought with a knight of your skill and power."

"Why, my name is Sir Lancelot," replied his opponent, "and what is yours?"

"I am Sir Percivale, son of King Pellinore and brother of Sir Lamorak and Sir Aglovale."

With that, Sir Lancelot groaned and threw his sword and shield away from him. "Good grief," he exclaimed, "why am I fighting with a fellow Knight of the Round Table?"

Then Sir Percivale realized that it truly was Sir Lancelot. He begged Lancelot to forgive him and told him that Sir Ector was waiting outside the castle. They immediately sent for Sir Ector. When he came in, Sir Ector and Lancelot hugged like long-lost brothers. Then all three went into the castle and spent the evening catching up on everything that had happened. Sir Percivale and Sir Ector asked Sir Lancelot if he was ever going to return to King Arthur's court.

"No," replied Sir Lancelot sadly. "I have been forbidden by the Queen."

Then Sir Ector and Sir Percivale told Lancelot how much King Arthur and Queen Guenevere missed him, not to mention all the other knights and ladies of the court. After much persuasion, Sir Lancelot finally gave in. "I will go with you," he said.

When Dame Elaine heard about his departure, she was very unhappy. But she loved him too much to stand in his way and so she let him go.

Five days later, the three knights arrived at Camelot. When the arrival of Sir Lancelot was announced, the court went mad with joy. A great feast was prepared and King Arthur and Queen Guenevere and all the knights and ladies attended. At the feast, Sir Percivale and Sir Ector told about all that had happened to Sir Lancelot. And as they related his adventures, Queen Guenevere cried for happiness. Then King Arthur spoke: "I am curious about why you went mad, Sir Lancelot. I and many others thought it was because of your love for Dame Elaine. We hear that you and she have a son named Galahad who shows great promise."

"My lord," replied Lancelot, "if I have acted foolishly, I have paid dearly for it." The King wondered what he meant by that, but he said no more about it. Everyone else at court, though, knew why Sir Lancelot had gone mad,

and over whom. But now it was time to celebrate and all the lords and ladies gladly
passed the rest of the night in feasting and
merrymaking.

Not long after, Queen Guenevere decided to
give a special dinner for the Knights of the
Round Table. She invited twenty-four of her
favorite knights to the dinner, and to make it
even more special, she decided to prepare the
meal herself. Now, one of the knights invited
was Sir Gawaine. He was a great favorite of
the Queen, who knew that above all other
foods, Sir Gawaine enjoyed fresh fruit. With
that in mind, Queen Guenevere made certain
there was plenty of fruit on the table when
the knights sat down to eat.

Unfortunately, Sir Gawaine had an enemy at
court. His name was Sir Pinel, and he hated
Sir Gawaine because Gawaine had killed his
brother in a tournament. Now Sir Pinel saw
his chance for revenge. Knowing that Sir
Gawaine loved fruit, Sir Pinel crept quietly
into the dining hall before dinner and poisoned the fruit near Sir Gawaine's place at the
table.

Soon after, all the knights came in and took
their places. Queen Guenevere welcomed
them all and thanked them for coming. She
was a little sad, however, for Sir Lancelot was

not there. She and Sir Lancelot had quarreled and the great knight had decided to leave Camelot for a while.

Meanwhile, the knights were eating hungrily, complimenting Queen Guenevere on the meal she had prepared with her own hands. Then something terrible happened. Sir Patrice, a cousin of Sir Mador, took an apple and ate it. Almost immediately, he gasped, his hands clutching at his throat. The other knights rushed to his side, but it was too late. With a groan of agony, Sir Patrice closed his eyes and died.

Suddenly everyone turned and stared at Queen Guenevere. They knew Sir Patrice had been poisoned and she had cooked the meal! Sir Gawaine spoke first: "My Queen, everyone knows how much I like fruit. Therefore, it seems to me that this poison was meant for me!" Queen Guenevere was so shocked at this, she could not utter a word. Then Sir Mador spoke up: "My cousin has been murdered and I demand revenge. I think the Queen is guilty!"

At this, the Queen burst into tears and sank into a chair, hiding her face in her hands. All the noise and commotion brought King Arthur to the dining hall in a hurry. "What's going on?" he demanded. When the knights explained

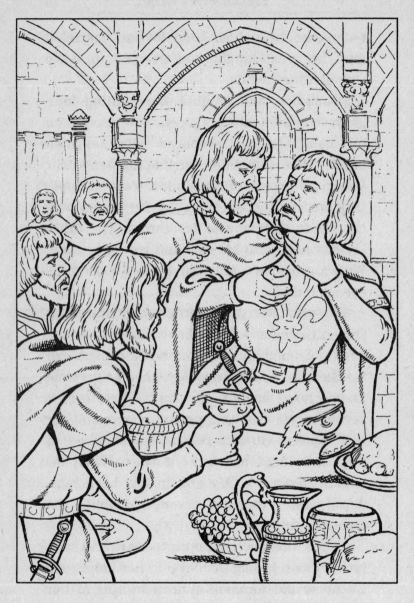

Almost immediately, he gasped, his hands
clutching at his throat.

what had happened, King Arthur was upset and angry. Since Queen Guenevere had prepared the food herself, it looked very bad. And all the while, Sir Mador continued to accuse her.

"My lords," said King Arthur, "I do not believe the Queen did this terrible thing, but I cannot very well defend her myself, because she is my wife. I am sure," continued the King, looking around at the stern and angry knights before him, "that a worthy knight will defend my Queen and save her from a death sentence!"

"King Arthur," replied Sir Mador, "none of the knights here will defend her because they all think she is guilty."

The knights agreed that this was so. By this time, Queen Guenevere had recovered a little. "I swear on my honor to everyone here that I did nothing wrong!" cried the tearful Queen. "It is true I prepared the meal, but I did not poison anyone!"

"My lord," said Sir Mador, "I demand that you decide on a day of justice. That day, the Queen's champion must meet me in battle. If I win, the Queen is guilty and must be burned at the stake. If I lose, the Queen may go free."

Reluctantly, King Arthur agreed to the terms, for that is how questions of guilt or innocence were decided in those days. With a heavy heart, King Arthur set a day two weeks from then as the Queen's day of judgment. On that day, in a meadow beside Westminster, the Queen's champion would meet Sir Mador in battle. If he lost, the Queen would die.

Later, when they were alone, King Arthur asked his wife how the whole thing had come about. "I tell you I don't know anything about it," she said.

"Where is Sir Lancelot?" asked King Arthur. "He would defend you."

"I don't know where he is," responded the Queen sadly. "They tell me he is nowhere to be found in Camelot."

"Then send for Sir Bors," said the King. "Perhaps he will agree to help."

As King Arthur suggested, Queen Guenevere met with Sir Bors and threw herself on his mercy. But Sir Bors was reluctant to assist the Queen because he knew what the other knights would think. But finally, after much persuasion, he agreed to be the Queen's champion. But only if no other knight came to her rescue. The Queen was overjoyed. "Oh thank you, Sir Bors!" she cried, "you will not regret this!"

After leaving the Queen, Sir Bors rode straight to a hermit's hut in the woods. He happened to know Sir Lancelot was staying there. He told Sir Lancelot all that had happened. "Go to the battlefield on the appointed day," said Lancelot, "but delay the fight a little until you see me come. I have a plan." Sir Bors agreed and left Lancelot in the hermit's hut.

On the appointed day, King Arthur and Queen Guenevere and all the Knights of the Round Table gathered in the meadow at Westminster to watch the contest. Nearby was a great iron stake surrounded by firewood. If Sir Mador won, the Queen would be burned at the stake. If Sir Bors won, she would be free.

It was time, at last. The two knights rode to opposite ends of the field and prepared for battle. As Sir Bors placed his spear in position, he noticed a knight riding toward him from a little wood near the edge of the field. He was astride a splendid white horse and carried a shield with strange markings. When he reached Sir Bors, the knight spoke: "Fair knight, allow me to do battle in your place. I have ridden hard to be here this day and I beg you to do as we agreed a short time ago."

"Gladly," replied Sir Bors, delighted to be relieved of a fight he did not want. He then rode to where King Arthur was sitting and explained that the knight on the white horse had offered to fight in his place.

"Who is he?" asked King Arthur.

"I don't know," replied Sir Bors, "but he has kindly offered to be the Queen's champion."

"Very well," said the King, beginning to grow impatient at the delay. "Let the contest begin!"

When both knights were in position, a trumpet blast sounded and the two charged toward each other as hard as they could. With a mighty crash, Sir Mador's spear splintered in a hundred pieces, but the other knight's spear held and he knocked Sir Mador backwards over the tail of his horse. With a great clatter, Sir Mador landed on his back in the dirt. But quick as lightning, he leaped to his feet and drew his sword. "Get off your horse and fight me on foot!" he cried.

"Very well," responded the other knight, nimbly jumping down and pulling out his own sword. The two then fought like madmen, each giving the other many terrible blows. But at last, the other knight dealt Sir Mador a mighty blow on the side of the helmet that knocked him head over heels. While he lay there, dizzy from the ringing in his ears, the other knight reached down and yanked off his helmet.

"I surrender," gasped Sir Mador, "you are too strong. I beg you to spare my life."

"On one condition," replied the other knight softly: "that you drop all charges against

Queen Guenevere and never mention the matter again."

"It shall be as you wish," whispered Sir Mador. Then, in a louder voice that everyone could hear, he agreed to take back all that he had said against the Queen.

With that, the fight was over. The Queen was saved. "Hurrah!" shouted the crowd as the victorious knight made his way to the stand where King Arthur and Queen Guenevere were waiting to greet him. After the King and Queen had both thanked the knight profusely, the King invited him to take off his helmet and have some refreshment. "Well!" exclaimed the King, "it's none other than Sir Lancelot!" Once again, the greatest Knight of the Round Table had won a noble victory. When she saw who it was that had saved her life, Queen Guenevere shed many tears of joy and gratitude. All the other Knights of the Round Table gathered round and clapped Lancelot on the back. King Arthur shook his hand again and again.

Later on, it was discovered that Sir Pinel was actually the one who had poisoned the apples. When he found out his crime had been brought to light, he fled the kingdom in disgrace. Even Sir Mador was forgiven, after Sir Lancelot had put in a good word for him, and once again, peace reigned in Camelot.

VIII
The Death of King Arthur

BUT UNFORTUNATELY, those golden days of harmony in the court of King Arthur came to an end all too soon. It happened in this way: because Sir Lancelot and Queen Guenevere were such good friends, they spent a lot of time together, talking and enjoying each other's company. After a time, people who were enemies of Sir Lancelot planted the seed of jealousy in King Arthur's heart. And as time went on, he grew angrier and more jealous with each passing day, until finally he threatened to have Queen Guenevere put to death if she continued to see Sir Lancelot.

The Queen was very frightened. After talking with Sir Lancelot, they decided to leave Camelot and go to Joyous Gard, Sir Lancelot's castle. At least the Queen would be safe there until King Arthur calmed down. But instead, the Queen's departure had just the opposite effect: King Arthur was enraged. Gathering his knights about him, he vowed to lay siege to Joyous Gard until Sir Lancelot should restore the Queen to him.

In a short time King Arthur had gathered a strong army and marched right up to the walls of Sir Lancelot's great stone castle. Meanwhile, Lancelot had heard about the King's plans to attack, and had gathered his own army of knights who were loyal to him. When word came that King Arthur's army was approaching the gates, Sir Lancelot went to a high tower and looked down. King Arthur saw him immediately and shouted: "Come out, if you dare, and meet me in battle!"

"My lord," replied Sir Lancelot, "I will never fight with the noble King who made me a knight!"

"Never mind your pretty words," sneered the King, "you have dishonored my Queen and taken her by force."

Then Sir Lancelot reminded King Arthur of how he had saved the Queen from death when she was falsely accused by Sir Mador and how he and the King had been good and loyal friends for many years. At first, King Arthur seemed to listen, but then Sir Gawaine and other enemies of Sir Lancelot persuaded him that Lancelot was an evil knight who must be punished. And so it was decided that King

Arthur and his men would meet Sir Lancelot and his knights in battle the very next day.

As soon as it was light, the two armies came together with a great crashing of spears and shields. All day the battle raged, with many knights slain on both sides. And always King Arthur looked for a chance to slay Sir Lancelot. But as soon as he managed to get near Sir Lancelot, that knight moved away— not because he was afraid, but because he did not want to fight against the King he still loved and respected.

Finally, Sir Bors, who was on Lancelot's side, challenged King Arthur to fight. "With pleasure!" cried the King, spurring his horse forward. But to his great surprise, Sir Bors knocked him off his horse with one blow. As King Arthur lay stunned in the dust, Sir Bors drew his sword and looked at Sir Lancelot as if to say, "Shall I end this war right here and now?"

"No," cried Sir Lancelot, "I will not stand by and let you kill the noble King who made me a knight!"

With that, he jumped off his horse, pulled King Arthur to his feet and helped him back on his own horse. With great feeling, Sir Lancelot spoke: "For God's sake, my King, let us stop fighting. This war will do nobody any good!"

King Arthur looked sadly down at the knight he had loved so well. He thought to himself about Sir Lancelot's courage and kindness, even in the heat of battle, and the words stuck in his throat. Unable to speak and unable to bear the sight of Lancelot any longer, he turned away with tears in his eyes and rode from the battlefield. The fighting was over for that day.

During the siege of Joyous Gard, news of the fighting reached the Pope in Rome. Disturbed by the reports of battle and bloodshed between such old friends as King Arthur and Sir Lancelot, the Pope decided to use his influence to help stop the war. He sent urgent messages to them both, urging them to forget their differences and to make peace. And he asked Sir Lancelot to return Queen Guenevere to the King.

It worked. Both sides agreed to stop fighting and Sir Lancelot promised to bring Queen Guenevere back to Camelot. And so it happened. On a beautiful spring day, Sir Lancelot and Queen Guenevere set out on their journey, each splendidly dressed in white cloth with gold embroidery. Along with them rode a hundred knights, all dressed in green, each holding an olive branch as a sign of peace.

When they arrived, Sir Lancelot led Queen

Guenevere before the King. With great ceremony, Lancelot explained that there had been
many lies told about him and the Queen. And
once again he reminded the King of all the
services he had performed in the past. When
he was through speaking, everyone there realized the truth of what he had said, and many
wept for happiness to see the King and Queen
together again.

But there was one knight who was not
happy. Sir Gawaine could not forgive Sir
Lancelot because Lancelot had slain his
brother, Sir Gaheris, during the fighting. Even
though Sir Lancelot had not realized it
was Sir Gaheris, Sir Gawaine nevertheless
privately vowed to revenge himself on Sir
Lancelot as soon as he got the chance.

Sir Lancelot looked about sadly and then he
spoke: "I am greatly saddened by all that has
happened, and I think it might be best if I left
this noble fellowship of knights forever." Then
he turned to Queen Guenevere: "I bid you
farewell, my Queen. Speak well of me, and if
you ever need my help, you have only to ask."
Then, with a last wave to the knights and
ladies of the court, Sir Lancelot slowly rode
out through the gates of Camelot. It was the
beginning of the end of the fellowship of the
Knights of the Round Table.

After leaving the court, Sir Lancelot returned to Joyous Gard and from there, he traveled over the sea to the land of Benwick, where he also had a castle. There he lived with many of the knights who had been loyal to him during his battles with King Arthur. Unfortunately, those battles were not over yet. After Sir Lancelot had left Camelot, Sir Gawaine again managed to persuade the king that Sir Lancelot was a traitor. King Arthur decided to take an army and pursue Sir Lancelot in Benwick. Before he left, King Arthur put Morgan le Fay's son, Sir Mordred, in charge of the kingdom.

But Sir Mordred was an evil man. Secretly, he wanted to get rid of King Arthur, crown himself King and marry Queen Guenevere. So he told all the knights at Camelot a terrible lie. He told them that King Arthur had been killed in a battle with Sir Lancelot. Then Sir Mordred persuaded the knights to appoint him King. When King Arthur heard what Mordred had done, he was furious. He immediately made plans to return to England.

When King Arthur and his army landed at Dover, Sir Mordred was there with an army of his own. In the great battle that followed, King Arthur's forces defeated Sir Mordred, but Sir Gawaine was fatally wounded. As he lay near death, he told King Arthur that none of this would have happened if he hadn't insisted that the King pursue Sir Lancelot into Benwick. After urging the King to send for Sir Lancelot and make peace with him, Sir Gawaine died. King Arthur was broken-hearted. The two knights he had loved the most, Sir Gawaine and Sir Lancelot, were both gone from him, and that in the bitterest of circumstances.

He had little time to worry about it, however, for Sir Mordred and his army had issued a new challenge to King Arthur. This time King Arthur and Sir Mordred were to bring their armies to Salisbury and there they would face each other again. The night before the battle, King Arthur dreamed that the ghost of Sir Gawaine warned him that if he fought the next day, he would be killed. But he put the warning out of his mind as a bad dream and soon forgot about it.

The next day, both armies came together in furious battle. The air was filled with the sounds of sword on sword and spears crashing against shields. Many knights on both sides had already been killed when King Arthur spotted Sir Mordred leaning on his sword near some fallen knights. Snatching up a great spear, he ran toward Sir Mordred, crying "Traitor! This day you will die!"

When he saw King Arthur coming, Sir Mordred quickly raised his sword and ran to meet him. With a mighty thrust, King Arthur plunged his spear into Sir Mordred, just below his shield. At the same time, Sir Mordred struck Arthur a terrible blow on the head with his sword. The blade split his helmet wide open and pierced King Arthur's brain.

Sir Mordred fell to the ground, dead. King Arthur, badly wounded, was helped by a young knight off the field where he could rest. "Ah, Sir Lancelot," groaned the King in great pain, "I needed you today. I am sorry I was ever against you, for I fear I am going to die as Sir Gawaine warned me in my dream."

Then King Arthur called one of his knights, Sir Bedivere, to his side. "Sir Bedivere," said the King, "take my sword, Excalibur, and throw it in that lake you see yonder. Then come back and tell me what you saw there." Sir Bedivere did as he was told. When he reached the lake, he threw the sword as far as he could out over the water. To his astonishment, an arm, clad all in white, rose out of the water and caught the sword in mid-air. Then, as Sir Bedivere watched, the arm shook the sword three times and disappeared beneath the waves.

Shaking with disbelief, Sir Bedivere hurried back to King Arthur and told him what he had

seen. "Take me there immediately," gasped
the King, "for I fear I have waited too long."
Sir Bedivere obeyed the King's orders and led
the dying monarch to the waterside. There,
floating gently near the shore, was a beautiful
barge, draped in colorful silks and decorated
with precious jewels. And in the barge were
three queens: Queen Morgan le Fay, Arthur's
sister, the Queen of Northgalis and the Queen
of the Waste Lands. Also in the barge was the
Lady of the Lake, who had done so much for
Arthur. Slowly and gently, Sir Bedivere helped
King Arthur into the barge. Morgan le Fay cra-
dled the King's head in her lap and spoke gently to him. Then the boat began to move away
from the shore. Sir Bedivere shouted after the
King, "My lord Arthur, what shall I do now
that you're leaving me here with my enemies?"

Weakly, the King raised his head and
replied: "Do the best you can, for I cannot
help you any more. I am going to the Vale of
Avalon to be healed of my wound."

And with that, the barge slowly vanished
into the mists hovering over the lake, taking
with it the noble Arthur, founder and leader of
the Knights of the Round Table and the greatest of all Kings.

That night, four ladies were spied bringing a
corpse into a tomb in the chapel at Canterbury, lighting a hundred candles around it,

There, floating gently near the shore, was a
beautiful barge.

and leaving behind a thousand gold-pieces for the bishop. Everyone knew whose body it was, and above the tomb was written:

HERE LIES ARTHUR, THE ONCE AND FUTURE KING.

Later, when Queen Guenevere heard that King Arthur, Sir Mordred and many other knights had been killed, she fell into a deep sadness. Because of this sadness and perhaps because she felt that she herself had caused a great deal of unhappiness, the Queen decided to devote herself to a religious life. Leaving the court and giving up her crown, she went to a convent in Almesbury where she spent her days praying and doing good deeds.

When Sir Lancelot heard the news of King Arthur's death, he, too, was greatly saddened. He returned to England, where he learned of all that had happened. After paying his respects at Sir Gawaine's tomb, Sir Lancelot went to Almesbury to see Queen Guenevere. Although she was glad to see him, Guenevere found that just looking at him reminded her of all the terrible things that had happened and of the death of King Arthur. And though it was very painful for her, she asked him to leave and not to return. Sir Lancelot felt as if his heart would break, but he understood why they had to part. Before he left, he promised Guenevere that he, too, would devote himself to a life of prayer and service. Then, sadly, he

departed from Queen Guenevere for the last
time.

Not long after Sir Lancelot had left, Queen
Guenevere fell ill. She was unable to get her
strength back, and within a short time, the
unhappy woman passed out of this life. Just
before she died, she asked that Sir Lancelot
be summoned and that after her death he
bury her beside King Arthur. When he learned
that Guenevere was dying, Sir Lancelot
rushed to her side, but he arrived a half hour
too late. With a heavy heart, Lancelot did as
she requested and saw to it that her body was
laid in King Arthur's tomb.

Then, weary and dejected, the grieving
knight returned to Joyous Gard. Now that
both Guenevere and King Arthur were dead,
Sir Lancelot found himself with little reason
to live. Nearly everyone he loved and cared
about was gone. As time went by, he began
eating less and less. Over the months, his
body slowly wasted away. Finally, he, too,
became very sick and in his weakened condition he could not get well. Soon after, Sir
Lancelot died. His body was prepared for
burial at Joyous Gard as he had wished. And
as his loyal knights stood weeping over his
tomb, Sir Ector murmured these final words:

"You were never defeated in battle by any
earthly knight. You were the truest friend we

ever had. You were always courteous and gentle with women, and you were stern, but fair, with your enemies. You were the greatest knight of all and we shall not look upon your like again."

THE END

DOVER
CHILDREN'S THRIFT CLASSICS

Robin Hood

RETOLD BY
BOB BLAISDELL

Illustrated by Thea Kliros

Dover Publications, Inc.
New York

Bibliographical Note

Robin Hood is a new work, first published by Dover Publications, Inc., in 1994.

Library of Congress Cataloging-in-Publication Data

Blaisdell, Bob.
    Robin Hood / retold by Bob Blaisdell ; illustrated by Thea Kliros.
        p.   cm. — (Dover children's thrift series)
    Summary: Recounts the life and adventures of Robin Hood, who, with his band of followers, lived in Sherwood Forest as an outlaw dedicated to fighting tyranny.
    ISBN 0-486-27573-6 (pbk.)
    1. Robin Hood (Legendary character)—Legends. [1. Robin Hood (Legendary character) 2. Folklore—England.] I. Robin Hood (Legend). English. II. Kliros, Thea, ill. III. Title.   IV. Series.
PZ8.1.B5826Ro   1994
398.22—dc20
[E]
                                                                        94-9381
                                                                           CIP
                                                                            AC

Manufactured in the United States of America
Dover Publications, Inc., 31 East 2nd Street, Mineola, N.Y. 11501

Note

ROBIN HOOD is one of the great folk figures in English tradition. Our information about his legend comes from brief old poems in which single adventures are told. Part of the tradition was also created much later by Sir Walter Scott in his novel *Ivanhoe*. In the nineteenth and twentieth centuries there have been many books telling a continuous story about Robin Hood (and, of course, a number of very successful movies), but there is no one accepted unified version; every complete story is an individual author's imaginative regrouping of the separate elements of the legend.

For the present volume Robert Blaisdell has written a new text based closely on authentic old material. He does not attempt to narrate all the incidents that have been connected with Robin Hood, but concentrates on the most familiar and basic ones, making sure that all the favorite characters are included.

Contents

List of Illustrations

Robin Hood and Little John

ROBIN HOOD was born long, long ago in Locksley town, not far from Nottingham. As a boy Robin worked in Sherwood Forest with his father, a forester who planted and nursed the trees in the King's woodlands. Robin's father was an expert with the bow and arrow, and Robin learned to shoot a bow from him. Robin's mother was the niece of a knight, Sir Jervey. Her brother was Gamwell, a squire of famous degree, of Great Gamwell Hall. Robin was sixteen when his parents died of an illness. So unhappy was he that he wandered the forest for several days. Finally he grew so hungry he shot his bow and killed a deer.

In Sherwood Forest all the deer belonged to the King and, unluckily for young Robin, the Sheriff of Nottingham, a young man then himself, captured and arrested him for the killing of that deer and of many others. Robin pleaded innocent to the killing of all but the one, saying that he had been lost and hungry, grieving for his parents. Nevertheless, the Sheriff sentenced Robin to death by hanging.

At the last moment a band of men, bold thieves and hunters who lived in a lodge in the forest, rescued Robin from the scaffold. He then joined them in their adventures and, thanks to his wits and skill in archery, soon became their leader.

When Robin Hood was about twenty years old, he met Little John. Though called "Little," his limbs were large and his height was seven feet, and wherever he went, people quaked in their shoes.

The day they met, Robin said to his jolly men, "Wait here in this grove and listen for my signal. I shall search the forest for deer to shoot or a rich man to rob."

When he came to a small stream, he happened to meet an enormous young stranger halfway across the narrow footbridge. Neither man would make way for the other, and so they had a standstill. Robin Hood, who had a temper, said, "I'll show you," and drew an arrow to his bow.

The black-bearded stranger answered, his voice a growl, "I'll thrash you well, my puny man, if you dare to twitch your bowstring."

"You donkey!" said Robin. "If I bend my bow at you, in an instant I can send an arrow through your heart."

"You are a coward," the stranger replied.

"You have a bow with arrows to shoot at me, while I have nothing but a staff in my hand."

"A coward!" said Robin, who had never been addressed so. "Not I! I'll set down my bow and fetch myself a staff."

Robin Hood went back along his path and found a staff of oak, and returned to his place on the bridge. "I'm ready, bold man. Look at my staff, and here on this bridge, we'll have a contest. Whoever falls in, the other shall win, and so by that we'll settle this."

"I agree," said the stranger. "I'm happy to compete."

They fell into battle and swung their strong staffs. At first Robin gave the stranger a bang so hard it made the big man's bones ring. The staggered stranger said, "I'll give as good as I got."

So to it again they went, their staffs in a whirl, and the giant of a man gave Robin such a crack on the skull that Robin saw red. Then Robin Hood, enraged, went at it more fiercely, and struck at the stranger harder. The stranger laughed at Robin's fury. Robin, too mad to see straight, because this man seemed to mock him, lost his balance, was struck by the stranger's powerful staff, and tumbled into the stream.

"I ask you, friend," laughed the stranger, "where are you now?"

They fell into battle and swung their strong staffs.

"I see I'm in the stream," said Robin, his temper now cooled in the cold, rushing stream. "I must acknowledge your strength. I shall no longer fight you—you have won."

Robin waded up onto the bank, and then blew his horn. His men came, clothed in green, to the spot.

"What's the matter?" said Midge the miller's son. "Good master, you're wet to the skin."

"This man knocked me in," said Robin.

"We'll get him for that," said Will Stutely.

Robin cried out, "You will find he's tough." Will took a swing at the stranger, but soon found himself taking a bath in the stream. Midge the miller's son tried to outsmart the big stranger, but the stranger's great strength was smarter than Midge's smarts. Midge, too, was soon sitting in the stream.

"Who else?" cried the stranger.

Now Robin said, "No one will attack you again, my friend. But why not join us and wear our cloak of green? I'll teach you how to use the bow and arrow to shoot at fat deer."

"I like deer," said the stranger. "But where do you find deer that don't belong to the King?"

"Right here in my forest," said Robin Hood. "The deer belong to the forest, and the forest belongs to those who live in it. I and my men live here, and these are our deer."

"And what about the Sheriff of Nottingham?" asked the stranger. "He does not see it the way you do. He serves the King and sets traps and hangs those who hunt the King's deer."

"The Sheriff is our foe, and the deer are ours to eat, as they are any honest man's. The deer belonged to the forest before they belonged to any king. We defend the rights of poor, hungry men to hunt for their food. The King will have to bear this. Please join us."

"I'll join you," said the stranger. "I swear I'll serve you faithfully. I'm a poor man, too. My name is John Little."

"His name should be changed," said Midge. "It's backwards, I think." At the feast which then followed, Robin and the men, as a joke, rechristened him Little John.

"We live here like squires," Robin told him. "We feast on good meat, wine and ale. We have the forest at our command. You are so grand and fine a fellow, you shall be my right-hand man."

"Very good," replied Little John. "And you shall be my lord."

Sir Richard and His Castle

ONE AFTERNOON Little John said to Robin Hood, "Master, it's about time you ate. It would do you good."

Robin Hood answered, "I do not feel like eating today, unless I have some rich and worthy knight as my guest, a man who might pay us for a feast."

"Tell us, then," said Little John, "where to go and whom to rob."

"Of course you must not rob any poor men, nor any good men that are squires. But rich churchmen, nobles and knights are fair game," said Robin Hood. "Take your good bow in your hand, Little John, and let Midge and Will Stutely go with you. Wait for our unknown guest, be he an earl, baron, bishop or knight, and bring him here to me."

Little John led the men and waited by the highway, till finally riding from the town there came a sad and grieving knight. Little John stepped out into the highway and went down on one knee. "Welcome, sir knight," politely said Little John. "Welcome to Sherwood

7

Forest. My master is waiting for you to come to dinner."

"Who is your master?" asked the knight.

Little John said, "Robin Hood."

"I have heard good things of Robin Hood. I agree to go with you, my friends." Even so, the knight was sad as he followed Little John, Midge and Will. There was some trouble on his mind that Little John could not discover. They brought him to the lodge door where Robin and all the men lived. When Robin saw him, he too went down on his knee. "Welcome, sir knight, you are welcome to our home. I have been waiting to serve you dinner."

The knight answered, "Thank you, Robin, and all your good men."

They washed and then sat down together to dine. They had bread and wine, and good deer steaks, swans, pheasants and waterfowl.

"Did you enjoy your meal?" asked Robin.

"Thank you," said the knight. "Such a dinner I have not had in many a year. If I ever come to your country again, Robin, I shall prepare for you a dinner as splendid as this you made me."

"Whenever I serve a dinner, sir knight, I am never so greedy as to eat it alone. Tell me your name now. But I must tell you, I expect you to pay for this dinner. Our rule here is that the rich must pay."

"My name is Sir Richard," said the sad knight, "but I am ashamed to say that I have no more than ten pennies."

"If you have no more than ten, I will not charge you a penny. And if you have need of any money, I shall lend it to you," said Robin Hood. "Little John, please look and see if what the knight says is so."

Little John looked through the knight's moneybox, and then went to his master. "It is true," he said.

"How is it," said Robin to the knight, "that you have lost your riches?"

"I had a son, good Robin, who jousted with a knight. When in that fight my son was killed, I paid out money to find his slayer, one Guy of Gisborne. The money that I paid out to marksmen and Sheriff's men was never returned. I had to borrow more from a rich bishop nearby to continue my search, but the bishop now demands his money when he knows I have nothing with which to repay him. He will take my land and my castle and put myself and my daughter out."

"What is the sum you owe him?" asked Robin. "Please tell me."

"Four hundred gold pieces," said the knight.

Tears fell out of his eyes, and he turned to go away.

"Where are your friends?" asked Robin Hood.

"Robin," said Sir Richard, "they do not know me any more, for shame of my poverty."

"Come here," said Robin Hood to Little John, "and go to my treasure room, and bring me four hundred gold pieces. We are going to help a sad knight who has fallen into poverty."

Sir Richard blessed Robin, and thanked him countless times. Robin felt glad to help such a knight.

On that very evening Little John accompanied the knight on his way to the bishop's palace. The bishop was waiting there to take possession of the castle nearby unless Sir Richard paid him in full by sunset the next day.

When morning came, Sir Richard's daughter Marian was in the castle gathering up their few remaining goods, for she believed that they were losing the castle and land that day.

The bishop was sitting at his dinner table at home, when knocks on the door announced the knight was at the gate.

"Welcome, Sir Richard," said the porter. "The bishop and his men are waiting for you now."

The knight went forth and into the bishop's

hall, and kneeled down and saluted the bishop and his men, including Robin's enemy, the Sheriff of Nottingham. "I have come on the day of payment," said Sir Richard.

"Have you brought me my money?" said the bishop.

"Not one penny," said the knight.

"You are terribly in my debt," said the bishop, laughing. "Why are you here if you do not mean to pay me for the loan?"

"I ask you," said Sir Richard, "to give me more time."

"Your time is up," said the Sheriff, the bishop's friend.

"Please, good Sheriff," said Sir Richard, "won't you speak for me?"

"I will not do that," said the Sheriff.

"Then, good bishop," said Sir Richard, "allow me to be your servant till I may pay you back in full."

"No," said the bishop. "I have a fancy for your land."

"Do you not know," asked Sir Richard, "that it is good to help a friend in need?"

"Get out, poor man!" cried the bishop. "Get out of my hall!"

Sir Richard now jumped up and strode toward the bishop. At the bishop's feet he dropped a heavy sack. "Here is your gold, bishop," said the knight. "It is all the money that you loaned to me. Had you been decent to me I would have paid you more!"

The bishop sat still at his table, and could not eat another bite. Sir Richard turned and left the bishop's hall and rode home in triumph on his horse.

"Welcome, father," sweet Marian greeted him. "Is it true, then, that all we have is lost?"

"Be happy, my daughter," said Sir Richard. "And let us thank Robin Hood. He gave me gold to pay the bishop. If not for Robin's kindness, we would be beggars now."

Sir Richard then managed his land and estate so well that within one year he was able to return to Sherwood Forest and repay Robin all of his gold. In addition, as a present, he gave Robin a splendid feast and one hundred beautiful silver arrows, which very much pleased Robin's merry men. So began Robin's friendship with Sir Richard, and so began the fondness that Marian, the knight's daughter, felt for Robin.

Friar Tuck

IN SUMMERTIME, when the leaves grow green, and the flowers are fresh and bright, Robin Hood and his men were disposed to play. Some would leap, some would run, and some would shoot their bows. Will Stutely shot a target from three hundred feet, and Midge shot one from four hundred, and finally Little John shot one from five hundred.

"That's such a good shot," remarked Robin Hood, "I'd ride my horse a hundred miles to find an archer as fine as you, Little John."

This made Will Stutely laugh. "There lives a Friar Tuck who will beat both him and you. He can draw a bow so well, he'll beat all of us in a row." Will said the friar lived beyond Sherwood Forest by a stream, and he described the enormous and powerful friar so that anyone might know him.

Robin vowed then he wouldn't eat or drink till he saw this Friar Tuck. He put on his gear and his sword, and took his bow in hand. Wearing a sheaf of arrows at his belt, he set out on his horse.

When he passed through Sherwood Forest and came to the wide, cold stream he saw a strong, big man, whose head was round and shaved on top, though his face was bearded. He wore a loose brown robe and a string of prayer beads—these signs showed he was a friar. At his side he had a broadsword and a small shield.

Robin Hood saw that he had found his man and leapt off his horse. Then he approached the friar and said, "Carry me over this stream, Friar Tuck, or else your life is done."

The friar said nothing but set Robin Hood on his back and strode out into the water. When he got to the middle of the stream, without saying a word, he tossed Robin off his back into the water. "It's your choice," now said the friar, "whether you will sink or swim."

Robin Hood swam to the bank of the stream and so did Friar Tuck.

But Robin was angry and took his bow in hand and let fly an arrow at the friar. Friar Tuck blocked that arrow with the shield at his belt. Robin Hood shot till his arrows were gone. Then he and the friar took their swords and shields and fought like fierce beasts from ten o'clock that day till four in the afternoon.

Without saying a word, he tossed Robin off his
back into the water.

Finally Robin sank to his knees with weariness and asked the friar for a favor. "O Friar Tuck, I beg for a favor on my knees. Allow me to set my horn to my mouth and to blow a blast three times."

"That I will allow," said the friar. "I hope, indeed, you'll blow so hard your eyes and cheeks pop out."

Robin Hood set his horn to his mouth and blew loud three times. Fifty of his merry men with bows in hand came running from the forest. "Whose men are these," asked Friar Tuck, "that come so fast?"

"They are mine," said Robin. "What is it to you?"

"A favor, a favor," said the friar. "Grant me one, just as I granted one to you. Let me put my fingers to my mouth to whistle three times."

"I will let you," said Robin, "or else I should seem unfair."

The friar put two fingers to his mouth and whistled loudly three times. And just as soon as he did, fifty-two savage dogs came running to the friar. "For every man there's a dog," said Friar Tuck. "And for you, I myself and two!" The dogs at once went for Robin and tore off his cloak. Robin was bitten and nipped so hard he yelped.

Little John, seeing his master's danger, cried out to the friar, "Call off your dogs, or else I'll shoot them down."

"Hold your bow, friend," said Friar Tuck, for he loved his dogs quite well. "Do not shoot my pets, and your master and I will make a deal."

So Robin said, "Friar, if you will forsake this life by the stream, you may come and live with us in Sherwood, be our chaplain, and share our merriness, wine and gold."

Now Friar Tuck had lived here by the stream for more than seven years, and no one had been able to persuade him to leave ... until Robin did this day. "I like your service, I think I'll join."

"Welcome, friend. My name is Robin Hood."

"And I am, as you know, good Friar Tuck."

Robin Hood and Allen a Dale

ROBIN HOOD was an outlaw, but he did poor men many good deeds. One day as Robin Hood stood under the leaves of the greenwood tree, he saw a young man come drooping along the way. Every step the young man took he sighed, "Oh, what a woeful day!"

Out from the trees at him stepped Little John and Midge the miller's son. The young man saw them, bent his bow and said, "Stand back! What do you want with me?"

"You need to come see our master under yonder greenwood tree," said Midge.

The young man nodded at the well-armed men and went along, and Robin asked, "Have you money to spare my men and me?"

"I have no money," the young man said, "except five pennies and a ring, a ring I've held for seven long years, to have it at my wedding. But yesterday, I was supposed to marry a maid, and she was taken from me and chosen to be, instead, an old knight's delight today."

"What is your name?" asked Robin Hood.

"My name is Allen a Dale."

18

"What will you give me, young Allen a Dale, to get you to your true love and your true love to you?"

"I have no money," the young man said, "but I would become one of your merry men if you could make that happen."

"How many miles is it to your true love, Allen?"

"It is only five miles."

Then Robin and his men and Allen set out across the plain. When Robin came to the church where Allen was to have been married, he left the men behind and entered.

"Why are you here?" the bishop asked Robin. The bishop was fat and rich and was there to perform the wedding ceremony.

"I am a good harper," said Robin Hood, "the best in the north of England."

"O welcome, o welcome," the bishop then said, clasping Robin by the hand. "Harp music delights me."

"But you shall have no music," said Robin Hood, pulling away. He did not like fat bishops. "You shall have no music till I see the bride and groom."

And just then in came a wealthy knight, Sir Twaddle, who was solemn, gray and old, and after him came a splendidly dressed young lady, Suzanne Marie, who was as beautiful and bright as gold.

"This is not a fitting match," said Robin Hood.

"How dare you," said Sir Twaddle. "Who are you to say such a thing?"

"The bride's protector," said Robin, "that's who."

"I have her consent," said the knight.

"Consent is not desire," said Robin. "I declare that the bride shall choose her own dear one."

"Thank you, good man," said Suzanne Marie, well pleased.

Then Robin Hood put his horn to his mouth and blew two or three blasts. Twenty-four of his archers leaped over the churchyard walls and came marching into the church. The first to come in was Allen a Dale.

"He is my dear one," cried the beautiful bride, "Allen a Dale."

"She is my dear one," said Allen a Dale, "Suzanne Marie."

"You each have found your true love," said Robin to Allen. "And you shall be married today."

"That shall not be," said the bishop, "for you have no right. Your blessing will not count."

"No right? Why not?"

"Because I am the bishop, I am a man of the cloth! This coat gives me my right."

Robin Hood clutched the bishop's arm, said, "Excuse me, please," and pulled off the bishop's coat and handed it to Friar Tuck. He was as large as the bishop was fat, and was able to pull it on. "I declare," said Robin, "this coat makes you the right man, Friar Tuck."

"Then I may marry the true loves?" asked Friar Tuck.

"Does the coat give him the right?" Robin Hood asked the bishop.

Now the bishop was not a brave man, and the men's swords and bows scared him quite a lot. He agreed and said, "Yes, he has the right, beggarly friar though he be."

"And you, Sir Twaddle, do you agree that Suzanne Marie should marry the man she loves, a man as fresh as spring, and not a man in the depth of winter?"

Sir Twaddle was a good man, but an old man, and he could not help but see that Suzanne Marie and Allen a Dale were as matched as matched could be. "I resign my claim," he said sadly. "I admit defeat. I see where love is and where it is not. I bless both him and Suzanne Marie."

"You are very gracious," said Robin.

"I am very sad," said Sir Twaddle. "If you don't mind," he said now, his head low, "I will take myself away before the wedding begins."

"I, too, will go my way," said the bishop.

"Sir Twaddle, please take your leave," said Robin, "and we are sorry for your sorrow. But as for you, dear bishop, we like your company. We shall be glad of your seal and signature when the wedding is over. Please stay."

And now Robin bent his bow at the bishop and asked if the bishop would like to hear the twang of his harp.

"No, not at all," said the bishop. "That is not the harp music I enjoy."

When humble Friar Tuck in a bishop's coat went to take his position, the people began to laugh. "Who gives this maid to be married?" asked Friar Tuck.

"I do!" said Robin Hood. The bride looked like a queen.

"And who gives this man?"

No one answered, so Robin nudged the bishop, who stuttered and then sang, "I do!"

Allen a Dale returned with his wife to Sherwood Forest, where the merry men built them a little house beside the lodge. Allen a Dale enjoyed his life as an outlaw, and Suzanne Marie enjoyed her life as the wife of the happiest outlaw in Robin's troop. The men envied Allen's happiness, and Robin did too. "I think we merry men need wives," said Robin. "Or we all shall be miserable."

Guy of Gisborne

ONE MORNING in springtime Robin Hood had a dream. He woke and told it to his men.

"I thought two men, one who seemed a wild beast, the other someone I know, beat and bound me and took my bow from me." Robin thought a moment and said, "If my name is Robin Hood, I'll take revenge on those two."

"Indeed that's your name, good master," said Little John. "But don't be hasty to read your dream. Dreams are strange and as unpredictable as the wind, which blows quickly over a hill tonight and yet tomorrow may be still."

But Robin Hood would not heed such talk. "I'm going to seek these men of my dream in the forest. Little John will go with me." They covered themselves in their green cloaks and went till they came within sight of the greenwood tree. There they saw a hulking man, clothed in horsehide from head to toe, who was leaning against the tree. The sword and dagger at the man's side had been the death of many men. It was from his dream that Robin recognized this loathsome man!

"Stay here," said Little John to Robin, "behind this grove, and I will go to this man and find out what he wants."

"How often have I sent my men ahead and stayed behind, John? Why shouldn't I go myself to this man and discover his business?" Now Robin, in bad spirits from his disturbing dream, was cruel to his friend and said, "If I thought my bow wouldn't break, John, I'd hit it over your head."

These words so angered Little John, that he scowled and stalked away. He sulkily wandered till he heard a shout, and near the town he found his fellows chasing after the Sheriff's men, who had just shot two of Robin's. Little John swore to himself, "I'll shoot that Sheriff, and please my friends and master."

Little John went after the Sheriff on his own, and discovered him safe in Nottingham's town square. Little John, undisguised and unhidden, bent his bow at the Sheriff and made to shoot, but the bow was made of poor wood and snapped in two. This attracted the attention of the Sheriff's men. "Woe to you, wicked wood," said Little John. "Today you have vexed me when I needed your help."

The Sheriff's men rushed at Little John and captured him and tied him to a post.

"You shall be chopped up and down till you are dead and then hanged upon a tree," said the Sheriff to Little John. The Sheriff hated Robin and Robin's men more than any man should hate.

Let us leave talking of Little John, for he is tied up for now, and speak instead of the fearsome Guy of Gisborne and Robin Hood, under the greenwood tree.

"Good morning, good man," said Sir Guy of Gisborne.

"Good morning, good sir," said Robin Hood. "By the look of your bow, I think you must be a good archer."

Guy of Gisborne nodded and said, "I am fair enough. But I'm unsure of my way."

"Then I'll guide you through the forest, friend," said Robin Hood.

"I'm looking for an outlaw," said Sir Guy. "Men call him Robin Hood. I'd rather meet him than find a pile of gold."

"It might be better for you if you don't," said Robin. "Let's have a contest, meanwhile, friend. We'll walk in the woods and shoot at marks."

Robin wanted to test his foe and so led the fierce man along.

"That bump on the log," said Robin, pointing his arm. "Whoever comes closest, will win the first round." Guy of Gisborne was an expert archer, but he could not at first see the mark.

"What log?" said Sir Guy.

"Through those trees, and beyond that meadow, there lies a log."

"Ah," said Sir Guy, narrowing his eyes. "Ah, I think I see. But what bump?"

"On the left, down along the side. There it is," said Robin, pointing again, "about the size of a nut."

"Hmm," said Guy of Gisborne. "I cannot see it."

"There!" said Robin. He plucked his bow and sent off an arrow. In a moment, Sir Guy could see the log and the arrow, like a flag, waving from it. "There is the bump," said Robin.

Sir Guy was surprised at the wonderful shot, and he strung his bow and himself let an arrow fly. Sir Guy hit the log, but they discovered, when they had walked out from the trees and over the meadow, that it was Robin's arrow only that struck the bump.

"You shoot very well," said Sir Guy.

"No," said Robin, "not I. I'm just fair enough."

"Let me choose the target this time," said Sir Guy.

"Please do," said Robin.

"I choose," said Guy of Gisborne, thinking evil thoughts, "I choose the cap upon your head. That will be our mark."

"Very well," said Robin. "Who shall shoot first?"

"I shall," said Sir Guy. "Please stand by that tree."

Robin strode over to the tree, and stood his ground. He lifted his chin, tapped his cap down tight on his head, folded his arms across his chest, and called out, "Shoot away!"

Guy of Gisborne thought this man was quite silly. He was tempted to shoot the man and not the cap. He notched his arrow, he squinted at Robin, he pulled the string, and the arrow shot out. At the last moment Robin ducked and then shouted, "Good shot, my friend, good shot!" For Robin's cap was stuck dead to the tree.

"Now," said Robin, "it's my turn. I don't think I can top that."

Sir Guy turned pink. He was very angry with this clown. He had tried to kill Robin with that shot, and now he had to allow Robin to shoot at him!

Robin handed Sir Guy his torn cap, and Sir Guy, patting it up, put it gently on his head.

"Now hold still," called out Robin. "No moving." Robin made ready, but then held his string. "Good, sir," he called. "Sir? If I shoot the cap from further away, does that mean I win?"

"No," called back Sir Guy. "We shall shoot till someone misses." Sir Guy planned to miss his next shot and strike his foe in the heart.

"Here she flies!" cried Robin. Sir Guy was brave yet he could not help but close his eyes. Robin plucked his bow and away flew the arrow.

Sir Guy waited and waited and then waited some more, his eyes still closed. He was waiting for the sound of the arrow to pass by. "Shoot!" he cried out. "Shoot the arrow, young man!"

"I shot it," said Robin quietly. "Now open your eyes."

Sir Guy opened his eyes and then felt for the cap upon his head. It was there, the cap was still on his head! "Ha, ha, young fellow, you have missed your mark!"

As Sir Guy gleefully held out Robin's cap to return it, out of the blue sky, high from above the greenwood tree, dropped an arrow, straight down through the cap! Sir Guy was so startled, his eyes bulged out.

"Who are you?" he cried. "What a shot! Tell me your name, friend." Now Guy of Gisborne was the most terrible man ever to set foot in Sherwood Forest, and yet this fool had amazed him. "Tell me."

"No, no," said Robin, "not till you've first told me yours, my friend."

"I come from far away, over the hills and dales. I've done many wicked deeds, I must admit. Today I murder Robin Hood for a bounty from the Sheriff. The Sheriff, indeed, is rounding up that outlaw's men right now, to rid him of all pests. My name," he said bowing, "is Guy of Gisborne."

"My name," bowed Robin, "is Robin Hood, the man you seek."

It was a splendid sight then, to see how these two men went at each other with their shining swords for two hours that summer day. Neither man could hit the other, but their swords sang out like angry steel.

"You are a dead man!" cried Sir Guy.

"Not before you will be," said Robin.

Both warriors began to stagger, their swords screeched up and down. Robin seemed the weaker at first, but then it seemed Sir Guy. Finally they had battled so that their swords were crossed, and Sir Guy gave Robin Hood a shove, and Robin went tumbling down.

"Oh," cried Robin, "it can't have been my

fate to die today." With these words, and with Guy about to strike him dead, Robin leaped up again and found a target on his foe. He swung his sword and killed the fearsome Guy.

Weary Robin stood over his foe. "Lie there, wicked Guy of Gisborne, and don't be angry with me if you've received worse wounds than I. You will now receive better clothes." And so Robin switched his clothes with Sir Guy, and clad himself head to toe in his foe's leather, bloody though it was. "I need a new disguise," said Robin Hood, "to repay that Sheriff who offered you a prize."

Robin took up Sir Guy's bow and arrows and horn, and went off to Nottingham, where Little John was tied to a post awaiting death. When Robin entered the town he blew Sir Guy's horn and sent a blast the Sheriff heard.

"Listen," said the Sheriff, "I hear good news. Sir Guy's horn has blown, and he has killed Robin Hood."

At this Little John groaned.

"Here comes Sir Guy in his suit of horse-hide," said the Sheriff. "Greetings, my fearsome Sir Guy of Gisborne. Ask for your reward and you'll receive it."

"I don't want gold," said Robin Hood. "And I

don't want land. Now that I have slain the master, let me strike down his second in command. That's all I ask."

"You're a madman," said the Sheriff. "You could have had riches. But since you've so asked, so will you receive."

Now Little John had heard his master speak and knew well it was his voice. The disguise could not hide his true friend Robin from him, and he knew he would soon be freed.

As Robin Hood went towards Little John, the Sheriff and his men followed to watch Little John's death.

"Get back," cried Robin Hood. "Why are you crowding me? It's not the custom where I come from for others to hear a man's last words."

The Sheriff and his men retreated, and Robin pulled out a knife and cut loose Little John. He gave Little John Sir Guy's bow and arrows and told him to flee. But John took Sir Guy's bow and bloody arrows and took an aim at the Sheriff. The Sheriff turned to run away and so did the Sheriff's men. The Sheriff received an arrow high up on his thigh, and tumbled to the ground. His men had to pull him up and take him home, and Little John felt avenged.

Robin pulled out a knife and cut loose Little John.

"Friends again?" asked Little John, offering Robin his hand.

Robin Hood said, laughing, "Of course, my fellow. The blame was all on me." Forever after Robin remembered his insult to Little John, and greatly regretted his temper.

Robin Hood and Little
John Meet Their Kin

IN NOTTINGHAM there lived a tanner, a man who turned hides into leather. His name was Arthur a Bland, and he was as tough as the leather he made. One summer morning he went into Sherwood Forest to see the King's deer that range among the trees, and there he met Robin Hood.

"Hold on there, young fellow," said Robin Hood, bending his bow at the tanner. "What is your business here? You look to me like a thief, one who comes to shoot at the King's deer. I must ask you to halt."

"I think I will not," said the tanner. "But if you try to stop me I shall put a knot on your head with my long oak staff."

At this Robin Hood unbuckled his belt and laid down his longbow and arrows. He took up his own staff of oak that was both stiff and strong. "I shall use your weapon," said Robin, "since you will not back down from mine."

"My staff is made of oak, and it will knock down a bull, and I think it will also knock down you. So take care," said Arthur a Bland.

Robin Hood was angry at these words and swung his long oak staff. He clipped the tanner on the head so hard that Arthur wandered in a short circle before he could shake himself back awake. He brushed the blood from off his face and took a swing at Robin.

The tanner's club found its mark, and toppled Robin Hood to the ground. The blood now dyed Robin Hood's dark hair red, but before Arthur could deliver another blow, up leapt Robin, and about and about they went, darting and lunging, like two wild beasts.

Finally, Robin Hood said, "Hold your hand, hold your hand, and let us end our quarrel. From now on, you are free to roam the woods of Sherwood."

"I have my staff to thank for that gift, not you," said Arthur, still rather angry.

"Come, come," said Robin Hood, "tell me what you do for a living. And where do you live?"

"I am a tanner," Arthur answered, "and I have worked for a long time in Nottingham. I give you my promise that if you come into town, I will tan your hide for free."

Robin laughed. "Well, good friend, since you are willing to be so kind to me, I will return the favor. But if you give up this tanning trade, and live in the green forest with me and my men, I swear by my name, which is Robin

Hood, that I will pay you gold and dress you in our Lincoln green."

"If you are Robin Hood," said Arthur a Bland, "then I will never leave. Because, please tell me, where is Little John? He is the one of whom I want to hear. For his mother is my aunt, and my mother is his aunt, and we are cousins."

Robin Hood blew on his bugle horn loudly and quite shrilly, and Little John quickly appeared running down a grassy hill. "What has happened?" cried out Little John. "Master, tell me what is the matter?"

"It's this tanner," said Robin Hood. "He is a strong young man and master of his business. He has tanned my hide quite well."

"He is to be praised," said Little John, "if he really did do that. But if he is that strong, then he and I shall have a fight, and he can try to tan my hide as well." Little John pounded his staff upon the ground and nodded at the man.

"No, dear Little John," said Robin Hood, "I understand that this man is a relative of yours. His name is Arthur a Bland."

Then Little John tossed the staff as far away as he could fling it, and threw himself upon Arthur a Bland and hung around his neck. Little John and Arthur wept for joy. Then Robin Hood smiled and called them back to join him under the greenwood tree to celebrate.

The summer went on, and the forest had not yielded many people for Robin Hood and his men to rob. The deer were scarce, as they had been killed by many besides Robin and his men. "We have no vittles," announced Robin. So he and the men set out separately to see what they each could find.

It was in the middle of the day when Robin met the fanciest man that had ever walked through the forest. The man's shirt was made of silk, and his stockings were scarlet red. As he walked on along his way, he did not notice Robin, but instead spied a fine herd of deer.

"Now the best of all you deer," declared the stranger, "I shall have for my dinner."

The stranger took no time at all to pull out his bow and bend it deep. And in an instant he shot, from a long distance, the best of the herd.

"Good shot! Good shot!" called out Robin Hood then. "That shot was as good as a man can make, and if you will accept, you shall become one of my merry men."

"Rather than that, why don't you go cut up and prepare my deer? Get to it now, or with my fist I'll make you sore," said the stranger.

"You had better not try that," said Robin

Hood, "because though I seem an easy mark, all alone, if I just blow my horn I can have several dozen men who will join my side."

"No matter how fast you blow your horn," the stranger said, "I can pluck my bow just as fast and stop your breath."

Robin Hood was angry and pulled out his bow to shoot, and the stranger just as quickly bent his bow at Robin. They stood poised, ready to shoot, each waiting for the other to flinch. "Hold on, hold on!" said Robin Hood, lowering his bow. "We are at a standstill. Let's instead take our swords and shields and fight our fight under that tree."

"Fair enough," said the stranger. "I will not flee."

They swung their swords and gave each other a powerful blow across the shield. They both almost fell over faint. "Let's take a rest," said Robin. And then he and the stranger sat down under the greenwood tree.

"Oh, my goodness," said Robin. "You are a mighty man, aren't you? Tell me who you are, and tell me why you have come."

"I shall tell you," said the stranger. "I was born and bred in Maxfield, and my name is Young Gamwell. I am looking for an uncle of mine, some call him Robin Hood."

"You are a relative of Robin Hood's? We should not have fought at all."

"I am his sister's son."

"Then I am your mother's brother!" said Robin Hood. And he and Young Gamwell leapt to their feet and hugged and cried.

Little John now came along this trail near the tree and said, "Oh, master, where have you been all day?"

"I met this stranger," said Robin Hood, all bloody. "He has given me a terrible drubbing."

"Then I shall have a fight with him," said Little John, "and see if he can beat me."

"Oh no, oh no," said Robin Hood. "Little John, that may not be. For he is my own sister's son, my nephew who is dear to me. He shall become one of our merry men, and Scarlet shall we call him. We will be the bravest outlaws in all of England."

"Very well," said Little John. "Now who shot that deer over there? For the men are hungry."

"My nephew did the deed," said Robin Hood. "Let us shoot several more and make a feast."

"Very good, dear master," said Little John. And Little John and Robin Hood and Scarlet plucked their bows and killed deer for their feast.

The Monk and the
Capture of Robin Hood

"THIS IS a merry morning," said Little John. "And a merrier man than I does not live. Pluck up your heart, dear master, and see that it's a beautiful morning in May."

"No, there is something that grieves my heart," said Robin Hood. "It makes my heart ache. I haven't been to church for two weeks. Today I will go to Nottingham."

"Then take twelve of your men, well armed, master, so no one dare try to kill you," said Midge.

"No," said Robin, "I will take no men but Little John, who shall bear my bow till I need it."

"You shall bear yours and I shall bear mine, and along our way we shall shoot at marks for pennies," said Little John. They shot at targets until Little John had won five pennies from his master. Now Robin Hood was the best of shots, but this morning shot much worse than usual.

Little John was proud and laughed at his

luck, and started thinking of ways to spend his pennies in town. But Robin Hood grew riled and called Little John a cheat, and slapped his friend's broad face.

"If you were not my master," cried Little John, "I'd clobber you or run you through. Get yourself a new man, for you have lost me now."

So Robin Hood went alone to Nottingham that morning, and Little John made his way back to his friends.

When Robin walked into Nottingham, he prayed that he would get out safe again. In St. Mary's Church he listened to a sermon. Everyone at church looked at him, and wondered that he was there. Down along the aisle strode a huge monk, who knew Robin Hood as soon as he saw him. He stopped at Robin's pew and gaped for one moment, before continuing past. The monk, who once was robbed by Robin, hoped to take revenge. He sneaked out now and had all the gates of Nottingham locked, and then went and found the Sheriff, who was fast asleep. "Get up, hurry, get ready!" cried the monk. "I have spotted the outlaw Robin Hood, he is in at the Mass. It's your fault, lazy Sheriff, if he gets away."

The Sheriff got up and quickly got ready, and gathered around himself many men. They came to the church and burst through the doors. Robin turned and saw the men, and said to himself, "Alas! Now I miss the company of my friend Little John."

As the Sheriff's men approached, Robin gave up, rather than fight in church. The Sheriff was gleeful. Crowing over the man he had long sought, he said, "Try to escape me this time, you outlaw!"

Indeed, Robin now doubted that he should be able to escape, and did not answer the Sheriff. Robin remembered how he himself had been cruel to Little John and, without Little John's help, Robin thought he was sure to die on the gallows or in prison.

The Sheriff set sorry Robin into the farthest, deepest cell in the jail. The Sheriff then sent off the happy monk on a trip to the King with a letter about the capture, requesting the King's wishes as to the fate of the famous bandit.

When Robin Hood did not return that day to the greenwood tree in Sherwood Forest, his men grew uneasy, especially Little John. He had not forgiven Robin Hood the slap on the cheek, but he also had not forgiven himself for allowing his friend to enter Nottingham alone. He and Midge stopped a passing carter on the road from town and asked for any news. "News?" said the carter. "Yes, the Sheriff has captured the good man Robin Hood. The monk, the one who hated Robin Hood, has set out for the King in London to tell him of the news. The Sheriff and monk expect rewards—"

"And I will be sure to give one to them," said Little John, thinking of revenge. "Thank you, carter."

Midge and Little John set out to block the monk's path. They stole two horses and made great haste, and caught up to the monk the next morning. They greeted him as if they were his friends, and asked him from where he had journeyed.

"I come from Nottingham," said the monk. He did not trust these men and wondered who they were. "And from where might you two come?" he asked.

"We come from the south, and yet we heard some news that cheered our hearts," said Midge, for Little John was too angry with the monk to speak. "We want to hear about that outlaw Robin Hood who was captured yesterday. He robbed me and my friend last year of a sack of gold. If that outlaw has been taken, we'll be quite content."

"So did he rob me of more than that," said the monk. He now trusted these men of

Robin's. "I was the one who caused his arrest. You may thank me for it."

"Yes," said Little John, his voice a growl, "indeed we soon will."

Midge spoke up, "We would like to go with you on your way. You know that outlaw Robin Hood has many wild men, and if you ride this way alone, you'll almost certainly be killed."

"Oh!" said the monk.

Before they went very much further, Midge took the bridle of the monk's horse, and Little John took the monk by the cowl and pulled him off the horse. The monk cried out for mercy.

"Mercy?" said Little John. "That was my master that you brought to harm. You'll never get to our King to tell him your tale."

"No, indeed," said Midge. "You'll be spending the rest of your life among Robin's men, unless indeed Robin returns to us." They took the Sheriff's letter to the King that the monk had kept under his shirt, and then Midge tied the monk's horse to his and led him back to Sherwood Forest while Little John, as the monk's substitute, went on to London.

When Little John arrived at the King's court, he fell on his knees. "God save the King," he said, and handed over the Sheriff's letter.

The King, reading the letter, cried out, "Hurrah!" When he finished, however, he was puzzled and asked, "But where is the monk who was supposed to bring this news?"

"He was too frightened of Robin Hood's men to pass through the forest, and so he asked me if I would take his place," said Little John. "I myself am not afraid of those merry outlaw men."

The King said Little John was a brave man, made him a present of a bag of gold, and named him a Royal Officer. His highness bid him return to Nottingham and tell the Sheriff to bring Robin Hood, unharmed, to him.

Little John, outfitted as a Royal Officer, now took the road back to Nottingham. When he arrived, however, the gates were barred, and Little John called out to the gatekeeper, "Why are the gates barred?"

"Because of Robin Hood," said the gatekeeper. "He's been tossed in our prison and Robin Hood's men have been trying to break in to free him."

"They haven't been able to rescue him, then?" said Little John.

"No, not even close," said the gatekeeper. "And are you the Royal Officer who has come as his escort?"

"That I am. I shall escort him out of Nottingham as soon as I can."

Little John went through the town then and found the Sheriff to give him the King's orders.

"And what happened to the good monk I sent to the King?" asked the Sheriff. He did not recognize this hulking man as Little John, the man he had once hired, the man he had once tied to a post and was about to hang.

"The King is so fond of the monk," lied Little John, "that he has made him the abbot of Westminster."

The Sheriff was delighted with the news of such a reward. If the monk had earned such a prize, what would the Sheriff's be? The Sheriff was too excited to suspect Little John any longer. He gave him a grand dinner and served him the finest wine. That night, after the Sheriff went to bed, Little John slipped through the town to the prison, called out to the jailer and asked him to get up.

"Get up?" cried the jailer. "Why should I?"

"Because," said Little John, "I am a Royal Officer, and your prisoner Robin Hood has escaped."

The jailer ran out to Little John and begged for pardon. "Please help me," said the jailer.

"Perhaps you may help me," said Little John.

"If ever I may, I will," said the jailer.

"Let us go see the cell from which he escaped," said Little John.

"Yes," said the jailer. "Let us see."

When they arrived at the cell, the jailer took his keys and opened the door. The dark, heavy door creaked. The cell was pitch black. But the jailer was surprised that when he held up a torch, there was Robin Hood fast asleep, sharing with a mouse a bed of straw.

"Why," whispered the jailer, with surprise and relief, "this is Robin Hood indeed."

"Go see," said Little John. "Go wake him and see."

As the jailer trembled, Robin Hood sat up and saw his dear Little John at the door.

"Little John!" said he.

"Hello, Robin," said Little John.

"It is he! Robin Hood!" said the jailer, jumping back.

"So I am!" said Robin Hood. "But for the rest of the night, you shall take my place."

Little John laughed with joy and said, "Thank you, jailer, for your help. We mean no harm to you, so if you stay here quietly, we shall let you live."

"I shall be quiet," said the jailer, "as quiet as this mouse." And he sat down on the straw where Robin Hood had been and watched Little John and Robin Hood close the door.

There was Robin Hood fast asleep, sharing with a
mouse a bed of straw.

When the Sheriff came that morning with his men to take Robin Hood away to the King, he found instead the jailer and a mouse asleep inside. "Where is Robin Hood?" cried the Sheriff.

"The King's deputy has already taken him, sir," said the jailer.

"But when? And why are you here?"

"This morning, sir, before the cock did crow. I admit I did not know, sir, that the King had made one of Robin Hood's men, Little John, the messenger for his fate."

"Little John!" said the Sheriff. He and his men ran out to the town gates, and the gate-keeper gave them the news that Robin Hood had been safely escorted out several hours before.

Already, Robin Hood and his men were celebrating under the greenwood tree deep in Sherwood Forest. Robin had apologized to Little John for his slap on the cheek and had offered to be Little John's own servant, but that was something Little John would not allow.

The men were glad to have Robin Hood back safe and sound. They released the monk, who felt lucky to still have his life, and he returned to Nottingham. "If I ever see Robin

Hood in church again," said he, "then I will walk by and say nothing but 'Bless him!' "

The Sheriff could get no one to go after Robin Hood in the forest, and he had no one to send to the King. And so he went to London himself with the distressing news that Robin Hood, the kingdom's most famous outlaw, had escaped again. He expected the King would have his head, and sad as could be was he.

But the King had mercy on the Sheriff. "This Little John, Sheriff, has tricked you, but he also tricked me. And so I pardon you, I pardon me, and I now also pardon Little John and Robin Hood, for there are no such heroes in all England. Little John was true to his master and fooled us all!"

Robin Hood and the Tinker

ONE DAY, as Robin Hood was walking towards Nottingham, he met a tinker, a man who fixed pots and pans. The tinker was a large, strong man, and Robin Hood politely said hello and asked, "Have you any news? You go from town to town, tell me what you have heard."

"All the news I have is my own," said the tinker. "I have a warrant from the King to arrest the daring outlaw Robin Hood wherever I find him. If you can tell me where he is, I will give you a small reward. The King will give me a hundred gold coins if I can bring that man before him, so if we can now arrest him, we shall be as rich as rich can be."

"Let me see that warrant, friend," said Robin Hood. "If it looks right, I will do the best I can so that we might catch him tonight."

"I will not show you," said the tinker. "I will not trust anyone with it. If you will not tell me where he is, I must go and try to trap him on my own."

"If you will go to Nottingham with me," said Robin, "I know we shall find him."

The tinker squinted at Robin Hood and Robin squinted at the tinker. "May I trust you?" asked the tinker.

"As well as I may trust you," said Robin.

The tinker had a long, knotty staff and Robin had a good long knife, and, looking each other over again, they nodded and set out for Nottingham. In the town they came to an inn where they might spend the night and drink. They both called for beer and wine. But the tinker drank so fast he lost his wits and fell asleep.

Robin Hood searched the tinker's coat till he found the warrant and the tinker's money-bag. "I shall keep both of these for you," said Robin to his dozing friend.

"Who is paying the bill for the beer and wine?" the innkeeper asked Robin.

"My friend will pay the bill," said Robin. "He also needs a room in which to sleep. Good-night."

When the tinker woke up in the morning and saw that his companion was gone, he called for the innkeeper. "I had a king's warrant for the arrest of the daring outlaw Robin Hood, and now it is gone. I had a bag of money, and now that is gone. I cannot pay you. The man who promised to be my friend has run away and robbed me."

"That friend you mention," said the innkeeper, "they call him Robin Hood. When you met him, you should have known he would do you no good."

"Had I known it was he, I would have arrested him and had my reward. In the meantime, innkeeper, I must go away. I will go and find him, whatever happens to me. Now, how much do I owe you?"

"Ten pennies," said the innkeeper.

"I will pay very soon," said the tinker, "or else you may keep my workbag, and my good tinkering hammer too."

"The only way you might find him and catch him," said the innkeeper, "is while he's out alone in the forest shooting the King's deer."

The tinker ran off into the forest until he found Robin Hood hunting deer. The tinker did not hide himself at all, but strode directly at his foe.

"Who is this fool," said Robin Hood, "that is coming toward me here?"

"No fool, no fool," said the tinker. "If you want to know who has done whom most wrong, just watch my crab-tree staff."

Robin drew his sharp steel sword, but the tinker got his blows in fast and bruised Robin black and blue.

"One moment, one moment!" cried out Robin Hood. "Grant me, please, one moment."

"Before I grant you a moment, I'll hang you from this tree," said the tinker. But when he turned to see if any of Robin's men were approaching, Robin blew his horn, and in three instants Little John and Will Stutely came.

"What is the matter again?" said Little John. Robin Hood often got himself into difficulties like these.

"This tinker here has hammered my body," said Robin.

"Let us see," said Little John, "what he can do with me."

"No," said Robin. "I wish to see this quarrel cease. I want us all to live in peace. Let us give the jolly tinker a reward, as much as the King offered in ransom for me. He is a mighty man, and I should prefer he be on our side than against us."

The tinker was quite content with this and made his peace with Robin. He took the bag of gold that Little John offered and returned to Nottingham to pay the innkeeper and claim his tools.

The Sheriff's Man

IT WAS a bright, sunny day, and the young men who lived in Nottingham town held a shooting contest. Little John was wandering through the forest seeking to shoot the King's deer when he overheard shouts and cheers. His face was newly shaven and he was sure no one would know him, so he made his way down to the town and went among the young men, asking if he might shoot with them. A contest was as irresistible to Little John as it was to Robin Hood.

Three times Little John shot and each time he slit the mark. The Sheriff of Nottingham, who also enjoyed contests, had come to watch and was standing by the target. He did not recognize Little John as one of Robin Hood's men, and exclaimed, "Astounding! This man is the best archer that I ever saw."

He said to Little John, "Tell me now, brave young man, what is your name? Where were you born, and where do you live?"

"In Yorkshire, sir, I was born," said Little John, "and men call me ... " (Little John was thinking up a false name) "Reynold Greenleaf."

"Tell me, Rey Greenleaf, won't you work for me? It's good service and good pay. As one of my men, you just might win the reward for capturing the outlaw Robin Hood."

Little John thought it would be a good joke on the Sheriff to let himself be hired, and he agreed. The Sheriff granted him a good horse and a servant, and Little John began to live in the quarters next to the Sheriff's house. Even with the luxuries of a town life, Little John soon missed Robin Hood and the fellows. He asked the Sheriff if he could return to his old master.

"And who is your old master?" asked the Sheriff.

"A ranger," said Little John. For it was true, Robin Hood ranged far and wide over Sherwood Forest.

"You may return to your ranger," said the Sheriff, "as soon as the year is up."

"A year? But I am unhappy, master. This life does not suit me. I prefer an outdoor life."

"You are mine for a year, wretch. Is the duty too hard, or are you too lazy? I thought highly of you, young man, and now I do not. Even so, you are not leaving my service."

"Then," grumbled Little John to himself,

"then I shall be the worst servant you have ever had."

The next day, the Sheriff went out hunting, and Little John, instead of accompanying him, as was his duty, swore he had a stomachache and stayed in bed. Thinking of the jolly old days under the greenwood tree, which were not so very far in the past, Little John became hungry. "Good steward," he called out to the man who served the Sheriff's men their meals. "I beg you, bring me my lunch."

After a few moments, the steward, a small, earnest, hard-working man, loyal to the Sheriff, came into Little John's room and shook his head at him. "No lunch for those who don't work," said the steward. "No lunch for those with bellyaches. So says the Sheriff, lazy Reynold Greenleaf."

"Bring me my lunch, steward," said Little John, "or I'll crack your head."

The steward, who was two feet shorter than Little John and wise with his years, quickly returned to the kitchen and locked the food cupboards. When Little John slowly rose from bed to come crack his head, he ran out of the house. Then Little John gave one of the cupboards such a kick, it opened like a door. Little John helped himself to a stock of food, ale and wine. He was eating like a bear when the cook, a stout, sturdy man, walked in. "Who crashed in my cupboard door, Rey Greenleaf?"

"That must have been I," calmly said Little John.

"Who told you you could help yourself to the Sheriff's food?" said the cook.

"I must have told myself," said Little John, not stopping in his feast but eating even more.

The cook walked over to Little John and smacked him on the head three times with a spoon. "Get out of my kitchen," said the cook.

"Oh," said Little John, "three times you smacked me, and three times will you be smacked. And then I will finish my meal."

After Little John had smacked the cook with a spoon three times in return, he meant to sit down, but the cook pulled out his sword, and so Little John did the same. They fought bitterly, but neither could harm the other, though they went on for an hour. "I vow," said Little John, "you're one of the best swordsmen that ever yet I saw. If you could shoot as well with a bow as you duel with a sword, you should come back with me to the forest, where I return today, to live again with Robin Hood and his merry fellows."

"Put away your sword," said the cook, "and friends we will be." Then he cooked up a bigger feast than five men usually eat, and he and Little John shared the best meat, bread and wine in the Sheriff's kitchen. Before they set out to join Robin Hood, they went to the Sheriff's treasure drawers and broke open the steel locks. They took away all the Sheriff's silverware, money and drinking cups and went off on the Sheriff's horses to Robin Hood in Sherwood Forest.

"How do you do, master?" said Little John.

"Welcome to you, Little John," said Robin Hood, "and welcome to the good man you have brought. Have you enjoyed your service with the Sheriff?"

"Of course not, master," said Little John. "It was a change of pace for two weeks, but when I asked to be allowed to return to my old life, he would not allow it. But look, today the Sheriff himself sends me back to you with his own cook, his own silverware, money, drinking cups and horses."

"He sent you and the cook and the goods willingly? I doubt this," said Robin Hood.

"He's happy to be rid of me, I assure you," said Little John.

Little John decided to go find the Sheriff in the forest and get his consent. He did not want Robin to doubt his word, which, as we know, was so far quite false. He ran off five miles along trails and through woods until he found the Sheriff hunting with hounds and horn. Little John rushed towards him and knelt down. "My dear master!" he exclaimed.

"Lazybones Reynold Greenleaf," said the Sheriff, "why are you here and not asleep with an aching belly as I left you?"

"I am better and have been in the forest, and I have seen a beautiful sight. Over there, not far, I saw a gorgeous deer, whose color is green! Green, indeed! And that deer has one hundred and forty in his herd with him. Their horns are so sharp, master, that I dared not shoot at them for fear they would have slashed me."

"I tell you," said the Sheriff, "I have got to see this."

"Come along, then, dear master, and I'll lead you."

The Sheriff rode, and Little John ran, and when they came to the greenwood tree, out leaped Robin Hood. Little John said, "Look, sir Sheriff, there's the leader of the deer!"

The Sheriff, a sorry man, sat still on his horse. "Curse you, Reynold Greenleaf, you have betrayed me!"

"I swear," said Little John, "it is your own fault, because you ordered the steward not to serve me my lunch. After all, you would not allow me to leave your service, and a man in service needs to eat."

"I wish that I had allowed you to leave, certainly," said the Sheriff.

"Then have I your consent to leave your service and to collect my pay?" asked Little John.

"I wish I had never seen you," said the Sheriff. "Of course you should leave my service. As for your pay, you hardly earned a penny."

"Too cheap," said Little John. "Too cheap."

Soon enough, as was the custom when Robin Hood detained any man, the Sheriff was seated at Robin Hood's table and served a supper. But when the Sheriff saw his own cups and silver on the table, he was so sad he could not eat. "Cheer up," said Robin Hood, "because, Sheriff, I shall spare your life."

When they had all eaten well, the day was gone, and Robin Hood told the Sheriff to put on the green cloak of the merry men. "As Little John was made to serve you, so shall you serve me. I shall teach you how to be an outlaw."

"Before I am here another night, Robin Hood, living such a life," said the Sheriff, "I pray to you to kill me. I would forgive you for doing so. Or better yet, be charitable, and let me go, and I shall be the best friend you and your men ever had."

"Swear me an oath, then," said Robin, "on my sword, that you shall never plot harm to me or to any of my men."

The Sheriff, lying in his heart, swore the oath and was allowed to go, though without his gold or silver, which, said Robin Hood, was a good trade for Little John's service.

The Golden Arrow

THE SHERIFF of Nottingham grieved and grieved about the trick that Little John and Robin Hood had played on him. He lamented to all and finally went to London to tell the King.

But the King said, "Why, Sheriff, what would you have me do? Aren't you my Sheriff? Isn't it your duty to deal with such outlaws? You have the power, you have the law, to help you crush that man. Invent some way to draw him and his crew into your town and then you can try to catch them all."

The Sheriff was spurred to think now and devised a luring game. All the archers in the north of England should come one day that autumn. Those who shot the best would take home prizes. He that shot the very best would win a silver arrow tipped with gold, the like of which did not exist in England.

When Robin Hood heard of this contest, he said, "Get ready, my men, for I am going to win."

Now Midge the miller's son had heard from

his father, who heard through a friend, who heard through one of the Sheriff's many men, that the purpose of this contest was to draw out Robin Hood and his men from the forest and into the town, and that, once there in Nottingham, the Sheriff and his men would shoot them down.

But Robin Hood was keen to have that prize arrow, and he turned his mind this way and that. "Listen to me, my men, my friends, my Midge, my Little John: come what may, I have to try my skill at that archery. But this shall we do. We shall not wear our Lincoln green cloaks. We shall dress so that the Sheriff's men will not find us. One shall wear white, another red, one yellow, one blue."

So out through the forest they went, all with steady hearts and minds. They mixed themselves with the people who came to Nottingham for the contest, and the Sheriff, who looked and looked for the Lincoln green cloaks that identified Robin Hood's men, saw none and was vexed. "I thought he would have been here," said the Sheriff, scratching his head. To the herd of contestants, he announced, "Though Robin Hood is brave, he's not so brave as to appear."

When Robin Hood, whose red cloak masked him, heard these words, he winced with pain. "Not brave! I, not brave?"

Standing beside the Sheriff on this day was his pretty fiancée. Christine was as bright and kind as the Sheriff was dark and mean. As they watched the contest he said to her, "If Robin Hood were here, and all of his men to boot, surely none of them could shoot better."

"That man in red," said Christine, "is clearly the best of all." And as she said this, Robin Hood, the man she meant, turned and smiled at the Sheriff. The Sheriff said, "Every shot you take is sure and on the spot. So the arrow with the golden head and the shaft of silver-white is yours, my friend. But tell me, archer, what is your name?"

"His name?" said the bishop, who had come to town to see the contest. The bishop was a man with a sharp eye for faces and remembered Robin's from Allen a Dale's wedding. "Robin Hood!" he exclaimed.

"Indeed it is," said Robin Hood. "You and the bishop were both once my guests. But remember, dear Sheriff, that not long ago, under the greenwood tree, we made a deal."

"Robin Hood!" said the Sheriff. "I hold to nothing said in a robber's nest. Men! My men, kill this thief!" And he himself would have run Robin Hood through with his sword, but his Christine, dear woman, checked his arm.

"Let him go, my darling," she said, "if you

ever gave him your word. A promise is a promise."

"No!" said the Sheriff. "A thief is a thief." He was angry, yet he held his arm and did not run Robin through.

"Woe to you, Sheriff," said Robin Hood, "for betraying your oath to me in the forest. Thank you, good lady, for reminding the Sheriff of his vow. But, Sheriff, will you let me and my men go, or shall I return your golden arrow to you in the chest and make your bright, good fiancée a widow before she is wed?" For Robin Hood had notched the golden arrow in his bow and had it aimed at his foe.

"I shall let you go," said the Sheriff. "I shall let you go—as far as the gates of Nottingham. Beyond those gates and within the forest, as you have made the King's deer your game, you and your men will be mine."

"Very well," said Robin Hood.

As soon as Robin and his men had left the town the Sheriff called together his men and his hounds. The Sheriff offered rewards to any man who killed a man of Robin Hood's, and a king's treasure to any who killed Robin Hood.

Now Robin Hood's men were hard sought after but managed their escape. Robin, however, was cut off in the forest by many Sheriff's men and dogs. He was like a deer, sensing danger on all sides. Unluckily, as he ran this way and that, a Sheriff's man saw him and shot an arrow that pierced his leg. Even so Robin managed to escape, and painfully crawled over the forest floor until he came near the castle of the man Robin had saved, Sir Richard. There, on the outskirts of the forest, Robin fell asleep with weariness, and in slumber's relief from pain he had a dream.

He dreamt of a woman. Her body was graceful, her body was straight, and her face free from pride. A bow was in her hand, and quiver and arrows hung dangling by her side. Her eyebrows were black and so was her hair, and her skin was as smooth as glass. Her face expressed wisdom and modesty too. Robin asked his dream vision, "Fair woman, where are you going?" And she answered, "To kill a fat buck, for tomorrow is a holiday." Robin said, "Fair woman, wander with me, down to the greenwood tree. You should sit down to rest." And as they were going toward the greenwood tree, they spied two hundred good bucks. She chose out the fattest in the herd and shot it through the side. "I swear," said Robin Hood, "I never saw a woman like you."

When he awoke, one of Sir Richard's men had found him and was carrying him from the edge of the forest and through the fields and into the castle, where Robin was put into a bed.

Sir Richard came to him and said, "I had heard that you won a contest and then were caught."

"Yes," said Robin Hood, gladly remembering his triumph. "I won the contest, but a Sheriff's archer then pierced my leg. I now beg of you a favor, my friend."

"I owe you favors forever," said Sir Richard. "You are hurt and I and my servants and my daughter will help you recover."

"That was just what I would ask. Thank you."

Now Marian was Sir Richard's daughter, and as beautiful as sunlight. When Robin Hood saw her, though he was almost faint with pain in his leg, the pain went to his heart, and he exclaimed to himself, "A Sheriff's man has shot my leg, but this goddess has shot my heart. I am in love. This is the woman of my dream."

Little John and Robin Hood's men were troubled and grieved that their master had disappeared, and they searched high and low for him and listened at the town walls for news, but no one, it seemed, had seen him. Robin Hood himself, who had never before

When Robin Hood saw her, the pain went to his
heart.

forgotten his men, forgot them now as Sir Richard's daughter helped nurse him back to health. But while his leg became well, his heart was still sore and tender.

"Sir Richard," said Robin one day. "I do not think I shall recover from my pain unless you grant me one favor more."

"Anything, my friend. You must be anxious for your friends. Let me send a messenger to them and tell them of your health."

"Tell them . . . that an archer has pierced my heart and that I shall never recover."

"But that is not true. It was your leg, and you are recovered nearly completely now."

"Sir Richard, please be generous to me. I ask you for your daughter's hand."

Never had Robin Hood seen his friend so confused, nor so sad. No, not even when the bishop was trying to turn Sir Richard out of his castle. Good Sir Richard staggered and sat down, and then said, "Forgive me, Robin. Forgive me, my friend. I did not expect this. My daughter, you say? My dearest? The comfort of my old age? The image of her mother, my departed wife?" He shook his head and wept.

"Sir Richard!"

"I would sooner give you my castle," said Sir Richard. "She is all I have."

"Then return, you yourself, with me and

Marian to the forest. My men and I are not knights, but we try to live well."

"Please let me consider," said Sir Richard. "My heart is stricken. I shall tell you tomorrow. I owe you almost everything, but it is my woe that you have chosen my daughter. And Marian, has she chosen you?"

"That is my heart's dream," said Robin. He was troubled also, because he did not know for certain that Marian was in love with him.

When the next day came, Sir Richard said to his daughter, "Marian, what would you have? Would you become the wife of our friend Robin Hood?"

"But if I married him," she said, "what would become of you, my father?"

"That is not the question," said the knight. Sir Richard called Robin Hood into the room, and now said again to Marian, "Would you become the wife of Robin?"

Marian bowed her head and closed her eyes, and said, "I will not, unless you, my father, live with us, wherever that might be."

"Six months," said Sir Richard, taking Marian's hand, "I will live with you and your husband, the good Robin Hood, in the forest. And six months will I live here alone. You shall marry Robin, my dear Marian."

And so Sir Richard consented to the wedding between the hero and the hero's delight, Marian. All of the merry men came to the ceremony, performed by Friar Tuck, and there were celebrations and contests that lasted many days. And then Sir Richard joined with Robin's men and learned some of the skills of the happy woodsmen, and he still enjoyed his daughter's care and devotion, though it was shared now between himself and Robin.

After six months, Sir Richard returned to his castle, and was able to live almost happily amongst his servants, because Marian would visit regularly and because he had the happy springtime to look forward to when he would join again with Robin's merry men.

Robin Hood and the Potter

THE BIRDS were singing merrily, and there were blossoms on every tree, when one morning, in Sherwood Forest, Robin Hood and his men spied a cocky potmaker riding on his cart.

"Here comes that potter," said Robin Hood. "He's the one who has long used our trails and yet never has been kind enough to pay us a single penny for his toll."

"I met him once on the west-end bridge," said Little John. "He gave me three knocks so hard my sides still ache. I'll bet forty pieces of gold that there's not one of us who can make that potter pay us a toll."

"Here's the forty pieces," said Robin Hood. "I will make that potter pay." Robin Hood now rushed through the trees and stopped in the potter's way. Robin took the horse's bridle and ordered the potter to stop.

The angry potter said, "What do you want, outlaw?"

"For the last three years, you have traveled this way, and yet have never been kind enough to pay us a penny."

"Who are you," said the potter, "that you should ask me to pay a toll?"

"Robin Hood is my name, I am keeper of this forest, and a bag of gold is the fee."

"I will not pay you a cent. Now unhand my horse, or I'll beat you black and blue." The potter hopped off his seat, went to the back of his cart and pulled out a long staff. Robin pulled out a sword and his small round shield. The potter walked up toward Robin now and said, "Listen, my man, let my horse go."

Robin let go but set out to fight, and he with his sword and the potter with his staff went fiercely at it, like a dog and cat.

Robin's men were standing under their meeting tree and they laughed as they watched this battle. Little John said to his fellows, "That potter there will stand up to him." At that moment the potter knocked the shield out of Robin Hood's hand. Before Robin could pick up his shield, the potter clubbed him with his staff and Robin fell to the ground.

"Let's help our master," said Little John, "so the potter does not kill him." He and the other men went down to the trail where the potter stood over poor Robin.

Little John nodded to the potter, who took a step away, and Little John leaned over his master and tapped Robin on the shoulder.

"Who has won the bet, master? Shall you have my forty gold pieces, or shall I have yours?"

"What was mine, Little John," said Robin Hood, as dizzy as in a dream, "is now yours." And now Robin stood up.

"I have heard," said the potter, "that it is hardly courteous to stop a poor workingman and rob him of his goods."

"You speak the truth," said Robin. "You are a good man, and every day for ever more, you shall drive and never pay a toll. Indeed, dear potter, will you become my friend? Let me do your job today, and you shall do mine. Give me your clothes and I will give you mine, and I will go to Nottingham."

"I agree to that," said the potter. "And you shall find me a good friend to you. But how can you sell my pots for me, as you hardly know my trade?"

"I vow," said Robin, "I will take all your pots today to town, and return again with all of them sold." The potter and the outlaw changed their clothes, and the potter lay down under the tree.

But then spoke Little John, "Master, if you must go to Nottingham, take care to avoid the Sheriff, because as you know he is not our friend."

"The Sheriff will never know me. He will

take me for a potter," said Robin Hood, dabbing his face with clay. He left for Nottingham to sell those pots, while the potter stayed with Robin's men and enjoyed himself quite well.

When Robin Hood came to Nottingham, he fed the horse some oats and hay. "Pots! Pots!" he began to cry out. "The more you buy the less you pay!"

In the middle of the town lived the Sheriff, and Robin had parked his cart against the Sheriff's front gate. Wives and widows surrounded Robin and quickly bought his pots. Robin Hood continued to call out, "Pots, real cheap! I would hate to stand here all day and not sell all my pots! Pots! Pots, real cheap! The more you buy the less you pay!"

The pots that were worth five pennies Robin Hood sold for three. He sold two pots for five, three for seven, five for ten. A man and wife who watched him sell, said to each other, "That potter is not too smart."

But in this way Robin Hood sold his pots quite fast, till he had just five pots left. And those five he took from off his cart and sent up to the Sheriff's bride.

When Christine got those pots, she smiled and laughed. "Oh, good potter," she called from her window, "thank you. The next time you come to Nottingham, I shall buy your pots if I can."

"You will have only my best," said Robin.

"Kind potter," said Christine, "come dine with the Sheriff and me. That would truly make me glad."

"Because you ask," said Robin, "I shall accept." The Sheriff did not recognize Robin in his role as a potter, and gently and nicely asked Robin Hood into his house. The Sheriff's manners since marriage had greatly improved.

"Look, my dear," said Christine to her husband, "what the potter has given to you and to me. Five fine pots."

"You are generous, potter," said the Sheriff. "Let us wash up for dinner and then eat."

As they sat down at their meal, with pleasant and happy conversation, Robin Hood and the Sheriff overheard two of the Sheriff's men outside speak of a great big bet. "We shall have a contest of the bow and arrow," said one, "and bet forty gold pieces."

Robin loved all contests and was, of course, a master of the bow. The Sheriff and his wife watched him as he listened to the men, for he looked like a fox who has picked up a scent, his ears twitching and listening.

"May we watch your good men in their contest?" asked Robin Hood.

"For your entertainment, indeed," said the Sheriff.

The Sheriff gently and nicely asked Robin Hood
into his house.

He led his wife and Robin Hood out of doors to watch his men. But neither of the Sheriff's men shot very well at all. Robin itched to take a try and win for himself the gold. "If I had a bow," he said, "I bet that in one shot I could beat these men."

"You shall have a bow, then," said the Sheriff. "You shall have the choice of three." He sent his steward to retrieve his bows, and the best that the steward brought back was the one Robin chose. He weighed the bow, he looked along its edge, he studied it carefully.

"Now let's see if you are any good," said the Sheriff. "You seem to know your bows."

"Indeed," said Robin Hood, "this is very fine gear." Robin strung the bow as easily as a musician strings his lute. And now he went to the quiver of arrows and took out a good sharp shaft. He let the arrow fly and hit the target in the middle. The Sheriff's men shot again, and so did he. This time Robin again hit the very center, and split the wooden plug in three.

The Sheriff's men felt ashamed that the potter had won. The Sheriff laughed, clapped Robin on the back and said, "Potter, you are a real man. You are worthy to bear a bow anywhere you go."

"At home," said Robin, "I do have a bow, and it is the one that Robin Hood gave me."

"You know Robin Hood?" said the Sheriff. "Tell me how."

"I have shot with him a hundred times under his greenwood tree," said Robin Hood.

"I would rather have such a chance to stand beside that outlaw," said the Sheriff, "than to have a hundred pieces of gold."

"Then, if you take my advice," said Robin, "and will dare to go with me, tomorrow, before breakfast, we will see Robin Hood."

"I will repay you for this favor," said the Sheriff.

But when the Sheriff's wife Christine heard from her husband this plan, she said, "I am not as happy as you about this, dear. Robin Hood, you know, is a cunning thief. He shall not allow you, much less even our clever potter, to approach him by disguise."

"We shall see," said the Sheriff, unhappy with his wife's words.

As soon as it was morning, the Sheriff and Robin Hood got ready for the forest. Robin called goodbye to the Sheriff's wife and thanked her for her dinner. "My good lady," he said, bowing, "please accept this gold ring as a sign of my respect and good wishes to you."

"This is too much," said the good lady. "Five pots and now a ring!"

"No," said Robin Hood. "It is a trade for your kindness."

The Sheriff agreed and said, "Accept it, my dear, and I shall repay the potter when I am able."

"Then, thank you, potter, and may you get what you deserve," said the lady. The ring was very fine, and once had belonged to a lord who had paid his way out of Sherwood Forest with it.

The Sheriff rode along with Robin and was keen to meet his foe and arrest him. He peered this way and that, and Robin led him slowly. The leaves in the forest were green and bright, and birds were singing joyously among the boughs.

"It is delightful to be here," said Robin. "But I swear to you, if a man has a cent more than he needs, he will here meet Robin Hood." Robin put his horn to his mouth and blew a blast, and when his men heard it they started running through the woods. Little John came, reaching his master first, and said, "How have you done in Nottingham? Have you sold all your pots?"

"Yes, I certainly have," said Robin. "And see what I have brought in return, the Sheriff of Nottingham, as a prize for us all."

"He is quite welcome," said Little John. "This is good news."

The Sheriff, seeing that the potter was no potter, but Robin Hood, wished he had never left town. "If I had known, in Nottingham, that you were no potter but Robin Hood, I would not have let you return to the forest for a thousand years."

"I believe that," said Robin Hood. "And so I am pleased that you and I are here. And now that you are my guest, I must ask that you leave your horse with us, as well as all your other gear."

"I object to this robbery," said the Sheriff. "I will not allow it."

"But you must." And Robin's men surrounded the Sheriff and took from him all he had. "You came here," said Robin Hood, "on a horse to bring harm to me, my wife and my men, and home you shall go on foot. And when you get home, nicely greet your wife, because she is so very good—as you are not. Marian sends her a fine, white gentle horse. If not for the respect and gratitude I owe your wife, you would have more to suffer than that I take your goods."

And so Robin Hood told the Sheriff goodbye, and the Sheriff, leading the gentle white horse home to his wife, sadly went on his way to Nottingham.

"My dear," his wife Christine greeted him, "how was your journey into the forest? Have you brought the outlaw Robin Hood home to jail?"

"I curse that man, for Robin was the potter! I wish he were dead," said the Sheriff. "He has made me a fool! Everything I brought into that forest he has taken from me. I have nothing now but this white horse his wife has sent to you."

"Oh, my dear," said Christine, kissing his brow. "I see that you have paid for all the pots and the fancy ring Robin Hood gave to me. What he robbed from us he gave us back in trade."

Robin, meanwhile, was with his men and the potter under the greenwood tree drinking and eating and telling long stories. Finally, as evening set in, Robin asked, "Potter, what were your pots worth, the ones that I sold in Nottingham?"

"Altogether," said the potter, "two gold pieces."

"You shall have ten gold pieces for them," said Robin, paying out the money. "Thank you, and whenever you come back through Sherwood Forest, come visit us again."

Robin Hood and the Beggar

ONE DAY, while Marian was at the castle visiting her father, Sir Richard, Robin Hood was restless missing her, so he got upon his horse and set out riding toward Nottingham, looking for something to amuse him. On the outskirts of the town he saw a man.

The man was wearing an old, patched coat, and had several small sacks slung over his shoulders.

"Hello, hello," said Robin Hood. "Where are you from?"

"I am from Yorkshire, sir. But before you go on your way, will you please give me some charity?"

"Why, what would you like?" said Robin.

"No prayers, no advice," said the man, "but perhaps just a penny."

"I have no money," said Robin then. "I am a ranger of the forest. I am an outlaw, and my name is Robin Hood. But I ask you, my friend, that to change the pace, let's swap our clothes each for the other's. Your old coat for my green cloak. My horse for your bags."

"Very good, very good," said the man. "You offer more than you expect."

When Robin Hood had put on the man's clothes, he looked at himself and laughed. "I think I seem a big, brave beggar. And you," Robin said to the man, "you look quite dashing."

"Indeed, I will dash now, on this horse. And you, make use of those bags," said the man.

"I see," said Robin. "Now I have a bag for my bread, another for wheat, one for salt and one for my horn. And what shall I do with this empty one?"

"Go begging," said the man.

"Have you a penny?" asked Robin.

"Yes," said the man, "I have several, but I never give money to beggars." The man laughed and went on his way.

As Robin started on another way, with the bags hanging about him, and the man's long staff and the old patched coat, he felt as jolly as could be. Along the path, riding fine horses, came two tubby priests, all dressed in black.

"I beg you," said Robin Hood, "have pity on me. Please give me a penny, for our dear Lord's sake. I have been wandering all day, with nothing offered, and not so much as one little drink nor bit of bread to eat."

"Get out of the way," said one priest, a red-headed fellow. "Neither of us has a penny."

"Yes," said the other, a blond-bearded man. "Not a penny. This morning were we robbed."

"I am very much afraid," said Robin, "that you are both telling a lie. Before you ride on, I am resolved to find out the truth."

When the priests heard this beggar say that, they kicked at their horses, but Robin Hood took hold of the bridles. Then he reached up and pulled down the men and they spilled to the ground with a thud.

"Spare us, beggar," said the redheaded priest.

"Have pity," said the blond-bearded one.

"You said you have no money," said Robin. "Therefore, right now, we three will go to our knees, and pray as hard as we can for some gold."

The priests could not run, they could not fight, and so they went to their knees to do as the beggar told them. "Send us, O send us," they prayed aloud, "some money to serve our needs." After they had prayed for a few hours, Robin said, "Now let's see what money heaven has sent. We shall be sharers all alike of the money that we have."

The priests put their hands in their pockets but found no money at all.

"Let's search each other," said Robin. "One by one."

Then Robin took pains to search them both, and hidden within their cloaks, coats, hats and shoes, as if by miracle, he found a good sum of money. There were five hundred gold pieces, in fact, that he emptied upon the grass.

"This is amazing," said Robin, "to see such a vast amount. You have both prayed so well that you shall each have a part."

He gave them fifty coins apiece and kept the rest for himself. They got up to leave, but Robin Hood said no. "I have one more thing to say," said Robin. "I want you both to swear that you will never tell lies again, wherever you go, wherever you are. The other promise I want you to keep is this, that you shall be charitable to the poor. I am a holy beggar, and that is all I say."

The priests said they promised. Robin nodded, set them upon their horses once more and watched them ride away.

"What would Marian think of me?" wondered Robin Hood. "Have I done bad or good? I miss her and I am aimless. I shall venture now to Nottingham, and go to church."

Outside the church, he met a sobbing woman, and he said, "What is it, good lady? May I help you somehow?"

"You are a beggar, are you not?" she said, her eyes quite full of tears.

"I am, but I am sturdy. I am strong and I am good. I am at your service."

"Then rescue, please, my sons," the good lady said. "The Sheriff means to hang them for shooting the King's deer."

"The King's deer?" said Robin. This reminded Robin of when he was a young man, and was to be punished for just this crime in just this way. "The King's deer are mine."

"Are you the King?" asked the woman.

"No, but within Sherwood Forest, I am as good as one. My name is Robin Hood."

"Then, please, good Robin Hood, save my boys. They do no more harm than you do, and they only killed the deer so that I and their sisters could eat."

"I will save them, good lady, if it is up to me."

Robin, who looked to the Sheriff like a beggar, made his way to the gallows, where the Sheriff was preparing to hang the young men.

"Tell me, Sheriff," said Robin, "what did these men do?"

"They are robbers, as bad as Robin Hood," said the Sheriff. "They will receive what that outlaw should get."

"We shall see," said Robin. He now edged through the crowd that came to watch this horrible sight. But before the hangman could perform his work, Robin begged a long stick from a dog, and from a woman a piece of string, and from a boy three broken arrows. He still had his horn, and as the young men put their heads near the ropes that would hang them, Robin Hood strung his make-shift bow and fired his three arrows, cutting the ropes in two. He pulled out his horn and blew, and dodged the Sheriff's men, until Little John and Will and Allen and Arthur and the others came running, rescuing him and the boys.

The Sheriff retreated into his house, and his wife Christine said sadly, "I told you you should not try to hang young men. No good could come of that. They killed deer only because they needed food for their family's table."

"I hate Robin Hood," said the Sheriff.

"You ought to forgive him for helping you not make an error."

"Ought I to pardon him, too?"

"Perhaps," said his wife.

"I cannot do that," said the Sheriff.

"Then let us enjoy our supper, and thank our good fortune we have food enough," said Christine.

"That I may do," said the Sheriff. He admired his wife for her good sense and fine feeling, and resolved to pardon the hungry young men.

When Robin and his merry men returned to the forest, Marian was there awaiting him.

"I have shot you a deer, and brought you wine and beer," she said. "I hope you have missed me, my poor beggar man. You have done a fine deed for those young men, and I love you."

They kissed and hugged, and Robin's men laughed and cheered.

"Good master," said Little John. "We shall leave you in peace for the rest of the week. We are going hunting."

And so ends our tale of Robin Hood, who, with his jolly men and Marian, lived happily ever after under the greenwood tree in England's Sherwood Forest.

CHILDREN'S THRIFT CLASSICS

Robinson Crusoe

DANIEL DEFOE

Adapted by
Bob Blaisdell

Illustrated by
John Green

DOVER PUBLICATIONS, INC.
New York

DOVER CHILDREN'S THRIFT CLASSICS
EDITOR OF THIS VOLUME: CANDACE WARD

Copyright

Copyright © 1995 by Dover Publications, Inc.
All rights reserved under Pan American and International Copyright Conventions.

Published in Canada by General Publishing Company, Ltd., 30 Lesmill Road, Don Mills, Toronto, Ontario.
Published in the United Kingdom by Constable and Company, Ltd., 3 The Lanchesters, 162–164 Fulham Palace Road, London W6 9ER.

Bibliographical Note

This Dover edition, first published in 1995, is a new abridgment of the work based on a standard text. The introductory Note and illustrations have been specially prepared for this edition.

Library of Congress Cataloging-in-Publication Data

Defoe, Daniel, 1661?–1731.
    Robinson Crusoe / Daniel Defoe ; abridged by Bob Blaisdell ; illustrated by John Green.
        p.   cm. — (Dover children's thrift classics)
    Summary: During one of his several adventurous voyages in the 1600s, an Englishman becomes the sole survivor of a shipwreck and lives for nearly thirty years on a deserted island.
    ISBN 0-486-28816-1 (pbk.)
    [1. Shipwrecks—Fiction. 2. Survival—Fiction.] I. Blaisdell, Robert. II. Green, John, 1948–   ill. III. Title. IV. Series.
PZ7.D36Ro   1995
[Fic]—dc20   95-36752
                                                                           CIP
                                                                            AC

Manufactured in the United States of America
Dover Publications, Inc., 31 East 2nd Street, Mineola, N.Y. 11501

Note

DANIEL DEFOE (1661[?]–1731) was born in London. He was raised as a Nonconformist, or Dissenter, and since he could not attend Oxford or Cambridge because of his religious beliefs, he was educated at the Dissenters' academy at Newington Green. Defoe's first career was as a merchant, and he remained in trade for much of his adulthood. He began writing political pamphlets on economic, religious and other issues as early as 1683, but it wasn't until 1719 that Defoe wrote his first and most famous novel, *Robinson Crusoe*. Based on the adventures of the Scottish adventurer Alexander Selkirk, who was rescued in 1709 after being marooned on a desert island for five years, Defoe's novel first appeared as a true narrative. In its first year, the book went through three printings. Today, Robinson Crusoe remains one of literature's most fascinating fictional characters and his story remains a literary classic for children and adults.

This edition, specially adapted by Bob Blaisdell, retains all the excitement of the original, while condensing Defoe's text especially for young readers.

Contents

List of Illustrations

1

I Go to Sea

I WAS BORN in the year 1632, in the city of York,
England, of a good family. My parents named me
Robinson Crusoe. I had two older brothers, one of
whom was killed in a war. What happened to my
second brother I never knew, any more than my
father or mother later knew what happened to me.

My father, who was a merchant and very old, had
given me a good education, and wanted me to become a lawyer. I, however, would be happy with
nothing but becoming a sailor, and so my father
called me one morning into his room, and lectured
me very harshly about my seafaring desires. Then he
said that he would do very kind things for me if I
would stay and settle at home. To close all, he told
me I had my older brother for an example, to whom
he had used the same arguments to keep him from
going to war. My brother, instead, had entered the
army and was killed.

When he mentioned my brother's fate, I saw the
tears run down his face, and then he broke off his
lecture, saying he was so sad he could no longer
speak to me.

In spite of my father's wishes, I decided, a few

weeks after, to run away. But first I told my mother that I was determined to do so; that I was now eighteen years old; and if she would speak to my father to let me go on one voyage, and I did not like it, I would go no more, and I would promise to work doubly hard to regain the time I had lost.

She said there was no sense speaking to my father; and that, if I wanted to ruin myself, there was no help for it; they would never give their consent to such a plan.

It was not till almost a year after this that I broke loose. One day a friend, who was about to go to sea to London in his father's ship, encouraged me to go with them. I agreed to do so. I did not inform my parents. And so, on the first of September, 1651, I went on board a ship bound for London. The ship was no sooner out of the port but the wind began to blow, and the sea to rise in a most frightful manner. As I had never been at sea before, I was very sick. I decided if I ever got my foot upon dry land again, I would go directly home to my father and never set it into a ship again.

These thoughts continued all during the storm; but the next day the wind died down and the sea was calmer, and I began to get used to it. Towards night the weather cleared up, and a fine evening followed; the sun went down perfectly clear, and rose so the next morning. I entirely forgot the decision I had made in my distress to return to my father and give up the sea.

My friend's father, when I met him soon after, scolded me when he heard of my father's protests against my going on a ship. "Young man," said he, "depend upon it, if you do not go back, wherever you go, you will meet with nothing but disasters and disappointments, till your father's warnings come true."

I refused to go home. I disliked the idea of being laughed at by my neighbors for being turned back so quickly by the sea. In London I went on board a vessel bound to the coast of Africa.

This was the only voyage which I may say was successful in all my adventures, and which I owe to the captain, who taught me mathematics and the rules of navigation—things that were necessary to be understood by a sailor.

On my next voyage I fell into terrible misfortunes. Our ship was making her course towards the Canary Islands, and we were surprised in the gray of morning by a Turkish pirate ship. They chased us for several hours. They caught us and boarded our ship, killing a few of our men and wounding several others, and so we had to surrender. We were carried as prisoners into a Moorish port.

I was kept by the captain of the pirate ship and made his slave. When he went back to sea, he left me on shore to look after his little garden and do the common work around his house. When he came home again from his cruise, he ordered me to sit in the ship cabin to safeguard his vessel.

For two years, though I often tried to think of a way to escape, I found no help to do so. But then, after my master got used to sending me out in a small boat to do his fishing for him, I and one of his Moorish servant boys made our getaway in this boat. "Xury," I told the boy, "if you will be faithful to me, I'll make you a great man." Xury swore to be faithful to me and to go all over the world with me. For five days, as we were well-supplied with food, I would not stop or go on shore.

Finally, I ventured to the coast and put out our anchor in the mouth of a little river. I neither saw, or desired to see, any people; the main thing I wanted was fresh water. Xury said if I would let him go on shore with one of the empty water jars, he would find if there was any water and bring some to me. I asked him, "Why should not I go, and you stay in the boat?" The boy answered, "If wild mans come, they eat me, and you get away."

"Well, Xury," I said, "we will both go, and if the wild mans come, we will kill them; they shall eat neither of us." We hauled the boat in near the shore, and waded onto shore, carrying nothing but our guns and two jars for water.

A little higher up the creek, we found the water fresh when the tide was out, which flows but a little way up. So we filled our jars and feasted on a rabbit we had caught, and went on our way, having seen no footsteps of any human creature.

Several times I was obliged to land for fresh water

after we had left this place. We went southward for
many days, living very tightly on our food. My plan
was to get to the river Gambia or Senegal, anywhere
close to Cape Verde, where I was in hopes to meet
with some European ship.

One day, as we came within sight of the Cape
Verge islands, Xury cried out, "Master, master, a ship
with a sail!"

I jumped out of the cabin and immediately saw a
Portuguese ship. With all the sail power I could make,
I found we would not be able to cross their path and
that they would be gone before I could make any
signal to them. But they, it seems, saw me by the help
of a spyglass and lay in wait for me to catch up.

I immediately offered all I had to the captain of the
ship as a return for my rescue. He generously told me
he would take nothing from me, that all I had would
be delivered safe to me when I came to Brazil. "I will
carry you there, Mr. Englishman," he said, "and those
things will help you to buy your food and lodging and
your passage home again."

He offered me a sack of money for my boy Xury,
which I did not want to take. I did not want to sell the
poor boy's liberty after he had helped me so well in
gaining my own. When I let the captain hear my
reason, he suggested a compromise, that he would
give the boy his freedom after ten years. With this,
and Xury saying he was willing to go to him, I let the
captain have him.

We had a very good voyage to Brazil and arrived in

All Saints' Bay about twenty-two days after. I had not been long here before I met a good honest man who owned a plantation and sugar house. Seeing how well the planters lived and how they grew rich suddenly, I decided I would become a planter myself.

But alas! for me to do wrong that never did right was no great wonder. I was a planter for three years and discovered that I was doing what I did not enjoy. I might as well have stayed at home and never have tired myself in the world as I had done. And I used often to say to myself, I could have done this as well in England among my friends as have gone five thousand miles off to do it among strangers and savages in a wilderness.

I had nobody to talk with but now and then a neighbor. All the work that had to be done, I had to do it. I used to say I lived just like a man cast away upon some desolate island where no one lived but himself.

In the fourth year I prospered. I had not only learned the Portuguese language, but had made friends with fellow planters and merchants. In my talk with them, I told them of my voyages to Africa, and the manner of trading with the natives there, and how easy it was to purchase gold and ivory. My friends were so attentive, they decided they wanted me to go to Africa for them and carry on this trading for themselves, for which I would receive an equal share of the goods I bargained for.

I had a plantation of my own to look after; for me

to think of such a voyage was the most preposterous thing that I could have done. But I, who was born my own worst enemy, could not resist my friends' offer. They agreed to take care of my plantation while I was gone.

2

I Arrive on the Desert Island

THE SHIP being fitted out and cargo put aboard, I departed the first of September, 1659, the same day as eight years before I went from my father and mother. Our ship carried six cannons and fourteen men, besides the master of the ship, his servant boy, and myself.

We had good weather all the way up Brazil's coast till we turned east and a violent hurricane took us sailing into unknown parts. For twelve days we could do nothing but let the fury of the winds direct us whatever way it wanted.

Besides the terror of the storm, one of our men died of a tropical fever, and one man and the servant boy washed overboard. About the twelfth day, the weather letting up a little, the shipmaster made an observation as well as he could, and found that we were upon the coast of Guiana, or the north part of Brazil, beyond the Amazon River, towards the Orinoco River. He asked me what course he should take, for the ship was leaky and disabled, to return to the coast of Brazil.

We concluded there was no inhabited country for us to land upon until we came within the circle of the

Caribbean Islands, and therefore decided to make for Barbados, which we might do in about fifteen days' sail.

But our voyage brought us into another storm and drove us so far off our course that were we able to land, we were more likely to be eaten by savages than to ever return to our country.

In this distress, the wind still blowing very hard, one of our men early in the morning cried out, "Land!" We had no sooner run out of the cabin than the ship struck upon the sand, and in a moment, the sea broke over her. We rushed back within our close quarters to shelter us from the waves. We did not know where we were or upon what land it was we were driven, whether an island or mainland, inhabited or not inhabited. We sat looking at each other and expecting death every moment.

The ship having struck upon the sand, and sticking too fast for us to expect her getting off, we were in a dreadful condition. The mate of our ship, however, lay hold of the life boat, and with the help of the rest of the men, they got her slung over the ship's side and, getting all into her, let go and committed ourselves to God's mercy and the wild sea.

We worked at the oars towards the land. But we all felt that when the boat came nearer the shore, she would be dashed in a thousand pieces by the break of the sea. As we made nearer and nearer the shore, the land looked more frightful than the sea.

After we had rowed a few miles, a raging wave,

But our voyage brought us into another storm.

mountain-like, came rolling from behind us. It overset the boat at once, and hardly gave us time to say, "O God!" We were all swallowed up in a moment.

Though I swam very well, I could not get out from under the waves so as to draw breath, till that wave went back, and left me upon the land almost dry, but half dead with the water I swallowed. I got upon my feet and tried to get on towards the land as fast as I could, before another wave should return and take me up again. But I soon found it was impossible to avoid it. I saw the sea come after me as high as a great hill, and as furious as an enemy.

The sea dashed me against a piece of a rock, and with such force that it left me senseless. I held fast to the rock till the wave went back, and then I ran for the shore. I got to the mainland, where, to my great comfort, I clambered up the cliffs to the shore and sat myself down upon the grass, free from danger, and quite out of reach of the water.

I was now landed and safe on shore, and began to look up and thank God that my life was saved. I walked about on the shore, lifting up my hands, reflecting upon all my comrades that were drowned and that there was not a single person left alive but myself. I never saw any sign of them, except three of their hats, one cap, and two unmatched shoes.

I looked out towards the stranded ship, where I could hardly see it, it lay so far off. Lord! how was it possible I could get on shore!

After this I began to look round me to see what

kind of place I was in, and what was next to be done. I was wet, I had no clothes to change into, nor anything to eat or drink. I did not see anything ahead of me but perishing with hunger or being devoured by wild beasts. I had nothing with me but a knife, a tobacco pipe, and a little tobacco in a box. Night was coming upon me. I walked a ways from the shore to see if I could find any fresh water to drink, which I did, to my great joy. Having drunk, I went to a thick, bushy tree and climbed up into it. I put myself into a position so that if I happened to fall asleep, I would not tumble down. I soon fell fast asleep.

When I waked it was broad daylight, the weather clear, and the storm gone. But what surprised me most was the ship had been lifted off in the night from the sand where she had lain, and was driven up almost as far as the rock I first mentioned, where I had been so bruised by being dashed against it. This was within about a mile from the shore where I was and, the ship seeming to stand upright, I wished myself on board, so that I might save some necessary things for my use.

In the afternoon I found the sea very calm and the tide so far out that I could come within a quarter of a mile of the ship. I resolved to get to it, so I pulled off my clothes and swam through the water. When I came to the ship I found a small piece of rope hanging down by which, with great difficulty, I pulled myself up.

My first work was to search and to see what

remaining goods on board were spoiled and what
was not. I went to the kitchen and filled my pockets
with biscuits. I was very hungry, and ate them as I
went about, for I had no time to lose. I also found
some rum in the great cabin. Now I needed nothing
but a boat to furnish myself with many things which I
foresaw would be very necessary to me.

It was no use wishing for a boat, so I built myself a
strong raft. I loaded it with boards, seaman's chests
filled with provisions (that is, bread, rice, cheese,
dried goat meat, grains). While I was doing this, I
found the tide began to flow, and I had the disappointed surprise of seeing my coat, shirt, and
waistcoat, which I had left on shore upon the sand,
swim away. As for my pants, which were only linen,
and open-kneed, I swam on board in them and my
stockings. However, this got me to rummage for
clothes, of which I found enough, but I took no
more than I wanted for present use. I had other
things which my eye was keener on, for instance
tools to work with on shore. I found the carpenter's
chest of tools—more valuable to me than a ship
full of gold would have been, and got it down to my
raft.

My next care was for some ammunition and guns. I
secured two small guns and two pistols, with some
gunpowder horns and a small bag of gunshot, and
two old rusty swords. I found two barrels of dry
gunpowder. Now I thought my raft pretty well loaded,
and began to think how I should get to shore with

this cargo, having neither sail, oar, or rudder. A breeze would have upset the raft.

I had, however, three signs of encouragement: 1. A smooth, calm sea. 2. The tide rising and setting in to shore. 3. What little wind there was blew me towards the land.

And so, having found two or three broken oars belonging to the boat, I set out. I found a strong current of the tide setting into a creek, so I guided my raft as well as I could to keep it in the middle of the stream. But, knowing nothing of the coast, I ran my raft aground upon a sandbank, and all my cargo nearly slipped off. When the tide rose further, after half an hour, the raft floated again, and I at length found myself in the mouth of the little river, with land on both sides. I guided my raft to a little cove and anchored her till the water ebbed away and left my raft and all my cargo safe on shore.

My next piece of work was to view the country, and seek a proper place to live and stow my goods. Where I was I did not know, whether on the continent or on an island; whether inhabited or uninhabited; whether in danger of wild beasts or not. There was a hill not more than a mile from me, which rose up very steep and high, and which seemed to overtop some other hills. I took out one of the small guns and one of the pistols, and a horn of gunpowder, and thus armed I travelled for discovery up to the top of that hill. After I had with great labor and difficulty got to the top, I saw that I was on an island, no land to be seen in any direction across the sea except some rocks that lay a great way off.

I found also that the island was uninhabited, except by wild beasts, of whom, however, I saw none. Yet I saw many birds. On returning from the hilltop I shot a large bird I saw sitting upon a tree near a forest. I believe it was the first gun that had been fired there since the creation of the world. I had no sooner fired than from all parts of the forest there arose innumerable birds of many sorts, making a confused screaming, and crying every one according to his usual note. Not one of them was of any kind that I knew.

I went back to my raft and went to work to bring my cargo on shore, which took me the rest of that day. What to do with myself at night, I did not know. I was afraid to lie down on the ground, thinking that some wild beast might devour me.

However, as well as I could, I barricaded myself round with the chests and boards that I had brought on shore, and made a kind of hut for that night's lodging.

The next day I resolved to make another voyage to the ship and get myself many useful things. I knew that the first storm that blew must necessarily break her all in pieces. My raft appeared unmanageable, so I resolved to swim out as before, when the tide was down.

I got on board the ship as before, and prepared a second raft, and having had experience of the first, I made this more simple. I did not load it as much, but yet I brought back several things useful to me. In the carpenter's storeroom I found two or three bags of nails and spikes, a jack, a dozen or two hatchets and a grindstone. All these I tied together, with several guns and bags of ammunition belonging to the gunner. Besides these things I took all the men's clothes that I could find, and a spare sail, hammock and bedding. With this I loaded my second raft, and brought it all safe on shore.

I went to work to make myself a little tent with the sail and some poles that I had cut for that purpose, and into this tent I brought everything that I knew would spoil, either with rain or sun, and I piled all the empty chests and casks up in a circle round the tent, to fortify it from man or beast. When I had done this, I blocked up the door of the tent with some boards inside, and an empty chest set up on end outside. Spreading one of the beds upon the ground, laying my two pistols just at my head and my gun at length by me, I went to bed for the first time since my arrival, and slept very quietly all night, for I was very weary.

I had the largest store of goods of all kinds now that ever was laid up, I believe, for one man. But I was not satisfied. For while the ship sat upright, I thought I ought to get everything out of her that I could. After I had made five or six voyages, and thought I had nothing more to expect from the ship, I found a great container of bread, and three large casks of rum, a box of sugar, and a barrel of fine flour. After this I went every day on board and brought away what I could get.

After thirteen days on shore, I had been eleven times on board the ship. Preparing the twelfth time to go on board, I found the wind began to rise. However, at low water I went on board, and though I thought I had rummaged the cabin so effectually, as that nothing more could be found, yet I discovered a locker with drawers in it, in one of which I found two or three razors and one pair of large scissors, with some dozen good knives and forks.

I began to think of making another raft, but while I was wrapping up these goods, I found the sky overcast, and the wind began to rise. In a quarter of an hour it blew a fresh gale from the shore. It occurred to me it was folly to make a raft, and that it was my business to be gone before the tide of flood began, otherwise I might not be able to reach the shore at all. And so I let myself down into the water and swam across the channel, which lay between the ship and the sands, and even that with difficulty, partly with the weight of the things I had wrapped up about me, and partly the roughness of the water. The wind rose very quickly. Before it was quite high water, it blew a storm.

But I got home to my little tent, where I lay with all my wealth about me very secure. It blew very hard all that night, and in the morning, when I looked out, behold, no ship was to be seen.

3

I Build My Fortress

MY THOUGHTS were now wholly employed about securing myself against either savages or wild beasts. I had many thoughts of the method how to do this, and what kind of dwelling to make. I wondered whether I should make a cave in the earth, or a tent upon the ground. And, in short, I resolved upon both. I soon found the place I was in was not right for my settlement, particularly because there was no fresh water near it.

I wanted several things for my place. Firstly, health and fresh water. Secondly, shelter from the heat of the sun. Thirdly, security from hungry creatures, whether man or beast. Fourthly, a view to the sea, so that if any ship came in sight, I might not lose a chance for my rescue.

I found a little plain on the side of a hill. The rocky hillside facing the plain was very steep. This was good, because nothing then could come down upon me from the top. On the side of this rock there was a hollow place worn a little way like the entrance or door of a cave, but there was not really any cave or way into the rock at all.

On the flat of the green just before this hollow

place, I pitched my tent. This plain was not more than a hundred yards wide, and about twice as long, and lay like a lawn before my door, and at the end of it dropped every which way down into the low grounds by the seaside. It was on the north-northwest side of the hill, so that I was sheltered from the heat every day.

Before I set up my tent I drew a half circle before the hollow place. In this half circle I drove two rows of strong stakes, the longer end being out of the ground about five foot and a half, and sharpened on the top. Then I took the pieces of cable I had cut from the ship, and laid them in rows one upon another, within the circle between these two rows of stakes. This fence was so strong that neither man nor beast could get into it or over it.

The entrance into this place I made to be not by a door but by a short ladder to go over the top. The ladder, when I was in, I lifted over after me. In this way I was completely fenced in, and fortified from all the world, and so slept well in the night.

Into this fence or fortress I carried, with much labor, all my riches, all my provisions, ammunition and goods. I made a large doubled tent to protect me from the rains that in one part of the year are very violent there. Now I lay no more in the bed which I had brought on the shore, but in a hammock, which was indeed a very good one.

When I had brought into the tent all my goods, I began to work my way into the rock. I made a cave just behind my tent, which then served me like a cellar to my house.

In the many days which this took me, I went out at least once every day with my gun, as much to amuse myself as to see if I could kill anything fit for food. The first time I went out, I discovered there were goats on the island. But they were so shy, so swift, that it was the most difficult thing in the world to get near them. However, after I had found their haunts, I laid in wait for them. I observed, if they saw me in the valleys, they would run away. But if they were feeding in the valleys, and I was upon the rocks, they took no notice of me. Their eyes were so directed downward, that they did not see objects that were above them. I then always climbed the rocks first, to get above them, and then was able to shoot them for my food somewhat easily.

It was, by my account, the thirtieth of September when I first set foot upon this horrid island. After I had been there about ten or twelve days, it came into my thoughts that I should lose my reckoning of time and should even be unable to tell the Sabbath days from the working days. To prevent this forgetfulness, I cut with my knife upon a large post, on the shore where I landed: "I CAME ON SHORE THE 30TH OF SEPTEMBER 1659." Upon the sides of this square post I cut every day a notch with my knife, and every seventh notch was twice as long as the rest. Every first day of the month was twice as long as that long one. In this way I kept my calendar.

I discovered there were goats on the island.

Among the many things I brought off the ship in the several voyages I made to it, I got several useful things I have not mentioned: pens, ink and paper, compasses, perspectives, charts and books of navigation. Also I found three very good Bibles; some Portuguese books also. I must not forget that we had on the ship a dog and two cats, of whose story I may say something. I carried both the cats with me. As for the dog, he jumped out of the ship by himself, and swam on shore to me the day after I went on shore with my first cargo. He was a trusty servant to me for many years.

While my ink lasted, I kept things very exact. After it was gone, I could not find any way to make more.

My lack of enough tools made every job I did difficult, and it was near a whole year before I had entirely finished the little wall in front of my settlement. I have already described my habitation, which was a tent under the side of a rock, surrounded with a strong wall of posts and cables. After a year and a half, I raised rafters from the wall to the rock, and thatched them with boughs of trees and such things as I could get to keep out the rain.

I also set to enlarge my cave farther into the hillside. It was composed of loose sandy rock, which gave in easily to the work I put in at it. And so, when I found I was pretty safe from beasts of prey, I worked sideways to the right hand into the rock; and then turning to the right again, worked quite out, and made a door to come out on the outside of my wall.

This gave me not only entry and retreat but gave me room to store my goods.

Now I began to make such necessary things as I found I most wanted, particularly a chair and a table. Without these I was not able to enjoy the few comforts I had in the world. I could not write or eat with so much pleasure without a table.

So I went to work. Here I must say that every man may in time be master of every mechanical art. I had never handled a tool in my life, and yet in time, by labor, persistence, and contrivance, I found at last that whatever I needed, I could have made it, especially if I had tools. However, I made many things even without tools, and some with no tools but an adze[1] and hatchet. For example, if I wanted a board, I had no other way than to cut down a tree, set it on an edge before me, and hew it flat on either side with my axe, till I had made it as thin as a plank, and then smooth it with my adze.

And now it was when I began to keep a journal of every day's activity. At first I was in too much of a hurry in my work and in my mind. But having settled my household, I wrote as long as my ink lasted.

(I shall omit from this journal most of those details which I have already related.)

---

[1]*adze*] a cutting tool used for shaping wood.

4
The Journal

October 31. In the morning I went out into the island with my gun to look for some food. I killed a goat, and her kid followed me home.

November 3. I went out with my gun and killed two fowls like ducks, which were very good food. In the afternoon I went to work to make a table.

November 4. This morning I began to order my times of work, of going out with my gun, time of sleep, and time of amusement. Every morning I walked out with my gun for two or three hours, if it did not rain, and worked till about eleven o'clock. Then I ate what I had, and from twelve to two I lay down to sleep, the weather being too hot to be outside. Then in the evening I set to work again.

November 5. This day I went out with my gun and my dog, and killed a wild cat. Every creature I killed, I took off the skins and preserved them. Coming back by the seashore, I was surprised, and almost frightened, by two or three seals, which, while I was gazing at them, not knowing what they were, got into the sea and escaped.

November 6. After my morning walk, I went to work on making my table again, and finished it, though not to my liking.

· *November 7.* Now it began to be fair weather. The 7th, 8th, 9th, 10th, and part of the 12th (for the 11th was a Sunday) I took to make a chair, and with much effort brought it to a passable shape, but not good enough to please me, and even in the making I pulled it to pieces several times. NOTE: I soon gave up taking my Sundays off. Having failed to make my mark for them on my calendar post, I forgot which day was which.

November 13. This day it rained, which refreshed me very much, and cooled the earth, but it came with terrible thunder and lightning, which frightened me dreadfully, for fear of my gunpowder. As soon as it was over, I resolved to separate my stock of gunpowder into as many little packets as possible, that it might not be in danger of exploding.

November 14, 15, 16. These three days I spent in making little square boxes, which might hold about a pound or two pounds, at most, of gunpowder. And so, putting the powder in, I stowed it in places as safe and far from one another as possible.

* * *

December 17. From this day to the 20th, I placed shelves and knocked nails into the posts to hang everything up that could be hung up. And now I began to have some order inside my cave.

December 20. Now I carried everything into the cave, and began to furnish my house, and set up some pieces of boards like a dresser, to arrange my food supplies. But boards began to be very scarce with me. Also I made me another table.

December 24. Much rain all night and all day; no stirring out.

December 25. Rain all day.

December 26. No rain, and the earth much cooler than before, and pleasanter.

December 27. Killed a young goat, and lamed another, so that I caught it, and led it home on a string. When I had it home, I bound and splintered up its leg, which was broken. I took such care of it that it lived, and the leg grew well, and as strong as ever. But by nursing it so long it grew tame, and fed upon the little green at my door, and would not go away. This was the first time that I thought of breeding some tame goats, so that I might have food when my gunpowder and gunshot was all gone.

December 28, 29, 30. Terrible heat and no breeze. There was no going out, except in the evening for food. This time I spent putting all my things in order.

January 1. Very hot still, but I went out early and late with my gun, and lay quiet during the day. This evening going farther into the valleys, which lay towards the center of the island, I found there were plenty of goats, though very shy and hard to get at.

From the 3rd of January to the 14th of April, I was working, finishing and perfecting the wall outside my habitation.

During this time, I made my rounds in the woods for food every day when the rain let me, and made many discoveries in these walks of something or other for my own good. Particularly, I found a kind of wild pigeon, which had very good meat.

In the managing of my household affairs, I found myself in need of many things, which I thought at first it was impossible for me to make, as indeed for some of them it was. I was in great need for candles. As soon as it was dark, which was generally by seven o'clock, I had to go to bed. The only solution I had was that, when I would kill a goat, I saved the fat, and with a little dish I made of clay, which I baked in the sun, to which I added a wick of rope fiber, I made me a lamp. This gave me light, though not a clear, steady light like a candle.

In the middle of all my projects it happened that, rummaging through my things, I found a little bag, which had been filled with grain for birds. I saw nothing in the bag now but husks and dust. Wanting the bag for some other use, I shook the husks of grain out of it to one side of my fort.

It was a little before the great rains that I threw this stuff away, taking no notice of anything, and not so much as remembering that I had thrown anything there. About a month after, I saw some few stalks of something green shooting out of the ground, which I imagined might be some plant I had not seen. But I was surprised when after a little longer time I saw about ten or twelve ears of green barley, of the same kind as our English barley.

I carefully saved the ears of this grain, you may be sure. Storing up every seed, I resolved to plant them all again, hoping in time to have enough to supply myself with bread. It was not until the fourth year that I could let myself eat the smallest part of this crop.

But to return to my journal.

June 16. Going down to the seaside, I found a large turtle. This was the first I had seen, which it seems was only my bad luck, not any fault of the place or lack of them. Had I happened to be on the other side of the island, I might have had hundreds of them every day.

June 17. This day I spent in cooking the turtle. I found in her sixty eggs. This turtle was to me the best and most pleasant meat that I ever tasted in my life, having eaten nothing but goats and birds since I had landed on this horrid place.

June 21. Very ill, frightened almost to death with my fears of my sad condition, to be sick and have no help. Prayed to God for the first time since my first ship adventure, but hardly knew what I said, my thoughts being all confused.

From the 4th of July to the 14th I was mostly busy in walking about with my gun in my hand, a little at a time, as I was a man that was gathering up his strength after a fit of sickness.

I had been now on this miserable island more than ten months. All possibility of rescue seemed gone. I firmly believed that no human shape had ever set foot upon that place. Having now made my home safe, I had a great desire to make a fuller discovery of the island and to see what other things I could find.

It was the 15th of July when I began to take a closer look at the island. I went up the creek first, where I had brought my rafts from the wrecked ship on shore.

I found, after I went about two miles up, that the tide did not flow any higher, and that it was no more than a brook of running water, and very fresh and good. But this was the dry season, and there was hardly any water in some parts of it.

On the bank of this brook, I found many pleasant meadows.

The next day, the 16th, I went up the same way again, and after going somewhat farther than I had gone the day before, I found the brook and the meadows began to disappear, and the country became more woody than before. In this part I found different fruits, and particularly I found melons upon the ground in great abundance, and grapes upon the trees, and the clusters of grapes were just now in their prime, very ripe and rich. I found an excellent use for these grapes, and that was to dry them in the sun and keep them as raisins, which I thought would be, as indeed they were, as wholesome and good to eat when no grapes might be had.

I spent all that evening there. In the night I got up into a tree, where I slept well. The next morning I proceeded on my discovery, travelling near four miles, keeping due north, with a ridge of hills on the south and north side of me. I came to a clearing where the country seemed to descend to the west, and a little spring of fresh water, which issued out of the side of the hill by me, ran due east. The country appeared to me so fresh, so green, so flourishing, that it looked like a planted garden.

I went down a little on the side of that beautiful valley, looking it over with a secret kind of pleasure, to think that this country was all my own, that I was king and lord of all this country. I saw here many cocoa trees, orange and lemon and citron trees. But all of them were wild and very few were bearing any fruit, at least not then. However, the limes that I gathered were not only pleasant to eat but very wholesome. I mixed their juice afterwards with water, which made it very wholesome and very cool and refreshing.

When I came home from this journey, I thought with great pleasure about the fruitfulness of that valley and the pleasantness of the place, the security from storms on that side of the water and the forest.

I spent much of my time there for the whole remaining part of the month of July. I built myself a little kind of a shelter and surrounded it at a distance with a strong fence, being a double hedge as high as I could reach. And here I lay very secure, sometimes two or three nights in a row. I fancied now I had my country house and my seacoast house. And this work took me up to the beginning of August.

I had recently finished my fence and began to enjoy the efforts of my work. The 3rd of August I found the grapes I had hung up were perfectly dried, and were excellent raisins. No sooner had I taken them down and carried most of them to my cave than it began to rain and from here on, which was the 14th of August, it rained more or less every day, till the middle of October; and sometimes so violently that I could not stir out of my cave for several days.

From the 14th of August to the 26th, there was such steady rain that I could not stir, and I was now very careful not to get too wet. In this confinement I began to be short of food, but venturing out twice, I one day killed a goat. And the last day, which was the 26th, I found a very large turtle, which was a treat to me. I ate a bunch of raisins for my breakfast; a piece of broiled goat or turtle meat for my lunch; and two or three of the turtle's eggs for my supper.

September 30. I was now come to the unhappy anniversary of my landing. I counted up the notches on my calendar post, and found I had been on shore three hundred and sixty-five days. I kept this date as a solemn fast day, setting it apart to religious exercise, confessing my sins to God, and praying to Him to have mercy upon me. Having not tasted the least bit of food for twelve hours, I then ate a biscuit and a bunch of grapes, and went to bed.

A little after this my ink began to fail me, and so I forced myself to use it less, and to write down only the most remarkable events of my life, without continuing a daily journal.

I mentioned before that I wanted to see the whole island, and that I had travelled up the brook, and so on to where I built my second shelter. I now resolved to travel quite across to the seashore on that side. When I had passed the valley where my shelter stood, I came to within view of the sea to the west. It was a very clear day, and I saw land. I knew it must be part of South America. Perhaps it was inhabited by savages, and if I had landed there, I would have been in a worse condition than I was now. For they are cannibals and fail not to murder and devour all the human bodies that fall into their hands.

I found this side of the island, where I now was, much pleasanter than mine, the open meadows sweet, adorned with flowers and grass, and full of fine woods. I saw many parrots. After some painstaking, I did catch a young parrot, and I brought it home. It was, however, some years before I could make him speak.

I travelled along the shore of the sea, towards the east, about twelve miles; and then setting up a great pole upon the shore for a marker, I decided I would go home again; and that the next journey I took should be on the other side of the island, east from my dwelling, and so round till I came to the post again.

I was very impatient to be at home, from where I had been gone more than a month. I cannot express what a satisfaction it was to me to come into my old home and lie down in my hammock. I relaxed here for a week, to rest myself after my long journey. During that week, most of the time was taken up with making a cage for my parrot.

When the rainy season came again, I kept the 30th of September in the same manner as before. This date was the anniversary of my landing on the island, and I had now been there two years.

5

I Am Very Seldom Idle

THUS I began my third year. It may be observed that I was very seldom idle. I had regularly divided my time, going out every day for food, which generally took me three hours every morning. Then I was organizing, preserving and cooking what I had killed or caught for my supply. These duties took up a great part of the day. My labors took many hours, as I lacked tools, help and skill. For example, it took forty-two days for me to make a long shelf for my cave; whereas two carpenters with their tools would have cut six of them out of the same tree in half a day.

My case was this: it was a large tree which I had to cut down, because my board was to be a wide one. This tree I was three days cutting down, and two more cutting off the boughs, and reducing it to a log. With hacking and shaving, I reduced both sides of it into chips, till it began to be light enough to move. Then I turned it and made one side of it smooth and flat; then turning that side downward, cut the other side, till I made the plank about three inches thick and smooth on both sides.

I was now in the months of November and December, expecting my crop of barley and rice which I had planted earlier. The ground I had manured and dug up for them was not large, but I found I was in danger of losing it all to enemies of several kinds. At first, it was the goats and the rabbits. I got my plot totally well fenced in in about three weeks' time. Having shot some of the raiding creatures in the daytime, I set my dog to guard it in the night, tying him up to a stake at the gate, where he would stand and bark all night long. In a little time the enemies gave up the place, and the grain grew very strong and well, and began to ripen.

But as the beasts ruined me before, while my grain was growing, the birds were as likely to ruin me now, when it was ripening. I foresaw that in a few days they would devour all my hopes. I killed three of the birds and hanged them to frighten away the others, and this was very effective.

At the latter end of December, I reaped my crop. I had a hard job, as I did not have a sickle to cut it down, and all I could do was to make one as well as I could out of one of the swords I had saved from the ship.

I foresaw that in time it would please God to supply me with bread. And yet here I was perplexed again, for I neither knew how to grind or make meal of my grain, or indeed how to clean it and separate it. Even if I had had meal, I did not know how to make bread of it. And even if I had known how to make it, I did not know how I would be able to bake it. I preserved this crop all for seed for the next season, and in the meantime tried to figure out a way to make bread for myself.

At the latter end of December, I reaped my crop.

But first I had to prepare more land, for I had now seed enough to plant more than an acre. I planted my seed in two large flat pieces as near my house as I could find them, and fenced them in with a good hedge. This work took me nearly three months, because a large part of that time was during the wet season, when I could not go out.

When I stayed inside and while I was at work on something, I amused myself with talking to my parrot and teaching him to speak. I quickly taught him to know his own name and at last to speak it out loud, "Poll," which was the first word I ever heard spoken on the island by any mouth but my own.

I had long been studying how to make myself some clay vessels, which indeed I wanted very much, but did not know how to do so. It would make the reader pity me, or rather laugh at me, to tell how many awkward ways I took to make this pasty clay. What odd, misshapen, ugly things I made! How many of them fell in, and how many fell apart, the clay not being stiff enough to bear its own weight. How many of the vessels cracked by the too hot sun. After having worked so hard to find the clay, to dig it, to bring it home and work it, I could not make more than two large clay ugly things, I cannot call them jars, in about two months' labor.

Though I botched so much in my design for large pots, yet I made several smaller things with better success; such as little round pots, flat dishes, pitchers and anything my hand turned to, and the heat of the sun baked them hard.

But all this would not satisfy my need, which was to get a clay pot to hold a liquid and bear the fire, which none of these could do. It happened after some time, making a pretty large fire for cooking my meat, when I went to put it out after I had done with it, I found a broken piece of one of my clay vessels in the fire, burnt hard as a stone, and red as a tile. I was surprised to see it, and said to myself that certainly they might be made to burn whole, if they would burn broken.

This set me to studying how to arrange my fire, so as to make it burn some pots. I placed several large pots in a pile one upon another and placed my firewood all around it with a great heap of embers under them; I added to the fire with fresh fuel round the outside and on top, till I saw the pots in the inside red hot quite through, and observed that they did not crack at all. When I saw them clear red, I let them stand in that heat about five or six hours, till I found one of them, though it did not crack, did run, for the sand which was mixed with the clay melted, and would have run into glass if I had gone on. So I slacked my fire, and found in the morning I had five very good, I will not say handsome, pots. One of them, indeed, was perfectly glazed with the running of the sand.

No joy was ever equal to mine, when I found I had made a clay pot that would bear the fire. I had hardly patience to wait till they were cold, before I set one upon the fire again, with some water in it, to boil me some meat, which it did well. With a piece of goat I made some very good broth.

My next concern was to get a mortar to grind some grain in it. I found a great block of hard wood, and I rounded it and formed it to make a hollow place in it. To separate the bran from the husk of the grain I made a sieve from some muslin neckerchiefs. I made some very wide clay vessels and used these as ovens for my bread, which I had learned to make.

It need not be wondered at, if all these things took me the most part of the third year of my life here.

I began thinking whether it was not possible to make myself a canoe, such as the natives of these climates make, even without tools, from the trunk of a large tree.

I pleased myself with the plan for one, without figuring out whether I would ever be able to complete it and get the boat from its place to the water. "Let's first make it," I told myself. "I'll find some way or other to get it out of here, once it's done."

This was a ridiculous method. But the eagerness of my imagination won out, and to work I went. I chopped down a cedar tree. It took me twenty days of hacking and chipping at its base to chop it down. I was two weeks more getting the branches and limbs off. After this it cost me a month to shape it and get it something like the bottom of a boat, that it might swim upright as it ought to do. It cost me near three months more to clear the inside, and work it out so as to make an exact boat of it. This I did without fire, with mere mallet and chisel. I made it a very hand-some canoe, big enough to have carried twenty-six men, or big enough to have carried me and all my cargo.

I was extremely delighted with it. The boat was really much bigger than I ever saw a canoe that was made of one tree. There remained nothing but to get it into the water. Had I gotten it into the water, I have no doubt but I should have begun the craziest voyage ever undertaken.

But all my attempts to get it into the water failed me. The boat lay about one hundred yards from the water.

In the middle of this work I finished my fourth year in this place, and kept my anniversary with the same devotion as before.

6

I Travel Around the Island

MY CLOTHES began to decay. It was a very great help to me that I had among all the men's clothes of the ship almost three dozen shirts. There were also several thick seamen's coats, but they were too hot to wear. Though it is true that the weather was so violently hot that there was no need of clothes, yet I could not go quite naked. No, even had I wanted to, which I did not, I could not bear the heat of the sun so well when quite naked, as with some clothes on. With my shirt on, the air itself made some motion, and under that shirt I was twice as cool than without it. I could not bring myself to go out in the heat of the sun without a cap or a hat.

I have mentioned that I saved the skins of all the creatures that I killed, and I hung them up and stretched them out with sticks in the sun, by which means some of them were so dry and hard that they were fit for little, but others were very useful. The first thing I made of these was a cap for my head, with the fur on the outside, to put off the rain. I made this so well, that after this I made a suit of clothes out of these skins. That is to say, a waistcoat, and pants open at the knees, and both loose, for they were more for keeping me cool than to keep me warm. I must not fail to say that they were poorly made; for if I was a bad carpenter, I was a worse tailor. However, they were such as I did very well by them; and when I was out, if it happened to rain, the fur of my waistcoat and cap kept me very dry.

After this I spent a great deal of time and pains to make an umbrella. The main difficulty I found was to make it let down. I could make it spread, but if it did not let down too and draw in, it was not portable for me any way but just over my head, which would not do. However, at last, I made one that worked, and covered it with skins.

I cannot say that after this, for five years, any extraordinary thing happened to me, but I lived on in the same way, in the same place. The chief thing I was busy with, besides my yearly labor of planting my barley and rice and drying my raisins and my daily labor of going out with my gun, was to make me a canoe, which at last I finished. As for the first canoe, which was so big that I was never able to bring it to the water, I had to let it lie where it was. However, though my little canoe was finished, it was not big enough to do what I had wanted my boat to do, which was to venture from my island to the mainland forty miles off across the sea. But as I had a boat, my next plan was to make a tour around the island.

For this, I fitted up a little mast to my boat, and made a sail to it out of some of the pieces of the ship's sail. I found the boat would sail very well. Then

I made little boxes at either end of my boat, to put provisions, necessities, and ammunition, etc., into, to be kept dry.

I fixed my umbrella also in a slot at the stern, like a mast, to stand over my head, and keep the heat of the sun off of me like an awning. In this way I every now and then took a little voyage upon the sea, but never went far out, nor far from the little creek. But at last being eager to see all the way around my little kingdom, I resolved upon my tour and so packed for the voyage, putting in two dozen of my cakes of barley bread, a clay pot full of cooked rice, a little bottle of rum, half a goat, and gunpowder and gunshot for killing more goats, and two large coats to use as blankets in the night.

It was the 6th of November, in the sixth year of my kingship, that I set out on this voyage, and I found it much longer than I expected. For though the island was not very large, yet when I came to the east side of it, I found a great ledge of rocks lie out a few miles into the sea, some above water, some under it, so that I had to go a great way out to sea to get around the point.

A current carried my boat along with it with such strength that all I could do could not prevent my being driven into the vast ocean. I was taken a frightful distance from the island, and had the least cloud or hazy weather come between me and it, I should have been lost, for I had no compass on board, and should never have known how to have steered towards the island, if I had lost sight of it.

When I finally got back to shore, I fell on my knees and gave God thanks for my deliverance, resolving to give up all thoughts of my escape from the island by my boat.

After I slept near the beach that night, I had no idea how I would get home with my boat. I had been in so much danger that I would not think of going back the way I had come there. What might be on the other side, I did not know, and did not desire to take any more chances. So I coasted along the shore about three miles, and came to a bay, which narrowed until it became a brook, where I found a safe harbor for my boat.

I soon found I had barely passed by the place where I had been when I travelled on foot to the shore. So, taking nothing out of my boat but my gun and my umbrella, I began my march to my country shelter, where I found everything as I had left it.

I got over the fence and laid me down in the shade to rest my limbs, for I was very weary, and fell asleep. But think of what a surprise I felt, when I was waked out of my sleep by a voice calling me by my name several times, "Robin, Robin, Robin Crusoe, poor Robin Crusoe! Where are you, Robin Crusoe? Where are you? Where have you been?"

I was so dead asleep at first, being tired with paddling the first part of the day, that I did not wake completely. But dozing between sleeping and waking, I thought I dreamed that somebody spoke to me. But as the voice continued to repeat "Robin Crusoe, Robin Crusoe," at last I began to wake fully, and was at first dreadfully frightened and started up in confusion. But no sooner were my eyes open, but I saw my Poll sitting on the top of the hedge; and immediately I knew that it was he that spoke to me. It was just in such language I had used to talk to him, and teach him. He had learned it so perfectly that he would sit upon my finger and lay his bill close to my face, and cry, "Poor Robin Crusoe! Where are you? Where have you been? How did you come here?"

However, even though I knew it was the parrot, and that indeed it could be nobody else, it was a while before I could calm down. But when I got over it, I called out, "Poll," and he came to me, and sat upon my thumb, and continued talking to me, "Poor Robin Crusoe! How did you come here? Where have you been?" It was just as if he had been overjoyed to see me again. And so I carried him home along with me.

For the next year I lived a very calm life. I arrived at an unexpected skill in my pottery. I made things round and well-shaped which before were filthy things indeed to look at. But I think I was never more vain of my own work than for being able to make a tobacco pipe. And though it was a very ugly, clumsy thing when it was done, it was firm, and would draw the smoke, and I was very comforted with it.

Being now in the eleventh year of my residence, and my ammunition growing low, I set myself to study some art to trap and snare the goats, to see whether I could catch some of them alive. I particularly wanted a pregnant she-goat. I made pits and caught three kids, and taking them one by one, I tied them with strings together and brought them all home.

It was a while before they would feed, but by throwing them some sweet grain, it tempted them and they began to be tame. And now I found if I expected to supply myself with goat-meat when I had no gunpowder or gunshot left, breeding some up tame was my only way.

But then it occurred to me that I needed to have some enclosed ground, well-fenced, to keep them penned in. This was a great chore for one pair of hands, yet as I saw the need for doing it, I did it. It took me about three months to hedge in my first piece of ground. In about a year and a half I had a flock of about twelve goats, kids and all. In two years more I had forty-three, besides several that I ate. Now I had not only goat meat to eat when I liked, but milk too. I set up my dairy and had sometimes a gallon or two of milk a day.

I was finally impatient to have the use of my boat again, though not wanting to have any more dangerous adventures. At length I resolved to travel to the other side of the island by land, following the edge of the shore. Had anyone in England to meet such a man as I looked, it must either have frightened them or caused a great deal of laughter. Imagine how I appeared:

I had a large, high shapeless cap, made of a goat's skin, with a flap hanging down behind, as well to keep the sun from me as to ward off the rain from running down my neck. I had a jacket of goatskin that came down to about the middle of my thighs, and a pair of open-kneed pants of the same material. I did not have any shoes or socks, but I had made myself a pair of somethings, I hardly know what to call them, to flap over my legs, and lace on either side.

I had a broad belt of goatskin, and loops, where I hung a little saw and a hatchet. I had another belt, over my shoulder, and at the end of it, under my left arm, hung two pouches. In one of the pouches was my gunpowder, and in the other my gunshot. At my back I carried a basket, on my shoulder my gun, and over my head a large, clumsy, ugly goatskin umbrella. My beard I once allowed to grow till it was about a foot long. But as I had both scissors and razors, I cut it pretty short, except for my moustache, which I trimmed to look the way a Turk's would.

7

I Find the Print of a Man's Naked Foot

IT HAPPENED one day about noon, going towards my boat on the other side of the island. I was very surprised with the print of a man's naked foot on the shore, which was very plain to be seen in the sand. I stood like one thunderstruck, or as if I had seen a ghost. I listened, I looked round me, I could hear nothing, nor see anything. I went up to a rising ground to look farther. I went up the shore and down the shore, but I could see no more prints than that one. I went to it again to see if there were any more, and to check if it might not be my imagination. But there it was, the exact print of a foot, toes, heel and every part of a foot. How it came to be there I did not know, nor could in the least imagine. But after many confusing thoughts, I went home, terrified, looking behind me every two or three steps, mistaking every bush and tree, and imagining every stump at a distance to be a man.

When I arrived at my castle, I fled into it like one pursued. There had never been a more frightened rabbit or fox fleeing to cover, than I had been returning to my fort.

I did not sleep at all that night. After convincing

I was very surprised with the print of a man's naked foot
on the shore.

myself that the print had not been left by the Devil, I
concluded that then it must be an even more dangerous creature, that is, some of the savages of the
mainland, who had wandered out to sea in their
canoes. Then terrible thoughts racked my imagination
about their having found my boat, and that there were
people here. If so, they would certainly come again in
larger numbers and devour me.

For three days and nights I stayed within my cave,
and then it came into my head that all these thoughts
about the footprint might have been the result of an
illusion, that this foot might be the print of my own
foot, when I came on shore from my boat. I began to
gain courage and to peep outside again. After I
resumed my former routine, and began venturing to
my goats, I decided to return to the shore and see this
print of a foot, and measure it against my own, that I
might know if it was indeed my foot. But when I came
to the place, first it appeared obvious to me that
when I laid up my boat, I could not possibly have
been on shore anywhere near there. Secondly, when I
came to measure the mark with my own foot, I found
my foot much smaller. Both these things filled my
head with new fancies, and gave me the terrors again.
I went home again, filled with the belief that some
man or men had been on shore there. I imagined that
the island was inhabited, and I might be surprised
before I was aware. What I should do for my safety, I
did not know.

I concluded that this island, which was so pleasant,

fruitful and not so very far from the mainland, was not so entirely desolate as I had imagined. I had lived here fifteen years now, and had not met with the least shadow or figure of any people yet. If at any time the savages should be driven here, it was probable they went away again as soon as ever they could.

I had nothing to do but to think of some safe retreat, in case I should see any savages land upon the spot. I made a second wall of trees around my first wall, and in two years had a thick grove. In five or six years' time I had an impassable forest in front of my dwelling. No man of any kind would ever imagine there was anything beyond it. As for the way I got in and out, I now had two ladders; one to a part of the rock which was low and had a ledge, where I placed another ladder.

While all this was going on, I was not careless of my other affairs; for I had great concern for my little herd of goats. I decided to separate my goats into two remote, hidden spots, that the savages might not find them. One spot I found was a little piece of open ground in the middle of the thick woods.

All this effort and labor came about because of my fears on account of the man's footprint, and for the next two years I lived with less comfort than before. After I had found the one hidden pen for half of my goats, I went around the whole island searching for another private place. When wandering more to the west point of the island than I had ever done yet, and looking out to sea, I thought I saw a boat upon the sea, at a great distance. I had found a spyglass in one of the seaman's chests from the ship; but I did not have it with me.

When I came down the hill to the shore, I was horrified and amazed to see the shore covered with skulls, hands, feet and other bones of human bodies. I observed a place where there had been a fire, and a circle dug in the earth, where I supposed the savages had sat down to their terrible feastings upon the bodies of their fellow creatures.

I turned and ran up the hill again, and then walked home to my castle. I felt that as I had been here now almost eighteen years, I might be here eighteen more if I stayed as hidden as I had been. Within a few days, I began to live in the same calm way as before. It was only with this difference, that I used more caution, and kept my eyes more alert than I did before. I was more cautious about firing my gun, to prevent any of them, did they happen to be on the island, from hearing it. It was therefore fortunate that I had provided myself with a herd of tame goats, so that I did not have to hunt any more for them through the woods or shoot at them. For two years after this, I believe I never fired my gun off once, though I never went out without it. What was more, as I had saved three pistols out of the ship, I always carried them out with me, or at least two of them, sticking them in my goatskin belt. I was now a most imposing looking fellow when I went out, if you add to the earlier description of myself the two pistols and a large sword, hanging at my side by the belt.

I seldom went out from my cave other than to milk my she-goats and manage my little flock in the woods. I had the care of my safety more now upon my hands than that of my food. I did not want to drive a nail or chop a piece of wood now, for fear the noise I should make should be heard. Above all, I was worried about making a fire, as the smoke, which is visible at a great distance in the day, should betray me. And for this reason I moved that part of my business which required fire, such as burning pots, into a natural cave in the earth, which was deep, and where, I dare say, no savage, had he been at the mouth of it, would be so courageous as to go in.

I was now in my twenty-third year of living on this island and was so used to the place and to the way of living that could I have been certain that no savages would come, I could have been content to spend the rest of my life here. I had also managed some amuse-ments, which made the time pass more pleasantly than it did before. I had taught my parrot, Poll, to speak. He did it so well, that it was very pleasant to me. My dog was a very pleasant and loving com-panion to me for no less than sixteen years of my time, and then died of mere old age. Besides these, I always kept two or three household kids about me, which I taught to feed out of my hand. And I had two more parrots, which talked pretty well, and would all call "Robin Crusoe," but none like my first. I had also several tame sea birds, which I caught along the shore, and clipped their wings. These birds now lived among the wall of trees in front of my home and bred there.

8

I Meet Friday

I WAS SURPRISED one morning to see at least five canoes all on shore together on my side of the island. The people who had come in on them all had landed and were out of my sight. I retreated to my fort and climbed the rock above my cave with my ladders and spied the site with my glass. There were about thirty savages, and they had a fire started and were cooking meat. They were all dancing round the fire.

While I was watching them, I saw two miserable men dragged from the boats, where, it seemed, they had been kept, and were now brought out for killing. One of the two immediately fell, being knocked down, I suppose, with a club, and while two or three of the savages killed him, the other victim was left standing by himself till they should be ready for him. In that very moment, the remaining victim saw his chance and dashed away and ran across the sands in my direction.

I saw a group run after him. There was between them and my castle the creek which I mentioned often at the first part of my story, when I landed my cargoes out of the ship. This creek I saw he must swim over, or the poor man would be captured there.

The escaping savage made nothing of the obstacle, but plunged into the creek, swam through it in about thirty strokes, landed and ran on with great strength and swiftness. When the three savages in pursuit came to the creek, two swam after, but the third did not and returned to the others, which, as it happened, was very lucky for him.

I saw that it was now my time to get a friend or servant, and that I was called by God to save this poor escaping creature's life. I immediately ran down the ladders, fetched my two guns, went back up over the ladders, and down hill towards the sea. I hurried to put myself in between the pursuers and the pursued, helloing aloud to the one that was fleeing, who, looking back, was at first perhaps as frightened of me as of them. But I beckoned with my hand to him to come back, and in the meantime I slowly went towards the two that followed. Then, rushing at once upon the first of them, I knocked him down with the butt of my gun. I did not want to fire my gun, because I did not want the others to hear. Having knocked this fellow down, his comrade stopped, as if he was frightened. I now went towards him. But as I came nearer, I saw he had a bow and arrow, and was getting it ready to shoot me. So I had to shoot at him first; which I did, and I killed him at the first shot.

The poor savage who had escaped, though he saw both his enemies fallen, yet was so frightened by the fire and noise of my gun, that he stood still and neither came forward or went away. I helloed again to him, and made signs to come forward, which he understood and came a little way, then stopped again, and then a little farther, and stopped again. And I could see that he stood trembling, as if he had been taken prisoner by me and was about to be killed, as his two enemies were. I beckoned him again to come to me, and gave him all the signs of encouragement I could think of. He came nearer and nearer, kneeling down every ten or twelve steps in thanks for my saving his life.

I smiled at him and looked pleasantly and beckoned him to come still closer. Finally, he came close to me, and then he kneeled down again, kissed the ground, and laid his head upon the ground, and taking me by the foot, set my foot upon his head. I made him get up and tried to make him more at ease. But there was more work to do yet, as I saw the savage whom I knocked down was not killed, but stunned with the blow, and began to come to. So I pointed to him, and showed him the savage, that he was not dead. Upon this he spoke some words to me, and though I could not understand them, yet I thought they were pleasant to hear, for they were the first sound of a man's voice that I had heard, not counting my own, for more than twenty-five years. The savage who was knocked down recovered himself so well as to sit up on the ground. When I pointed my gun at the man as if I would shoot him, my savage made a motion to me to lend him my sword, so I did. He no sooner had it, but he ran to his enemy and at one

blow cut off his head. When he had done this, he
came laughing to me in triumph and brought me the
sword again, and with many gestures I did not understand, laid it down in front of me.

He then buried his two enemies, and then I called
him to follow me, and I brought him to my cave, on
the farther side of the island. Here I gave him bread
and a bunch of raisins to eat, and a drink of water.
Having fed him, I made signs for him to go lie down
and sleep, pointing to a place where I had put down
a great load of straw, and a blanket upon it. So the
poor creature lay down and went to sleep.

He was a handsome fellow, with straight, strong
limbs, tall, and well-shaped, and about twenty-six
years old. He had a manly face, and a sweet and soft
look, especially when he smiled. His hair was long
and black, and his skin was dark. His face was round
and plump; his nose was small, his lips were thin,
and his fine teeth were white as ivory.

After he had napped for half an hour, he woke up
and came out of the cave to me, where I had been
milking the goats, who had their pen nearby. When
he saw me he came running, then lay himself down
again on the ground, with all the possible signs of a
humble, thankful feeling, to let me know he would
serve me as long as he lived. In a little while, I began
to speak to him and teach him to speak to me. First, I
made him know his name should be Friday, which
was the day I saved his life. I likewise taught him to
say "Master," and then let him know that was to be

my name. I likewise taught him to say "yes" and "no" and to know their meaning.

I stayed there with him all that night, but as soon as it was day, I asked him to come with me, and led him up to the top of the hill, to see if his enemies were gone. Pulling out my spyglass, I looked, and saw plainly the place where they had been, but no sight of them or their canoes. It was plain they were gone, and had left their two comrades behind them, without any search for them.

I was not content with this discovery, but having now more courage, and more curiosity, I took my man Friday with me, giving him the sword in his hand, and the bow and arrows we had from the dead savages at his back, which I found he could use very easily. I also made him carry one gun for me. I carried two for myself, and away we marched to the place where these creatures had been. When I came to the place, my blood ran cold, and my heart sunk within me at the horror of the spectacle. Friday, by his signs, made me understand that they brought over four prisoners to feast upon. He indicated three of them were eaten up, and that he, pointing to himself, was to have been the fourth.

When we came back to our castle, I let him know I would give him some clothes, for he was stark naked. I gave him a pair of linen pants, which, with a little alteration, fitted him very well. Then I made him a goatskin jacket and a rabbit-fur cap. He was mightily pleased to see himself almost as well clothed as his

I gave him a pair of linen pants, which, with a little
alteration, fitted him very well.

master. It is true, he went awkwardly in these things at first. Wearing pants was very awkward to him, and the sleeves of the coat bothered his shoulders and arms.

Never did a man have a more faithful, loving, sincere servant than Friday was to me. I was greatly delighted with him, and made it my business to teach him everything that was proper to make him useful, handy and helpful. The most important thing was to make him speak and understand me when I spoke. He was the best student that ever was, and so cheerful, hardworking and so pleased when he could understand me or make me understand him, that it was very pleasant to talk to him.

I set him to work to beating some grain, and sifting it in the manner I used to do. He soon understood how to do it, especially after he had seen what the meaning of it was, and that it was to make bread. After that I let him see me make my bread, and bake it too, and in a little time Friday was able to do all the work as well as I could do it myself.

Having two mouths to feed now instead of one, I needed to provide more ground for my harvest and plant a larger quantity of grain than I used to do. So I marked out a larger piece of land, and began the fence in the same manner as before, in which Friday not only worked very willingly and very hard, but did it very cheerfully. I told him what it was for, that it was for grain to make more bread, because he was now with me, and that I might have enough for him and myself too.

This was the pleasantest year of all the life I led in this place. Friday began to talk a great deal to me. I began now to have some use for my tongue again, which indeed I had very little use for before; that is to say, for speaking. Besides the pleasure of talking to him, I had a real satisfaction in the fellow himself. His simple honesty appeared to me more and more, and I began to love the creature. On his side, I believe he loved me.

Having taught him English so well that he could answer me almost any questions, I asked him whether the nation that he belonged to ever won their battles. He smiled and said, "Yes, yes, we always fight the better."

"You always fight the better," said I; "how was it that you were taken prisoner then, Friday?"

"My nation beat much, for all that," he replied.

"How beat?" I wondered. "If your nation beat them, how were you taken?"

"They more many than my nation in the place where me was. They take one, two, three and me. My nation overbeat them in the far place, where me no was. There my nation take one, two, great thousand," he said.

"But why," I continued, "did not your side recover you from the hands of your enemies then?"

Friday explained, "They run one, two, three and me, and make go in the canoe. My nation have no canoe that time."

"Well, Friday, what does your nation do with the men they take? Do they carry them away, and eat them, as these did?"

"Yes, my nation eats mans too, eat all up."

"Do they come here?"

"Yes, yes, they come here."

"Have you been here with them?"

Friday, pointing to the northwest side of the island, which, it seems, was their side, answered, "Yes, I been here."

By this I understood that my man Friday had been among the savages who used to come on shore on the farther part of the island. I asked him how far it was from our island to the shore, and whether canoes were not often lost. He told me there was no danger, no canoes ever got lost; but that after a little way out to the sea, there was a current, and a wind, always one way in the morning, the other in the afternoon.

I afterwards understood this current was controlled by the great outflow and inflow of the mighty Orinoco River, in the gulf of which river our island lay. The land which I could see to the west was, I found, the great island Trinidad.

I asked Friday a thousand questions about the country, the people who lived there, the sea, the coast and what nations were near. He told me all he knew.

I asked him once, after he had been with me a long time, who made him. He did not understand me at all, but thought I had asked who his father was. I took it by another route, and asked him who made the sea, the ground we walked on and the hills and woods. He told me it was one old Benamuckee, that lived beyond all. He could describe nothing of this great person but that he was very old; much older, he said, than the sea or the land, than the moon or the stars. I asked him then, if this old person had made all things, why did not all things worship him? He looked very serious, and with a perfect look of innocence, said "All things said O!" to him. I asked him if the people who die in this country went away anywhere. He said yes, they all went to Benamuckee. Then I asked him whether these men they eat went there too. He said yes.

After Friday and I got to know each other better, and he could understand almost all I said to him and speak fluently, though in broken English, I told him my own story, how I had lived there, and how long. I let him into the mystery of gunpowder and gunshot, and taught him how to shoot. I described to him Europe, and particularly England, which I came from. I told him how we lived, how we worshipped God, how we behaved to one another; and how we traded in ships to all parts of the world.

9

We Stop a Mutiny

I WAS NOW in my twenty-seventh year of living on this island. I kept the anniversary of my landing here with the same thankfulness to God for His mercies as at first. I had the feeling that my escape from this island would be soon, and that I should not be another year here. However, I went on with my farming, digging, planting, fencing, as usual. I gathered and dried my grapes, and did every necessary thing, as before.

After the rainy season, I was busy one morning, when I called to Friday and asked him to go to the seashore and see if he could find a turtle, a thing we generally got once a week, for the sake of the eggs as well as the meat. Friday had not been long gone when he came running back and flew over my outer wall. Before I had time to say a word, he cried out to me, "O Master! O Master! O sorrow! O bad!"

"What's the matter, Friday?"

"Master, master, they are come, they are come!"

I jumped up, and, not thinking of the danger, went out through my little grove, without my guns, which was not my custom to do. But I was surprised when, turning my eyes to the sea, I soon saw a boat a few miles away, heading for shore, with a short sail, and the wind blowing pretty well to bring them in. I called to Friday and told him to lie low, that we did not know yet whether they were friends or enemies.

I went in to fetch my spyglass, to see what I could make of them. Having taken the ladder out, I climbed to the top of the hill to take my view without being seen.

I had hardly got up on the hill when my eye easily discovered a ship lying at anchor at about five miles distance from me, but not more than a few miles off shore. It appeared to be an English ship.

I cannot express the confusion I was in, though the joy of seeing a ship, and one I had reason to believe was manned by my own countrymen, and therefore friends, was such as I cannot describe. And yet I had some caution. I had to wonder why an English ship should be in that part of the world.

I watched the boat draw near the shore, as they looked for a creek for easier landing. However, as they did not come quite far enough, they did not see the little inlet where I used to land my rafts, but ran their boat on shore upon the beach, about a half a mile from me.

When they were on shore, I saw that they were indeed Englishmen, or at least most of them. There were in all eleven men, with three of them unarmed and tied up. When the first four or five of them jumped onto shore, they took those three out of the boat as prisoners.

Friday cried out to me in English, "O master! You see English mans eat prisoner as well as savage mans."

"Why," I said, "Friday, do you think they are going to eat them then?"

"Yes," said Friday, "they will eat them."

"No, no," I said, "I am afraid they will murder them, indeed, but you may be sure they will not eat them."

After I had observed the outrageous usage of the three men by the rude seamen, I observed the fellows run scattering about the land, as if they wanted to see the country. I observed that the other three men had been untied and were at liberty to go also where they pleased; but they sat down on the ground.

It was just at high water when these people came on shore, and while talking and rambling about the island, they had carelessly stayed till the tide was gone, and now their boat was grounded. It would be at least ten hours before the boat could be floated again, and by that time it would be dark.

In the meantime I fitted myself up for a battle. I ordered Friday also to load himself with guns. I took two bird guns and I gave him three muskets. I had my goatskin coat on, with the large cap, a sword by my side, two pistols in my belt, and a gun upon each shoulder.

I had planned not to make any move till it was dark. But about two o'clock, I found that they were all in the woods and fallen asleep. The three hostages, worried about their fate, did not sleep, but were sitting under the shelter of a large tree, out of sight of the rest.

I resolved to go to them and learn something of their condition. Immediately I set out towards them, my man Friday at a good distance behind me. Before any of them saw me, I called aloud to them, "What are you, gentlemen?"

They started at my words, but were more surprised by my appearance. I saw that they were about to run away, so I said to them: "Gentlemen, do not be surprised by me. I may be your friend."

One of them said, "Am I talking to God, or man? Is it a real man, or an angel?"

"I am a man," I said, "an Englishman, who would like to help you. I have one servant only. We have guns and ammunition. Tell us, can we help you? What is your story?"

"Our story," said he, "sir, is too long to tell you, while our murderers are so near. But in short, sir, I was commander of that ship. My men have mutinied against me, they have hardly held themselves back from killing me. Instead they have set me on shore in this desolate place, with these two men with me, one my mate, the other a passenger, where we expect to die."

"Have the brutes any guns?" I asked.

He answered that they had only two guns, one of which they left in the boat.

"Shall we take them as prisoners?" I asked.

He told me there were two desperate villains among

I resolved to go to them and learn something of their condition.

them, but that if those two were captured, he believed all the rest would return to their duty.

"Sir," said I, "if I help you to escape, are you willing to make pledges to me?"

He said he knew what I would ask, and that if the ship were recovered, he would be at my command. If it were not recovered, he declared he would live and die with me. The other two men said the same.

"Well, then," I said, "here are three muskets for you, with gunpowder and bullets."

He took the musket, and with his two men approached the slumbering mutineers. One of the seamen woke up and cried out. The captain's two men fired their guns and killed one man and wounded another. The others gave up and begged for mercy. The captain told them he would spare their lives, if they would swear to be faithful to him in recovering the ship and afterwards sailing her back to Jamaica, from where they had come. They promised, and he believed them, which I was not against, only I asked the captain to keep them bound hand and foot while they were upon the island.

I now told the captain my whole history, which amazed him. He was particularly amazed at the way I had furnished myself with goods and guns. Indeed, as my story is a whole collection of wonders, it affected him deeply. I then took him and his two men into my castle, where I fed them and gave them drink, and showed them my many works. All I showed them, all I said to them, was perfectly amazing. Above all, the captain admired my fort, and how well I had hidden my retreat with a grove of trees.

At present, however, our business was to consider how to recover the ship. He told me he did not know what to do, that there were still twenty-six men on board who would fight us.

We went back to the shore and saw, with the use of the spyglass, that the mutineers on board ship were launching another boat for the island. We found, as they approached, that there were ten men in the boat, and that they had guns with them.

We hid and watched them come on shore, hauling the boat up after them. After they looked around for a while, they let out two or three great shouts, helloing with all their might, to try to get their companions to hear. They fired off guns as a signal, but there was no response. They were so surprised, they went back to their boat and launched it to return to the ship. But they were not far off before they returned to the shore. This time they left three men in the boat, and seven got out to search the island for their mates.

After the seven were amongst the woods, we surprised the men in the boat, and captured it. By the time the other seven returned to the shore from the woods, it was night.

We came upon the mutineers in the dark, so that they could not see us. After a short fight in which two of the mutineers were killed, we forced the others to surrender.

Our next work was to think of how to seize the

ship. Our captives, in order to try to regain the captain's sympathy and thus make their case before a judge in Jamaica go easier, agreed to help us. The captain put himself at the head of one boat, and his passenger the captain of the other, with four men in each. They rowed out to the ship and arrived about midnight. As soon as they came within call of the ship, he made one of the captive mutineers hail them and tell them they had brought off the first men who had gone over, and the boat. But then, upon entering the ship, the captain and his mate knocked down two mutineers aboard ship, and began locking down the hatches to keep the other mutineers below the deck.

When this was done, and all safe upon deck, the captain ordered the mate with three good men to break into the cabin where the leader of the mutineers was hiding. As they borke down the door, guns went off, and though the captain's mate was wounded, he continued his charge and shot dead the chief mutineer. The rest of the mutineers surrendered, and no more lives were lost.

As soon as the ship was thus recovered, the captain ordered seven guns to be fired, which was the signal agreed upon with me, to give me notice of his success. Having heard the signal, I went to sleep. In the morning I awoke, hearing the captain's voice from atop the hill near my castle. He came to me, hugged me, and told me, "My dear friend, there's your ship, for she is all yours, and so are we and all that belong to her."

At first, for some time, I was not able to answer him one word. He said a thousand kind things to me, to calm me and bring me around. But such was the flood of joy in my heart that I was confused. At last I broke out into tears, and a little while after I was able to speak. I told him that I saw him as my rescuer.

From the ship he brought me presents: wine, tobacco, pork, peas, biscuits, sugar, flour, lemons and an abundance of other things. But even more useful to me, he brought me six clean new shirts, two pairs of gloves, one pair of shoes, a hat, one pair of stockings and a very good suit of clothes of his own, which had been worn very little. He clothed me from head to foot.

Some time after this the boat was ordered on shore, the tide being up. When Friday and I took leave of this island, I carried on board for souvenirs the large goatskin cap I had made, my umbrella, and one of my parrots. And thus I left the island, the 19th of December, in the year 1686, after I had been upon it twenty-eight years, two months and nineteen days.

In this vessel, after a long voyage, I arrived in England the 11th of June, in the year 1687, having been thirty-five years absent.

When I came to England, I was a perfect stranger, as if I had never been known there. I went down to Yorkshire. My father and my mother, however, and all my family were dead except two sisters and two of the children of one of my brothers.

The owners of the ship, after the captain told them

how I had saved the ship and its cargo, gave me a present of money. But after thinking about my life, and how little this money would go towards settling me in the world, I resolved to return to my plantation in Brazil. My man Friday accompanied me on all my ramblings, and proved a most faithful servant upon all occasions.

DOVER
CHILDREN'S THRIFT CLASSICS

Tom Sawyer

MARK TWAIN

Adapted by Bob Blaisdell
Illustrated by John Green

DOVER PUBLICATIONS, INC.
Mineola, New York

DOVER CHILDREN'S THRIFT CLASSICS

Bibliographical Note

This Dover edition, first published in 1996, is a new abridgment by Bob Blaisdell of *The Adventures of Tom Sawyer* (original publication: American Publishing Company, Hartford, 1876). The illustrations by John Green and the introductory Note have been specially prepared for this edition.

Library of Congress Cataloging-in-Publication Data

Twain, Mark, 1835–1910.
    [Adventures of Tom Sawyer]
    Tom Sawyer / Mark Twain ; abridged [by Bob Blaisdell] ; illustrated by John Green.
        p.   cm. — (Dover children's thrift classics)
    "This Dover edition, first published in 1996, is a new abridgement by Bob Blaisdell of The adventures of Tom Sawyer"—T.p. verso.
    Summary: The adventures of a mischievous young boy and his friends, growing up in a Mississippi River town in the nineteenth century.
    ISBN 0-486-29156-1 (pbk.)
    [1. Mississippi River—Fiction. 2. Missouri—Fiction.] I. Blaisdell, Robert. II. Green, John, 1948– ill. III. Title. IV. Series.
PZ7.C584Ad   1996
[Fic]—dc20   95–40294
                                                     CIP
                                                     AC

Manufactured in the United States of America
Dover Publications, Inc., 31 East 2nd Street, Mineola, N.Y. 11501

Note

THE CHARACTER Tom Sawyer is a creation of the master storyteller and humorist Mark Twain, who also gave us "The Celebrated Jumping Frog of Calaveras County," *The Adventures of Huckleberry Finn* and *A Connecticut Yankee in King Arthur's Court,* as well as many other books. Twain was born Samuel Langhorne Clemens in 1835, and grew up in Hannibal, Missouri, a frontier town on the Mississippi River. His frontier youth, diverse job experience (newspaper writer, steamboat pilot) and wide travels all provided material for his many novels and short stories, which express the spirit of the American West in all its moods. When *The Adventures of Tom Sawyer* was published in 1876, Twain was already one of America's most beloved authors.

This book takes place in the sleepy Missouri town of St. Petersburg, where Tom Sawyer lives with his old Aunt Polly, prowls with his comrade Huckleberry Finn and meets his sweetheart Becky Thatcher. Tom, who is a curious mixture of innocence and mischief, heroism and laziness, is soon pulled into a series of romantic and dangerous adventures having to do with piracy, tedious chores and the cutthroat Injun Joe.

Mark Twain died in 1910, leaving the world a bounty of exuberant, witty prose which it will probably never tire of. This abridged version of his classic novel, which contains the chief nuggets of Tom Sawyer's adventures, will surely leave young readers greedy for more, of which, fortunately, there is plenty.

Contents

1

Tom Whitewashes a Fence

"TOM!"

No answer.

"Tom!"

No answer.

"What's wrong with that boy, I wonder? You, TOM!"

No answer. The old lady pulled her spectacles down and looked over them about the room.

"Well, if I get hold of you I'll—"

She did not finish, for by this time she was bending down and punching under the bed with the broom.

"I never did see the likes of that boy!"

She went to the open door and stood in it and looked out among the tomato vines and weeds that made up her garden. No Tom. So she lifted her voice and shouted:

"Y-o-u-u, Tom!"

There was a slight noise behind her and she turned just in time to seize a small boy by the slack of his jacket and stop his flight.

"There! I might 'a' thought of that closet. What you been doing in there?"

"Nothing."

"Nothing! Look at your hands. And look at your mouth. What *is* that business?"

Aunt Polly seized Tom by his jacket.

"*I* don't know, aunt."

"Well, I know. It's jam—that's what it is. Forty times I've said if you didn't let that jam alone I'd skin you. Hand me that switch."

The switch hovered in the air above the boy—the peril was near—

"My! Look behind you, aunt!"

The old lady whirled round, and snatched her skirts out of danger. The lad fled, instantly, scrambled up the high board fence, and disappeared over it.

His aunt Polly stood surprised a moment, and then broke into a gentle laugh.

"Hang the boy, can't I never learn anything? Ain't

he played me tricks enough like that for me to be looking out for him by this time? But my goodness, he never plays them alike, two days, and how is a body to know what's coming? He 'pears to know just how long he can torment me before I get my dander up, and he knows if he can make out to put me off for a minute or make me laugh, it's all down again and I can't hit him a lick. I ain't doing my duty by that boy, and that's the Lord's truth, goodness knows. Spare the rod and spile the child, as the Good Book says. But laws! he's my own dead sister's boy, poor thing, and I ain't got the heart to lash him, somehow. He'll play hooky this afternoon, and I'll be obliged to make him work, tomorrow, to punish him. It's mighty hard to make him work Saturdays, when all the boys is having holiday, but he hates work more than he hates anything else."

Tom did play hooky, and he had a very good time. He got back home barely in time to help Jim, a small black boy, saw next day's wood and split the kindlings before supper—at least he was there in time to tell his adventures to Jim while Jim did three-fourths of the work. Tom's younger brother (or rather, half brother), Sid, was already through with his part of the work (picking up wood chips), for he was a quiet boy and had no adventurous, troublesome ways.

When Saturday morning came, all the summer world was bright and fresh, and brimming with life. There was a song in every heart; and if the heart was young the music issued at the lips. There was cheer in every face and a spring in every step.

Jim said he was forbidden to help Tom paint the fence.

Tom appeared on the sidewalk with a bucket of whitewash and a long-handled brush. He surveyed the fence, and all gladness left him and a deep sadness settled down upon his spirit. Thirty yards of board fence nine feet high. Sighing he dipped his brush and passed it along the topmost plank;

repeated the operation; did it again; compared the tiny whitewashed streak with the far-reaching country of the unwhitewashed fence, and sat down on a tree-box discouraged. Jim came skipping out at the gate with a tin pail, and singing. Bringing water from the town pump had always been hateful work in Tom's eyes before, but now it did not strike him so. He remembered that there was company at the pump. White, mulatto, and Negro boys and girls were always there waiting their turns, resting, trading playthings, quarreling, fighting, fooling.

Tom said: "Say, Jim, I'll fetch the water if you'll whitewash some."

Jim shook his head and said: "Can't, Marse Tom. Ole missis, she tole me I got to go an' git dis water an' not stop foolin' round wid anybody. She say she 'spected Marse Tom gwine to ax me to whitewash, an' so she tole me go 'long an' 'tend to my own business—she said *she'd* tend to de whitewashin'.' "

"Oh, never you mind what she said, Jim. That's the way she always talks. Gimme the bucket—I won't be gone only a minute. *She* won't ever know. I'll give you a white marble! I'll show you my sore toe."

Jim was only human—this attraction was too much for him. He put down his pail, took the marble, and bent over the toe while the bandage was being un-wound. In another moment he was flying down the street with his pail and tingling rear, Tom was white-washing, and Aunt Polly was returning to the house with a slipper in her hand.

But Tom's energy did not last. He began to think of

the fun he had planned for this day, and his sorrows increased. Soon the boys would come tripping along on all sorts of wonderful outings, and they would make a world of fun of him for having to work. And then inspiration burst upon him!

He took up his brush and went calmly to work. Ben Rogers came in sight soon—the very boy, of all boys, whose teasing he had been dreading. Ben was eating an apple, and giving long, cheerful whoops.

Tom went on whitewashing—paid no attention to Ben. The boy stared a moment and then said: "Hi-*yi!* *You're* up a stump, ain't you!"

No answer. Tom looked over his last touch with the eye of an artist, then he gave his brush another gentle sweep and looked over the result, as before. Ben went up alongside of him. Tom's mouth watered for the apple, but he stuck to his work. Ben said, "Hello, old chap, you got to work, hey?"

Tom wheeled suddenly and said, "Why, it's you, Ben! I warn't noticing."

"*Say*—I'm going in a-swimming, *I* am. Don't you wish you could? But of course you'd druther *work*—wouldn't you? Course you would!"

Tom looked at the boy a bit, and said, "What do you call work?"

"Why, ain't *that* work?"

Tom began again his whitewashing, and answered, "Well, maybe it is, and maybe it ain't. All I know is, it suits Tom Sawyer."

"Oh, come now, you don't mean to let on that you *like* it?"

The brush continued to move.

"Like it? Well, I don't see why I oughtn't to like it. Does a boy get a chance to whitewash a fence every day?"

That put the thing in a new light. Ben stopped nibbling his apple. Tom swept his brush daintily back and forth—stepped back to note the effect—added a touch here and there—Ben watching every move and getting more and more interested, more and more pulled in. Soon he said, "Say, Tom, let *me* whitewash a little."

Tom considered, was about to say yes; but he changed his mind: "No—no—I reckon it wouldn't hardly do, Ben. You see, Aunt Polly's awful particular about this fence—right here on the street, you know— but if it was the back fence I wouldn't mind and *she* wouldn't. Yes, she's awful particular about this fence; it's got to be done very careful; I reckon there ain't one boy in a thousand, maybe two thousand that can do it the way it's got to be done."

"No—is that so? Oh, come now—lemme just try. Only just a little—I'd let *you*, if you was me, Tom."

"Ben, I'd like to, honest Injun; but Aunt Polly—well, Jim wanted to do it, but she wouldn't let him; Sid wanted to do it, and she wouldn't let Sid. Now don't you see how I'm fixed? If you was to tackle this fence and anything was to happen to it—"

"Oh, shucks, I'll be just as careful. Now lemme try. Say—I'll give you the core of my apple."

"Well, here— No, Ben, now don't. I'm afeared—"

"I'll give you *all* of it!"

Tom sat on a barrel while the other boys worked.

Tom gave up the brush. While Ben worked and sweated in the sun, Tom sat on a barrel close by, dangled his legs, munched his apple, and planned the trap of more boys. There was no lack of them; they came to jeer, but remained to whitewash. By the time Ben was tired out, Tom had traded the next chance to Billy Fisher for a kite; and when *he* played out, Johnny Miller bought in for a dead rat and a string to swing it with—and so on, and so on, hour after hour. And when the middle of the afternoon came, Tom was literally rolling in wealth. He had besides the things before mentioned, twelve marbles, part of a jew's-harp, a piece of blue bottle glass to look through, a spool, a key that wouldn't unlock anything, a piece of chalk, a glass stopper of a bottle, a tin soldier, a couple of tadpoles, six firecrackers, a kitten with only one eye, a brass doorknob, a dog collar—but no dog—the handle of a knife, four pieces of orange peel, and an old window sash.

He had had a nice, good, idle time all the while— plenty of company—and the fence had three coats of whitewash on it! Tom had discovered a great law of human action, without knowing it—namely, that in

Tom had a kite, twelve marbles, a key and a kitten with one eye.

order to make a man or a boy want a thing, it is only necessary to make the thing difficult to get.

Tom presented himself before Aunt Polly, who was sitting by an open window in a pleasant rear room. The warm summer air, the quiet, and the odor of the flowers had had their effect, and she was napping over her knitting. She had thought that of course Tom had run off long ago, and she was surprised to see him place himself in her power again.

He said, "Mayn't I go and play now, aunt?"

"What, a'ready? How much have you done?"

"It's all done, aunt."

"Tom, don't lie to me—I can't bear it."

"I ain't, aunt; it *is* all done."

Aunt Polly went out to see for herself. She was astonished!

"Well, I never! There's no getting around it, you can work when you're a mind to, Tom.—But it's powerful seldom you're in mind to, I'm bound to say. Well, go 'long and play."

As Tom was passing by the house where Jeff Thatcher lived, he saw a new girl in the garden—a lovely little blue-eyed creature with yellow hair plaited into two long tails, and white summer dress.

He admired this angel without letting on that he was till he saw that she had seen him. Then he pretended he did not know she was there, and began to show off in all sorts of silly boyish ways, in order to win her admiration. He kept up this foolishness for some time; but by and by, while he was in the middle of some dangerous gymnastic stunts, he glanced over and saw that the little girl was making her way toward the house. Tom came up to the fence and leaned on it, hoping she would wait a while longer. She halted a moment on the steps and then moved toward the door. Tom heaved a great sigh as she put her foot on the threshold. But his face lit up right away, for she tossed a pansy over the fence a moment before she disappeared.

2

Tom Meets Becky Thatcher

MONDAY MORNING found Tom Sawyer miserable. Monday mornings always found him so—because it began another week's slow suffering in school. He generally began that day with wishing he had had no holiday, it made the going into prison and chains again so much more hateful.

Tom lay thinking. Soon he thought that he wished he was sick. Here was a possibility. He tried to find a stomach ache, but no, he was fine. Suddenly he discovered something. One of his upper front teeth was loose. This was lucky; he was about to begin to groan as a "starter," as he called it, when it occurred to him that if he told his aunt about it, she would pull it out, and that would hurt. So he thought he would hold the tooth in reserve and look for another trouble. Then he remembered hearing the doctor tell about a thing that laid up a patient for two or three weeks and almost made the patient lose a finger. So the boy drew his sore toe from under the sheet and held it up. He fell to groaning.

But Sid, lying beside him, slept on.

Tom groaned louder, and imagined that he began to feel pain in the toe.

No result from Sid.

Tom was aggravated. He said, "Sid, Sid!" and shook him. Tom began to groan again. Sid yawned, stretched, then brought himself up on his elbow with a snort, and began to stare at Tom. Tom went on groaning.

Sid said, "Tom! Say, Tom!" (No response.) "Here, Tom! *Tom!* What is the matter, Tom?" And he shook him and looked in his face.

Tom moaned out, "Oh, don't, Sid. Don't joggle me."

"Why, what's the matter, Tom? I must call auntie."

"No—never mind. It'll be over by and by, maybe. Don't call anybody."

"But I must! *Don't* groan so, Tom, it's awful. How long you been this way?"

"Hours. Ouch! Oh, don't stir so, Sid, you'll kill me."

"Tom, why didn't you wake me sooner? Oh, Tom, *don't!* What *is* the matter?"

"I forgive you everything, Sid. (Groan.) Everything you've ever done to me. When I'm gone—"

"Oh, Tom, you ain't dying, are you? Don't, Tom— oh, don't. Maybe—"

"I forgive everybody, Sid. (Groan.) Tell 'em so, Sid. And, Sid, you give my window sash and my cat with one eye to that new girl that's come to town, and tell her—"

But Sid had snatched his clothes and gone. He flew downstairs and said, "Oh, Aunt Polly, come! Tom's dying!"

"Dying!"

"Yes'm. Don't wait—come quick!"

"Rubbage! I don't believe it!"

But she fled upstairs with Sid and Mary at her

Aunt Polly gasped, "Tom, what's the matter?"

heels. And her face grew white, too, and her lip trembled. When she reached the bedside she gasped out, "You, Tom! Tom, what's the matter with you?"

"Oh, auntie, I'm—"

"What's the matter with you, child?"

"Oh, auntie, my sore toe's mortified!"

The old lady sank down into a chair and laughed a little, then cried a little, then did both together. "Tom, what a turn you did give me. Now you shut up that nonsense and climb out of this bed."

The groans stopped and the pain disappeared from the toe. The boy felt a little foolish, and he said, "Aunt Polly, it *seemed* mortified, and it hurt so I never minded my tooth at all."

"Your tooth, indeed! What's the matter with your tooth?"

"One of them's loose, and it aches perfectly awful."

"There, there, now, don't begin that groaning again. Open your mouth. Well—your tooth is loose, but you're not going to die about that. Mary, get me a silk thread, and a chunk of hot coal out of the kitchen."

Tom said, "Oh, please, auntie, don't pull it out. It don't hurt any more. I wish I may never stir if it does. Please, don't, auntie. *I* don't want to stay home from school."

"Oh, you don't, don't you? So all this was because you thought you'd get to stay home from school and go a-fishing? Tom, Tom, I love you so, and you seem to try every way you can to break my old heart." By this time the dental instruments were ready. The old lady tied one end of the silk thread to Tom's tooth with a loop and tied the other to the bedpost. Then she seized the chunk of coal and suddenly thrust it almost into the boy's face. The tooth hung dangling by the bedpost now.

But all suffering brings its rewards. As Tom went to school after breakfast, he was the envy of every boy he met because the gap in his upper row of teeth enabled him to spit in a new way. He gathered quite a following of lads interested in this show.

Shortly Tom came upon the young outcast of the

Shortly Tom came upon Huckleberry Finn.

village, Huckleberry Finn, son of the town drunkard.
Huckleberry was hated and dreaded by all the mothers of the town, because he was idle and lawless and

crude and bad—and because all their children admired him so, and delighted in his company, and wished they dared to be like him. Tom was like the rest of the respectable boys, in that he envied Huckleberry and was under strict orders not to play with him. So he played with him every time he got the chance. Huckleberry was always dressed in the cast-off clothes of full-grown men, and they were fluttering and ragged. His hat had a wide crescent torn out of its brim; his coat, when he wore one, hung nearly to his heels and had the rear buttons far down the back; only one suspender supported his pants; the seat of his pants bagged low and contained nothing; the fringed legs dragged in the dirt when not rolled up.

Huckleberry came and went, at his own free will. He slept on doorsteps in fine weather and in empty barrels in wet weather; he did not have to go to school or church, or call anybody master or obey anybody. He could go fishing or swimming when and where he chose, and stay as long as it suited him; nobody forbade him to fight; he could sit up as late as he pleased. He was always the first boy that went barefoot in the spring and the last to put on shoes in the fall. He never had to wash, nor put on clean clothes; he could swear wonderfully. In a word, everything that goes to make life good that boy had. So thought every respectable boy in St. Petersburg.

Tom called out, "Hello, Huckleberry!"

"Hello, yourself, and see how you like it."

"What's that you got?"

"Dead cat."

"Lemme see him, Huck. My, he's pretty stiff. Where'd you get him?"

"Bought him off a boy."

"Say—what is dead cats good for, Huck?"

"Good for? Cure warts with."

"But say—how do you cure 'em with dead cats?"

"Why, you take your cat and go and get in the graveyard 'long about midnight when somebody that was wicked has been buried; and when it's midnight a devil will come, or maybe two or three, but you can't see 'em, you can only hear something like the wind, or maybe hear 'em talk; and when they're taking that fellow away, you heave your cat after 'em and say, 'Devil follow corpse, cat follow devil, warts follow cat, *I*'m done with ye!' That'll fetch *any* wart."

"Sounds right. D'you ever try it, Huck?"

"No, but old Mother Hopkins told me."

"Well, I reckon it's so, then. Say, Hucky, when you going to try the cat?"

"Tonight. I reckon they'll come after old Hoss Williams tonight."

"But they buried him Saturday. Didn't they get him Saturday night?"

"Why, how you talk! How could their charms work till midnight?—and *then* it's Sunday. Devils don't slosh around much of a Sunday, I don't reckon."

"I never thought of that. That's so. Lemme go with you?"

"Of course—if you ain't afeared."

"Afeared! 'Tain't likely. Will you meow?"

"Yes—and you meow back, if you get a chance."

Tom sat down next to the new girl.

When Tom reached the little schoolhouse, he hurried in. He hung his hat on a peg and flung himself into his seat. The teacher, sitting in his armchair, was dozing, but the interruption woke him up. "Thomas Sawyer!"

Tom knew that when his name was pronounced in full, it meant trouble.

"Sir!"

"Come up here. Now, sir, why are you late again, as usual?"

Tom was about to lie, when he saw the girl with the

yellow hair that he had showed off for. And beside this girl was the only vacant space on the girls' side of the schoolhouse. He instantly said, "I STOPPED TO TALK WITH HUCKLEBERRY FINN."

The teacher said, "You—you did what?"

"Stopped to talk with Huckleberry Finn."

"Thomas Sawyer, this is the most astounding confession I have ever listened to. Go and sit with the *girls!* And let this be a warning to you."

He sat down upon the end of the pine bench next to the girl. Soon he began to make secret looks at her. She noticed, "made a mouth" at him and gave him the back of her head for the space of a minute.

When she turned, Tom whispered, "What's your name?"

"Becky Thatcher. What's yours? Oh, I know. It's Thomas Sawyer."

"That's the name they lick me by. I'm Tom when I'm good. You call me Tom, will you?"

When school broke up at noon, Tom whispered in Becky Thatcher's ear:

"Put on your bonnet and let on you're going home; and when you get to the corner give the rest of 'em the slip and turn down through the lane and come back. I'll go the other way and come back."

So the one went off with one group of students, and the other went with another. In a little while the two met at the bottom of the lane, and when they reached the school they had it all to themselves. Then they sat together and fell to talking. Tom was swimming with bliss. He said, "Do you love rats?"

"No! I hate them!"

"Well, I do, too—*live* ones. But I mean dead ones, to swing round your head with a string."

"No, I don't care for rats much, anyway. What *I* like is chewing gum."

"Oh, I should say so. I wish I had some now."

"Do you? I've got some. I'll let you chew it awhile, but you must give it back to me."

That was fine, so they chewed it turn about and dangled their legs against the bench.

3

Adventure in the Graveyard

AT HALF past nine, that night, Tom and Sid were sent to bed, as usual. They said their prayers, and Sid was soon asleep. Tom lay awake and waited. When it seemed to him that it must be nearly daylight, he heard the clock strike ten! So he lay still, and stared up into the dark. By and by, he began to doze, in spite of himself. The clock chimed eleven, but he did not hear it. And then there came, mingling with his dreams, a sad moaning. A minute later, Tom was dressed and out the window and creeping along the roof of the house on all fours. He meowed once or twice as he went, then jumped to the roof of the woodshed and then to the ground. Huckleberry Finn was there, with his dead cat. The boys moved off and disappeared in the gloom. At the end of half an hour they were wading through the tall grass of the graveyard.

It was a graveyard of the old-fashioned western kind. It was on a hill, about a mile and a half from the village. It had a crazy board fence around it, which leaned inward in places, and outward the rest of the time, but stood upright nowhere. Grass and weeds grew over the whole cemetery. All the old graves were

Tom crept along the roof to join Huck Finn.

sunken in, there was not a tombstone on the place; round-topped, worm-eaten boards staggered over the graves, leaning for support and finding none.

A faint wind moaned through the trees, and Tom feared it might be the spirits of the dead, complaining of being disturbed. The boys talked little. They found the new heap of earth they were seeking, and placed themselves within the protection of three great elms that grew in a bunch within a few feet of the grave.

Then they waited in silence for what seemed a long time. Tom said in a whisper, "Hucky, do you believe the dead people like it for us to be here?"

Huckleberry whispered, "I wisht I knowed. It's awful gloomy like, *ain't* it?"

Some figures approached the boys through the gloom.

"I bet it is." Suddenly Tom grabbed his friend's arm and said, "Sh!"

"What is it, Tom?"

"Sh! There 'tis again. Didn't you hear it?"

"Lord, Tom, they're coming! They're coming sure. What'll we do?"

"I don't know. Think they'll see us?"

"Oh, Tom, they can see in the dark, same as cats. I wisht I hadn't come."

A sound of voices floated up from the far end of the graveyard. Some figures approached through the gloom, swinging an old-fashioned tin lantern that freckled the ground with little spangles of light. Huckleberry whispered, "It's the devils, sure enough. Three of 'em! Lordy, Tom, we're goners!—Wait, they're humans! One of 'em's old Muff Potter's voice."

"Say, Huck, I know another o' them voices; it's Injun Joe."

"That's so—that murderin' half-breed! I'd druther they was devils. What kin they be up to?"

The whispering died out now, for the three men had reached the grave and stood within a few feet of the boys' hiding place.

"Here it is," said the third voice; and the owner of it held the lantern up and revealed young Dr. Robinson.

Potter and Injun Joe were carrying a handbarrow with a rope and couple of shovels on it. They cast down their load and began to open the grave. The doctor put the lantern at the head of the grave and came and sat down with his back against one of the elm trees. He was so close the boys could have touched him.

"Hurry, men!" he said. "The moon might come out at any moment."

They growled in response and went on digging.

Finally a spade struck upon the coffin, and within another minute or two the men had pulled it up and out on the ground. They pried off the lid with their shovels, got out the body and dumped it on the ground. The moon came out from behind the clouds and shone on this scene. The corpse was placed on the barrow and covered with a blanket.

"Now the cussed thing's out, Sawbones, and you'll just pay us out another five, or here it stays," said Potter.

"Look here, what does this mean?" said the doctor. "You asked for your pay in advance, and I've paid you."

"Yes, and you done more than that," said Injun Joe, approaching the doctor, who was now standing. "Five years ago, you drove me away from your father's kitchen one night, when I come to ask for something to eat, and you said I warn't there for any good; and when I swore I'd get even with you if it took a hundred years, your father had me jailed for a vagrant. Did you think I'd forget?" He was threatening the doctor, with his fist in his face, by this time. The doctor struck out suddenly and knocked the ruffian to the ground.

"Here, now, don't you hit my pard!" said Potter, dropping his knife. The next moment he had grabbed the doctor and they were struggling. Injun Joe sprang to his feet, his eyes flaming, snatched up Potter's knife, and went round and round the fighters, seeking a chance. All at once the doctor flung himself free, picked up the heavy headboard of Williams' grave

The doctor swung the headboard of the grave.

and knocked Potter down with it—and in the same instant the half-breed saw his chance and drove the knife to the hilt in the young man's breast. The doctor tumbled over and fell partly on Potter, dashing him with his blood. In the same moment the clouds blotted out the scene and the two frightened boys went speeding away in the dark.

Soon, when the moon came out again, Injun Joe was standing over the two men. He robbed the doctor's dead body. After which he put the fatal knife in Potter's open right hand, and sat down on the coffin. Five minutes passed and then Potter began to stir and moan. His hand closed upon the knife; he raised it and glanced at it, and let it fall. Then he sat up, pushing the body from him, and gazed at it, and then around him. His eyes met Joe's.

"Lord, how is this, Joe?" he said.

"It's a dirty business," said Joe. "What did you do it for?"

"I! I never done it!"

"Look here! That kind of talk won't wash."

Potter trembled and grew white. "I thought I'd got sober. I'd no business to drink tonight. But it's in my head yet. I'm all in a muddle; can't recollect anything of it, hardly. Tell me, Joe—*honest*, now, old feller—did I do it? Joe, I never meant to—'pon my soul and honor, I never meant to, Joe. Tell me how it was, Joe. Oh, it's awful—and him so young and promising."

"Why, you two was scuffling, and he fetched you one with the headboard and you fell flat; and then up you come, all reeling and staggering, like, and snatched the knife and jammed it into him, just as he fetched you another awful clip—and here you've laid, as dead as a wedge till now."

"Oh, I didn't know what I was a-doing. I wish I may die this minute if I did. It was all on account of the whisky; and the excitement, I reckon. I never used a weapon in my life before, Joe. Joe, don't tell! Say you won't tell, Joe—that's a good feller. I always liked you and stood up for you, too. Don't you remember? You *won't* tell, *will* you, Joe?" And the poor creature dropped on his knees before the murderer, and clasped his hands.

"No, you've always been fair and square with me, Muff Potter, and I won't go back on you. There, now, that's as fair as a man can say."

"Oh, Joe, you're an angel. I'll bless you for this the longest day I live." And Potter began to cry.

"Come now, that's enough of that. This ain't any time for blubbering. You be off yonder way and I'll go this."

The two boys, meanwhile, had flown on and on, toward the village.

They stopped in the old tannery, panting hard.

"Huckleberry," Tom whispered, "what do you reckon'll come of this?"

"If Dr. Robinson dies, I reckon hanging'll come of it."

"Who'll tell? We?"

"What are you talking about? S'pose something happened and Injun Joe didn't hang? Why he'd kill us some time or other, just as dead sure as we're a-laying here. Now, look-a-here, Tom, let's take and swear to one another—that's what we got to do—swear to keep mum. But there orter be writing 'bout a big thing like this. And blood."

Tom picked up a clean pine shingle that lay in the moonlight, took a fragment of chalk out of his pocket, got the moon on his work, and painfully scrawled these lines:

"Huck Finn and Tom Sawyer swears they will keep mum about this and they wish they may drop down dead in their tracks if they ever tell and rot."

Huckleberry was filled with admiration of Tom's writing, and the grandness of the language. Tom unwound the thread from one of his needles, and each boy pricked the ball of his thumb and squeezed out a drop of blood. In time, after many squeezes, Tom managed to sign his initials, using the ball of his finger for a pen. Then he showed Huckleberry how to make an H and an F, and the oath was complete. They buried the shingle close to the wall.

Then they separated. When Tom crept in at his bedroom window the night was almost gone. He undressed and fell asleep.

Close upon the hour of noon the whole village was suddenly electrified with the ghastly news. A gory knife had been found close to the murdered man, and it had been recognized by somebody as belonging to Muff Potter.

All the town was drifting toward the graveyard, even Huck and Tom. Poor Muff Potter was caught nearby, and his eyes showed the fear that was upon him. When the sheriff brought him to the site, Potter stood before the murdered man, put his face in his hands and burst into tears.

"I didn't do it, friends," he sobbed, " 'pon my word and honor I never done it." He saw Injun Joe there, and exclaimed, "Tell 'em, Joe, tell 'em!"

Then Huckleberry and Tom stood dumb and staring and heard the liar reel off his statement that Potter had killed the doctor. Potter was hauled off to jail.

Tom's fearful secret and conscience disturbed his

sleep for as much as a week after this. Every day or two, during this time of sorrow, Tom watched his opportunity and went to the little jail window and smuggled any small comforts through to Potter, the "murderer," as he could get hold of.

4

Life as a Pirate

ONE OF the reasons why Tom's mind finally drifted away from its secret troubles was that it had found a new matter to interest itself about. Becky Thatcher had stopped coming to school. She was ill. What if she should die? The charm of life was gone.

Finally, one morning at school, Becky passed in at the gate, and Tom's heart gave a great bound. The next instant he was "going on"; yelling, laughing, chasing boys, jumping over the fence at risk of life and limb, throwing handsprings, standing on his head—doing all the heroic things he could think of, and keeping an eye out all the while, to see if Becky was noticing. But she never looked. Could it be possible that she was not aware that he was there? He went closer; came war-whooping around, snatched a boy's cap, hurled it to the roof of the schoolhouse, broke through a group of boys, tumbling them in every direction, and fell sprawling, himself, under Becky's nose, almost upsetting her—and she turned, with her nose in the air, and he heard her say: "Mf! some people think they're smart—always showing off!"

Tom's mind was made up now. He was gloomy. He

Tom did handsprings, watching to see if Becky noticed.

was a forsaken, friendless boy, he said; nobody loved him; when they found out what they had driven him to, perhaps they would be sorry; he had tried to do right and get along, but they would not let him; since nothing would do them but to be rid of him, let it be so.

By this time he was far down Meadow Lane, away from school. Just at this point he met his soul's sworn comrade, Joe Harper. Tom, wiping his eyes with his sleeve, began to blubber out something about escaping from hard usage and lack of sympathy at home by roaming abroad into the great world never to return.

Jackson's Island.

It happened that Joe had come to Tom to declare such a thing himself. Joe's mother had whipped him for drinking some cream; it was plain that she was tired of him and wished him to go. If she felt that way, there was nothing for him to do but give in; he hoped she would be happy, and never regret having driven her poor boy out into the unfeeling world to suffer and die.

As the two boys walked along, they made a deal to stand by each other and be brothers and never separate till death. Then they began to lay their plans. Joe was for being a hermit, and living on crusts of bread in a remote cave; but after listening to Tom, he agreed that there were some advantages about a life of crime, and so he went along with becoming a pirate.

Three miles below St. Petersburg, at a point where the Mississippi River was a trifle over a mile wide, there was a long, narrow, wooded island. No one lived there; it lay far over toward the farther shore, near a dense forest. So Jackson's Island was chosen. Who were to be the subjects of their piracies was a matter that did not occur to them. Then they hunted Huckleberry Finn, and he joined them, for all careers were one to him. They separated to meet at a lonely spot two miles above the village at the favorite hour—which was midnight. There was a small log raft there which they meant to capture. Each would bring hooks and lines, and such food as he could steal.

About midnight Tom arrived with a boiled ham and stopped on a small bluff overlooking the meeting place. It was starlight and very still. The mighty river lay like an ocean at rest. Tom gave a low whistle. It was answered from under the bluff.

"Who goes there?"

"Tom Sawyer, the Black Avenger of the Spanish Main. Name your names."

"Huck Finn the Red-Handed, and Joe Harper the Terror of the Seas." Tom had given them these titles, from his favorite books.

Then Tom tumbled his ham over the bluff and let himself down after it.

The Terror of the Seas had brought a side of bacon. Finn the Red-Handed had stolen a skillet and a lot of tobacco, and had also brought a few corncobs to make pipes with. The Black Avenger of the Spanish Main said it would never do to start without some fire. Matches were hardly known there in that day. They saw a fire smoldering upon a great raft a hundred yards above, and they sneaked there and helped themselves to a chunk.

The raft drew beyond the middle of the river.

They shoved off, soon after, Tom in command, Huck at the after oar and Joe at the forward. The raft drew beyond the middle of the river; the boys pointed her head right and then lay on their oars. The river was not high, so there was not more than a two- or three-mile current. Hardly a word was said during the next three-quarters of an hour. Now the raft was passing before the distant town. Two or three glimmering lights showed where it lay.

About two o'clock in the morning the raft grounded on a sand bar two hundred yards above the head of Jackson's Island, and they waded back and forth until they had moved their cargo onto the island.

They built a fire against the side of a great log twenty or thirty steps within the dark depths of the forest, and then cooked up some bacon in the frying pan for supper, and used up half of the corn pone stock they had brought. It seemed glorious to be feasting on that uninhabited island, far from the haunts of men, and they said they would never return to civilization.

"Ain't it great?" said Joe.

"It's the best," said Tom. "What would the boys say if they could see us?"

"Say? Well, they'd just die to be here—hey, Hucky!"

"I reckon so," said Huckleberry. "Anyways, *I'm* suited. I don't want nothing better'n this."

"It's just the life for me," said Tom. "You don't have to get up, mornings, and you don't have to go to school, and wash, and all that blame foolishness. You see a pirate don't have to do *anything*, Joe, when he's ashore, but a hermit *he* has to be praying considerable, and then he don't have any fun, anyway, all by himself that way."

"Oh, yes, that's so," said Joe. "But I hadn't thought much about it, you know. I'd a good deal rather be a pirate, now that I've tried it."

Gradually their talk died out and sleepiness began to steal upon them. Huck fell asleep easily, but Joe and Tom began to feel a fear that they had been doing wrong to run away. And next they thought of the stolen meat. They decided that so long as they remained in the pirate business, their piracies should not again involve the crime of stealing. Now they fell peacefully to sleep.

When Tom awoke in the morning, he wondered

where he was. He sat up and rubbed his eyes and looked around. Then he remembered. It was the cool gray dawn, and there was a beautiful feeling of peace in the woods. Tom stirred up the other pirates, and in a minute or two they were stripped and chasing after and tumbling over each other in the shallow water of the white sand bar. They felt no longing for the little village sleeping in the distance beyond the river. A current or rise in the river had carried off their raft, but they were pleased, since its going was something like burning the bridge between them and civilization.

They came back to camp and soon had the camp-fire blazing up again. Huck found a spring of clear cold water close by, and the boys made cups of oak or hickory leaves and felt that water would be a good enough substitute for coffee. While Joe was slicing bacon for breakfast, Tom and Huck asked him to hold on a minute; they stepped to a promising nook in the riverbank and threw in their lines; almost immediately they had their reward. They came back with some handsome bass, a couple of sun perch, and a small catfish. They fried the fish with the bacon, and were astonished, for no fish had ever seemed so delicious before.

They lay around in the shade, after breakfast, while Huck had a smoke, and then went off through the woods on an exploring expedition. They found plenty of things to be delighted with. They discovered that the island was about three miles long and a quarter of a mile wide, and that the shore it lay closest to was only separated from it by a narrow channel hardly

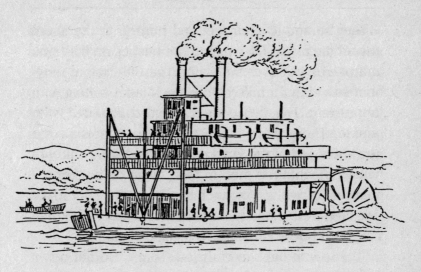

The boys could not figure out what the ferryboat was doing.

two hundred yards wide. They took a swim every hour, so it was close to the middle of the afternoon when they got back to camp. They were too hungry to stop to fish, but they ate well upon cold ham and then threw themselves down in the shade to talk. The stillness of the woods and the sense of loneliness began to affect the spirits of the boys. They fell to thinking. A longing crept upon them—it was budding homesickness. Even Finn the Red-Handed was dreaming of his doorsteps and empty barrels. But they were all ashamed to speak of their missing home.

The boys began to notice a strange sound in the distance. There was a long silence, then a deep boom came floating down out of the distance.

" 'Tain't thunder," said Huckleberry.

They sprang to their feet and hurried to the shore toward the town. They parted the bushes on the bank and peered out over the water. The little steam ferry-boat was about a mile below the village, drifting with the current. Her broad deck seemed crowded with people. There were a great many rowboats in the neighborhood of the ferryboat, but the boys could not figure out what the men in them were doing. Soon a great jet of white smoke burst from the ferryboat's side, and as it expanded and rose in a lazy cloud, that same dull boom came to the listeners again.

"I know now!" exclaimed Tom. "Somebody's drownded!"

"That's it!" said Huck. "They done that last summer, when Bill Turner got drownded; they shoot a cannon over the water, and that makes him come up to the top. Yes, and they take loaves of bread and put quicksilver in 'em and set 'em afloat, and wherever there's anybody that's drownded, they'll float right there and stop."

"By jings, I wish I was over there, now," said Joe.

"I do too," said Huck. "I'd give heaps to know who it is."

"Boys," said Tom, "I know who's drownded—it's us!"

They felt like heroes in an instant. Here was a great triumph; they were missed; they were mourned; hearts were breaking; and best of all, the dead boys were the talk of the whole town, and the envy of all the boys. This was fine. It was worth while to be a pirate.

As twilight drew on, the ferryboat went back and

the rowboats disappeared. The pirates returned to their camp. They were jubilant with their new fame and the great trouble they were making. They caught fish, cooked supper and ate, and then fell to guessing at what the village was thinking and saying about them. But when the shadows of night closed them in, they gradually stopped talking, and sat gazing into the fire. The excitement was gone now, and Tom and Joe could not keep back thoughts of certain persons at home who were not enjoying this fine frolic as much as they were. They grew troubled and unhappy; a sigh or two escaped.

As the night deepened, Huck began to nod, and soon to snore. Joe followed next. Tom lay upon his elbow for some time, watching the two. At last he got up. Then he tiptoed his way among the trees till he felt that he was out of hearing, and broke into a keen run in the direction of the sand bar.

A few minutes later Tom was wading toward the shore. Before the depth reached his middle he was halfway over; the current would permit no more wading, now, so he swam the remaining hundred yards. He went through the woods, following the shore. Shortly before ten o'clock he came out into an open place near the village. He flew along alleys, and shortly found himself at his aunt's back fence. He climbed over and looked in at the sitting-room window, for a light was burning there. There sat Aunt Polly, Sid, Mary, and Joe Harper's mother, grouped together, talking. They were by the bed, and the bed was between them and the door. Tom went to the

Tom looked in at the sitting-room window.

door and began to softly lift the latch; then he pressed gently, and the door yielded a crack; he continued pushing, and quaking every time it creaked, till he judged he might squeeze through on his knees.

"What makes the candle blow so?" said Aunt Polly. "Why, that door's open, I believe. Go 'long and shut it, Sid."

Tom disappeared under the bed just in time. He then crept to where he could almost touch his aunt's foot.

"But as I was saying," said Aunt Polly, "he warn't *bad*, so to say—only misch*ee*vous. Only just giddy, and harum-scarum, you know. He warn't any more responsible than a colt. *He* never meant any harm, and he was the best-hearted boy that ever was"—and she began to cry.

"It was just so with my Joe—always full of his devilment and up to every kind of mischief, but he was just as unselfish and kind as he could be—and laws bless me, to think I went and whipped him for taking that cream, never once recollecting that I throwed it out myself because it was sour, and I never to see him again in this world!" And Mrs. Harper sobbed as if her heart would break.

"Oh, Mrs. Harper," said Aunt Polly, "I don't know how to give him up! I don't know how to give him up! He was such a comfort to me, although he tormented my old heart out of me, 'most. But he's out of all his troubles now—"

This was too much for the old lady, and she broke entirely down. Tom was snuffling, now, himself—and more in pity of himself than anybody else. He went on listening, and gathered by odds and ends that it was thought the boys had been drowned mid-channel, since the boys, being good swimmers, would otherwise have escaped to shore. This was Wednesday night. If the bodies continued missing until Sunday, all hope would be given over and the funerals would be preached on that morning.

Mrs. Harper gave a sobbing goodnight and turned to go. Then the two bereaved women flung themselves into each other's arms and had a good cry, and then parted.

Aunt Polly knelt down and prayed for Tom so touchingly, so appealingly, and with such measureless love in her words and her old trembling voice, that he was in tears long before she was through.

He had to keep still long after she went to bed, for she kept making brokenhearted sighs from time to time. But at last she was still, only moaning a little in her sleep. Now the boy stole out, rose gradually by her bedside, and stood regarding her. His heart was full of pity for her. He bent over and kissed her lips, and right away made his exit, latching the door behind him.

He threaded his way back to the shore opposite the island and swam across and returned to the pirate camp.

For the next couple of days they hunted and played and swam and ran a circus starring three clowns. But by Friday, they were all so homesick they could hardly endure the misery of it.

Joe said, "Oh, boys, let's give it up. I want to go home. It's so lonesome."

"Oh, no, Joe, you'll feel better by and by," said Tom. "Just think of the fishing that's here."

"I don't care for fishing, I want to go home."

"But, Joe, there ain't such another swimming place anywhere."

"Swimming's no good. I don't seem to care for it, somehow, when there ain't anybody to say I shan't go in. I mean to go home."

"Oh, shucks! Baby! You want to see your mother, I reckon."

"Yes, I do want to see my mother—and you would, too, if you had one. I ain't any more baby than you are." And Joe snuffled a little.

"Well, we'll let the crybaby go home to his mother, *won't* we, Huck? *You* like it here, don't you, Huck? We'll stay, won't we?"

Huck said "Y-e-s"—but without any heart in it.

"Go 'long home, Joe," said Tom, "and get laughed at. Oh, you're a nice pirate. Huck and me ain't no crybabies. We'll stay, won't we, Huck?"

Huck now said, "I want to go, too, Tom. It was getting so lonesome anyway, and now it'll be worse. Let's us go, too, Tom."

"I won't! You can all go, if you want to. I mean to stay."

"Tom, I wisht you'd come too. Now you think it over. We'll wait for you when we get to shore."

"Well, you'll wait a blame long time, that's all."

Huck started away, and Tom stood looking after him. He hoped the boys would stop, but they still waded slowly on.

He darted after his comrades, yelling, "Wait! Wait! I want to tell you something!"

They stopped and turned around. When he got to

where they were, he began unfolding his secret, and
they listened till at last they saw the point he was
driving at, and then they set up a war whoop of
applause and said it was "splendid!" and said if he
had told them at first they wouldn't have started away.

The lads came merrily back and went at their
sports again with a will, chattering all the time about
Tom's stupendous plan and admiring the genius of it.
The next day, Saturday, the boys played Indians all
afternoon.

When the Sunday-school hour was finished, the
next morning, the bell began to toll, instead of ringing
in the usual way. It was a very quiet Sunday. The
villagers began to gather, pausing a moment outside
the church to whisper about the sad event. But there
was no whispering in the church. None could remember when the little church had been so full before.
When Aunt Polly entered, followed by Sid and Mary,
and the Harper family, all in deep black, the congregation rose and stood until the mourners were seated in
the front pew.

Then the minister prayed. A moving hymn was
sung, and then the sermon followed.

As the service proceeded, the clergyman drew such
pictures of the qualities, the winning ways, and the
great promise of the lost lads that every soul there,
thinking he recognized those pictures, felt a pang in
remembering that he had seen only faults and flaws
in the poor boys. The minister related many a touching event in the lives of the departed, too, which

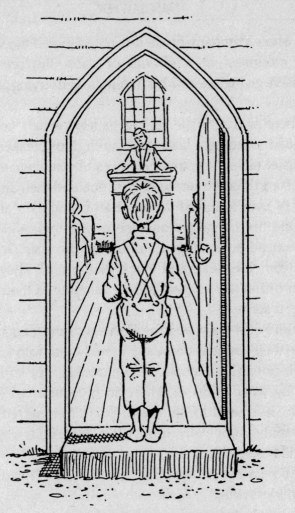

Tom led the march up the aisle.

illustrated their sweet, generous natures, and the people could easily see, now, how noble and beautiful those times were. The congregation became more and more moved, as the sad tale went on, till at last

the whole company broke down and joined the weeping mourners in a chorus of sobs, the preacher
himself giving way to his feelings and crying in the
pulpit.

There was a rustle in the gallery, which nobody
noticed; a moment later the church door creaked; the
minister raised his streaming eyes above his handker-
chief, and stood transfixed! First one and then another
pair of eyes followed the minister's, and then almost
as one the congregation rose and stared while the
three dead boys came marching up the aisle, Tom in
the lead, Joe next, and Huck in the rear! They had
been hid in the unused gallery listening to their own
funeral sermon!

Aunt Polly, Mary, and the Harpers threw themselves
upon their restored ones, smothered them with kisses,
while poor Huck stood uncomfortable, not knowing
exactly what to do or where to hide from so many
eyes. He started to slink away, but Tom seized him
and said: "Aunt Polly, it ain't fair. Somebody's got to
be glad to see Huck."

"And so they shall. I'm glad to see him, poor
motherless thing!"

Suddenly the minister shouted at the top of his
voice: "Praise God for whom all blessings flow—
SING!—and put your hearts in it!"

And they did. While the hymn shook the rafters,
Tom Sawyer the Pirate looked around him and confessed in his heart that this was the proudest moment
of his life.

Tom got more knocks and kisses that day—according to Aunt Polly's moods—than he had earned before in a year.

What a hero about the village Tom was become, now! He did not go skipping and prancing, but moved with the swagger of a pirate. Smaller boys than himself flocked at his heels, as proud to be seen with him as if he had been the drummer at the head of a parade. Boys of his own size pretended not to know he had been away at all; but they were envious. They would have given anything to have Tom's fame. At school the children made so much of him and of Joe that the two heroes were not long in becoming stuck up.

5
Muff Potter's Trial

VACATION CAME. Becky Thatcher, who had been overjoyed to see Tom again after his "drowning," was gone to her home to stay with her parents during vacation—so there was no bright side to life anywhere for Tom.

The dreadful secret of the murder was a terrible misery. The murder trial came on in the court. It became the talk of the village immediately and Tom could not get away from it. Every reference to the murder sent a shudder to his heart. This gossip kept him in a cold shiver all the time, and so he took Huck to a lonely place to have a talk with him. It would be some relief to unseal his tongue for a little while.

"Huck, have you told anybody about—that?"

"'Bout what?"

"You know what."

"Oh—course I haven't."

"Never a word?"

"Never a solitary word, so help me. We wouldn't be alive two days if that got found out. *You* know that."

"Huck, they couldn't anybody get you to tell, could they?"

"Get me to tell? Why, if I wanted that half-breed

devil to drownd me they could get me to tell. They ain't no different way."

"Well, that's all right, then," said Tom. "I reckon we're safe as long as we keep mum."

"But the talk's just Muff Potter, Muff Potter, Muff Potter all the time. It keeps me in a sweat."

"That's just the same way they go round me. I reckon he's a goner. Don't you feel sorry for him, sometimes?"

"Most always—most always," said Huck. "He hain't ever done anything to hurt anybody. Just fishes a little, to get money to get drunk on—and loafs around considerable; but, Lord, we all do that—leastways most of us. But he's kind of good—he gave me half a fish, once, when there wasn't enough for two; and lots of times he's kind of stood by me when I was out of luck."

"Well, he's mended kites for me, Huck, and knitted hooks onto my line. I wish we could get him out of there."

"My! we couldn't get him out, Tom. And besides, 'twouldn't do any good; they'd ketch him again."

The boys had a long talk, but it brought them little comfort. They did as they had often done before—went to the cell grating and gave Potter some tobacco and matches. He was on the ground floor and there were no guards.

His gratitude for their gifts had always made them feel guilty—it cut deeper than ever this time, when Potter said: "You've been mighty good to me, boys—better'n anybody else in this town. And I don't forget

Huck and Tom often went to the cell to visit Potter.

it, I don't. Well, boys, I done an awful thing—drunk and crazy at the time—that's the only way I account for it—and now I got to swing for it, and it's right. Right, and best, too, I reckon—hope so, anyway. Well, we won't talk about that. I don't want to make *you* feel bad."

Tom went home miserable, and his dream that night was full of horrors. The next day and the day after, he hung about the courtroom, drawn to go in, but forcing himself to stay out. Huck was having the same experience. At the end of the second day the village talk was to the effect that Injun Joe's evidence stood firm and unshaken, and that there was not the slightest question as to what the jury's verdict would be.

Tom was out late that night, doing something, and came to bed through the window. He was in a tremendous state of excitement. It was hours before he got to sleep. All the village flocked to the court-house the next morning, for this was to be the great day. After a long wait the jury filed in and took their places; shortly afterward, Potter, pale and haggard, timid and hopeless, was brought in, with chains upon him, and seated where all the curious eyes could stare at him; no less conspicuous was Injun Joe, quiet as ever. There was another pause, and then the judge arrived and the sheriff proclaimed the opening of the court.

Now a witness was called who testified that he found Muff Potter washing in the brook, at an early hour of the morning that the murder was discovered, and that he immediately sneaked away. After some further questioning, counsel for the prosecution said:

"Take the witness."

The prisoner raised his eyes for a moment, but dropped them again when his own counsel said, "I have no questions to ask him."

The next witness proved the finding of the knife near the corpse. Counsel for the prosecution said, "Take the witness."

"I have no questions to ask him," Potter's lawyer replied.

A third witness swore he had often seen the knife in Potter's possession.

"Take the witness."

Counsel for Potter declined to question him. The faces of the audience began to show annoyance. Did this attorney mean to throw away his client's life without an effort?

Several witnesses talked about Potter's guilty behavior when brought to the scene of the murder. They were allowed to leave the stand without being cross-examined.

Every detail of what occurred in the graveyard upon that morning was brought out by believable witnesses, but none of them were cross-examined by Potter's lawyer.

The prosecution now said, "By the oaths of citizens whose simple word is above suspicion, we have fastened this awful crime, beyond all possibility of question, upon the unhappy prisoner. We rest our case."

A groan escaped from poor Potter, and he put his face in his hands and rocked his body softly to and fro, while a painful silence came over the courtroom. Many men were moved, and many women cried. Counsel for the defense rose and said, "Your honor, in our remarks at the opening of this trial, we gave

Tom took his place upon the witness stand.

our purpose as proving that our client did this fearful deed while under the influence of too much alcohol. We have changed our mind. We shall not offer that plea." He turned to the clerk and said, "Call Thomas Sawyer!"

A puzzled amazement awoke in every face in the house, not even excepting Potter's. The boy was very scared as he rose and took his place upon the stand.

"Thomas Sawyer, where were you on the seventeenth of June, about the hour of midnight?"

Tom glanced at Injun Joe's iron face and his tongue stopped. The audience listened breathless, but the

words refused to come. After a few moments, however, the boy got a little of his strength back, and said:
"In the graveyard!"

"A little louder, please. Don't be afraid. You were—"

"In the graveyard."

A savage smile went across Injun Joe's face.

"Were you anywhere near Horse Williams's grave?"

"Yes, sir."

"Speak up—just a trifle louder. How near were you?"

"Near as I am to you."

"Were you hidden, or not?"

"I was hid."

"Where?"

"Behind the elms that's on the edge of the grave."

Injun Joe gave a start.

"Anyone with you?"

"Yes, sir, I went there with—"

"Wait—wait a moment. Never mind mentioning
your companion's name. We will bring him up to the
stand at the proper time. Did you carry anything there
with you?"

Tom hesitated and looked confused.

"Speak out, my boy—don't be shy. The truth is
always respectable. What did you take there?"

"Only a—a—dead cat."

There was laughter, which the court officers
stopped.

"We will produce the skeleton of that cat. Now, my
boy, tell us everything that occurred—tell it in your
own way—don't skip anything, and don't be afraid."

Tom began—hesitatingly at first, but as he warmed

Injun Joe tore through the crowd and was gone.

to his subject his words flowed more and more easily; in a little while every sound stopped but his own voice; every eye fixed itself upon him; with parted lips and held breath the audience hung upon his words, taking no note of time, fascinated by the tale. The climax came when the boy said, "—and the doctor fetched the board around and Muff Potter fell, Injun Joe jumped with the knife and—"

Crash! Quick as lightning the half-breed sprang for a window, tore his way through all opposers, and was gone!

Tom was a glittering hero once more—the pet of the old, the envy of the young. His name even went into print, for the village paper wrote about him. The village took Muff Potter to its bosom now.

6
Hunting for Treasure

TOM'S DAYS were days of splendor, but his nights were seasons of horror. Injun Joe was in all his dreams, and always with doom in his eye. Poor Huck was in the same state of terror, for Tom had told the whole story to the lawyer the night before the great day of the trial, and Huck was sore afraid that his share in the business might come out too.

Every day Muff Potter's gratitude made Tom glad he had spoken; but nightly he wished he had sealed up his tongue. Half the time Tom was afraid Injun Joe would never be captured; the other half he was afraid he would be. He felt sure he never could draw a safe breath again until that man was dead and he had seen the corpse.

Rewards had been offered, the country had been looked over, but no Injun Joe was found.

The slow days of summer drifted on, and each left behind a slightly lightened weight of fear on Tom.

There comes a time in every boy's life when he has a raging desire to go somewhere and dig for hidden treasure. This desire came upon Tom one day. He stumbled upon Huck, and told Huck about it, and Huck was willing.

"Where'll we dig?" he asked.

"Oh," said Tom, "most anywhere."

"Why, is it hid all around?"

"No, indeed it ain't. It's hid in mighty particular places, Huck—sometimes on islands, sometimes in rotten chests under the end of a limb of an old dead tree, just where the shadow falls at midnight; but mostly under the floor in haunted houses."

"Who hides it?"

"Why, robbers, of course—who'd you reckon?"

"I don't know. If 'twas mine I wouldn't hide it; I'd spend it and have a good time."

"So would I. But robbers don't do that way. They always hide it and leave it there."

"Don't they come after it any more?"

"No, they think they will, but they generally forget the marks, or else they die. Anyway, it lays there a long time and gets rusty. There's the old haunted house up the Still-House branch, and there's lots of dead-limb trees."

"Is it under all of them?"

"How you talk! No!"

"Then how you going to know which one to go for?"

"Go for all of 'em!"

"Why, Tom, that'll take all summer."

"Well, what of that? S'pose we tackle that old dead-limb tree on the hill t'other side of Still-House branch?"

"I'm agreed."

So they got a pick and a shovel, and set out on their three-mile tramp.

"Say, Huck, if we find a treasure here, what you going to do with your share?"

"Well, I'll have pie and a glass of soda every day, and I'll go to every circus that comes along. What you going to do with yourn, Tom?"

"I'm going to buy a new drum, and a sword, and a red necktie and a bull pup, and get married."

"Married!"

"That's it."

"Tom, you—why, you ain't in your right mind."

"Anyway, let's go to digging."

They worked and sweated for half an hour. No result. They toiled another half hour without result. Huck said, "Do they always bury it as deep as this?"

"Sometimes—not always. Not generally. I reckon we haven't got the right place."

So they chose a new spot and began again. By and by Huck said, "Blame it, we must be in the wrong place again."

"It is mighty curious, Huck. I don't understand it.— Oh, I know what the matter is! What a blamed lot of fools we are! You got to find out where the shadow of the limb falls at midnight, and that's where you dig!"

"Then consound it, we've fooled away all this work for nothing. Well, I'll come around and meow tonight."

"All right."

The boys were there that night, about the appointed time. They marked where the shadow fell, and began to dig. The hole deepened and still deepened. At last Tom said, "It ain't any use, Huck, we're wrong again."

Huck dropped his shovel. "That's it," said he. "We

got to give this one up. Besides this kind of thing's too awful, here this time of night with witches and ghosts a-fluttering around so. I feel as if something's behind me all the time; and I'm afeared to turn around, becuz maybe there's others in front a-waiting for a chance. I been creeping all over, ever since I got here."

"Well, I've been pretty much so, too, Huck."

"Say, Tom, let's give this place up, and try somewheres else."

"All right, I reckon we better. The haunted house. That's it!"

"Blame it, I don't like haunted houses, Tom. And you know mighty well people don't go about that haunted house in the day nor the night."

"But ghosts don't come around in the daytime, so what's the use of our being afeared?"

"Well, all right. We'll tackle the haunted house if you say so—but I reckon it's taking chances."

They had started down the hill by this time and took their way homeward through the woods.

About noon the next day the boys arrived at the dead tree; they had come for their tools. When they reached the haunted house there was something so weird about the dead silence, that they were afraid, for a moment, to venture in. Then they crept to the door and took a peep. They saw a weed-grown, floorless room, an ancient fireplace, empty windows, a ruinous staircase; and here, there, and everywhere hung cobwebs. They entered, talking in whispers. They wanted to look upstairs. They threw their tools

For a moment they were afraid to venture in.

into a corner and made the climb. Up there were the same signs of decay. They were about to go down and begin work when—

"Sh!" said Tom.

"What is it?" whispered Huck.

"They're coming right toward the door."

The boys stretched themselves upon the floor with their eyes to knotholes in the planking.

Two men entered the house. Each boy said to himself, "There's the old deaf-and-dumb Spaniard that's been about town lately—never saw t'other man before."

"T'other" man was a ragged creature, with nothing very pleasant in his face. The Spaniard was wrapped in a serape; he had bushy white whiskers; long white hair flowed from under his sombrero. When they came in, "t'other" was talking in a low voice. "No," said he, "it's dangerous."

"Dangerous!" grunted the "deaf-and-dumb" Spaniard—to the vast surprise of the boys. "Coward!"

The voice made the boys gasp and quake. It was Injun Joe's!

The two men got out some food and made a lunch. Injun Joe said, "Look here, lad—you go back up the river where you belong. I'll take the chances on dropping into this town just once more. We'll do that 'dangerous' job after I've spied around a little. Then for Texas! We'll leg it together!"

"All right." Both men fell to yawning, and Injun Joe said, "I'm dead for sleep! It's your turn to watch."

Soon enough, however, both men began to snore.

The boys drew a long, grateful breath. Tom whispered: "Now's our chance—come!"

Huck said, "I can't—I'd die if they was to wake."

Tom urged—Huck held back. At last Tom rose slowly and softly, and started alone. But the first step he made wrung such a hideous creak from the crazy floor that he sank down almost dead with fright.

Now one snore ceased. Injun Joe sat up, stared around—smiled grimly upon his comrade, whose head was drooping upon his knees—stirred him up with his foot and said, "You're a watchman, ain't you! All right, though—nothing's happened."

"My! have I been asleep?"

"Oh, partly. It's sunset, nearly time for us to be moving, pard. What'll we do with what little dough we've got left?"

The coins were gold!

"I don't know—leave it here as we've always done, I reckon. No use to take it away till we start south. Six hundred in silver's something to carry."

"Well—all right—it won't matter to come here once more. We'll just bury it."

"Good idea."

The boys forgot all their fears, all their miseries in an instant. With gloating eyes they watched every movement. Luck! Six hundred dollars was money enough to make half a dozen boys rich! Here was the best sort of treasure hunting—they would not be wondering where to dig!

As Joe dug with his knife, it struck upon something.

"Hello!" said he.

"What is it?" said his comrade.

"It's a box, I believe." He reached his hand in through a hole in the wooden plank and drew it out—"Man, it's money!"

The two men examined the handful of coins. They were gold!

Joe's comrade said, "We'll make quick work of getting the rest of the box out. There's an old rusty pick over in the corner." He ran and brought the boys' pick and shovel. Injun Joe took the pick and unearthed the box.

"Pard," said Injun Joe, "there's thousands of dollars here."

"What'll we do with this—bury it again?"

"Yes."

At this answer Tom and Huck were delighted.

Then Injun Joe declared, "No! by the great sachem, no! I'd nearly forgot. That pick had fresh earth on it. What business has a pick and shovel here? Who brought them here—and where are they gone? What! bury it again and leave them to come and see the ground disturbed? Not exactly. We'll take it to my den."

"Why, of course! You mean Number One?"

"No—Number Two—under the cross. The other place is bad—too common."

"All right. It's nearly dark enough to start."

Injun Joe got up and went about from window to window peeping out. Then he said, "Who could have brought those tools here? Do you reckon they can be upstairs?"

The boys' breath left them. Injun Joe put his hand

Injun Joe turned toward the stairway.

on his knife and then turned toward the stairway. The steps came creaking up the stairs—when there was a crash of rotten timbers and Injun Joe landed on the ground amid the debris of the ruined stairway.

"Now what's the use of that?" said his comrade. "If it's anybody, and they're up there, let them *stay* there—who cares? If they want to jump down now, who objects? It will be dark in fifteen minutes—and then let them follow us if they want to. In my opinion, whoever left those tools in here caught a sight of us and took us for ghosts or devils or something. I'll bet they're running yet."

Joe grumbled awhile; then he agreed with his friend that they ought to get ready to leave. Shortly afterward they slipped out of the house and moved toward the river with their precious box.

Tom and Huck rose up, weak, and stared after them through the chinks between the logs of the house. Follow? Not they. They were content to reach ground again without broken necks, and take the townward track over the hill.

7
The Cave

THE NEXT week Tom heard that Judge Thatcher's family had come back to town. Both Injun Joe and the treasure sank into secondary importance for a moment, and Becky took the chief place in the boy's interest. He saw her, and they had an exhausting good time playing with a crowd of their schoolmates. The day was crowned in a fine way: Becky managed to get her mother to name the next day, a Saturday, as a picnic for all her friends.

By eleven o'clock the next morning a giddy company were gathered at Judge Thatcher's, and everything was ready for a start. The children were escorted by young ladies of eighteen and a few young gentlemen. The old steam ferryboat was chartered for the occasion. Sid was sick and had to miss the fun; Mary remained at home to entertain him.

Three miles below town the ferryboat stopped at the mouth of a woody hollow and tied up. The crowd swarmed ashore and soon there were shouts and laughter. After the feast there was a time of resting and chatting in the shade of the spreading oaks. By and by somebody shouted: "Who's ready for the cave?"

Everybody was. Bundles of candles were passed around, and right away there was a general scamper up the hill. The mouth of the cave was up the hillside—an opening shaped like the letter A. Its massive oaken door stood unbarred. Within was a small chamber, chilly as an icehouse, and walled by nature with solid limestone that was dewy with a cold sweat.

It was romantic and mysterious to stand here in the deep gloom and look out upon the green valley shining in the sun. But then the romping began again. The procession of children and young men and women went filing down the steep descent of the main path, the flickering candle lights dimly revealing the lofty walls of rock. McDougal's Cave was a vast labyrinth, a maze of crooked aisles that ran into each other and out again and led nowhere. It was said one might wander days and nights through its tangle of pathways and never find the end of the cave; and that one might go down and down, and still down, into the earth, and it was just the same—maze underneath maze.

The parade moved along the main path some three-quarters of a mile, and then groups and couples began to slip aside into branch avenues. By and by one group after another came straggling back to the mouth of the cave, panting, entirely delighted with the success of the day. They were astonished to find that they had been taking no note of time and that night was about at hand. The ferryboat with her wild passengers pushed into the stream and headed for home.

Becky and Tom wandered into the depths of the cave.

Meanwhile, Tom and Becky had been left behind.
They had visited the familiar wonders of the cave
with the rest of the company. Then the hide-and-seek
had begun, and Tom and Becky had played along
until they got tired of it and wandered down a curving
path. They held their candles up and read the web-

The bats chased the children a good distance.

work of names, dates, and mottoes with which the rock walls had been stained with candle smoke. Still drifting along and talking, they scarcely noticed that they were now in a part of the cave whose walls were not decorated with personal marks. They smoked their own names under an overhanging shelf and moved on. Soon they came to a place where a little stream of water trickled over a ledge. They found a steep natural stairway behind it. They made a smoke mark for their future guidance, and started upon their quest to explore further into the cave. They wound this way and that, far down into the secret depths of the cave, made another mark, and branched off in search of novelties to tell the others about.

They came to a spring in the midst of a cavern, whose walls were supported by many fantastic pillars which had been formed by the joining of great stalactites and stalagmites, the result of the ceaseless water-drip of centuries. Under the roof vast knots of bats had packed themselves together, thousands in a bunch; the lights disturbed the creatures, and they came flocking down by hundreds, squeaking and darting at the candles. Tom seized Becky's hand and hurried her into the first corridor they found; and none too soon, for a bat struck Becky's light out with its wing while she was passing out of the cavern. The bats chased the children a good distance; but Tom and Becky plunged into every new passage they found and at last got rid of the perilous things. Tom found an underground lake, shortly, and they sat down by it and rested awhile.

Becky said, "It seems ever so long since I heard any of the others."

"Come to think, Becky, we are away down below them—and I don't know how far away north, or south, or east, or whichever way it is. We couldn't hear them here."

"I wonder how long we've been down here, Tom. We better start back."

"Yes, I reckon we better. But if the bats put both our candles out it will be an awful fix. Let's try some other way, so as not to go through there."

"Well, I hope we won't get lost."

But indeed they did get hopelessly lost.

They were finally so weary with hiking through the tunnels and along the underground paths that they lay down and slept. When they woke they walked further and drank some spring water. They were down to their last candle.

Becky said, "They'll miss us and hunt for us!"

"Yes, they will! Certainly they will!"

The children fastened their eyes upon their bit of candle and watched it melt slowly away, and then— the horror of utter darkness!

Both held their breath and listened. There was a sound like the faintest, far-off shout. Instantly Tom answered it, and, leading Becky by the hand, started groping down the corridor in its direction. Soon he listened again; again the sound was heard a little nearer.

"It's them!" said Tom. "They're coming! Becky, we're all right now!"

Their joy was almost overwhelming. They had to move slowly, however, because pitfalls were common, and had to be watched for. They soon came to one and had to stop. It might be three feet deep, it might be a hundred—there was no passing it. The children groped their way back to the spring. The weary time

The hand was followed by the body it belonged to—Injun Joe's!

dragged on; they slept again and awoke famished. Tom believed it must be Tuesday by this time.

Now an idea struck him. There were some side passages near at hand. It would be better to explore some of these than bear the weight of the heavy time in idleness. He took a kite string from his pocket, tied it to a rock, and he and Becky started, Tom in the lead, unwinding the line as he groped along. At the end of twenty steps the corridor ended in a "jumping-off place." Tom got down on his knees and felt below, and then as far around the corner as he could reach with his hands. He made an effort to stretch yet a little farther to the right, and at that moment, not twenty yards away, a human hand, holding up a candle, appeared from behind a rock! Tom lifted up a glorious shout, and instantly that hand was followed by the body it belonged to—Injun Joe's. Tom could not move. He was happy the next moment to see Joe take to his heels and get himself out of sight. Tom wondered that Joe had not recognized his voice and come over and killed him for testifying against him in court. But the echoes must have disguised the voice. He was careful to keep from Becky what he had seen. He told her he had only shouted "for luck."

They waited and waited by the spring and had another long sleep. The children awoke tortured with a raging hunger. Tom believed that it must be Wednesday of Thursday or even Friday or Saturday now, and that the search had been given up. He proposed to explore another passage. He felt willing to risk Injun Joe and all other terrors. But Becky was very weak. She said she would wait now, where she was, and die—it would not be long. She told Tom to go with the kite line and explore if he chose.

8

Finding Treasure

TUESDAY AFTERNOON came and went. The village of St. Petersburg mourned for the lost children. Still no good news came from the cave. The majority of the searchers had given up the quest and gone back to their daily lives, saying it was plain the children could never be found. Mrs. Thatcher was very ill. Aunt Polly had drooped into a settled sadness, and her gray hair had turned almost white.

Away in the middle of the night a wild peal burst from the village bells, and in a moment the streets were swarming with half-dressed people who shouted, "They're found! They're found!" Tin pans and horns were added to the din, and the population moved toward the river and met the children coming in an open carriage drawn by shouting citizens. The village was lit up; nobody went back to bed; it was the greatest night the little town had ever seen.

Aunt Polly's happiness was complete, and Mrs. Thatcher's nearly so. It would be complete, however, as soon as the messenger to the cave should get the word to her husband. Tom lay upon a sofa and told the history of the wonderful adventure and closed with a description of how he left Becky and went on an exploring expedition; how he followed two paths

Aunt Polly drooped into a settled sadness.

as far as his kite string would reach; how he followed a third to the fullest stretch of the string, and was about to turn back when he glimpsed a far-off speck that looked like daylight; dropped the line and groped toward it, pushed his head and shoulders through a small hole and saw the broad Mississippi rolling by! And if it had only happened to be night he would not have seen that speck of daylight and would not have explored that passage any more! He told how he went back for Becky and broke the good news and how she almost died with joy when she had groped to where she actually saw the blue speck of daylight; how he pushed his way out at the hole and then helped her out; how they sat there and cried for gladness; how some men came along in a rowboat and Tom hailed them and told them their troubles; how the men didn't believe the wild tale at first,

"Because," they said, "you are five miles down the river below the valley the cave is in"—then took them aboard, rowed to a house, gave them supper, made them rest till two or three hours after dark, and then brought them home.

Before dawn, Judge Thatcher and the handful of searchers with him were tracked out, in the cave, and informed of the news.

About two weeks after Tom's rescue from the cave, he stopped to see Becky. The judge and some friends set Tom to talking, and someone asked him, as a joke, if he wouldn't like to go to the cave again. Tom said he thought he wouldn't mind it.

The judge said, "Well, there are others just like you, Tom. But we have taken care of that. Nobody will get lost in that cave any more."

"Why?"

"Because I had its big door covered with iron two weeks ago, and triple locked—and I've got the keys."

"Oh, judge, Injun Joe's in the cave!"

Within a few minutes the news had spread, and a dozen rowboats of men were on their way to Mc-Dougal's Cave, and the ferryboat, well filled with passengers, soon followed. Tom Sawyer was in the rowboat that brought Judge Thatcher.

When the cave door was unlocked, a sorrowful sight presented itself in the dim twilight of the place. Injun Joe lay stretched upon the ground, dead, with his face close to the crack of the door. Tom was touched, for he knew by his own experience how this wretch had suffered. His pity was moved, but never-

Injun Joe was buried near the mouth of the cave.

theless he felt a sense of relief and security, now, which showed him how huge a weight of dread had been lying upon him since the day he testified against this bloody-minded outcast.

Injun Joe was buried near the mouth of the cave; and people flocked there in boats and wagons from the towns and from all the farms and hamlets for seven miles around.

The morning after the funeral Tom took Huck to a private place to have an important talk.

"Huck, that treasure's in the cave!"

"Say it again, Tom."

"The money's in the cave!"

"Tom—honest, now—is it fun or true?"

"True, Huck—just as true as ever I was in my life. Will you go in there with me and help get it out?"

"I bet I will! I will if it's where we can blaze our way to it and not get lost."

"Huck, we can do that without the least bit of trouble in the world. There's a mighty short cut that they don't anybody but me know about. I'll take you right to it in a rowboat."

"Let's start right off, Tom."

"All right. We want some bread and meat, and our pipes, and a little bag or two, and two or three kite strings, and some of these newfangled things they call matches. I tell you, many's the time I wished I had some when I was in there before."

They borrowed a rowboat and got under way at once. When they were several miles down the river, Tom said, "Now you see this bluff here looks all alike all the way down from the cave—no houses, no woodyards, bushes all alike. But do you see that white place up yonder where there's been a landslide? Well, that's one of my marks. We'll get ashore now."

They landed.

"Now, Huck, where we're a-standing you could touch that hole I got out of with a fishing pole. See if you can find it."

Huck searched all the place about, and found nothing. Tom proudly marched into a thick clump of sumac bushes and said, "Here you are! Look at it, Huck! It's the snuggest hole in this country."

They entered the hole, Tom in the lead. They toiled their way to the farther end of the tunnel, then tied their kite strings to rocks and moved on. A few steps brought them to the spring. They went on and soon entered and followed Tom's other corridor until they reached the "jumping-off place." The candles showed that it was not really a cliff, but only a steep clay hill twenty or thirty feet high. Tom whispered: "Now I'll show you something, Huck."

He held his candle high and said, "Look as far around the corner as you can. Do you see that? There—on the big rock over yonder—done with candle-smoke."

"Tom, it's a *cross*!"

" '*Under the cross,*' hey? Right yonder's where I saw Injun Joe poke up his candle!"

Huck stared at the sign awhile, and then said with a shaky voice: "Tom, let's git out of here!"

"What! and leave the treasure?"

"Yes—leave it. Injun Joe's ghost is round about there, certain."

"No, it ain't, Huck, no, it ain't. It would haunt the place where he died—away out at the mouth of the cave—five miles from here."

"No, Tom, it wouldn't. It would hang around the money. I know the ways of ghosts, and so do you."

Tom began to fear that Huck was right. But soon an idea occurred to him: "Looky-here, Huck, what fools we're making of ourselves! Injun Joe's ghost ain't a-going to come around where there's a cross!"

"Tom, I didn't think of that. But that's so. It's luck for us, that cross is. I reckon we'll climb down there and have a hunt for that box."

They searched everywhere, and then sat down discouraged. By and by Tom said, "I bet you the money is under the rock. I'm going to dig in the clay."

"That ain't no bad notion, Tom!" said Huck.

"My, but we're rich, Tom!" Huck said.

Tom's knife was out at once, and he had not dug four inches before he struck wood.

"Hey, Huck!—do you hear that?"

Huck began to dig and scratch now. Some boards were soon uncovered and removed. They had hidden a natural hole which led under the rock. Tom got into this hole and held his candle as far under the rock as he could, but could not see to its bottom. He stooped and passed under the rock. He followed its winding course, first to the right, then to the left, Huck at his heels. Tom turned a short curve and exclaimed, "My goodness, Huck, looky-here!"

It was the treasure box, sure enough, occupying a snug little cavern, along with an empty gunpowder keg, a couple of guns in leather cases, two or three pairs of old moccasins, a leather belt, and some other rubbish well soaked with the water-drip.

"Got it at last!" said Huck. "My, but we're rich, Tom!"

"Huck, I always reckoned we'd get it. It's just too good to believe, but we have got it, sure!"

They transferred the money from the box into the bags they had brought along, and the boys took it up to the cross rock.

They soon came out into the clump of sumac bushes, looked carefully out, found the coast clear, and were soon lunching in the rowboat. As the sun dipped toward the horizon they pushed out and got under way. They landed back in the village shortly after dark.

"Now, Huck," said Tom, "we'll hide the money in the loft of the widow's woodshed, and I'll come up in the morning and we'll count it and divide it, and then we'll hunt up a place out in the woods for it where it will be safe."

But just as soon as they had hid the money, a Mr. Jones saw them coming out and asked them to come along with him to the Widow Douglas's drawing room.

The place was grandly lighted, and everybody that was of any importance in the village was there. The Thatchers were there, the Harpers, the Rogerses, Aunt Polly, Sid, Mary, the minister, the editor, and a great many more, and all dressed in their best. The widow received the boys as heartily as anyone could well receive two such looking beings. They were covered with clay and candle grease. Aunt Polly blushed and frowned and shook her head at Tom.

Mr. Jones said, "I just brought them along in a hurry."

"And you did just right," said the widow. "Come with me, boys."

She took them to a bedroom and said, "Now wash and dress yourselves. Here are two new suits of clothes—shirts, socks, everything complete. Get into them. We'll wait—come down when you are slicked up enough."

After the widow had left the room, Huck said, "Tom, we can go out the window and down the slope of the roof. It ain't high from the ground."

"Shucks, what do you want to do that for?"

"Well, I ain't used to that kind of crowd. I can't stand it. I ain't going down there, Tom."

"Oh, bother! It ain't anything. I don't mind it a bit. I'll take care of you."

Some minutes later the widow's guests were at the supper table, and a dozen children propped up at little side tables in the same room, after the fashion of that country and that day. The widow now announced that she meant to give Huck a home under her roof and have him educated; and that when she could spare the money she would start him in business.

Tom's chance was come. He said, "Huck don't need it. Huck's rich. Maybe you don't believe it, but he's got lots of it. Oh, you needn't smile—I reckon I can show you. You just wait a minute."

Tom ran out of doors. The company looked at each other and at Huck, who was tongue-tied.

"Sid, what ails Tom?" said Aunt Polly. "He—well, there ain't ever any making of that boy out. I never—"

Tom entered, struggling with the weight of his sacks, and Aunt Polly did not finish her sentence. Tom poured the mass of yellow coin upon the table and said, "There—what did I tell you? Half of it's Huck's and half of it's mine!"

The spectacle took the general breath away. All gazed, nobody spoke for a moment. Then there was a call for an explanation. Tom's tale was long, but brimful of interest.

The money was counted. The sum amounted to a little over twelve thousand dollars. It was more than anyone present had ever seen at one time before.

The reader may rest satisfied that Tom and Huck's windfall made a mighty stir in the poor little village of St. Petersburg. So vast a sum, all in actual cash, seemed next to incredible. It was talked about, glorified, until every "haunted" house in St. Petersburg and the neighboring villages was pulled apart, plank by plank, and its foundations dug up and ransacked for hidden treasure—and not by boys, but men. Wherever Tom and Huck appeared they were admired, stared at. The village paper published stories of the boys' lives.

The Widow Douglas put Huck's money into a bank account, and Judge Thatcher did the same with Tom's at Aunt Polly's request. Each lad had an income, now, that was simply huge—a dollar for every weekday in

Judge Thatcher hoped to see Tom a soldier someday.

the year and half of the Sundays. A dollar and a
quarter a week would board, lodge, and school a boy
in those old simple days—and clothe him and wash
him, too, for that matter.

Judge Thatcher had a great opinion, now, of Tom.
He said that no commonplace boy would ever have
got his daughter out of the cave. The judge hoped to
see Tom a great lawyer or a great soldier someday.
He said he meant to look to it that Tom should be

Huck was kept clean, neat, brushed and combed.

admitted to the National Military Academy and afterward trained in the best law school in the country, in order that he might be ready for either career or both.

Huck Finn's wealth and the fact that he was now under the Widow Douglas's protection introduced him into society—no, dragged him into it, hurled him into it—and his sufferings were almost more than he could bear. The widow's servants kept him clean and neat, combed and brushed, and they bedded him nightly in fresh sheets. He had to eat with knife and fork; he had to use napkin, cup, and plate; he had to learn his book; he had to go to church; he had to talk so properly that his speech was becoming boring in his mouth.

He bravely bore his miseries three weeks, and then one day turned up missing. For forty-eight hours the widow hunted for him everywhere in great distress. Early the third morning Tom Sawyer wisely went poking among the old empty barrels down behind the abandoned slaughterhouse, and in one of them he found Huck. He had slept there; he had just break-fasted upon some stolen odds and ends of food, and was lying down, now, in comfort, with his pipe. He was dirty, uncombed, and wearing the same old rags that had made him so interesting to look at in the days when he was free and happy. Tom told him the trouble he had been causing, and urged him to go home. Huck's face turned sad. He said:

"Don't talk about it, Tom. I've tried it, and it don't work; it don't work, Tom. It ain't for me; I ain't used to it. The widder's good to me, and friendly; but I can't stand them ways. She makes me git up just at the same time every morning; she makes me wash, they comb me all to thunder; she won't let me sleep in the woodshed; I got to wear them blamed clothes that just smothers me, Tom; they don't seem to let any air git through 'em, somehow; and they're so rotten nice that I can't set down, nor lay down, nor roll around anywher's; I hain't slid on a cellar door for—well it 'pears to be years; I got to go to church and sweat

and sweat—I hate them ornery sermons! I can't ketch
a fly in there, I can't chaw. I got to wear shoes all
Sunday. The widder eats by a bell; she goes to bed by
a bell; she gits up by a bell—everything's so awful
reg'lar a body can't stand it."

"Well, everybody does that way, Huck."

"Tom, it don't make no difference. I ain't everybody,
and I can't *stand* it. It's awful to be tied up so. And
grub comes too easy—I don't take no interest in
vittles that way. I got to ask to go a-fishing; I got to
ask to go in a-swimming—derned if I hain't got to ask
to do everything. Well, I'd got to talk so nice it wasn't
no comfort—I'd got to go up in the attic and rip out
awhile, every day, to git a taste in my mouth, or I'd 'a'
died, Tom. The widder wouldn't let me smoke; she
wouldn't let me yell, she wouldn't let me scratch
before folks. And, dad fetch it, she prayed all the time!
I never see such a woman! I *had* to shove off—I just
had to. And, besides, that school's going to open, and
I'd 'a' had to go to it—well, I wouldn't stand *that.*
Looky-here, Tom, being rich ain't what it's cracked up
to be. It's just worry and worry, and sweat and sweat,
and a-wishing you was dead all the time. I wouldn't
ever got into all this trouble if it hadn't 'a' been for all
that money; now you just take my sheer of it along
with yourn, and gimme a ten-center sometimes—not
many times, becuz I don't give a dern for a thing
without it's tollable hard to git—and you go and beg
off for me with the widder."

"Oh, Huck, you know I can't do that. 'Tain't fair.
And, besides, if you'll try this thing just a while longer
you'll come to like it."

"I'll smoke private and cuss private," Huck promised.

"Like it! Yes—the way I'd like a hot stove if I was to set on it long enough. No, Tom, I won't be rich, and I won't live in them cussed smothery houses. I like the woods, and the river, and the barrels, and I'll stick to 'em, too. Blame it all!"

"But, Huck, we can't let you into the gang if you ain't respectable, you know."

Huck's joy disappeared. "Can't let me in, Tom? You wouldn't shet me out, would you, Tom? You wouldn't do that, now, *would* you, Tom?"

"Huck, I wouldn't want to, and I *don't* want to—but what would people say? Why, they'd say, 'Mf! Tom Sawyer's Gang! pretty low characters in it!' They'd mean you, Huck. You wouldn't like that, and I wouldn't."

Huck was silent for a time. Finally he said, "Well,

I'll go back to the widder for a month and tackle it and see if I can come to stand it, if you'll let me b'long to the gang, Tom."

"All right, Huck, it's a whiz! Come along, old chap, and I'll ask the widow to let up on you a little."

"Will you, Tom—now will you? That's good. If she'll let up on some of the roughest things, I'll smoke private and cuss private, and crowd through or bust. When you going to start the gang?"

"Oh, right off. We'll get the boys together and have the initiation tonight, maybe."

"Have the which?"

"Have the initiation."

"What's that?"

"It's to swear to stand by one another, and never tell the gang's secrets."

"That's fine—that's mighty fine, Tom, I tell you."

"Well, I bet it is. And all that swearing's got to be done at midnight, in the lonesomest, awfullest place you can find—a haunted house is the best, but they're all ripped up now."

"Well, midnight's good, anyway, Tom."

"Yes, so it is. And you've got to swear on a coffin, and sign it in blood."

"Now, that's something like! Why, it's a million times bullier than pirating. I'll stick to the widder till I rot, Tom; and if I git to be a reg'lar ripper of a robber, and everybody talking 'bout it, I reckon she'll be proud she brought me in out of the wet."

CHILDREN'S THRIFT CLASSICS

Kidnapped

ROBERT LOUIS STEVENSON

Adapted by Bob Blaisdell

Illustrated by Thea Kliros

DOVER PUBLICATIONS, INC.
Mineola, New York

DOVER CHILDREN'S THRIFT CLASSICS
EDITOR OF THIS VOLUME: CANDACE WARD

Published in Canada by General Publishing Company, Ltd., 30 Lesmill Road, Don Mills, Toronto, Ontario.
Published in the United Kingdom by Constable and Company, Ltd., 3 The Lanchesters, 162–164 Fulham Palace Road, London W6 9ER.

Bibliographical Note

This Dover edition, first published in 1996, is a new abridgment, by Bob Blaisdell, of the work first published in 1886 by Cassell & Co., London. The illustrations, by Thea Kliros, the introductory Note and the explanatory footnotes have been specially prepared for this edition.

Library of Congress Cataloging-in-Publication Data

Stevenson, Robert Louis, 1850–1894.
    Kidnapped / Robert Louis Stevenson : adapted by Bob Blaisdell ; illustrated by Thea Kliros.
        p.   cm. — (Dover children's thrift classics)
    Summary: After being kidnapped by his villainous uncle, sixteen-year-old David Balfour escapes and becomes involved in the struggle of the Scottish highlanders against English rule.
    ISBN 0-486-29354-8 (pbk.)
    1. Scotland—History—18th century—Juvenile fiction. [1. Scotland—History—18th century—Fiction. 2. Adventure and adventurers—Fiction.] I. Blaisdell, Robert. II. Kliros, Thea, ill. III. Title. IV. Series.
PZ7.S8482Ki 1996
[Fic]—dc20
                                            96-20060
                                           CIP
                                           AC

Manufactured in the United States of America
Dover Publications, Inc., 31 East 2nd Street, Mineola, N.Y. 11501

Note

___

ROBERT LOUIS STEVENSON (1850–1894) was born in Edinburgh, the son of Thomas and Margaret Isabella Balfour Stevenson. For much of his life, Stevenson suffered from poor health, but his physical frailties did not dampen his enthusiasm for travel and adventure. Though Stevenson's formal education was sporadic during his early years (again, due to ill health), he was an avid reader and somewhat precocious. He eventually attended Edinburgh University to study engineering—his father's and grandfather's occupation—and later law. He never practiced either profession, but turned instead to literature.

Stevenson had been publishing his writings since he was 16, but it wasn't until his university days, when he began contributing essays to various periodicals, that he attracted critical attention. Then in 1881, with the serialized publication of *Treasure Island,* he achieved popular success. Five years later Stevenson published two of his most successful works: *The Strange Case of Dr. Jekyll and Mr. Hyde* and *Kidnapped.* Set against the backdrop of the highland uprisings of the mid-eighteenth century, the latter reveals Stevenson's fascination with Scottish history. David Balfour, the young hero of the tale, encounters several historical figures—including Alan Breck Stewart, the Jacobite rebel. In Stevenson's novel, David's loyalties to the British crown conflict with his personal relationship to Alan, an outlaw with a price on his head. As the two are pursued through the Scottish highlands, David comes to appreciate Alan's code of honor, despite their political differences.

In this abridgment, Bob Blaisdell has preserved the sense of adventure and excitement that has made Stevenson's original a classic; young and old alike will be enthralled by the romance of these highland adventures.

Contents

CHAPTER 1

I Set Off upon My Journey to the House of Shaws

I WILL BEGIN the story of my adventures with a morning early in the month of June, 1751, when I took the key for the last time out of the door of my father's house.

Mr. Campbell, the minister of Essendean, was waiting for me by the garden gate, good man! He asked me if I had breakfasted; and hearing that I had, he took my hand in both of his and clapped it kindly under his arm.

"Well, Davie lad," said he, "I will go with you as far as the river-crossing, to set you on the way.—Are you sorry to leave Essendean?"

"Why, sir," said I, "if I knew where I was going, or what was likely to become of me, I would tell you. Essendean is a good place, and I have been very happy there; but then I have never been anywhere else. My father and mother, since they are both dead, I shall be no nearer to in Essendean than in Hungary. If I had a chance to better myself where I was going, I would go with a good will."

"Ay?" said Mr. Campbell. "Very well, Davie. Then I am bound to tell your fortune; or so far as I may. When your mother was gone, and your father (the worthy man) began to sicken for his end, he gave me a certain letter, which he said was your inheritance. 'So soon,' says he, 'as I am gone, and the house is cleared out and the gear disposed of' (all which, Davie, has been done), 'give my boy this letter, and start him off to the house of Shaws, not far from Cramond. That is the place I came from,' he said, 'and it's where my boy should return. He is a steady lad,' your father said, 'and clever; and I doubt not he will arrive safe, and be well liked where he goes.' "

"The house of Shaws!" I cried. "What had my poor father to do with the house of Shaws?"

"Who can know for sure?" said Mr. Campbell. "But the name of that family, Davie boy, is the name you bear— Balfours of Shaws: an old, honest house, perchance somewhat fallen. Your father, too, was a man of learning; no man better suited to conduct school; nor had he the manners or the speech of the common schoolmaster; wealthy and well-known gentlemen had pleasure in his company. Lastly, here is the letter itself."

He gave it to me, which was addressed in these words: "To the hands of Ebenezer Balfour, Esquire, of Shaws, in his house of Shaws, these will be delivered by my son,

David Balfour." My heart was beating hard at this great prospect suddenly opening before a lad of seventeen years, the son of a poor country schoolmaster in the Forest of Ettrick.

"Mr. Campbell," I stammered, "and if you were in my shoes, would you go?"

"Surely," said the minister. "A strong lad like you should get to Cramond (which is near Edinburgh) in two days of walk. If the worst came to the worst, and your high relations should send you from their door, you can but walk the two days back again. Davie laddie, I mean to set you on guard against the dangers of the world."

Here he sat down upon a big boulder under a tree near the path. With uplifted forefinger, he urged me to be constant in my prayers and reading of the Bible. That done, he drew a picture of the great house that I was bound to, and how I should conduct myself with the people who lived there.

"Bear this in mind, that, though well born, you have had a country upbringing. Don't shame us, Davie, don't shame us! In that great house, with all those servants, show yourself as quick at understanding as any. As for the lord of the house—remember he's the lord. It's a pleasure to obey a lord; or should be, to the young."

"Well, sir," said I, "I'll promise you I'll try to make it so."

"Very well said," replied Mr. Campbell. "And now I come to the little packet for you which contains four things." He tugged it, as he spoke, from the pocket of his coat. "Of these four things, the first is your legal due: the little money for your father's books and furnishings, which I have bought. The other three are gifts that Mrs. Campbell and myself would like you to accept. The first is but a drop of water in the sea; it'll help you but a step, and vanish in the morning—a shilling piece. The second, which is flat and square and written upon, will stand by you through life—

directions for making Lilly of the Valley Water, good for the body and the brain. And as for the last, which is cubical, that'll see you into a better land—a Bible."

With those words he got upon his feet, took off his hat, and prayed a little while aloud for a young man setting out into the world; then suddenly took me in his arms and embraced me; then held me at arm's length, looking at me with his face all working with sorrow; and then whipped about, and crying goodbye to me, set off backward by the way that we had come at a sort of jogging run. I watched him as long as he was in sight; and he never stopped hurrying, nor once looked back.

I then got my bundle on my staff's end and set out over the ford and up the hill upon the farther side; till, just as I came on the green road running wide through the heather, I took my last look of Kirk Essendean, the trees about the family home, and the big trees in the churchyard where my father and my mother lay.

In the morning of the second day, coming to the top of a hill, I saw all the country fall away before me down to the sea; and in the midst of this slope, on a long ridge, the city of Edinburgh. Soon after, I came by a house where a shepherd lived, and got a rough direction for the neighbourhood of Cramond.

A little while later, and I was told I was in Cramond parish, and began to ask for the house of Shaws. It was a name that seemed to surprise those of whom I asked the way. At first I thought the plainness of my appearance, in my dusty country clothes, compared poorly to the greatness of the place to which I was bound. But after two or three had given me the same look and the same answer, I began to take it in my head there was something strange about the Shaws itself.

So, upon spying an honest fellow coming along a lane on his cart, I asked him if he had ever heard of a house they called the house of Shaws.

He stopped the cart and looked at me, like the others.

"Ay," said he. "What for?"

"It's a great house?"

"The house is big."

"Ay," said I, "but the folk that are in it?"

"Folk?" cried he. "Are ye daft? There's no folk there—to call folk."

"What?" said I; "not Mr. Ebenezer?"

"Ay," said the man; "there's the lord, to be sure, if it's him you're wanting. What'll be your business, mannie?"

"I was led to think that I would get work," I said.

"What?" cried the carter. "Well, mannie, it's none of my business, but ye seem a decent lad, and if ye'll take a word from me, ye'll keep clear of the Shaws."

What kind of a great house was this, that all the parish should start and stare to be asked the way to it? Or what sort of a gentleman, that his bad character should be famous? If an hour's walking would have brought me back to Essendean, I would have left my adventure then and there, and returned to Mr. Campbell's. But little as I liked the sound of what I heard, and slow as I began to travel, I

still kept asking my way and still kept advancing.

It was near sundown when I met a stout, sour-looking woman coming down a hill; and she, when I asked my usual question, turned sharp about, led me back to the summit she had just left, and pointed to a large building standing very bare upon a green in the bottom of the next valley. The country was pleasant round about, with low hills, and streams and woods, and the crops good; but the house itself appeared to be a kind of ruin; no road led up to it; no smoke arose from any of the chimneys; nor was there any garden. My heart sank. "That!" I cried.

"That is the house of Shaws!" she cried. "Blood built it, blood stopped the building of it; blood shall bring it down. See here!" she cried again—"I spit upon the ground, and crack my thumb at it! If you see the lord, tell him this makes the twelve hundred and nineteenth time that Jennet Clouston has called down the curse on him and his house, barn and stable!"

And the woman turned with a skip, and was gone. I stood where she left me, with my hair on end. In those days folk still believed in witches and trembled at a curse.

I sat me down and stared at the house of the Shaws. The more I looked the pleasanter that countryside appeared. At last the sun went down, and then, right up against the yellow sky, I saw a thin scroll of smoke go up; that meant a fire, and warmth, and food, and someone living there that must have lit it.

So I set forward. Soon I was standing before stone uprights, with an unroofed lodge beside them, and coats of arms upon the top. A main entrance it was plainly meant to be, but never finished; instead of gates of iron, a rickety fence. I walked past on the right-hand side of the pillars, and went wandering on towards the house.

The nearer I got to that, the drearier it appeared. It seemed like the one wing of a house that had never been finished. What should have been the inner end stood open on the upper floors, and showed against the sky with steps and stairs of uncompleted masonry. Many of the windows had no glass, and bats flew in and out.

The night had begun to fall as I got close; and in the three of the lower windows, which were very high up and narrow, and well barred, the changing light of a little fire began to glimmer.

Was this the place I had been coming to? Was it within these walls that I was to seek new friends and begin great fortunes? Why, in my father's house, the fire and the bright lights would show a mile away, and the door open to a beggar's knock!

I came forward, and listened, hearing someone rattling with dishes, and a little dry cough; but there was no sound of speech, and not a dog barked.

The door was a great piece of wood all studded with nails; and I lifted my hand under my jacket, and knocked once. Then I stood and waited. The house had fallen into a dead silence; a whole minute passed, and nothing stirred but the bats overhead. I knocked again, and listened. By this time my ears had grown so accustomed to the quiet that I could hear the ticking of the clock inside as it slowly counted out the seconds.

I wondered whether to run away; but anger got the upper hand, and I began to rain kicks and knocks on the door, and to shout out aloud for Mr. Balfour. I heard the cough right overhead, and jumping back and looking up, beheld a man's head in a tall nightcap, and the wide mouth of a musket, at one of the second-story windows.

"It's loaded," said a voice.

"I have come here with a letter," I said, "to Ebenezer Balfour of Shaws. Is he here?"

"Well," was the reply, "ye can put it down upon the doorstep, and be off!"

"I will do no such thing," I cried. "I will deliver it into Mr. Balfour's hands, as it was meant I should. It is a letter of introduction."

"A what?" cried the voice, sharply.

I repeated what I had said.

"Who are ye yourself?"

"They call me David Balfour."

At that, the man started, for I heard the musket rattle on the windowsill; after a long pause, he asked, "Is your father dead?"

I was so much surprised at this, that I stood staring.

"Ay," the man went on, "he's dead, no doubt; and that'll be what brings ye to my door. Well, man, I'll let ye in"; and he disappeared from the window.

CHAPTER 2
I Meet My Uncle

SOON THERE CAME a great rattling of chains and bolts, and the door was cautiously opened.

"Go into the kitchen and touch nothing," said the voice; and while he set himself to replacing the chains and bolts, I made my way forward through the dark and entered the kitchen.

The fire was fairly bright, and showed me the barest room I think I ever saw. Half-a-dozen dishes stood upon the shelves; the table was laid for supper with a bowl of porridge, a spoon, and a cup of beer. There was not another thing in that great, stone room but chests arranged

along the wall and a corner cupboard.

As soon as the last chain was up, the man rejoined me. He was a mean, stooping, narrow-shouldered, clay-faced creature; and his age might have been anything between fifty and seventy. He was long unshaved; but what most distressed me, he would neither take his eyes away from me nor look me in the face.

"Are ye hungry?" he asked. "Ye can eat that porridge?"

I said I feared it was his own supper.

"Oh," said he, "I can do fine without it. I'll take the beer, though, for it wets my throat." He drank the cup, still keeping an eye upon me as he drank; and then suddenly held out his hand. "Let's see the letter."

I told him the letter was for Mr. Balfour; not for him.

"And who do ye think I am?" said he. "Give me Alexander's letter!"

"You know my father's name?"

"It would be strange if I didn't," he returned, "for he was my brother; and little as ye seem to like either me or my house, or my porridge, I'm your uncle, Davie my man. So give us the letter and sit down and fill your stomach."

If I had been younger, I believe I would have burst into tears. As it was, I could find no words, but handed him the letter.

My uncle, stooping over the fire, turned the letter over and over in his hands.

"Do ye know what's in it?" he asked.

"You see for yourself, sir," said I, "that the seal has not been broken."

"Ay," he said, "but what brought you here?"

"To give you the letter," said I.

"No," said he, "but ye'll have had some hopes, no doubt?"

"I confess, sir," said I, "when I was told that I had rich kinsfolk, I hoped they might help me in my life. But I am no beggar. For as poor as I appear, I have friends of my own that will be happy to help me."

"Oh ho!" said Uncle Ebenezer. "So, Davie my man, your father's been long dead?"

"Three weeks, sir."

"He was a secret man, Alexander—a secret, silent man," he went on. "He never said much when he was young. He'll never have spoken much of me?"

"I never knew, sir, till you told it me yourself, that he had any brother."

"To think o' that!" said he. He hit me a smack upon the shoulder, saying, "We'll get along fine! I'm glad I let you in. And now come away to your bed."

To my surprise he lit no lamp or candle, but set forth into the dark passage, groped his way, breathing deeply, up a flight of steps, and paused before a door, which he unlocked. I begged a light to go to bed with.

"Hoot-toot!" said Uncle Ebenezer, "there's a fine moon."

"Neither moon nor star, sir, and dark as a cave," said I. "I cannot see the bed."

"Hoot-toot!" said he. "Lights in a house is a thing I don't agree with. I'm afraid of fires. Good night to ye, Davie."

And before I had time to add a further protest, he pulled the door shut, and I heard him lock me in from the outside.

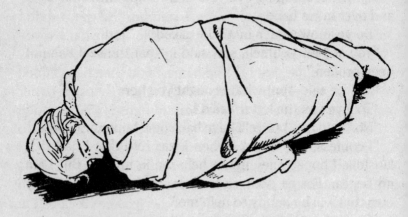

The room was as cold as a well, and the bed was damp; but by good fortune I had brought up my bundle, and rolled myself in my cloak, and lay down upon the floor and fell asleep.

With the first peep of day I opened my eyes, to find myself in a great chamber, lit by three fair windows. Perhaps twenty years ago, it must have been as pleasant a room as a man could wish; but damp, dirt, disuse, and the mice and spiders had done their worst since then. Many of the window panes, besides, were broken; and indeed this was a common feature in that house.

Meanwhile the sun was shining outside; and being very cold in that miserable room, I knocked and shouted till my jailer came and let me out. In the kitchen he had lit the fire and was making the porridge. The table was laid with two bowls and two horn spoons.

"Davie, my man," said he, "I think much of the family, and I mean to do right by you. Just you give me a day or two, and as sure as sure, I'll do the right by you."

"Very well," said I. "If you want to help me, there's no doubt but I'll be glad of it, and grateful." Then I began next to say that I must have the bed and bedding aired and put to sun-dry.

"Is this my house or yours?" said he. "No, no, I didn't mean that. What's mine is yours, Davie, and what's yours is mine. Blood's thicker than water; and there's nobody but you and me that has the name." And then he rambled on about the family, and its old greatness, and his father that began to enlarge the house, and himself that stopped the building as a sinful waste; and this put it in my head to give him Jennet Clouston's message.

"The witch!" he cried. "Twelve hundred and fifteen—that's how many days it's been since I had her thrown off the land! I swear, David, I'll have her roasted before I'm done with it! A witch—I'll go make a legal complaint against her."

And with that he opened a chest, and got out a very old blue coat, and a good hat. These he threw on, and taking a staff from the cupboard, locked all up again, and was for setting out, when a thought stopped him.

"I can't leave you by yourself in the house," said he. "I'll have to lock you out."

"If you lock me out," I said, "it'll be the last you'll see of me in friendship."

"This is not the way to win my favor, David."

"Sir," said I, "with all respect for your age and our common blood, I do not value your favor. If you were all the family I had in the world, I wouldn't buy your liking for two pence."

Uncle Ebenezer went and looked out the window for a while. I could see him trembling and twitching, but when he turned round, he had a smile on his face.

"Well, well," said he, "we must bear and forbear. I'll not go; that's all that's to be said of it."

"Uncle Ebenezer," I said, "I can make nothing out of this. You treat me like a thief; you hate to have me in this house; you let me see it, every word and every minute: it's not possible you can like me; and as for me, I've spoken to you as I never thought to speak to any man. Why do you seek to keep me, then? Let me go back to the friends I have, and that like me!"

"No, no," he said. "I like you fine; we'll get along fine yet. Stay here quiet, there's a good lad; just you bide here quiet a bittie, and ye'll find that we agree."

"Well, sir," said I, after I had thought the matter out in silence, "I'll stay a while. It's more just I should be helped by my own blood than strangers; and if we don't get along, I'll do my best it shall be through no fault of mine."

For a day that was begun so ill, the day passed fairly well. We had the porridge cold again at noon, and hot porridge at night. He spoke but little, shooting a question at me after a long silence. In a room next door to the kitchen, where he allowed me to go, I found a great number of books, both Latin and English, in which I took great pleasure all the afternoon.

After our late meal, he sat awhile smoking.

"Davie," he said at length, "I've been thinking. There's a wee bit silver that I half promised you before you were born, promised it to your father. O, nothing legal, you understand. Well, I kept that bit of money separate—and it has grown by now to be a matter of just precisely—just exactly—" and here he paused and stumbled, "—of just exactly forty pounds—*Scots* pounds!"

The Scots pound being the same thing as an English shilling, the difference made by his second thought was considerable; I could see, besides, that the whole story was a lie. "O think again, sir! Pounds sterling, I believe!"

"That's what I said," returned my uncle: "pounds ster-

ling! And if you'll step out the door a minute, I'll get it out
for you and call you in again."

It was a dark night, with a few stars low down; and as I
stood just outside the door, I heard a moaning of wind far
off among the hills.

When I was called in again, my uncle counted out into
my hand the golden guinea pieces.

"There," said he, "that'll show you! I'm a strange man,
and strange with strangers; but my word is my bond, and
there's the proof of it."

Now, my uncle seemed so miserly that I was struck
dumb by this sudden generosity, and could find no words
in which to thank him.

"Not a word!" said he. "I want no thanks. I do my duty.
It's a pleasure to me to do the right by my brother's son."
And now he looked toward me sideways. "And see here,"
said he, "tit for tat."

I told him I was ready to return a favor. He told me that

he was growing old and a little broken, and that he would expect me to help him with the house and the small garden. I expressed my readiness to serve.

"Well," he said, "let's begin." He pulled out of his pocket a rusty key. "There," said he, "there's the key of the stair-tower at the far end of the house. You can only get into it from the outside, for that part of the house is not finished. Go in there, and up the stairs, and bring me down the chest that's at the top. There's papers in it."

"Can I have a light, sir?"

"No," said he. "No lights in my house."

"Very well, sir," said I. "Are the stairs good?"

"They're grand," said he; and then as I was going: "Keep to the wall," he added; "there's no bannisters. But the stairs are grand."

Out I went into the night. The wind was still moaning. It was darker than ever; and I had to feel along the wall, till I came to the length of the stair-tower door at the far end of the unfinished wing. I had got the key into the keyhole and had just turned it, when all of a sudden, without sound of wind or thunder, the whole sky lighted up with wild fire and went black again.

It was so dark inside, that I pushed out with foot and hand, and soon struck the wall with the one, and the lowermost round of the stair with the other. The wall, by the touch, was of fine cut stone; the steps too, though somewhat steep and narrow, were polished, and regular and solid. Minding my uncle's word about the bannisters, I kept close to the tower side, and felt my way in the pitch darkness with a beating heart.

The house of Shaws stood some five full storeys high, not counting lofts. As I advanced, it seemed to me the stairway grew airier and a bit less dark; and I was wondering what might be the cause of this change, when a second blink of the summer lightning came and went. If I did

not cry out, it was because fear had me by the throat. The flash shone in on every side through breaches in the wall, so that I seemed to be climbing up an open scaffold, but the same passing brightness showed me the steps were of unequal length, and that one of my feet rested that moment within two inches of the edge.

This was the grand stair! I thought. My uncle had sent me here, certainly to run great risks, perhaps to die. I got down upon my hands and knees; and as slowly as a snail, feeling before me every inch, and testing each step, I continued to go up the stairs. The darkness, by contrast with the flash, appeared to have deepened; nor was that all, for there was a great stir of bats in the top part of the tower, and the foul beasts, flying downwards, sometimes beat about my face and body.

The tower, I should have said, was square; and in every corner the step was made of a great stone of a different shape, to join the flights. Well, I had come close to one of these turns, when, feeling forward as usual, my hand slipped upon an edge and found nothing but emptiness beyond it. The stairs had been carried no higher; to set a stranger mounting it in the darkness was to send him straight to his death.

I turned and groped my way down again, with anger in my heart. About half-way down, the wind sprang up in a clap and shook the tower, and died again; the rain followed; and before I had reached the ground level it fell in buckets. I put out my head in the storm, and walked softly along towards the kitchen. I came in unheard, and stood and watched him. He sat with his back towards me at the table. I stepped forward, came close behind him, and suddenly clapped my two hands down upon his shoulders.

My uncle gave a kind of broken cry, flung up his arms, and tumbled to the floor like a dead man. I let him lie as he had fallen. His keys were hanging in the cupboard; and it was my plan to furnish myself with arms before my uncle should come again to his senses. I turned to the chests. The first was full of meal; the second of money-bags and papers; in the third, with many other things (for the most part clothes), I found a rusty, ugly-looking knife. This, then, I hid inside my waistcoat, and turned to my uncle.

He lay as he had fallen, all huddled, with one knee up and one arm sprawling. I got water and dashed it in his face; and with that he seemed to come a little to himself, working his mouth and fluttering his eyelids. At last he looked up and saw me, and there came into his eyes a terror.

"Come, come," said I; "sit up."

"Are you alive?" he sobbed.

"That am I," said I. "Small thanks to you!"

I set him on a chair and looked at him. I numbered over
before him the points on which I wanted explanation: why
he lied to me at every word; why he had given me money
to which I was convinced I had no claim; and, last of all,
why he had tried to kill me. He heard me all through in
silence; and then, in a broken voice, begged me to let him
go to bed.

"I'll tell you in the morning," he said; "as sure as death I
will."

And so weak was he that I could do nothing but consent. I locked him in his room, however, and pocketed the
key; and then returning to the kitchen, made up such a
blaze as had not shone there for many a long year, and
wrapping myself in my plaid, lay down upon the chests
and fell asleep.

CHAPTER 3
I Go to the Queen's Ferry

Much rain fell in the night; and the next morning there blew a bitter wintry wind out of the northwest, driving scattered clouds.

I went upstairs and gave my prisoner his liberty. He gave me good-morning; and I gave the same to him. Soon we were set to breakfast.

"Well, sir," said I, "have you nothing more to say to me?" And then, as he did not answer, I continued, "It will be time, I think, to understand each other. You took me for a Johnnie Raw, with no more mother-wit or courage than a porridge-stick. I took you for a good man, or no worse than others at the least. It seems we were both wrong. What cause you have to fear me, to cheat me, and to attempt my life—"

He murmured something about a joke, and that he liked a bit of fun. We were then interrupted by a knocking at the door.

Bidding my uncle sit where he was, I went to open it, and found on the doorstep a half-grown boy in sea-clothes. He had no sooner seen me than he began to dance some steps, snapping his fingers in the air.

"What cheer, mate?" said he.

I asked him to name his business, but instead he sang two lines of nonsense.

"Well," said I, "if you have no business, I will be so rude as to shut you out."

"Wait, brother!" he cried. "Have you no fun about you? Or do you want to get me thrashed? I've brought a letter from old Heasyoasy to Mr. Belflower." He showed me a letter as he spoke. "And I say, mate," he added, "I'm awful hungry."

"Well," said I, "come into the house, and you shall have a bite."

With that I brought him in and set him down to my own place, where he fell-to on the remains of breakfast. Meanwhile, my uncle read the letter and sat thinking; then, suddenly, he got to his feet and pulled me to the farthest corner of the room.

"Read that," said he, and put the letter in my hand.

> The Hawes Inn, at the Queen's Ferry.
>
> Sir,—I lie here with my hawser up and down, and send my cabin-boy to inform. If you have any further commands for overseas, today will be the last chance, as the wind will serve us well. I have disputes with your agent, Mr. Rankeillor; of which, if not cleared up, you may look to see some losses. I have drawn a bill upon you, and am, sir, your humble servant,
>
> ELIAS HOSEASON.

"You see, Davie," resumed my uncle, "I have a venture with this man Hoseason, the captain of the trading brig, the *Covenant*, of Dysart. Now, if you and me was to walk over with that lad, I could see the captain at the Hawes, or maybe on board the *Covenant* if there was papers to be signed; and so far from a loss of time, we can go on to the lawyer, Mr. Rankeillor's. After all that's come and gone, you wouldn't believe me upon my word; but you'll believe Rankeillor. He's a respected old man, and he knew your father."

I stood awhile and thought. I was going to some place of shipping, which was doubtless busy, and where my uncle would dare not attempt to harm me. Besides, I was eager to take a nearer view of the sea and ships. You are to remember that I had lived all my life in the inland hills, and just two days before had my first sight of the firth lying like a blue floor, and the sailing ships moving on the face of it, no bigger than toys.

"Very well," said I, "let us go to the Ferry."

My uncle got into his hat and coat, and buckled an old rusty sword on; then we locked the door and went out.

It was the month of June; the grass was all white with daisies, and the trees with blossom; but to judge by our blue nails and aching wrists, the time might have been winter and the whiteness a December frost. Uncle Ebenezer trudged along, never saying a word the whole way; and I was left for talk with the cabin-boy. He told me his name was Ransome, and that he had followed the sea since he was nine, but could not say how old he was, as he had lost track. He showed me tattoo marks, baring his chest; he swore horribly, more like a silly schoolboy than a man; and boasted of many wild and bad things that he had done: stealing, false accusations, ay, and even murder; but all with such a lack of likely details, as made me pity him rather than believe him.

I asked him of the brig and of Captain Hoseason. Heasyoasy (for so he named the skipper) was rough, fierce, mean, and brutal; and all this the poor cabin-boy admired as something seamanlike and manly. He would only admit one flaw in his idol. "He ain't no seaman. It's Mr. Shuan that navigates the brig; he's the finest seaman in the trade, only he drinks too much. Why, look here"; and turning down his stocking he showed me a great, raw, red wound that made my blood run cold. "He done that—Mr. Shuan done it," he said, with an air of pride.

"What!" I cried, "do you take such savage treatment at his hands?"

"No," said the poor boy, "and so he'll find. See here"; and he showed me a case-knife, which he told me was stolen. "O," said he, "let me see him try; I dare him to; I'll get him sure! O, he ain't the first!"

I have never felt such pity for any one in this wide world as I felt for that half-witted boy; and it began to come over me that the brig *Covenant* was little better than a hell upon the seas.

"Have you no friends?" said I.

He said he had a father in some English seaport. "He was a fine man, too," he said; "but he's dead."

"In Heaven's name," cried I, "can you find no decent life on shore?"

"O no," said he, "they would put me to a trade."

I asked him what trade could be so dreadful as the one he followed, where he was in danger of his life, not alone from wind and sea, but by the cruelty of those who were his masters. He then began to praise the life, and tell what a pleasure it was to get on shore with money in his pocket, and spend it like a man, and buy apples and swagger. "And then it's not all as bad as that," said he; "there's worse off than me: there's the twenty-pounders. And then there's little uns, too. O, littler than me! I tell you, I keep them in order." And so he ran on, and it came to me what he meant by twenty-pounders were those unhappy criminals who were sent overseas to slavery in North America, or the still more unhappy innocents who were kidnapped.

Just then we came to the top of the hill, and looked down on the Ferry. The Firth of Forth narrows at this point to the width of a good-sized river. Right in the middle of the narrows lies an islet with some ruins; on the south shore they have built a pier for the service of the Ferry.

The town of Queensferry lies farther west, and the neighborhood of the inn looked pretty lonely at that time of day, for the boat had just gone north with passengers. A skiff lay beside the pier; this, as Ransome told me, was the brig's boat waiting for the captain; and about half a mile off he pointed out the *Covenant* herself. There was a sea-going bustle on board; and as the wind blew from that quarter, I could hear the song of the sailors as they pulled upon the ropes. I pitied all poor souls that were condemned to sail in the ship.

As soon as we came to the inn, Ransome led us up the stair to a small room. At a table by the chimney, a tall, dark man sat writing. In spite of the heat of the room, he wore a thick sea-jacket, buttoned to the neck, and a tall hairy cap drawn down over his ears.

He got to his feet at once, and offered his large hand to Ebenezer. "I am proud to see you, Mr. Balfour," said he, in a fine deep voice, "and glad that you are here in time. The wind's fair, and the tide upon the turn; we'll see the old coal-bucket burning on the Isle of May before tonight."

It was so warm in the room, away I went back outside, leaving the two men sitting down to a bottle and a great mass of papers; and crossing the road in front of the inn, walked down upon the beach. Little waves beat upon the shore. The smell of sea-water was salt and stirring; the *Covenant* was beginning to shake out her sails; and the spirit of all that I beheld put me in thoughts of far voyages and foreign places.

I returned to the inn and sat down. I asked the landlord if he knew Mr. Rankeillor.

"Ay," said he, "and a very honest man. And, O, by-the-by, was it you that came in with Ebenezer?" And when I had told him yes, "You're no relative of his?" he asked.

I told him no.

"I thought not," said he, "and yet you have a kind of look of Mr. Alexander."

I said it seemed that Ebenezer was ill-seen in the country.

"No doubt," said the landlord. "He's a wicked old man, and there are many would like to see him hanged. And yet he was once a fine young fellow. But that was before the word went around about Mr. Alexander."

"And what was it?"

"Oh, just that he had killed him," said the landlord, "to get the place."

"The Shaws? Is that so? Was my—Was Alexander the eldest son?"

"Indeed was he," said the landlord. "What else would Ebenezer have killed him for?"

And with that he went away.

I sat stunned with the news; my father was the elder brother, and therefore he had been, and now I myself was, the rightful owner of the house and lands that Ebenezer claimed as his own.

The next thing I knew. I heard my uncle calling me, and found him and the captain out on the road before the inn.

"Sir," said the captain, "Mr. Balfour tells me great things of you; and for my part I like your looks. I wish I was longer here, that we might make the better friends; but we'll make the most of what we have. You shall come on board my brig for half an hour, till the ebb sets, and drink a bowl with me."

Now I longed to see the inside of a ship more than words can tell; but I was not going to put myself in danger, and I told the captain that I had an appointment with the lawyer.

"Ay, ay," said he, "your uncle passed me word of that. But, you see, the boat'll set you ashore at the town pier, and that's but a stone's throw from Rankeillor's house." And here he suddenly leaned down and whispered in my ear: "Beware of the old man, he means trouble. Come aboard till I can get a word with you." And then, passing his arm through mine, he continued aloud, "But, come, what can I bring you from the Carolinas? A roll of tobacco? Indian feather-work? A skin of a wild beast?— Take your pick."

By this time we were at the boat-side, and he was handing me in. I did not dream of hanging back; I thought (poor fool!) that I had found a good friend and helper, and I was rejoiced to see the ship. As soon as we were all set in our places, the boat was thrust off from the pier and began to move over the waters.

As soon as we were alongside the ship, Hoseason, declaring that he and I must be the first aboard, ordered a tackle to be sent down from the main-yard. In this I was whipped into the air and set down again on the deck, where the captain stood ready waiting for me, and instantly slipped back his arm under mine.

"But where is my uncle?" said I.

"Ay," said Hoseason, "that's the point."

I felt I was lost. I pulled free of him and ran to the side of the ship. Sure enough, there was the boat pulling for the town, with my uncle sitting in the stern. I gave a piercing cry—"Help, help! Murder!"—and my uncle turned round where he was sitting, and showed me a face full of cruelty.

It was the last thing I saw before strong hands plucked me back from the ship's side; and now a thunderbolt seemed to strike me; I saw a great flash of fire, and fell senseless.

CHAPTER 4
I Go to Sea in the Brig *Covenant*

I CAME TO myself in darkness, in great pain, bound hand and foot. The whole world now heaved up, and now rushed downward; and so sick and hurt was I in body, and my mind so confounded, that it took me a long while to realize that I must be lying somewhere in the belly of the ship.

A small man of about thirty, with green eyes and a tangle of fair hair, came to me by the light of a lantern.

"How goes it?" said he.

I answered by a sob; and my visitor felt my pulse and temples, and set himself to wash and dress the wound upon my head.

"Ay," said he, "a hard hit. But cheer up! The world's not over; you've made a bad start of it, but it'll get better."

The next time he came to see me, I was lying with my eyes wide open in the darkness. I ached in every limb. He was followed by the captain. Neither said a word; but the first set to examining me, and dressed my wound as before, while Hoseason looked me in the face.

"Now, sir, you see for yourself," said the first man: "a high fever, no appetite, no light, no meat: you see for yourself what that means. I want that boy taken out of this hole and put in the forecastle."

"Mr. Riach, I have sailed with ye three cruises," replied the captain. "In all that time, sir, ye should have learned to know me: I'm a hard man; but if ye say the lad will die—"

"Ay, he will!" said Mr. Riach.

"Well, sir, is not that enough?" said Hoseason. "Put him where you please!"

Thereupon the captain went up the ladder; and moments afterwards my bonds were cut, and men came down to carry me up to the quarters under the raised deck, or forecastle, where they laid me in a bunk on some sea blankets. I fell asleep.

It was a blessed thing indeed to open my eyes again upon the daylight, and to find myself with men. The forecastle was a roomy place, set all about with berths, in which the men were seated smoking or lying down asleep. The day being calm and the wind fair, the scuttle—the hole in the ceiling—was open, and not only the good daylight, but from time to time (as the ship rolled) a dusty beam of sunlight shone in, and dazzled and delighted me.

Here I lay for the space of many days, and not only got my health again, but came to know my companions. They were a rough lot indeed, as sailors mostly are. But they had many virtues. They were kind when it occurred to them, simple, and had some glimmerings of honesty. There was one man, of maybe forty, that would sit on my berthside for hours and tell me of his wife and child.

Among other good deeds that they did, they returned my money, which had been shared among them. The ship was bound for the Carolinas; and you must not suppose that I was going to that place merely as an exile. In those days of my youth, white men were still sold into slavery on the plantations, and that was the destiny to which my wicked uncle had condemned me.

The cabin-boy Ransome came in at times from the round-house, where he served, now nursing a bruised leg or arm in silent agony, now raving against the cruelty of Mr. Shuan. It made my heart bleed. I did my best in the small time allowed me to make something like a man, or rather like a boy, of poor Ransome. But he could remember nothing of the time before he came to sea; only that his father had made clocks, and had a bird that could whistle, in the parlor; all else had been blotted out in these years of hardship and cruelty.

Soon the *Covenant* was meeting continual head-winds and tumbling up and down against head-seas, so that the scuttle was almost constantly shut, and the forecastle lighted only by a swinging lantern on a beam. There was constant labor for all hands; but as I was never allowed to set my foot on deck, you can picture to yourselves how weary of my life I grew to be, and how impatient for a change.

One night, about eleven o'clock, a man of Mr. Riach's watch (which was on deck) came below for his jacket; and instantly there began to go a whisper about the forecastle that "Shuan had done for Ransome at last." We had hardly time to get the idea in our heads, far less to speak of it, when the scuttle was flung open, and Captain Hoseason came down the ladder. He looked round the bunks in the tossing light of the lantern; and then, walking straight up to me, said, "My man, we want you to serve in the round-house. You and Ransome are to change berths. Run away aft with you."

Even as he spoke, two seamen appeared in the scuttle, carrying Ransome in their arms; and the ship at that moment giving a great sheer into the sea, and the lantern swinging, the light fell direct on the boy's face. It was as white as wax. The blood in me ran cold, and I drew in my breath as if I had been struck.

"Run away aft; run away aft with ye!" cried Hoseason.

I ran up the ladder on deck. The brig was sheering through a long, cresting swell. The round-house, where I was now to sleep and serve, stood some six feet above the decks. Inside were a fixed table and bench, and two berths, one for the captain and the other for the two mates, turn and turn about. It was all fitted with lockers from top to bottom, so as to stow away the officers' belongings and a part of the ship's stores; all the firearms, except two pieces of brass ordnance, were set in a rack in the aftermost wall of the round-house. The most of the cutlasses were in another place.

A small window with a shutter on each side, and a skylight in the roof, gave it light by day; and after dark there was a lamp always burning. It was burning when I entered, and Mr. Shuan was sitting at the table, with a brandy bottle and tin cup in front of him. He was a tall man, strongly made.

He took no notice of my coming in; nor did he move when the captain followed and leaned on the berth beside me, looking darkly at the mate. Soon Mr. Riach came in. He gave the captain a glance that meant the boy was dead as plain as speaking. We all three stood without a word, staring down at Mr. Shuan, and Mr. Shuan sat without a word, looking hard upon the table.

All of a sudden he put out his hand to take the bottle; and at that Mr. Riach started forward and took it away.

Mr. Shuan was on his feet in a second; he still looked dazed, but he meant murder, ay, and would have done it, for the second time that night, had not the captain stepped in between him and his victim.

"Sit down!" roared the captain. "Ye drunken pig, do ye know what ye've done? Ye've murdered the boy!"

Mr. Shuan seemed to understand; for he sat down again, and put up his hand to his brow.

"Well," he said, "he brought me a dirty cup!"

At that word, the captain and I and Mr. Riach all looked at each other for a second with a frightened look; and then Hoseason walked up to his chief officer, took him by the shoulder, led him across to his bunk, and told him to lie down and go to sleep, as you might speak to a bad child. The murderer cried a little, but he took off his sea-boots and obeyed.

"Ah!" cried Mr. Riach, "ye should have interfered long since. It's too late now."

"Mr. Riach," said the captain, "this night's work must never be known in Dysart. The boy went overboard, sir; that's what the story is; and I would give five pounds out of my pocket it was true!" The pair sat down to drink; and while they did so, the murderer, who had been lying and whimpering in his berth, raised himself upon his elbow and looked at them and at me.

That was the first night of my new duties; and in the course of the next day I had got well into the run of them. I had to serve at meals; all the day through I would be running with a drink to one or other of my three masters; and at night I slept on a blanket thrown on the deck boards at the far end of the round-house.

Though I was clumsy enough and sometimes fell with what I was bringing them, both Mr. Riach and the captain were unusually patient. I believed they were making up with their guilt, and that they would not have been so good with me if they had not been worse with Ransome.

As for Mr. Shuan, the drink, or his crime, had certainly troubled his mind. He never grew used to my being there, stared at me continually (sometimes, I thought, with terror) and more than once drew back from my hand when I was serving him. I was pretty sure from that he had no clear mind of what he had done. On my second day in the round-house, he got up from his seat, and came up close to me.

"You were not here before?" he asked.

"No, sir," said I.

"There was another boy?" he asked again.

"Yes, sir."

"Ah!" said he, "I thought so." He went and sat down, without another word, except to call for brandy.

You may think it strange, but for all the horror I had, I was still sorry for him. He was a married man, with a wife in Leith; but whether or not he had children, I hope not.

Altogether it was no very hard life for the time it lasted, which (as you are to hear) was not long. Mr. Riach, who had been to college, spoke to me like a friend when he was not sulking, and told me many curious things; and even the captain would sometimes unbuckle a bit, and tell me of fine countries he had visited.

Here I was, however, doing dirty work for three men that I looked down upon; that was for the present; and as for the future, I could only see myself slaving in the tobacco fields. As the days came and went, my heart sank lower and lower, till I was even glad of the work which kept me from thinking.

CHAPTER 5
The Man with the Belt of Gold

M ORE THAN A week went by, and some days the *Covenant* made a little way; others she was driven actually back. At last we were beaten so far to the south that we tossed and tacked to and fro the whole of the ninth day, within sight of Cape Wrath and the wild, rocky coast on either hand of it. The officers decided to make a fair wind of a foul one and run south.

The tenth afternoon there was a falling swell and a thick, wet, white fog that hid one end of the brig from the other. Maybe about ten at night, I was serving Mr. Riach and the captain at their supper, when the ship struck something with a great sound, and we heard voices singing out. My two masters leaped to their feet, and hurried out.

We had run down a boat in the fog, and she had parted in the middle and gone down to the bottom with all her crew but one. This man had been sitting in the stern as a passenger, while the rest were on the benches rowing. At the moment of the blow, the stern had been thrown into the air, and the man (having his hands free, yet encumbered with an overcoat that came below his knees) had leaped up and caught hold of the brig's bowsprit. It showed he had luck and much agility and unusual strength, that he should have thus saved himself from such a pass.

He was smallish, but well set and as nimble as a goat; his face was sunburnt very dark; his eyes were unusually light; and when he took off his overcoat, he laid a pair of fine silver-mounted pistols on the table, and I saw that he was belted with a great sword. He wore a hat with feathers, a red waistcoat, breeches of black plush, and a blue coat with silver buttons and handsome silver lace.

"I'm vexed, sir, about the boat," said the captain.

"There are some good men gone to the bottom," said the stranger, "that I would rather see on the dry land again than ten boats."

"You've a French soldier's coat upon your back and a Scotch tongue in your head," said the captain.

"So?" said the gentleman in the fine coat. "Well, sir, to be quite plain with you, I am one of those honest gentlemen that were in trouble about the years forty-five and six;* and if I got into the hands of any of the red-coated gentry, it's like it would go hard with me. Now, sir, I was headed for France; and there was a French ship cruising here to pick me up; but she gave us the go-by in the fog—as I wish from the heart that you had done yourself! And the best I can say is this: If you can set me ashore where I was going, I have that upon me will reward you highly for your trouble."

"In France?" said the captain. "No, sir; but where you come from—we might talk of that."

The gentleman took off a money-belt from about his waist, and poured out a guinea or two upon the table, saying, "Thirty guineas on the seaside, or sixty if you set me on the Linnhe Loch. Take it, if you will; if not, you can do your worst."

"Ay," said Hoseason. "And if I give you over to King George's soldiers?"

"You would make a fool's bargain," said the gentleman. "Bring this money within reach of Government, and how much of it'll come to you?"

"Little enough, to be sure," said Hoseason. "Well, what must be must. Sixty guineas, and done. Here's my hand upon it."

---

*The stranger is referring to the Jacobite rebellion of 1745, led by Charles Stuart, the grandson of James II of England. Charles was also known as Bonnie Prince Charlie and the Young Pretender. (His father was known as the Old Pretender.)

"And here's mine."

And then the captain went out, and left me alone in the round-house with the stranger.

"This bottle of yours is dry," he said to me. "It's hard if I'm to pay sixty guineas and be grudged a drink."

"I'll go and ask for the key," said I.

The fog was as thick as ever. The captain and the two officers were out with their heads together. The first word I heard, as I drew softly near, was Mr. Riach's saying, "Couldn't we lure him out of the round-house?"

"Hut!" said Hoseason. "We can get the man in talk inside, and pin him by the two arms."

At this I was seized with fear and anger at these greedy, bloody men that I sailed with.

"Captain," I called out, "the gentleman is seeking a drink, and the bottle's out. Will you give me the key?"

"Why, here's our chance to get the firearms!" Riach cried. And then to me, "Listen, David," he said, "do you know where the pistols are?"

"Ay, ay," put in Hoseason. "David knows; he's a good lad. You see, David my man, that wild Highlandman is a danger to the ship, besides being an enemy to King George.—The trouble is, that all our firearms, great and little, are in the round-house under this man's nose; likewise the powder. Now if I or one of the officers was to go in and take them, he would fall to thinking. But a lad like you might snap up a horn and a pistol or two without remark. And if you can do it cleverly, I'll bear it in mind when it'll be good for you to have friends; and that's when we come to Carolina.—And see here, David, that man has a beltful of gold, and I give you my word that you shall have your fingers in it."

I told him I would do as he wished; and so he gave me the key of the spirit locker, and I began to go slowly back to the round-house. What was I to do? They were dogs

and thieves; they had stolen me from my own country; and was I to hold a candle to a murder? Upon the other hand, what could a boy and a man do against a whole ship's company?

I came into the round-house and saw the man eating his supper under the lamp. I walked right up to the table and put my hand on his shoulder.

"Do you want to be killed?" said I.

He sprang to his feet.

"O!" cried I, "they're all murderers here; it's a ship full of them. They've murdered a boy already. Now it's you."

"Ay, ay," said he; "but they haven't got me yet.—Will you stand by me?"

"That I will!" said I.

"Why, then," said he, "what's your name?"

"David Balfour," said I.

"My name is Stewart. Alan Breck, they call me."

The round-house was built very strong to support the breaching of the seas. Of its five openings, only the skylight and the two doors were large enough for the passage of a man. One door was already closed, but Alan stopped me from closing the other.

"David, that door, being open, is the best part of my defences. You see, I have but one face; but so long as that door is open and my face to it, the best part of my enemies will be in front of me, where I would wish to find them."

Then he gave me from the rack a sword (of which there were a few besides the firearms); and next he set me down to the table with a powder-horn, a bag of bullets and all the pistols, which he asked me to charge.

"How many are against us?" he asked.

I reckoned them up. "Fifteen," said I.

"Well," said he, "that can't be cured. It is my part to keep this door, where I look for the main battle."

"But then, sir," said I, "there is the door behind you, which they may perhaps break in."

"Ay," said he, "and that is a part of your work. No sooner the pistols charged, than you must climb up into that bed where you're close to the window; and if they lift hand against the door, you're to shoot. But that's not all. There's the skylight. And when your face is at the one, you must listen to hear the bursting of the glass of the other."

Scarce had Alan spoken, when the captain showed his face in the open door.

"Stand!" cried Alan, and pointed his sword at him.

"This is a strange return for hospitality!"

"The sooner the clash begins," said Alan, "the sooner you'll taste this steel."

The captain said nothing to Alan, but he looked over at me. "David," said he, "I'll remember this." The next moment he was gone.

"And now," said Alan, "the battle is coming."

Alan drew a knife, which he held in his left hand in case

they should run in under his sword. I clambered up into the berth with an armful of pistols and set open the window where I was to watch. It was a small part of the deck that I could overlook, but enough for our purpose. The sea had gone down, and the wind was steady and kept the sails quiet; so that there was a great stillness in the ship, in which I heard the sound of muttering voices. A little after, and there came a clash of steel upon the deck, by which I knew they were dealing out the cutlasses and one had fallen; and after that, silence again.

All of a sudden, I heard a rush of feet and a roar, then a shout from Alan and a sound of blows. I looked back over my shoulder, and saw Mr. Shuan in the doorway, crossing blades with Alan.

"Look to your window!" said Alan; and as I turned back I saw him pass his sword through the mate's body.

My head was scarce back at the window, before five men, carrying a spare yard for a battering-ram, ran past me to drive the door in. I had never fired a pistol in my life. But it was now or never; and just as they swang the yard, I cried out: "Take that!" and shot into their midst.

I must have hit one of them, for he sang out and gave back a step, and the rest stopped. Before they had time to recover, I sent another ball over their heads; and at my third shot (which went as wide as the second) the whole party threw down the yard and ran for it.

Then I looked round again into the deck-house. The whole place was full of the smoke of my own firing. But there was Alan, standing as before; only now his sword was running blood to the hilt. Right before him on the floor was Mr. Shuan, on his hands and knees, sinking slowly lower; and just as I looked, some of those from behind caught hold of him by the heels and dragged him out.

I told Alan I had winged one, and thought it was the captain.

"And I've settled two," said he. "No, there's not enough blood let; they'll be back again. To your place, David. Unless we can give them a good distaste of us, there'll be no sleep for either you or me."

I settled back to my berth, recharging the three pistols I had fired, and keeping watch with both eye and ear.

There came single call on the sea-pipe, and that was their signal. A knot of them made one rush of it, cutlass in hand, against the door; and at the same moment, the glass in the skylight was dashed in a thousand pieces, and a

man leaped through and landed on the floor. Before he got to his feet, I had clapped a pistol to his back. He had dropped his cutlass as he jumped, and when he felt the pistol, whipped straight round and laid hold of me, roaring out an oath; and at that I gave a shriek and shot him in the midst of his body. He gave the most horrible, ugly groan and fell to the floor. The foot of a second fellow, whose legs were dangling through the skylight, struck me at the same time upon the head; and at that I snatched another pistol and shot him through the thigh, so that he slipped through and tumbled in a lump on his companion's body. I clapped the muzzle to him and fired.

I heard Alan shout as if for help. He had kept the door for so long; but one of the seamen, while he was engaged with the others, had run in under his guard and caught him about the body. Alan was knifing him with his left hand, but the fellow clung like a leech. Another had broken in and had his cutlass raised. The door was filled with their faces. I thought we were lost, and catching up my cutlass, came at them.

But I had not time to be of help. The wrestler dropped at last; and Alan, leaping back to get his distance, ran upon the others like a bull, roaring as he went. They broke before him like water, turning, and running, and falling one against another in their haste. The sword in his hands flashed like lightning; and at every flash there came the scream of a man hurt. I was still thinking we were lost, when lo! they were all gone.

The round-house was like a shambles; three were dead inside, another lay in agony across the threshold; and there were Alan and I victorious and unhurt.

He came up to me with open arms, and embraced me. "David," said he, "I love you like a brother. And O, man," he cried happily, "am I not a wonderful fighter?"

Then he turned to the four enemies, passed his sword clean through each of them, and tumbled them out of doors one after the other. As he did so, he kept humming and singing and whistling to himself, like a man trying to recall a tune; only what *he* was trying was to make one. Soon he sat down upon the table, sword in hand; the tune that he was making all the time began to run a little clearer; and then out he burst with a great voice into a Gaelic song.

In the meanwhile, the battle was no sooner over than I was glad to stagger to a seat. There was a tightness in my chest; the thought of the two men I had shot sat upon me like a nightmare; and all of a sudden, I began to sob and cry like any child.

Alan clapped my shoulder, and said I was a brave lad and needed nothing but a sleep.

"I'll take the first watch," said he. "You've done well by me, David."

So I made up my bed on the floor; and he took the first spell, pistol in hand and sword on knee, three hours by the captain's watch upon the wall. Then he roused me up, and I took my turn of three hours; before the end of which it was broad day, and a very quiet morning. At last, looking out of the door of the round-house, I saw the great stone hills of Skye on the right hand, and, a little more astern, the strange Isle of Rum.

Alan and I sat down to breakfast about six. The floor was covered with broken glass and blood.

"Depend upon it," said Alan, "we shall hear more of them before long."

He took a knife from the table, and cut me off one of the silver buttons from his coat. "I had them," he said, "from my father, Duncan Stewart; and now give you one of them to be a keepsake for last night's work. And wherever you go and show that button, the friends of Alan Breck will come around you."

We were hailed by Mr. Riach from the deck, asking for a talk. I climbed through the skylight and sat on the edge of it, pistol in hand.

"This is a bad job," said he.

"It was none of our choosing," said I.

"The captain would like to speak to your friend.—What we want is to be quits with him."

I consulted with Alan, and a meeting was agreed to.

The captain came and said to Alan, "You've made a sore hash of my brig; I haven't hands enough left to sail her. There is nothing left me, sir, but to put back into the port

of Glasgow after more sailors."

"No," said Alan, "that'll not do. You'll just have to set me ashore as we agreed."

"Ay," said Hoseason, "but my first officer is dead. There's none of the rest of us acquainted with this coast, sir; and it's one very dangerous to ships."

"Set me on dry ground, within thirty miles of my own country; except in the country of the Campbells," said Alan, "and you'll have sixty guineas."

CHAPTER 6
I Hear of the "Red Fox"

BEFORE WE HAD done cleaning out the round-house, a breeze sprang up. This blew off the rain and brought out the sun.

And here I must explain; and the reader would do well to look at a map. On the day when the fog fell and we ran down Alan's boat, we had been running through Little Minch. At dawn after the battle, we lay becalmed to the east of the Isle of Canna. Now to get from there to the Linnhe Loch, the straight course was through the Sound of Mull. But the captain had no chart; he was afraid to sail his brig so deep among the islands; and he preferred to go by west of Tiree and come up under the southern coast of the Isle of Mull.

By nightfall, we had turned the end of Tiree. Meanwhile, the early part of the day was very pleasant; sailing, as we were, in a bright sunshine and with many mountainous islands upon different sides. Alan and I sat in the round-house with the doors open on each side, and smoked a pipe or two of the captain's tobacco. It was at this time we heard each other's stories, and I gained some knowledge of that wild Highland country on which I was so soon to land.

I went first, telling him all my misfortune. But when I came to mention that good friend of mine, Mr. Campbell the minister, Alan cried out that he hated all that were of that name.

"Why," said I, "he is a man you should be proud to give your hand to."

"I know nothing I would help a Campbell to," said he, "unless it was a bullet. If I lay dying, I would crawl upon my knees to the window for a shot at one."

"Why, Alan," I cried, "what do you have against the Campbells?"

"Well," said he, "you know that I am an Appin Stewart, and the Campbells have long bothered and destroyed those of my name; ay, and stolen lands from us by treachery—but never with the sword! They used lying words, lying papers, and the show of it being legal, to make a man the more angry."

"You that are so wasteful of your buttons," said I, "I can hardly think you would be a good judge of business."

"Ah!" said he, smiling, "I got my wastefulness from the same man I got the buttons from; and that was my poor father, Duncan Stewart! He was the prettiest man of his kindred; and the best swordsman in the Highlands, David, and that is the same as to say, in all the world."

"I think he was not the man to leave you rich."

"And that's true," said Alan. "He left me my trousers to cover me, and little else besides. And that was how I came to enlist, which would be a hard lot for me if I fell among the red-coats."

"What," cried I, "were you in the English army?"

"That was I," said Alan. "But I deserted to the right side—and that's some comfort."

"Dear, dear. The punishment for desertion is death."

"Ay," said he, "if they got their hands on me."

I asked him, "You are a man of the French king's—what

tempts you back into this country?"

"Tut!" said Alan. "I have been back every year since forty-six!"

"And what brings you, man?"

"Well, you see, I weary for my friends and country," said he. "France is a fine place, no doubt; but I weary for the heather and the deer. But the heart of the matter is the business of my chief, Ardshiel, captain of the clan. Now the tenants of Appin have to pay a rent to King George; but their hearts are loyal, and what with love and a bit of pressure, and maybe a threat or two, the poor folk scrape up a second rent for Ardshiel. Well, David, I'm the hand that carries it back to France for him." And he struck the belt around his body, so that the guineas rang.

"I call it noble of those folk," I cried. "I'm loyal to King George, but I call it noble."

"Ay," said he, "you're a Whig, but you're a gentleman. Now if you were one of the cursed Campbells, or if you were the Red Fox . . . "

"And who is the Red Fox?"

"When the men of the clans were defeated at Culloden, and the good cause lost, Ardshiel had to flee like a poor deer upon the mountains—he and his lady and his children. A sad time of it we had before we got him shipped; and while he still lay in the heather, the English rogues, that could not kill him, were striking at his rights. They stripped him of his powers; they stripped him of his lands; they plucked the weapons from the hands of his clansmen; ay, and the very clothes off their backs—so that it's now a sin to wear a tartan plaid, and a man may be cast into prison if he has a kilt about his legs. One thing they couldn't kill. That was the love the clansmen had for their chief. These guineas are the proof of it. And now, in there steps a man, a Campbell, red-headed Colin of Glenure! In he steps, and gets papers from King George, to be King's agent on the lands of Appin. By-and-by, it came to his ears how the poor folk of Appin were wringing their very plaids to get a second rent, and send it over-seas for Ardshiel and his poor children. Well, the black Campbell blood in him ran wild. What! should a Stewart get a bite of bread, and him not be able to prevent it? No. Ardshiel was to starve: that was the thing he aimed at. And he would drive them that fed him out. Therefore he sent for lawyers, and papers, and red-coats to stand at his back. And the kindly folk of that country must all pack and tramp, every father's son out of his father's house, and out of the place where he was bred and fed!"

There was so much anger in Alan's voice that I thought it wise to change the conversation. I expressed my wonder how, with the Highlands covered with troops, a man in Alan's situation could come and go without arrest.

"It's easier than ye would think," he said. "A hillside is like one road; if there's a sentry at one place, ye just go by another. And then the heather's a great help. And everywhere there are friends' houses and friends' barns and haystacks. And besides, when folk talk of a country covered with troops, it's not truly so. A soldier covers no more of it than his boot-soles. I have fished a water with a sentry on the other side of the brook, and killed a fine trout; and I have sat in a heather bush within six feet of another, and learned a real bonny tune from his whistling. This was it," said he, and whistled me the air.

"And then, besides," he continued, "it's not so bad now as it was in forty-six. The Highlands are what they call pacified. But not for long, with men like Ardshiel in exile and men like the Red Fox harassing the poor at home. But it's not easy to know what folk'll bear, and what they will not. Or why would Red Colin be riding his horse all over my poor country of Appin, and never a fine lad to put a bullet in him?"

And with this Alan fell into a long silent thought.

It was already late at night, when Hoseason clapped his hand into the round-house door.

"Here," said he, "come out and see if you can pilot.—My brig's in danger!"

Alan and I stepped on deck.

The sky was clear; it blew hard, and was bitter cold; the moon shone brightly. Away on the lee bow, a thing like a fountain rose out of the moonlit sea, and immediately after we heard a low sound of roaring.

"What do you call that?" asked the captain.

"The sea breaking on a reef," said Alan.

"If it was only one," said Hoseason.

And sure enough, just as he spoke there came a second fountain farther to the south.

"There!" said Hoseason. "You see for yourself. If I had known of these reefs, or if Shuan had lived, it's not sixty guineas, no, nor six hundred, would have made me risk my brig in such a stoneyard!"

"It sticks in my mind there are ten miles of the Torran Rocks," said Alan.

"There's a way through them, I suppose?" said the captain.

"Doubtless," said Alan. "It somehow runs in my mind that it is a clearer near the land."

"Well," said the captain, "we're in for it now, and may as well crack on."

With that he gave an order to the steersman, and sent Riach to the foretop. There were only five men on deck, counting the officers.

"The sea to the south is thick," Riach cried; and then, after a while, "it does seem clearer in by the land."

"Well, sir," said Hoseason to Alan, "we'll try your way of

it. Pray God you're right."

As we got nearer to the turn of the land at the end of the Isle of Mull, the reefs began to appear here and there on our very path; and Mr. Riach sometimes cried down to us to change the course. Sometimes, indeed, none too soon; for one reef was so close that when a sea burst upon it the spray fell upon the deck and wetted us like rain.

"Goodness, David," said Alan, "this is not the kind of death I fancy!"

"What, Alan!" I cried, "you're not afraid?"

"No," said he, wetting his lips, "but you'll allow it's a cold ending."

By this time, now and then sheering to one side or the other to avoid a reef, but still hugging the wind and the land, we got round Iona and began to come alongside Mull. The tide at the tail of the land ran very strong, and threw the brig about.

"Keep her away a point," sang out Mr. Riach. "Reef to windward!"

And just at that time the tide caught the brig, and threw the wind out of her sails. She came round into the wind like a top, and the next moment struck the reef with such a crash as threw us all flat upon the deck, and came near to shake Mr. Riach from his place upon the mast.

I was on my feet in a minute. The reef on which we had struck was close in under the southwest end of Mull, off a little isle they call Earraid, which lay low and black upon the larboard. Sometimes a swell broke clean over us; sometimes it only ground the poor brig upon the reef, so that we could hear her beat herself to pieces; and as well there was the great noise of the sails, and the singing of the wind, and the flying of the spray in the moonlight, and the sense of danger.

I observed Mr. Riach and the seamen busy round the skiff, and ran over to assist them. All the time of our work-

ing to clear the boat, I asked Alan, looking across at the shore, what country it was; and he answered, it was the worst possible for him, for it was a land of the Campbells.

Well, we had the boat about ready to be launched, when one of the wounded men, keeping a watch on the seas, cried out, "For God's sake, hold on!"

There followed a sea so huge that it lifted the brig right up and turned her over on her beam. At the sudden tilting of the ship I was cast clean over the side into the sea.

I went down and drank my fill, and then came up, and got a blink of the moon, and then down again. I was being hurled along, and beaten upon and choked, and then swallowed whole. Soon I found I was holding to a spar, which helped me somewhat. And then all of a sudden I was in quiet water, and began to come to myself.

It was the spare yard I had got hold of, and I was amazed to see how far I had travelled from the brig. I hailed her, indeed; but it was plain she was already out of cry. She was still holding together; but whether or not they had yet launched the boat, I was too far off and too low down to see.

I now lay quite becalmed, and began to feel that a man can die of cold as well as of drowning. The shores of Earraid were close in. I had no skill in swimming, but when I laid hold upon the yard with both arms, and kicked out with both feet, I soon began to find that I was moving. After an hour of kicking and splashing, I had got well into a sandy bay surrounded by low hills. I thought in my heart I had never seen a place so deserted and desolate. But it was dry land.

CHAPTER 7
The Islet

WITH MY STEPPING ashore I began the most unhappy part of my adventures. I climbed a hill, and when I got to the top the dawn was come. There was no sign of the brig, which must have lifted from the reef and sunk. The boat, too, was nowhere to be seen.

I was afraid to think what had befallen my shipmates. I set off eastward, along the south coast, hoping to find a house where I might warm myself, and perhaps get news of those I had lost. After a little while my way was stopped by a creek or inlet of the sea, which seemed to run pretty deep into the land; and as I had no means to get across, I must needs change my direction to go about the end of it. It was the roughest kind of walking, nothing but a jumble of granite rocks with heather in among. At last I came to a rise, and it burst upon me that I was cast upon a little barren isle, and cut off on every side by the salt seas.

Instead of the sun rising to dry me, it came on to rain. It occurred to me that perhaps the creek was fordable. But not three yards from shore, I plumped in head over ears.

The time I spent upon the island, which I later learned was Earraid, is still so horrible a thought to me, that I must pass it lightly over. In all the books I have read of people cast away, they had either their pockets full of tools, or a chest of things would be thrown upon the beach along with them. My case was very different. I had nothing in my pockets but money and Alan's silver button.

The second day I crossed the island to all sides. There was no one part of it better than another; it was all desolate and rocky; nothing living on it but birds which I lacked the means to kill.

Now, from a little up a hillside over a bay, I could catch a sight of a great, ancient church and the roofs of the people's houses in Iona. Over the low country of the Ross, I saw smoke go up, morning and evening. This sight I had of men's homes and comfortable lives kept hope alive, and helped me eat my raw shell-fish.

The second day passed, but on the third in the morning I saw a red-deer standing in the rain on the top of the island. I supposed he must have swum the strait; though what should bring any creature to Earraid, was more than I could fancy. My clothes were beginning to rot; my stockings in particular were quite worn through. And yet the worst was not yet come.

All of a sudden, a fishing boat with a brown sail and a pair of fishermen aboard of it, came flying round a corner of the isle, bound for Iona. I shouted out, and then fell on my knees on the rock and reached up my hands and prayed to them. They were near enough to hear—I could even see the color of their hair; they cried out in Gaelic, and laughed. But the boat never turned aside, and flew on, right before my eyes, for Iona.

I ran along the shore from rock to rock, crying after them.

The next day I found my strength very low. But the sun shone, the air was sweet, and what I managed to eat of the shell-fish agreed well with me and revived my courage.

I was scarce back on the highest rock on Earraid (where I went always the first thing after I had eaten) before I observed a boat. I began at once to hope and fear. She was coming straight to Earraid!

I ran to the seaside and out, from one rock to another, as far as I could go. It was the same boat and the same two men as yesterday, but now there was a third man along with them.

As soon as they were come within easy speech, they let down their sail and lay quiet. The new man tee-hee'd with laughter as he talked and looked at me.

Then he stood up in the boat and addressed me a long while, speaking fast and with many wavings of his hand. I picked out a word, "tide." Then I had a flash of hope. I remembered he was always waving his hand towards the mainland of the Ross.

"Do you mean when the tide is out—?" I cried.

"Yes, yes," said he. "Tide."

At that I turned tail, leaped back the way I had come, from one stone to another, and set off running across the isle. In about half an hour I came out upon the shores of the creek; and, sure enough, it was shrunk into a little trickle of water, through which I dashed, not above my knees, and landed with a shout on the main island.

A sea-bred boy would not have stayed a day on Earraid; which is only what they call a tidal islet, and can be entered and left twice in every twenty-four hours. I had starved with cold and hunger on that island for close upon one hundred hours. But for the fishermen, I might have left my bones there.

The Ross of Mull, which I had now got upon, was rugged and trackless, like the isle I had just left. I aimed as well as I could for the smoke I had seen so often from the island, and came upon a house in the bottom of a little hollow about five or six at night. In front of it, an old gentleman sat smoking his pipe in the sun.

With what little English he had, he gave me to understand that my shipmates had got safe ashore, and had eaten in that very house on the day after. He said that I must be the lad with the silver button.

"Why, yes!"

"Well, then," said the old gentleman, "I have a word for you, that you are to follow your friend to his country, by Torosay." He and his good wife fed me, and let me sleep till the next day.

I set out and wandered, meeting plenty of people and, along the roads, many beggars. At night I paid for lodgings in lonely houses.

On my fourth day of travel, I overtook a great, ragged man, moving pretty fast but feeling before him with a staff. He was quite blind, and as we began to go along together, I saw the steel butt of a pistol sticking from under the flap of his coat-pocket. I could not see what a blind man could be doing with a pistol.

He told me he would guide me to Torosay for a drink of brandy.

I said I did not see how a blind man could be a guide; but at that he laughed aloud, and said his stick was eyes enough for an eagle.

"In the Isle of Mull, at least," said he, "where I know every stone and heather-bush. See, now," he said, striking right and left, "down there a creek is running; and at the head of it there stands a bit of a small hill with a stone cocked upon the top of that; and it's hard at the foot of the hill, that the way runs by to Torosay; and the way here is plainly trodden, and will show grassy through the heather."

I had to own he was right in every feature, and told my wonder.

He then began to question me, where I came from, whether I was rich, whether I could change a five-shilling piece for him, and all the time he kept edging up to me and I avoiding him. We were now upon a sort of green cattle-track which crossed the hills towards Torosay, and we kept changing sides upon that like dancers. I took a pleasure in this game of blindman's bluff; but he grew angrier and angrier, and at last began to swear in Gaelic and to strike for my legs with his staff.

Then I told him that, sure enough, I had a pistol in my pocket as well as he, and if he did not strike across the hill due south I would even blow his brains out.

He became at once very polite, and after trying to soften me for some time, but quite in vain, he cursed me once more and took himself off.

At Torosay, on the Sound of Mull and looking over to the mainland of Morven, there was an inn, where I stayed the night, having travelled the greater part of that big and crooked Island of Mull, from Earraid to Torosay, fifty miles as the crow flies, and (with my wanderings) much nearer a hundred, in four days.

CHAPTER 8
The Death of the Red Fox

THERE IS A regular ferry from Torosay to Kinlochaline on the mainland. The passage was a very slow affair. The skipper of the boat was Neil Roy Macrob; and since Macrob was one of the names of Alan's clansmen, and Alan himself had sent me to that ferry, I was eager to speak with him. At Kinlochaline, I did so.

He gave me my route. This was to lie the night in Kinlochaline in the public inn; to cross Morven the next day to Ardgour, and lie the night in the house of one John of the Claymore, who was warned that I might come; the third day, to be set across one loch at Corran and another at Balachulish, and then ask my way to the house of James of the Glens, at Aucharn in Duror of Appin. There was a good deal of ferrying, as you hear; the sea in all this part running deep into the mountains and winding about their roots. It makes the country strong to hold and difficult to travel, but full of startling sights.

I had some other advice from Neil: to speak with no one by the way, to avoid Whigs, Campbells, and the red-soldiers; to leave the road and lie in the bush if I saw any of the latter coming, "for it was never good to meet them"; and in brief, to conduct myself like a robber or a French spy, as perhaps Neil thought me.

On the last leg of that journey, into Appin, I set out with a fisherman across the Linnhe Loch. The mountains on either side were high, rough and barren. It seemed a hard country for people to care as much about as Alan did.

I was let off near the wood of birches, growing on a steep, craggy side of a mountain that overhung the loch. I sat down to eat some oat-bread and think about my situation. What I ought to do, why I was going to join myself with an outlaw like Alan, whether I should not be acting more like a man of sense to tramp back to the south country direct; these were the doubts that now began to come in on me.

As I was so sitting and thinking, a sound of men and horses came to me through the wood; and soon after, at a turning in the road, I saw four travellers come into view. The first was a great, red-headed gentleman, who carried his hat in his hand and fanned himself. The second, by his black garb and white wig, I took to be a lawyer. The third was a servant. The fourth, who brought up the tail, I had seen his like before and knew him to be a sheriff's officer. When the first came alongside of me, I rose up and asked him the way to Aucharn.

"And what do you seek in Aucharn?" said Colin Roy Campbell of Glenure, him they called the Red Fox; for he it was that I had stopped.

"The man that lives there," said I.

"Why does this honest man so far from his country come seeking the brother of Ardshiel?" As he said this he turned to look at the lawyer.

But just as he turned there came the shot of a firelock from higher up the hill; and with the very sound of it the Red Fox fell upon the road.

"O, I am dead!" he cried. With that he gave a great sigh, and passed away.

I stood staring in a kind of horror. The sheriff's officer had run back at the first sound of the shot, to hasten the coming of the soldiers. To help them I began to scramble away up the hill, crying out, "The murderer! the murderer!"

When I got to the top of the first steepness, and could

see some part of the open mountain, the murderer was moving away at no great distance. He was a big man, in a black coat, with metal buttons, and carried a long gun.

"Here!" I cried. "I see him!"

At that the murderer gave a little, quick look over his shoulder, and began to run. The next moment he was lost in a fringe of birches; then he came out again on the upper side, where I could see him climbing like a monkey, and then I saw him no more.

All this time I had been running, and had got a good way up, when a voice cried upon me to stop. I was at the edge of the upper wood, and so now when I halted and looked back, I saw all the open part of the hill below me.

The lawyer and the sheriff's officer were standing just

above the road, crying and waving to me to come back; and on their left, the red-coats, muskets in hand, were beginning to struggle out of the lower wood.

"Why should I come back?" I cried. "Come on!"

"Ten pounds if you take that lad!" cried the lawyer. "He's an accomplice. He was posted here to hold us in talk."

At that word (which I could hear quite plainly, though it was to the soldiers and not to me that he was crying it) my heart came in my mouth with a new kind of terror.

The soldiers began to spread, some of them to run.

"Duck in here among the trees," said a voice close by.

I obeyed; and as I did so, I heard the firelocks bang and the balls whistle in the birches.

Just inside the shelter of the trees I found Alan Breck standing, with a fishing-rod. He said, "Come!" and set off running along the side of the mountain towards Balachulish.

Now we ran among the birches; now stooping behind low humps upon the mountainside; now crawling on all fours among the heather. I had neither time to think nor speak. Every now and then Alan would straighten himself to his full height and look back; and every time he did so, there came a far-away cheering and crying of the soldiers.

At last we came to the upper wood of Lettermore, where we lay down panting like dogs.

"Well," he said finally, "that was a hot one, David."

I said nothing. I had seen murder done, and a great red-faced, jovial gentleman struck out of life in a moment. Here was murder done upon the man Alan hated; here was Alan hiding in the trees and running from the troops; and whether his was the hand that fired or only the head that ordered, meant little. My only friend in that wild country was guilty in the first degree; I could not look upon his face; I would have rather been alone in the rain on my cold isle, than in the warm wood beside a murderer.

"Are you still tired?" he asked.

"No," I said. "But you and I must part. I liked you very well, Alan, but your ways are not mine, and not God's."

"I will hardly part from you, David, without some kind of reason," said Alan.

"You know very well that the Red Fox lies in his blood upon the road. Do you mean to say you had no hand in it?"

"I will tell you, Davie, as one friend to another, if I were going to kill a gentleman, it would not be in my own country, to bring trouble to my clan; and I would not go without out a sword and gun, with a fishing-rod upon my back."

"Well," said I, "that's true."

"I swear I had no part in it."

"I thank God for that!" cried I, and offered him my hand.

He did not appear to see it. "But what a fuss you make about a Campbell," said he. "There are such a lot of them."

"But do you know who did it?" I asked. "Do you know that man in the black coat?"

"I have no clear mind about his coat," said Alan; "but it sticks in my head that it was blue."

"Blue or black, did ye know him?" said I.

"I couldn't swear to him," said Alan. "He went very close by me, to be sure, but it's a strange thing that I should just have been tying my shoes."

"Can you swear that you don't know him, Alan?"

"Not yet," said he; "but I've a grand memory for forgetting."

"Yet you exposed yourself and me to draw the soldiers away from him," I said.

"So would any gentleman," said Alan. "You and me were innocent of that event."

"The better reason, since we were falsely suspected, that we should get clear," I cried. "The innocent should surely come before the guilty."

"Why, David," said he, "the innocent have a chance in

court; but for the lad that shot the bullet, I think the best place for him will be the heather."

He then said we had not much time, but must both flee that country; he, because he was a wanted man, and the whole of Appin would now be searched, and I, because they would think I was certainly involved in the murder.

I asked him where we should flee; and as he told me "to the Lowlands," I was a little better inclined to go with him; for, indeed, I was growing impatient to get back and have the upper-hand of my uncle.

"I'll chance it, Alan," said I. "I'll go with you."

"But mind you," he said, "it's no small thing. Your life shall be like the hunted deer's, and you shall sleep with your hand upon your weapons. But if you ask what other chance you have, I answer: None. Either take to the heather with me, or else hang by their justice."

"And that's a choice very easily made," said I; and we shook hands upon it.

On the way to Aucharn, each of us narrated his adventures; and I shall here set down so much of Alan's as seems either curious or needful.

It appears he ran to the side of the ship as soon as the wave was passed; saw me, and lost me, and saw me again, as I tumbled in the roost; and at last had one glimpse of me clinging on the yard. It was this that put him in some hope I would maybe get to land after all, and made him leave those clues and messages which had brought me to that unlucky country of Appin.

In the meanwhile, those still on the brig had got the skiff launched, and one or two were on board of her already, when there came a second wave greater than the first, and heaved the brig out of her place, catching it on the reef. Water began to pour into her. All who were on deck tumbled one after another into the skiff and fell to their oars. They were not two hundred yards away, when there came a third great sea; and at that the brig lifted clean over the reef; her canvas filled for a moment, and she seemed to sail in chase of them, but settling all the while; and soon she drew down and down, as if a hand was drawing her; and the sea closed over the *Covenant.*

They had scarce set foot upon the beach when Hoseason told his men to lay hands upon Alan, saying that he had a lot of gold, that he had been the cause of losing the brig and drowning all their comrades. It was seven against one; and in that part of the shore there was no rock that Alan could set his back to; and the sailors began to spread out and come behind him.

"And then," said Alan, "Riach took up my defense, and argued against their attack. Then he cried to me to run, and indeed I thought it good advice, and ran. The last I saw they were all in a knot upon the beach, and the fists were going. So I set my best foot forward and got through the strip of Campbells in that end of Mull."

CHAPTER 9
The Flight in the Heather

NIGHT FELL as we were walking, and the clouds thickened, so that it felt extremely dark. The way we went was over rough mountainsides. At last, we came to the top of the valley, and saw lights below us. Alan whistled three times; having thus set the folks' minds at rest, we came down the valley, and were met at the yard gate by a tall man of more than fifty, who cried out to Alan:

"There has been a dreadful accident. It will bring trouble on the country."

"Hoots!" said Alan, "ye must take the sour with the sweet, James. Colin Roy is dead, and be thankful for that!"

"Ay," said James, "but now that it's done, Alan, who's to

bear the blame of it? The accident fell out in Appin—it's Appin must pay; and I am a man that has a family."

While he and Alan conversed, I looked about me at the servants. Some were on ladders, digging in the thatch of the house or the farm buildings, from which they brought out guns, swords, and different weapons of war; others carried them away; and by the sound of it farther down the valley, they were burying them.

"We're just setting the house in order, Alan," explained James. "They'll search Appin, and we must dig the guns and swords into the moss, ye see. And these French clothes you're wearing, we'll bury them, too."

"No, you won't!" cried Alan. He went off into the barn, and James took me into the house, and one of his sons gave me a change of clothing of which I had stood so long in need, and a pair of Highland shoes made of deer-leather, rather strange at first, but after a little practice very easy to the feet.

After Alan had told his story, it was understood that I was to escape with him, and they were all busy with our equipment. They gave us each a sword and pistols; and with these, some powder and bullets, a bag of oatmeal, an iron pan, and a bottle of brandy. Money, indeed, was lacking. I had about two guineas left, the rest having been lost in the sea off the islet; Alan's belt having been lost as well.

"This'll not do," said Alan.

"Ye must find a safe bit somewhere near by," said James, "and get word to me."

"Hoot, hoot," said Alan. "Tomorrow there'll be a fine to-do in Appin, a fine riding of soldier red-coats; and it would be well, Davie, for you and me to be gone."

We said farewell to James's family, and set out again, in a fine, mild night, and over much the same broken country as before.

Sometimes we walked, sometimes we ran; and as it drew

on to morning, walked ever the less and ran the more. Though that country appeared to be deserted, there were huts and houses of people, of which we must have passed more than twenty, hidden in quiet places of the hills. When we came to one of these, Alan would leave me, and go himself and rap upon the side of the house and speak a while at the window, passing the news of the murder.

For all our hurry, day began to come in while we were still far from any shelter. We were in a large valley, full of rocks and where ran a foaming river. Wild mountains stood around it; there grew neither grass nor trees.

"This is no place for you and me," said Alan. "This is a place they're bound to watch."

And with that he ran down to the waterside, in a part where the river was split in two among three rocks. Alan jumped clean upon the middle rock and fell there on his

hands and knees to check himself, for that rock was small and he might have pitched over on the far side. I had scarce time to measure the distance before I followed him, and he had caught and stopped me.

So there we stood, side by side upon a small rock slippery with spray, a far broader leap in front of us, and the river crashing upon all sides. When I saw where I was, I put my hand over my eyes. Alan took me and shook me; I saw he was speaking, but the roaring of the falls prevented me from hearing. Then, putting his hands to his mouth, and his mouth to my ear, he shouted, "Hang or drown!" and turning his back upon me, leaped over the farther branch of the stream, and landed safe.

I was now alone upon the rock, which gave me the more room. I bent low on my knees and flung myself forth. Sure enough, it was but my hands that reached the full length; these slipped, and I was sliddering back into the river, when Alan seized me, first by the hair, then by the collar, and with a great strain dragged me into safety.

Never a word he said, but set off running again for his life, and I must stagger to my feet and run after him. I kept stumbling as I ran; and when at last Alan paused under a great rock that stood there among a number of others, it was none too soon.

By rights it was two rocks leaning together at the top, both twenty feet high. Even Alan failed twice in an attempt to climb them; and it was only at the third trial, and then by standing on my shoulders and leaping up with such force as I thought must have broken my collar bone, that he secured a place. Once there, he let down his leather belt; and with that and the shallow footholds in the rock, I scrambled up beside him.

Then I saw why we had come there; for the two rocks, being both somewhat hollow on the top and sloping one to the other, made a kind of dish or saucer, where as many as three or four men might have lain hidden. The dawn had come clear; we could see the stony sides of the valley.

"Go you to your sleep, lad, and I'll watch," said Alan.

I lay down to sleep; the last thing I heard was the crying of eagles.

I was roughly awakened, and found Alan's hand pressed upon my mouth.

"Wheesht!" he whispered. "Ye were snoring." He peered over the edge of the rock, and signed to me to do the like.

It was now high day, cloudless, and very hot. About half a mile up the water was a camp of red-coats; a big fire blazed in their midst, at which some were cooking; and near by, on the top of a rock about as high as ours, there stood a sentry, with the sun sparkling on his arms. All the way down along the riverside were posted other sentries; but as the stream suddenly swelled by the water from a large brook, they were more widely set.

I took but one look at them, and ducked again.

"Ye, see," said Alan, "this was what I was afraid of, Davie: that they would watch the valley. They began to come in about two hours ago, and, man! but ye're a grand hand at sleeping! We're in a tight spot. If they get up the sides of the hill, they could easy spy us with a glass. Come night we'll try at getting by the posts down the water."

"And what are we to do till night?" I asked.

"Lie here," said he, "and toast."

The rock grew so heated, a man could scarce endure the touch of it; and the little patch between the two rocks of earth and fern, which kept cooler, was only large enough for one at a time. We took turn about to lie on the naked rock. All the while we had no water, only raw brandy, which was worse than nothing.

The boredom and pain of these hours upon the rock grew only the greater as day went on; the rock getting still the hotter and the sun fiercer.

At last, about two, there came a patch of shade on the east side of our rock, which was the side sheltered from the soldiers.

"As well one death as another," said Alan, and slipped over the edge and dropped on the ground on the shadowy side.

I followed him at once. Here, then, we lay for an hour or two, aching from head to foot, as weak as water, lying quite exposed to any soldier who should have strolled that way. None came, however, all passing by on the other side; so that our rock continued to be our shield.

Soon we began to get a little strength; and as the soldiers were now lying closer along the riverside, Alan proposed that we should try a start. We began to slip from rock to rock, one after the other, now crawling flat on our bellies in the shade, now making a run for it.

By sundown we had made some distance, even by our slow rate of progress, though the sentry on the rock was still plainly in our view. But now we came on a deep, rushing brook. We cast ourselves on the ground and plunged head and shoulders in the water.

We lay there (the banks hid us), drank again and again, and at last, being wonderfully renewed, we got out the meal-bag and made drammach in the iron pan. This, though it is but cold water mingled with oatmeal, yet makes a good enough dish for a hungry man.

As soon as the shadow of the night had fallen, we set forth again. The way was very tricky, lying up the steep sides of mountains and along the brows of cliffs.

Finally Alan judged us out of ear-shot of all our enemies; throughout the rest of our night-march he whistled many tunes on the great, dark, deserted mountain.

It was still dark when we reached our destination, a cleft in the head of the great mountain, with a stream running through the midst, and upon the one hand a shallow cave in a rock. The stream was full of trout; the wood of doves. From the mouth of the cleft we looked down upon a part of Mamore, and on the sea-loch that divides that country from Appin. The name of the cleft was the Heugh of Corrynakiegh; and although it was often covered with clouds, yet it was on the whole a pleasant place, and the five days we lived in it went happily.

We slept in the cave, making our bed of heather bushes, and covering ourselves with Alan's overcoat. There was a low concealed place, in the turning of the glen, where we were so bold as to make fire: so that we could warm ourselves when the clouds set in, and cook hot porridge, and grill the little trouts that we caught with our hands.

In the meanwhile, you are not to suppose that we forgot our chief business, which was to get away.

"It will be many a long day," Alan said to me on our first morning, "before the red-coats think upon seeking us here; so now we must get word sent to James, and he must find the silver for us."

"And how shall we send that word?" said I. "We are here in a deserted place, which we dare not leave."

"Ay?" said Alan. "Ye're a man of small imaginings, David."

Getting a piece of wood, he made it in a cross, the four ends of which he blackened on the coals. Then he asked, "Could ye lend me my button?"

I gave him the button; he strung it on a strip of his

overcoat which he had used to bind the cross; and tying in a little sprig of birch and another of fir, he said, "Now, there is a little hamlet not very far from Corrynakiegh. Many friends of mine are living there whom I could trust with my life, and some that I am not just so sure of. Ye see, David, there will be money upon our heads. So, I would rather they didn't see me. When it comes dark again, I will steal down into that hamlet, and set this that I have been making in the window of a good friend, John Breck Maccoll."

"If he finds it, what is he to think?"

"I am afraid he will think little enough of it! But this is what I have in mind. This cross is something like a fiery cross, which is the signal of gathering in our clans. Yet he will know the clan is not to rise, for there it is standing in his window, and he'd heard no word with it. Then he will see my button, and that was Duncan Stewart's. And then he will say to himself, 'The son of Duncan is in the heather, and has need of me.' "

"Well," said I, "it may be. But even supposing so, there is a good deal of heather between here and the Forth."

"But then John will see the sprig of birch and the sprig of pine; and he will say to himself, 'Alan will be lying in a wood which is both of pines and birches'; and then he will come and give us a look up in Corrynakiegh. And if he does not, the devil may take him, for what I care."

"But would it not be simpler," I asked, "to write him a few words in black and white?"

"It would certainly be much simpler for me to write to him, but it would be a sore job for John to read it. He would have to go to school for two-three years; and it's possible we might be wearied waiting for him."

So that night Alan carried down his fiery cross and set it in John's window.

About noon the next day we spied a man straggling up the open side of the mountain in the sun, and looking

round him as he came. No sooner had Alan seen him than he whistled; the man turned and came a little towards us: then Alan would give another "peep!" and the man would come still nearer.

He was a ragged, bearded man about forty, and looked both simple-minded and savage. Alan wanted him to carry a spoken message to James; but John said, "I would forget it."

We lacked the means of writing, but Alan was a man of resources; he searched the wood until he found the quill of a dove, which he shaped into a pen; made himself a kind of ink with gunpowder and water; and tearing a corner from his French military commission, he sat down and wrote:

> DEAR KINSMAN,—Please send the money by the bearer
> to the place he knows of.
>
> Your affectionate cousin,
>
> A. S.

John was three full days gone, but about five in the evening of the third, we heard a whistling in the wood, which Alan answered; and soon the man came up the waterside, looking for us.

He gave us the news of the country: that it was alive with red-coats; that weapons were being found, and poor folk brought in trouble daily; and that James and some of his servants were already in prison. It seemed it was said on all sides that Alan Breck had fired the shot; and there was a bill issued for both him and me, with one hundred pounds reward.

The little note John' had carried us from Mrs. Stewart asked Alan not to let himself be captured, assuring him, if he fell in the hands of the troops, both he and James were dead men. The money she had sent was all that she could beg or borrow. It was less than five guineas, more than I had, but he had to get as far as France, and I only to Queensferry.

"It's little enough," said Alan, putting the purse in his pocket, "but it'll do. And now, John Breck, if ye will hand me over my button, this gentleman and me will be for taking the road."

Doing so, John took himself off by one way; and Alan and I (getting our goods together) struck into another to resume our escape.

After a night of hard travelling, we lay down in a thick bush of heather to sleep. Alan took the first watch; and it seemed to me I had scarce closed my eyes before I was shaken up to take the second. We had no clock to go by; and Alan stuck a sprig of heath in the ground to serve instead; so that as soon as the shadow of the bush should fall so far to the east, I might know to rouse him. But I was by this time so weary that I could have slept twelve hours; my joints slept even when my mind was waking; the hot smell of the heather, and the drone of the wild bees, were

like a cup of warm milk to me; and every now and again I
would give a jump and find I had been dozing.

The last time I woke I seemed to have come back from
farther away, and thought the sun had taken a great start
in the heavens. I looked at the sprig of heath, and at that I
could have cried aloud: for I saw I had betrayed my trust.
My head was nearly turned with fear and shame; and at
what I saw, when I looked out around me on the moor, my
heart sank. For sure enough, horse-soldiers had come down
during my sleep, and were drawing near to us, fanned out
and riding their horses to and fro in the deep parts of the
heather.

When I waked Alan, he glanced first at the soldiers,
then at the mark and the position of the sun, and knitted
his brows with a sudden, quick look.

"What are we to do now?" I asked.

"We'll have to play at being hares," said he. "Do you see
that mountain?" pointing to one.

"Ay," said I.

"Well, then," said he, "let us strike for that."

"But, Alan, that will take us across the very coming of
the soldiers."

"I know that," said he; "but if we are driven back on
Appin, we are two dead men. So now, David man, be brisk!"

With that he began to run forward on his hands and
knees with an incredible quickness. All the time he kept
winding in and out in the lower parts of the moorland
where we were best concealed.

I had awakened just in time.

At length, in the first gloaming of the night, we heard a
trumpet sound, and looking back from among the heather,
saw the troop beginning to collect. A little after, they had
built a fire and camped for the night.

At this I begged that we might lie down and sleep.

"There shall be no sleep tonight," said Alan. "We got

through in the nick of time, and shall we hazard what we've gained? No, no, when the day comes, it shall find you and me in a safe place on the mountain."

"Lead away," said I. "I'll follow."

By daylight, we were able to walk upon our feet like men, instead of crawling like brutes. However, he must have been as stupid with weariness as myself, or we should not have walked into an ambush like blind men. It fell in this way. We were going down a heathery valley, when upon a sudden three or four ragged men leaped out, and the next moment we were lying on our backs, each with a knife at his throat.

I then heard Alan and another whispering in Gaelic; and the knives were put away.

"They are Cluny's men," said Alan. "We couldn't have fallen better."

Now Cluny Macpherson, the chief of the Vourich clan, had been one of the leaders of the great rebellion six years before; there was a price on his life; and I had supposed him long ago in France.

"What," I cried, "is Cluny still here?"

"Ay, is he so!" said Alan. "Still in his own country, and kept by his own clan. King George can do no more."

I was so tired I had to be carried by Cluny's men into the glens and hollows and into the heart of that dismal mountain hideout.

Alan and I remained a few days, gaining our strength, before going on. Cluny's men put us across the Loch Errocht under cloud of night, and we went down its eastern shore to another hiding-place near the head of Loch Rannoch. From there we got us up into the tops of the mountains, and for the best part of three nights headed for the lowlands by Kippen. There were troops in every district, and this route led us through the country of Alan's blood-foes, the Glenorchy Campbells.

By day we lay and slept in the drenching heather; by night, we clambered upon break-neck hills. We often wandered; we were often so involved in fog, that we must lie quiet till it lightened. A fire was never to be thought of. Our only food was drammach and a portion of cold meat we had carried from Cluny's; and as for drink, we had plenty of water.

The third night we were to pass through the western end of the country of Balquhidder. I was dead weary, deadly sick and full of pains and shiverings; the chill of the wind went through me. At last I put my pride away from me, and declared, "Alan, if you cannot help me, I must just die here." I spoke in a weeping voice that would have melted a heart of stone.

"Can you walk?" asked Alan.

"No," said I, "not without help. This last hour my legs have been fainting under me; I've a stitch in my side like a red-hot iron; I can't breathe right."

"Let me get my arm around you," he said; "that's the way. Now lean upon me. God knows where there's a house! We're in Balquhidder. We'll follow down the creek, where there's bound to be houses. My poor man!"

At the door of the first house we came to, Alan knocked. Chance served us very well, for it was a household of Maclarens, and the Maclarens followed Alan's chief in war. Alan was not only welcome for his name's sake but known by reputation. Here then I was got to bed without delay, and a doctor fetched, who found me in a very sorry plight. But whether because he was a very good doctor, or I a very young, strong man, I lay bedridden for no more than a week, and before a month I was able to take the road again with a good heart.

It was already far through August, and beautiful warm weather, with every sign of an early and great harvest, when I was pronounced able for my journey. Our money was now run so low that we must think first of all on speed; for if we came not soon to the lawyer Mr. Rankeillor's, or if when we came there he should fail to help me, we must surely starve. In Alan's view, besides, the hunt for us must have now greatly slackened; and the line of the Forth and even Stirling Bridge, which is the main pass over that river, would be watched with little interest.

"It's a chief principle in military affairs," said he, "to go where you are least expected."

The first night, accordingly, we pushed to the house of a Maclaren in Strathire, where we slept, and from there we set forth again about the fall of night to make another easy stage. The next day we lay in a heather bush on the hillside in Uam Var, within view of a herd of deer, the happiest ten hours of sleep in a fine, breathing sunshine and bone-dry ground, that I have ever tasted. That night we reached Allan Water, and followed it down; and coming to the edge of the hills saw the whole Carse* of Stirling underfoot, with the town and the castle on a hill in the midst of it, and the moon shining on the Links of Forth.

"Now," said Alan, "you're in your own land again. We passed the Highland Line in the first hour; and now if we could but pass that crooked water, we might cast our bonnets in the air."

I was for pushing straight across; but Alan was more wary.

"It looks too quiet," said he; "but for all that we'll lie down here behind a dyke, and make sure."

At last there came by an old, hobbling woman with a crutch. The woman was so little, and the night so dark, that we soon lost sight of her; only heard the sound of her steps, and her stick, and a cough that she had by fits.

And just then—"Who goes?" cried a voice, and we heard the butt of a musket rattle on the bridgestones. I must suppose the guard had been sleeping, so that had we tried, we might have passed unseen; but he was awake now.

"This'll never do for us, David," said Alan.

And without another word, he began to crawl away through the fields.

"Well?" said I.

"Well," said Alan, "what would you have us do? They're not the fools I took them for. We have still the Forth to pass, Davie, and if we cannot pass the river, we'll have to see what we can do for the firth."

"But a river can be swum."

"By them that have the skill of it," returned he, "I have yet to hear that either you or me is much of a swimmer."

*Carse is low, rich land, usually along a river, in this case the Forth River.

"But if it's hard to pass a river, it stands to reason it must be worse to pass a sea."

"But there's such a thing as a boat," said Alan.

By the next night, we had borrowed a boat from an innkeeper's kindly daughter, and we rowed across, setting down on the Lothian shore.

CHAPTER 10
I Come to Mr. Rankeillor

THE NEXT DAY, it was agreed that Alan should fend for himself till sunset; but as soon as it began to grow dark, he should lie in the fields by the roadside, and not stir until he heard me whistling. He taught me a little fragment of a Highland air, which has run in my head from that day to this. Every time it comes to me, it takes me off to that last day of my uncertainty, with Alan sitting up in the bottom of the den, whistling and beating the measure with a finger, and the gray of dawn coming on his face.

I was in the long street of Queensferry before the sun was up. It was a fairly built town, the houses of good stone, and I was ashamed of my tattered clothes.

As the morning went on, and the people began to appear out of the houses, I saw now that I had no clear proof of my rights over my uncle's. It might be no easy matter even to come to meet with the lawyer, far less to convince him of my story. I went up and down, and through the street, and down to the harbor-side. At last I chanced to have stopped in front of a very good house, from which came out a red-faced, kindly, important-looking man in a powdered wig and spectacles. This gentleman was so much struck with my poor appearance that he came straight up to me and asked me what I wanted.

I told him I was come to Queensferry on business, and asked him to direct me to the house of Mr. Rankeillor.

"Why," said he, "that is his house that I have just come out of; and for a rather surprising chance, I am that very man."

"Then, sir," said I, "I have to beg the favor of an interview. My name is David Balfour."

"And where have you come from, Mr. Balfour?"

"A great many strange places, sir."

He led me back into his house, cried out to someone whom I could not see that he would be busy all morning, and brought me into his little dusty chamber full of books and documents.

"I have reason to believe myself some rights on the estate of Shaws," I told him.

He asked me of where and when I was born, and of my parents, and finally, "Have you any papers proving who you are?"

"No, sir," said I, "but they are in the hands of Mr. Campbell, the minister. For that matter, I do not think my uncle Mr. Ebenezer Balfour would deny me."

"Did you ever meet a man of the name of Hoseason?" he asked.

"I did so, sir," said I; "for it was by his means and by pay of my uncle, that I was kidnapped within sight of this town, carried to sea, suffered shipwreck and a hundred other hardships, and stand before you today in these poor clothes."

"You were kidnapped? In what sense?"

"In the plain meaning of the word, sir," said I. "I was on

my way to your house, when I was kidnapped on board the brig, cruelly struck down, thrown below, and knew no more of anything till we were far at sea. I was destined for the plantations; a fate that I have escaped."

"The brig *Covenant* was lost on June the 27th," said he, looking in his book, "and we are now at August the 24th. Here is a considerable gap, Mr. Balfour, of nearly two months."

"Before I tell my story, I would be glad to know that I was talking to a friend," I said. "You are not to forget, sir, that I have already suffered by my trustfulness; and was shipped off to be a slave by the very man that is your employer."

"I *was* indeed your uncle's lawyer," he said. "But while you were gallivanting, a good deal of water has run under the bridges. On the very day of your sea disaster, your friend the minister Mr. Campbell stalked into my office, demanding you. I had never heard of you; but I had known your father. Mr. Ebenezer admitted having seen you; declared that he had given you much money; and that you had started for the continent of Europe. I am not exactly sure that anyone believed him," continued Mr. Rankeillor with a smile; "and in particular he so disliked my own suspicions, he fired me. Shortly thereafter, comes Captain Hoseason with the story of your drowning."

Thereupon I told him my story from the start. When I mentioned Alan Breck, we had an odd scene. The name of Alan had of course rung through Scotland, with the news of the Appin murder, and the offer of a reward; and his name had no sooner escaped me than the lawyer said, "We will call your friend, if you please, Mr. Thomson."

By this I saw he had already guessed I might be coming to the murder.

"Well, well," said the lawyer, when I had quite done, "this is a great Odyssey of yours. This Mr. Thomson seems

to me a gentleman of some choice qualities, though perhaps a little bloody-minded. But you are doubtless quite
right to stick to him; he stuck to you. He was your true
companion. Well, well, I think you are near the end of your
troubles."

He had another plate set at his table for my dinner, and
provided for me water, soap, and a comb; and laid out
some clothes that belonged to his son. I made what change
I could in my appearance.

When I had done, Mr. Rankeillor said, "Sit down, Mr.
David, and now that you are looking a little more like
yourself, you will be wondering, no doubt, about your
father and uncle. It is a strange tale, and the matter hinges
on a love affair."

"Truly," said I, "I cannot very well join that notion with
my uncle."

"But your uncle, Mr. David, was not always old," replied the lawyer, "and not always ugly. He had a fine, gallant air. In 1715 he ran away to join the rebels.* It was your father that pursued him, found him in a ditch, and brought him back. The two lads fell in love, and with the same lady. The end of it was, your mother preferred your father. Your uncle complained so loudly, so selfishly, that your father gave over his estate to Ebenezer, and took the lady. Now your father should have consulted his lawyer, myself, as this action was unjust. Your father and mother lived and died poor folk; and, in the meanwhile, what a time it has been for the tenants on the estate of the Shaws! Money was all Mr. Ebenezer got by his bargain. He was selfish when he was young, he is selfish now that he is old."

"Well, sir," said I, "and in all this, what is my position?"

"The estate is yours, beyond a doubt," replied the lawyer. "It matters nothing what your father signed, you are the lawful heir to the estate. My advice, however, is to make a very easy bargain with your uncle, perhaps even leaving him at Shaws, and contenting yourself till he dies with a fair sum."

I told him I was very willing to be easy, and began to see the outlines of that scheme on which we afterwards acted.

"The surest way to make the bargain," I asked, "is to get him to admit the kidnapping?"

"Surely," said Mr. Rankeillor.

"Well, sir," said I, "here is my plan."

Having told it to him, and obtained his liking for it, we set out from the house to meet with Alan, "Mr. Thomson." Mr. Rankeillor's clerk, Torrance, followed behind with a deed in his pocket, and a covered basket in his hand. All

*In 1715, there was a Jacobite rising in support of James Francis Edward Stuart, father of Charles Stuart and the son and heir of James II of England.

through the town the lawyer was bowing right and left, and being stopped by gentlemen on matters of town or private business. At last we were clear of the houses, and began to go along towards the Hawes Inn and the Ferry pier, the scene of my misfortune. I could not look upon the place without emotion, recalling how many that had been with me that day were now no more. All these, and the brig herself, I had outlived.

I was so thinking when, all of a sudden, Mr. Rankeillor cried out, clapped his hand to his pockets, and began to laugh. "Why, I have forgot my glasses!"

At that, I knew that he had left his spectacles at home on purpose, so that he might have the benefit of Alan's help without the legal awkwardness of recognizing him. For how could Rankeillor swear to my friend's identity?

As soon as we were past the Hawes, Mr. Rankeillor walked behind with Torrance and sent me forward as scout. I went up the hill, whistling from time to time the tune Alan had taught me; and at length I had the pleasure to hear it answered and to see Alan rise from behind a bush. At the mere sight of my clothes, he began to brighten up; and as soon as I had told him my plan, he was a new man.

I cried and waved on Mr. Rankeillor, who came up alone and was presented to my friend, Mr. Thomson.

Night was quite come when we came in view of the house of Shaws. It was dark and mild, with a pleasant, rustling wind that covered the sound of our approach; and as we drew near we saw no glimmer of light in the building. It seemed my uncle was already in bed, which was indeed the best thing for our arrangements. We made our last whispered plans some fifty yards away; and then the lawyer and Torrance and I crept quietly up and crouched down beside the corner of the house; and as soon as we were in our places, Alan strode to the door and began to knock.

At last we could hear the noise of a window gently thrust up, and knew that my uncle had come to his observatory. By what light there was, he would see Alan standing, like a dark shadow, on the steps; the three witnesses were hidden quite out of his view.

"What's this?" said he. "This is no kind of time of night for decent folk; I have no dealings with nighthawks. What brings you here? I have a gun."

"Is that you, Mr. Balfour?" returned Alan. "Have a care with that musket."

"What brings you here? and who are you?"

"I have no desire to shout my name to the countryside," said Alan; "but what brings me here is another story, being more your affair than mine."

"And what is it?"

"David," said Alan.

"What was that?" cried my uncle. "I'll come right down." He shut the window, and at last, we heard, downstairs, the creak of the door hinges.

"And now," said my uncle, "mind that I have my gun, and if you take a step nearer you're as good as dead."

"A very polite speech," said Alan, "to be sure."

"No," said my uncle, "but I'm bound to be prepared. And now you'll name your business."

"I am a Highland gentleman," said Alan. "My name has no business in my story; but the county of my friends is not very far from the Isle of Mull, of which you will have heard. It seems there was a ship lost in those parts; and the next day a gentleman of my family was seeking wreckwood for his fire along the sands, when he came upon a lad that was half drowned. Well, he brought him to; and he and some other gentlemen took and locked him in an old, ruined castle, where from that day to this he has been a great expense to my friends. My friends are a wee wild-

like, and not so particular about the law; and finding that
the lad was your born nephew, Mr. Balfour, they asked me
to give you a call and talk. And I may tell you, unless we
can agree upon some terms, you are little likely to set
eyes upon him. For my friends are not very well off."

My uncle cleared his throat. "I'm not very caring," said
he. "He wasn't a good lad, and I've no call to interfere."

"Ay, ay," said Alan, "I see what you're at: pretending you
don't care, to make the ransom smaller."

"No," said my uncle, "it's the simple truth. I take no
manner of interest in the lad, and I'll pay no ransom, and
you can do what you like with him, for what I care."

"Hoot, sir," said Alan. "Blood's thicker than water! You
cannot desert your brother's son; and if you did, and it
came to be known, you wouldn't be a very popular man."

"I'm not just very popular the way it is," returned
Ebenezer; "and I don't see how it would come to be known.
Not by me, anyway; nor yet by you or your friends."

"Then it'll have to be David that tells it," said Alan.

"How's that?"

"Oh, just this way," said Alan. "My friends would doubtless keep your nephew as long as there was any likelihood
of silver to be made of it, but if there was none, I am sure
they would let him go where he pleased. There are two
ways of it, Mr. Balfour: either you liked David and would
pay to get him back; or else you had very good reasons
for not wanting him, and would pay for us to keep him. It
seems it's not the first; well then, it's the second; and as I
see it, it should be a pretty penny in my pocket and the
pockets of my friends."

"I don't follow you there," said my uncle.

"No?" said Alan. "Well, see here: you don't want the lad
back; well, what do you want done with him, and how
much will you pay?"

My uncle made no answer, but shifted uneasily.

"Come, sir," cried Alan. "I would have you know that I am a gentleman, not a servant to be kept waiting. Answer me in civility, or by the top of Glencoe, I will ram three feet of iron through you."

"Just tell me about how much silver you'll want," said my uncle, "and you'll see if we can agree."

"Do you want the lad killed or kept?" asked Alan.

"O, sir," cried Ebenezer. "That's no kind of language!"

"Killed or kept!" repeated Alan.

"O, kept, kept!" wailed my uncle. "We'll have no blood-shed, if you please."

"Well," said Alan, "as you please; that'll cost more."

"More?" cried Ebenezer. "Would you stain your hands with crime?"

"Hoot!" said Alan. "They're both crimes! And the killing's easier, and quicker, and surer. Keeping the lad will be a troublesome job."

"I'll have him kept, though," returned my uncle. "I'm a man of principle, and if I have to pay for it, I'll have to pay for it."

"Well, well," said Alan, "and now about the price. It's not very easy for me to set a name upon it; I would have to know some small matters. I would have to know, for instance, what you gave Hoseason?"

"To Hoseason? What for?" cried my uncle.

"For kidnapping David," said Alan.

"It's a lie, a lie!" cried my uncle. "He was never kid-napped. He lied in his throat that told you that. Kidnapped? He never was!"

"What did you pay him?"

"Has Hoseason told you himself?"

"How else could I know?"

"Well," said my uncle, "I don't care what he said, he lied, and the solemn truth is this, that I gave him twenty pounds. But I'll be perfectly honest with you: for with that, he was

to have the price of the lad in Carolina, which would be as much more, but not from my pocket, you see."

"Thank you, Mr. Thomson," said the lawyer, stepping forward, "that will do excellently. Good-evening, Mr. Balfour."

And, "Good-evening, Uncle Ebenezer," said I.

And, "It's a fine night, Mr. Balfour," added Torrance.

Never a word said my uncle; but just sat where he was on the top doorstep and stared upon us like a man turned to stone. Alan took away his gun; and the lawyer, taking him by the arm, plucked him up from the doorstep, led him into the kitchen, where we all followed, and set him down in a chair beside the hearth.

"Come, come, Mr. Ebenezer," said the lawyer, "you must not be down-hearted, for I promise you we shall make easy terms." Mr. Rankeillor and my uncle passed into the next chamber to consult. They stayed there about an hour; at the end of which period they had come to a good understanding, and my uncle and I set our hands to the agreement in a formal manner. By the terms of this, my uncle bound himself to pay me two-thirds of the yearly income of Shaws.

So the beggar had come home; and when I lay down that night on the kitchen chests, I was a man of means and had a name in the country. Alan and Torrance and Rankeillor slept and snored on their hard beds; but for me who had lain out under heaven and upon dirt and stones, so many days and nights, and often with an empty belly, and in fear of death, I lay till dawn, looking at the fire and planning my future.

The next day Mr. Rankeillor supplied me with money and letters of introduction to his bankers and to the Advocate, whom I owed testimony about the murder. While Mr. Rankeillor and Torrance set out for the Ferry, Alan and I turned for the city of Edinburgh. As we went by the footpath and beside the gateposts, we kept looking back at the house of my fathers. It stood there, bare and great and smokeless, like a place not lived in.

Alan and I went slowly forward upon our way, having little heart either to walk or speak. The same thought was uppermost in both, that we were near the time of our parting; and remembrance of all the bygone days sat upon us sorely. We talked indeed of what should be done; and it was resolved that Alan should keep to the county, biding now here, now there, but coming once in the day to the particular place where I might be able to communicate with him. In the meanwhile, I was to seek out a lawyer, who was an Appin Stewart, and a man therefore to be wholly trusted; and it should be his part to find a ship and arrange for Alan's safe departure. No sooner was this business done, than the words seemed to leave us.

We came the by-way over the hill of Corstorphine; and when we got near to the place called Rest-and-be-Thankful, and looked down on bogs and over to the city and the castle on the hill, we both stopped, for we both knew

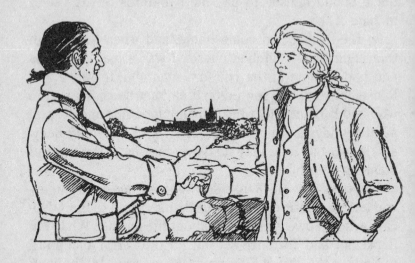

without a word said that we had come to where our ways
parted. I gave him what money I had, and then we stood a
while, and looked over at Edinburgh in silence.

"Well, good-bye," said Alan, and held out his hand.

"Good-bye," said I, and gave the hand a little grasp, and
went off down hill.

Neither one of us looked the other in the face, nor so
long as he was in my view did I take one back glance at
the friend I was leaving. But as I went on my way to the
city, I felt so lost and lonesome, that I could have found it
in my heart to sit down by the dyke, and cry and weep
like any baby.

It was coming near noon when I passed in by the West
Kirk and the Grassmarket into the streets of the capital.
And yet all the time I was thinking of Alan, and all the time
there was a cold gnawing in my inside like a remorse for
something wrong.

The hand of fate brought me in my drifting to the very
doors of the bank.

DOVER
CHILDREN'S THRIFT CLASSICS

Tarzan

EDGAR RICE BURROUGHS

Adapted by Bob Blaisdell
Illustrated by John Green

DOVER PUBLICATIONS, INC.
Mineola, New York

DOVER CHILDREN'S THRIFT CLASSICS
GENERAL EDITOR: STANLEY APPELBAUM
EDITOR OF THIS VOLUME: ADAM H. FROST

Bibliographical Note

This Dover edition, first published in 1997, is a new abridgment of a standard text of *Tarzan of the Apes,* which was originally published by A. C. McClurg & Co., Chicago, in 1914. The introductory Note and the illustrations were prepared specially for this edition.

Library of Congress Cataloging-in-Publication Data

Burroughs, Edgar Rice, 1875–1950.
    Tarzan / Edgar Rice Burroughs ; abridged by Bob Blaisdell ; illustrated by John Green.
        p.   cm. — (Dover children's thrift classics)
    Abridgment of: Tarzan of the apes.
    Summary: A baby boy, left alone in the African jungle after the deaths of his parents, Lord and Lady Greystoke, is adopted by an ape, whose own infant has died, and raised to manhood without ever seeing another human being.
    ISBN 0-486-29530-3 (pbk.)
    1. Tarzan (Fictitious character)—Juvenile fiction.   [1. Feral children—Fiction. 2. Apes—Fiction. 3. Africa—Fiction. 4. Jungles—Fiction.] I. Blaisdell, Robert. II. Green, John, 1948– ill. III. Title. IV. Series.
PZ7.B9453Tam   1997
[Fic]—dc21
                                                      96-49011
                                                         CIP
                                                           AC

Manufactured in the United States of America
Dover Publications, Inc., 31 East 2nd Street, Mineola, N.Y. 11501

Note

EDGAR RICE BURROUGHS (1875–1950) led a rich and varied life, of which his career as an author was but one part. He served in the U.S. Cavalry until it was discovered that he was underage; once discharged, Burroughs went on to work as a cowboy, gold miner, storekeeper, railway detective and newspaper correspondent. Deciding that he could improve upon the popular dime novel, Burroughs turned to writing fiction, eventually creating westerns, science fiction and popular stories for newspapers and magazines as well as for books, and becoming a millionaire in the process. He was a prolific writer and was able to compose a full-length novel in a weekend, as he proved once on a bet.

Tarzan of the Apes (from which this abridgment was taken) was originally published in 1914, the first in a long and highly successful series centered around that character. Through these books and their many adaptations, Tarzan and Jane have become deeply ensconced in the public imagination, and this retelling of Burroughs' classic retains all the adventure and suspense of their original story in a way that is sure to enthrall young readers.

Contents

1. Out to Sea

I HAD this story from one who had no business to tell it to me. I do not say the story is true, for I did not witness it, but my own belief is that it *may* be true. If you do not find it believable, you will at least agree that it is remarkable and interesting.

From the records of the Colonial Office and from a dead man's diary, we learn that a certain young English nobleman, whom we shall call John Clayton, Lord Greystoke, was sent to investigate the conditions in a British colony on the west coast of Africa, whose natives another European country was recruiting as soldiers to use in the collection of rubber and ivory from the tribes along the Congo and Aruwimi rivers.

John Clayton was a strong man—mentally, morally and physically. He was above average height; his eyes were gray, his features regular and strong. He was still young when he was entrusted with this important mission in the service of the Queen, a reward for his past good services. This would be a stepping stone to posts of greater importance and responsibility, he knew; on the other hand, he had been married to Alice Rutherford for scarcely three months, and the thought of taking this fair young girl into the dangers of tropical Africa dismayed him.

For her sake he would have refused the appointment, but she would not have it so. Instead she insisted that he accept and, indeed, take her with him.

On a bright May morning in 1888, Lord and Lady
Greystoke sailed from Dover for Africa. A month later
they arrived at Freetown, where they chartered a small
sailing ship, the *Fuwalda*, which was to bear them to
their destination. And here Lord and Lady Greystoke
vanished from the sight of the world.

Two months after the Greystokes left Freetown, a half
dozen British warships were scouring the south
Atlantic for trace of them or their ship, and it was
almost immediately that the wreckage of the *Fuwalda*
was found upon the shores of St. Helena.

The officers of the *Fuwalda* were bullies, hated by
and hating their crew. The captain was a brute in his
treatment of his men. So it was that, from the second
day out from Freetown, Lord Greystoke and his young
wife witnessed harrowing scenes upon the deck of the
Fuwalda. It was on the morning of the second day, while
two sailors were washing down the decks, that the captain stopped to speak with Lord and Lady Greystoke.

The sailors were working backwards toward the little
group, who faced away from them. Closer and closer
the sailors came, until one of them was directly behind
the captain. At that instant the officer turned to leave
his noble passengers, and, as he did so, he tripped
against the sailor and fell sprawling upon the deck.

His face red with rage, the captain got to his feet, and
with a mighty blow knocked down the sailor, who was
small and rather old.

The other seaman, however, was a huge bear of a
man, with a fierce, dark moustache, and a great bull
neck set between massive shoulders. As he saw his
mate go down he crouched, and, with a snarl, sprang
upon the captain, crushing him to his knees.

Without getting up, the officer whipped a revolver

With a snarl, the seaman sprang upon the captain.

from his pocket and fired point-blank at the great-muscled man before him. But, quick as he was, Lord Greystoke was almost as quick, striking the captain's arm, so that the bullet which was aimed at the sailor's heart struck him instead in the leg.

The captain was angry with Lord Greystoke, but turned on his heel and walked away.

The two sailors picked themselves up, the older man helping his wounded mate to rise. The big fellow, who was known as Black Michael, turned to Clayton with a word of thanks. He then limped off toward the sailors' quarters.

A few days later, at midafternoon, the little old sailor whom the captain had knocked down came along deck to where Lord and Lady Greystoke were watching the ocean. While he polished the ship's brass, he edged close to Lord Greystoke and said, in an undertone, "There's trouble to come, sir, on this here ship, and mark my word for it, sir. Big trouble."

"What do you mean, my good fellow?" asked Lord Greystoke.

"Why, hasn't you seen what's goin' on? Hasn't you heard that devilish captain and his mates has been knockin' the bloomin' lights out of half the crew? Black Michael's as good as new again, and he's not going to stand for it; mark my word for it, sir."

"You mean, my man, that the crew is thinking of mutiny?"

"Mutiny!" exclaimed the old fellow. "Mutiny! They means murder, sir!"

"When?"

"It's comin', sir, but I'm not a-sayin' when, and I've said too much now, but you was a good sort the other day, and I thought it right to warn you. So when you hear shootin', git below and stay there." And the old fellow went on with his polishing, which carried him away from where the Greystokes were standing.

"What are we to do, John?" asked his wife. "I shall not urge you to go to the captain. Possibly our best chance lies in keeping a neutral position. If the officers are able to prevent a mutiny, we have nothing to fear, while if the mutineers are victorious, our one slim hope lies in not having tried to stop them."

"Right you are, Alice. We'll keep to the middle of the road."

The next morning, as Lord Greystoke was coming up on deck for his walk before breakfast, a shot rang out, and then another, and another.

Facing the little group of officers was the entire crew of the *Fuwalda,* and at their head stood Black Michael.

At the first return of shots the men ran for shelter, and then shot again at the five officers. Two of the mutineers had been shot and lay where they had fallen. Soon the first mate, in his turn, was killed, and at the cry of command from Black Michael, the bloodthirsty ruffians charged the remaining four officers.

The captain was reloading his revolver when the charge was made. Both sides were cursing and swearing in a frightful manner, which, together with the gunshots and the screams of the wounded, turned the deck of the *Fuwalda* into a madhouse.

Before the officers had taken a dozen backward steps, the men were upon them. A burly sailor killed the captain with an axe, and an instant later the other officers were down.

Short and grisly was the work of the mutineers, and through it all Lord Greystoke stood aside, puffing on his pipe, as though watching a cricket match. As the last officer went down, Greystoke thought that it was time that he returned to his wife. He feared for her safety. As he turned to descend the ladder, he was surprised to see his wife standing on the steps, almost at his side.

"How long have you been here, Alice?"

"Since the beginning," she replied. "How awful, John. Oh, how awful!"

The men had by this time surrounded the dead and wounded officers, and began throwing both living and dead over the sides of the vessel. One of the crew spied the Lord and Lady Greystoke, and with a cry of: "Here's two more for the fishes," rushed toward them with an uplifted axe.

But Black Michael was even quicker, so that the fellow went down with a bullet in his back before he had taken a half dozen steps. With a loud roar, Black Michael pointed to Lord and Lady Greystoke, and cried: "These here are my friends, and they are to be left

On the fifth day land was sighted by the lookout.

alone. Do you understand? I'm captain of this ship now, and what I says goes!" Turning to Lord Greystoke, he said, "Just keep to yourselves, and nobody'll harm you." And then he looked threateningly on his fellows.

Lord and Lady Greystoke followed Black Michael's instructions, and thereafter saw little of the crew.

On the fifth day following the mutiny, land was sighted by the lookout. Black Michael announced to Lord Greystoke that, if the place was habitable, he and Lady Greystoke were to be put ashore with their belongings.

"You'll be all right there for a few months," he explained, "and by that time we'll have been able to make a coast somewheres and escape a bit. Then I'll see that your government's notified of where you be, and they'll soon send a ship to fetch you off."

Lord Greystoke protested against the inhumanity of landing them upon an unknown shore, to be left to the mercies of savage beasts and, possibly, still more savage men. But his words only angered the new captain, and so Lord Greystoke decided to make the best he could of a bad situation.

Before dark the ship lay peacefully at anchor in the sighted land's harbor. The surrounding shores were beautiful and green, while in the distance the country rose from the ocean in forested hills. No signs of human life were visible, but there was much bird and animal life, and a little river could be seen.

Black Michael told the Greystokes to prepare to land in the morning. "You saved my life once, and in return I'm going to spare yours, but that's all I can do," he said. "The men won't stand for any more, and if we don't get you landed pretty quick they may even change their minds about giving you that. I'll put all your stuff ashore with you. With your guns for protection, you ought to be able to live here easy enough until help comes."

After he had left them, they went to their room below deck, filled with gloomy thoughts. Lord Greystoke thought that if he had been alone, he might hope to survive for years, for he was a strong, athletic man. But what of Alice, and that baby to whom she would soon give birth?

2. Into the Jungle

EARLY THE next morning their numerous chests and boxes were hoisted on deck and lowered to the waiting boats for transportation to shore. Also loaded were salted meats and biscuits, with a small supply of potatoes and beans, matches, cooking pots, a chest of tools and old sails with which to make tents. Black Michael accompanied the Greystokes to shore, and there he wished them good luck.

Later, as the *Fuwalda* passed out of the harbor, Lady Alice threw her arms around her husband's neck and burst into sobs. "Oh, John," she cried, "the horror of it. What are we to do?"

"There is but one thing to do, Alice," he said quietly, "and that is work. Work must be our salvation. Hundreds of thousands of years ago our ancestors faced the same problems we must now face. What did they do that we may not do?"

"I only hope you are right, John. I will do my best to be a brave, primitive woman, a fit mate for a primitive man."

A hundred yards from the beach was a little level spot, fairly free of trees, and here they decided to build a permanent house, although for the time being they both thought it best to construct a little platform in the trees, out of reach of any savage beasts.

Greystoke selected four trees which formed a rectangle about eight feet square, and, cutting long branches

8

from other trees, he constructed a framework around them, about ten feet from the ground. Across this framework Greystoke placed other, smaller branches quite close together. Seven feet higher he constructed a lighter platform to serve as a roof, and from the sides of this he suspended the sailcloth for walls. When it was completed they had a rather snug little nest.

All during the day the forest about them had been filled with chattering monkeys and excited birds with brilliant feathers. That night, the Greystokes had scarcely closed their eyes when the terrifying cry of a panther rang out from the jungle behind them. For an hour or more they heard it sniffing and clawing at the trees which supported their platform, but at last it roamed away across the beach. They slept very little, and they were relieved when they saw the day dawn. As soon as they had made and finished their breakfast, Greystoke began work upon their home, for he realized that they could hope for no safety and no peace of mind until four strong walls barred the jungle life from them.

The task was a hard one and required the better part of a month, though Greystoke built but one small room. He constructed his cabin of small logs, with clay filling in the gaps. At one end he built a fireplace of small stones from the beach. These also he set in clay, and when the house had been entirely completed, he put on a coating of clay over the entire outside. In the window opening he set small branches, and wove them so that they could withstand the strength of a powerful animal. Thus they obtained air and ventilation. The A-shaped roof was thatched with small branches laid close together, and over these long grass and palm fronds, with a final coating of clay.

The door he built of pieces of the packing-boxes

which had held their belongings; he nailed one piece upon another until he had a solid door some three inches thick. After two days' hard work, he carved out two hardwood hinges, and with these he hung the door so that it opened and closed easily.

The building of a bed, chairs, table and shelves was a relatively easy chore, so that by the end of the second month they were well settled, and, but for the constant dread of attack by wild animals, they were not uncomfortable or unhappy. At night great beasts snarled and roared outside their tiny cabin, but they soon paid little attention to them, sleeping soundly the whole night through.

One afternoon, while Greystoke was working upon an addition to their cabin (for he thought about building several more rooms), a number of birds and monkeys came shrieking through the trees from the direction of the ridge.

Approaching through the jungle in a semierect position, now and then placing the backs of its closed fists upon the ground, was a great ape. As it advanced, it growled deeply and made an occasional low barking sound.

Greystoke was at some distance from the cabin, having come to cut down a perfect tree for his building. He had left his rifles and revolvers within the little cabin, and now that he saw the great ape crashing through the underbrush directly toward him, he felt a shiver of fear. He knew that, armed only with an axe, his chances against this monster were small indeed. There was yet a slight chance of reaching the cabin. He turned and ran toward it, shouting an alarm to his wife to run in and close the door.

Lady Greystoke had been sitting a little way from the

Armed only with an axe, his chances were small indeed.

cabin, and when she heard the cry, she looked up to see the ape springing with an almost incredible swiftness in an effort to cut off her husband. Greystoke cried out, "Close and bolt the door, Alice. I can finish this fellow with an axe." But he knew he was facing a horrible death, and so did she.

The ape was a great bull, weighing probably three hundred pounds. His close-set eyes gleamed beneath his shaggy brows, while his great fangs were bared in a snarl as he paused a moment before his prey.

The powerful brute seized the axe from Greystoke's grasp and hurled it away. With another snarl he reached for the throat of Greystoke, but suddenly there was a loud shot and a bullet entered the ape's back between his shoulders.

Throwing Greystoke to the ground, the beast turned upon his new enemy. Screaming with rage and pain, the ape flew at the woman, who immediately fainted.

Greystoke jumped to his feet and rushed forward to drag the ape away from his wife. He pushed him aside easily—for the ape was nearly dead. The bullet had done its work.

Gently, Greystoke lifted his wife's body and bore her to the little cabin, but it was two hours before she came to. When she awoke, her first words were: "O John, it is so good to really be home! I have had an awful dream, dear. I thought we were no longer in London, but in some horrible place where great beasts attacked us."

"There, there, Alice," he said, stroking her forehead, "try to sleep again, and do not worry your head with bad dreams."

That night a little son was born in the tiny cabin beside the forest. Lady Greystoke never recovered from the shock of the great ape's attack, and she was never again outside the cabin, nor did she ever fully realize that she was not in England. In other ways she was quite all right, and she took joy and happiness in her little son.

Lord Greystoke had long since given up any hope of rescue, and so he worked very hard to beautify the interior of the cabin. Skins of lions and panthers covered the floor. Cupboards and bookcases lined the walls. Odd vases made by his own hand from the clay of the jungle held beautiful tropical flowers. Curtains of grass and bamboo covered the windows, and, the most difficult task of all, he had fashioned lumber to neatly seal the walls and ceiling, and had laid a smooth floor within the cabin.

During the year that followed, Greystoke was several times attacked by the great apes which now seemed to continually pass by the neighborhood of the cabin, but he never again went outside without both rifle and revolver. He had been able at first to shoot many of the animals from the cabin windows, but toward the end they learned to fear the strange cabin from where the thunder of death roared.

Greystoke often read aloud to his wife, from the books he had brought for their new home. Among these were many for little children—picture books, first readers—for they had known that their little child would be old enough for these before they might hope to return to England.

The nobleman also wrote in his diary, which he had always kept in French, and in which he recorded the details of their strange life. This book he kept locked in a little metal box.

A year from the day on which her son was born, Lady Alice passed away in the night. Lord Greystoke now had the fearful responsibility of caring for that wee thing, his son, still a nursing babe.

The last entry in his diary was made the morning following her death: "My little son is crying for nourishment—O Alice, Alice, what shall I do?"

And as John Clayton, Lord Greystoke, wrote the last words, he dropped his head upon his arms. His wife lay still and cold in the bed beside him.

For a long time no sound broke the midday stillness of the jungle, save for the pitiful wailing of the tiny baby boy.

3. The Apes

IN THE forest a mile back from the ocean, old Kerchak the Ape was on a rampage. The younger and lighter members of his tribe scampered to the higher branches of the great trees to escape him. The other males scattered in all directions, but not before the brute had attacked and killed one.

Then he spied Kala, who, returning from a search for food with her young babe, did not know he was in such a state of rage. As he turned on her, she made a mad leap into a tree, climbing quickly away. But just as she reached a safe height, her baby lost its hold on her neck and fell to its death on the ground. With a cry of despair, Kala rushed down to its side, but it was too late. With low moans, she sat cuddling the body to her; Kerchak now left her alone. With the death of the infant his fit seemed to have passed.

Kerchak was a huge king ape, weighing perhaps three hundred and fifty pounds. His forehead was low, his eyes bloodshot, small and set close to his flat nose. There was no ape in all the forest that dared to contest his right to rule, nor did the other and larger animals try to bother him.

Old Tantor, the elephant, alone of all the savage beasts, did not fear him—and him alone did Kerchak fear. When Tantor trumpeted, the great ape scurried with his fellows high among the trees.

The tribe of apes over which Kerchak ruled numbered eight families, each family consisting of an adult male and his wives and their young, totaling some sixty or seventy apes. Kala was the youngest wife of a male called Tublat, meaning "broken nose," and the child she had seen dashed to death was her first, for she was but nine or ten years old. She was large and powerful, with a round, high forehead.

When the tribe saw that Kerchak's rage had ceased, they came slowly down from their trees and went back to their business. The young played among the trees and bushes. Some of the adults lay down upon the soft mat of leaves which covered the ground, while others turned over pieces of fallen branches in search of small bugs and reptiles, which formed part of their diet. Others searched the surrounding trees for fruit, nuts, small birds and eggs.

They had passed an hour or so at these activities when Kerchak called them together and, with a word of command to them to follow him, set off toward the sea. They traveled for the most part upon the ground, where it was open, following the paths of elephants, whose comings and goings broke the only roads through those tangled mazes of bushes, vines and trees.

When the apes walked, it was with a rolling motion, placing the knuckles of their closed hands upon the ground and swinging their bodies forward. But when the way was through the lower trees, they moved more swiftly, swinging from branch to branch. And all the way Kala carried her dead baby hugged closely to her breast.

It was shortly after noon when they reached a ridge overlooking the beach. Below them lay the tiny cottage which was Kerchak's goal. He had seen many of his kind go to their death there, killed by the loud noise

The instinct of mother love reached out.

that the white ape's little black stick made—the strange white ape who lived in that wonderful dwelling. Kerchak had made up his mind to own that stick, and to explore the interior of that mysterious den.

Today there was no sign of the man about, and from where they watched they could see that the cabin door was open. Slowly they crept through the jungle toward the little cabin. On, on they came until Kerchak slunk to the door and peered within. Behind him were two males, and then Kala, closely straining the little dead baby to her breast.

Inside the den they saw the strange white ape lying half across a table, his head buried in his arms; on the bed lay a figure covered by a sailcloth, while from the cradle came the wailing of a baby.

Kerchak entered, crouching for the attack, and John Clayton, Lord Greystoke, rose with a sudden start and faced him. But it was too late for him to grab his revolvers from the far wall. Kerchak charged at him and picked him up, crushing the noble Englishman to death.

Kerchak released the man from his arms and turned his attention toward the little cradle, but Kala was there before him. When he would have grasped the child, she snatched it up herself, and she had bolted through the door and into a high tree before he could stop her.

As she took up the little live baby of Alice Clayton, Lady Greystoke, Kala dropped the dead body of her own child into the empty cradle, for the wail of the living had answered the call of motherhood within her.

High up among the branches of a mighty tree, she hugged the shrieking infant to her bosom, and soon the instinct of mother love reached out to the tiny man-child, and he became quiet. Then the son of an English lord and an English lady nursed at the breast of Kala, the ape.

Below her, the beasts within the cabin were examining the contents of the strange dwelling. The rifle hanging upon the wall caught Kerchak's attention; he had yearned for this death-dealing thunderstick for months. He raised a huge hand and tore it from its hook. He began to examine it closely. He peered down the muzzle and fingered every part. During all these investiga-

tions the apes who had entered sat huddled near the
door, watching their chief, while those outside crowded in the doorway.

Suddenly Kerchak's finger closed upon the trigger.
There was a roar in the little room, and the apes fell
over one another in their hurry to escape. Kerchak was
equally frightened; so frightened, in fact, that he quite
forgot to throw aside the gun, and bolted for the door
with it tightly clutched in one hand. As he passed
through the doorway, the front of the rifle caught upon
the edge of the in-swung door so that it closed tightly
after the fleeing ape.

When Kerchak came to a halt a short distance from
the cabin, he discovered that he still held the rifle and
quickly dropped it.

It was an hour before the apes could bring themselves to approach the cabin again, and when they
finally did so, they found that the door was closed and
so securely fastened that they could not force it open.
The cleverly made latch which Clayton had designed
for the door had sprung as Kerchak passed through;
nor could the apes find a way to get in through the
heavily barred windows.

After roaming about the area for a short time, they
started back for the deeper forests and the higher land
from where they had come.

Kala had not once come to earth with her little adopt-
ed baby, but now Kerchak called to her to come along
with them, and as there was no note of anger in his
voice, she dropped lightly from branch to branch and
joined the others on their homeward march. Those of
the apes who tried to examine Kala's strange baby were
met with bared fangs and low, menacing growls.

It was as though she knew that this baby was frail
and delicate and she feared the rough hands of her

tribe. Remembering the death of her own little one, she clung desperately with one hand to the new babe whenever they were upon the march.

The other young rode upon their mothers' backs, their little arms tightly clasping the necks, and their legs locked beneath their mothers' arms. Not so with Kala's child; the ape held the small form of the little Lord Greystoke tightly to her breast. She had seen one child fall from her to a terrible death, and she would take no chances with this one.

Tenderly Kala nursed her little orphan, wondering why it did not gain strength as did the little babies of other mothers. It was nearly a year from the time the little fellow came to be her own before he would walk alone, and as for climbing—my, but how stupid he was! He could not even find food alone. Had she known that the child had seen thirteen moons before she had found it, she would have considered it absolutely hopeless, for the little apes in her tribe were as far advanced at two or three moons as was this little stranger after twenty-five.

Tublat, Kala's husband, disliked the newcomer. "He will never be a great ape," he said. "Always you will have to carry him and protect him. What good will he be to the tribe? None; only a burden. Let us leave him quietly sleeping among the tall grasses, that you may bear other and stronger apes to guard us in our old age."

"Never, Broken Nose," replied Kala. "If I must carry him forever, so be it."

And then Tublat went to Kerchak to urge him to force Kala to give up little Tarzan, which was the name they had given to the tiny Lord Greystoke, and which meant "white skin."

But when Kerchak mentioned this to her, Kala threatened to run away from the tribe if they did not leave her in peace with the child. And so he bothered her no more, for the tribe did not wish to lose her.

As Tarzan grew he developed quickly, so that by the time he was ten years old he was an excellent climber, and on the ground could do many wonderful things which were beyond the powers of his little brothers and sisters. In many ways did he differ from them, and they often marveled at his superior cunning, but in strength and size he was lacking, for at ten the great apes were fully grown, some of them over six feet in height, while Tarzan was still but a half-grown boy.

Yet such a boy! From early childhood he had used his hands to swing from branch to branch after the manner of his mother, and as he grew older, he spent hour upon hour speeding through the treetops with his brothers and sisters. He could spring twenty feet across space at the dizzy heights of the forest top, and grasp a wildly waving limb. He could drop twenty feet at a stretch from limb to limb to the ground, or he could swing to the top of the tallest tree with the ease of a squirrel. Though but ten years old, he was fully as strong as the average man of thirty.

His life among these fierce apes was happy, for he did not remember any other kind of life, and he did not know there was any other place than his forest. He was nearly ten before he began to understand that there was a great difference between himself and his fellows. His little body, brown from the sun, suddenly caused him feelings of shame, for he saw that it was entirely hairless, like some snake.

In the higher land his tribe went to a lake, and it was here that Tarzan first saw his face in the clear, still waters. It was on a hot day of the dry season. As he and his cousin leaned over the bank of the lake to drink, both little faces were mirrored in the water. Tarzan was disgusted. It had been bad enough to be hairless, but to have such a face! That tiny slit of a mouth and those puny white teeth! How they looked beside the mighty lips and powerful fangs of his lucky brothers! And the little pinched nose! But when he saw his own eyes, it was frightful. Not even the snakes had such hideous eyes as he.

So taken was he with this horrible sight that he did not hear the stirring of the tall grass behind him; nor did his companion, the ape, for he was drinking. Not thirty paces behind the two, Sabor, the huge lioness, crouched, lashing her tail. Slowly she advanced, her

Behind the two crouched Sabor, lashing her tail.

belly low, almost touching the ground—a great cat
preparing to spring upon its prey.

Now she was within ten feet of the two little playfel-
lows—carefully she drew her hind feet up beneath her
body. So low was she crouching now that she seemed
flattened to the earth. Then, with an awful scream, she
sprang.

At that sound, Tarzan leaped into the dreaded water.
He could not swim, and the water was very deep.
Rapidly he moved his hands and feet, and fell into the
stroke called the "dog paddle," so that within a few seconds his nose was above water. He found that he could
keep it there by continuing the strokes, and could also
make progress through the water.

He was now swimming parallel to the bank, where he
saw the cruel beast that would have seized him crouching upon the body of his little playmate. Tarzan raised
his voice in the call of distress common to his tribe,
adding to it the warning about Sabor.

Almost immediately there came an answer from the
distance, and soon forty or fifty apes swung rapidly
through the trees toward the scene of tragedy. In the
front was Kala, for she had recognized the voice of her
beloved.

Though more powerful and a better fighter than the
apes, the lioness had no desire to meet these enraged
adults, and with a snarl she sprang quickly into the
brush and disappeared.

Tarzan now swam to shore. The adventure with the
lioness was tragic, but it gave him another new skill,
something he, unlike his fellows, continued to pick up
through his experiences. Ever after he lost no chance
to take a daily plunge in the lake or a stream or the
ocean. But for a long time Kala could not get used to
the sight of him swimming.

The wanderings of the tribe brought them often near the cabin. Tarzan would peek into the curtained windows, or, climbing upon the roof, peer down the chimney. His childish imagination pictured wonderful creatures within. For hours he would attempt to get in, but he paid little attention to the door, for it seemed just another solid part of the walls.

It was during his next visit to the area near the cabin, following the adventure with old Sabor, that Tarzan noticed that, from a distance, the cabin door appeared to be separate from the wall in which it was set.

The story of his own connection with the cabin had never been told him. The language of the apes had so few words that they could talk but little of what they had seen in the cabin, having no words to describe either the strange people or their belongings. Only in a dim, vague way had Kala explained to Tarzan that his father had been a strange white ape, and he did not know that Kala was not his own mother.

On this day, then, he went to the door and spent hours examining it and fussing with the hinges, the knob and the latch. Finally he stumbled upon the right combination, and the door swung creakingly open. He slowly and cautiously entered.

In the middle of the floor lay a skeleton. Upon the bed lay another, though smaller, while in the tiny cradle nearby was a third, a tiny skeleton. He examined many things—strange tools and weapons, books, papers, clothing. He opened chests and cupboards, and among the other things he found was a hunting knife, on the sharp blade of which he immediately cut his finger. Unfrightened, he continued playing with his new toy.

But then in a cupboard filled with books he came across one with brightly colored pictures—it was a child's illustrated alphabet—

> *A is for Archer*
> *Who shoots with a bow.*
> *B is for Boy,*
> *His first name is Joe.*

The pictures interested him. There were many apes with faces similar to his own, and further along in the book he found, under "M," some little monkeys. But nowhere was pictured any of his own tribe; in all the book was none that looked like Kerchak or Kala.

At first he tried to pick the little pictures from the pages, but he soon saw that they were not real. The boats, trains, cows and horses were meaningless to him, but not quite so strange as the odd little figures which appeared beneath and between the colored pictures—some kind of bug he thought they might be, for many of them had legs, though nowhere could he find one with eyes and a mouth. It was his first introduction to the letters of the alphabet, and he was more than ten years old.

Of course he had never before seen print, and he was quite at a loss to guess the meaning of these strange marks. Near the middle of the book he found his old enemy, Sabor, the lioness, and further on was coiled Histah, the snake.

Oh, it was so interesting! It was approaching dusk when Tarzan put the book back in the cupboard and closed its door, for he did not wish anyone else to find and destroy his treasure. As he went out into the gathering darkness, Tarzan shut the door of the cabin behind him, but not before he had picked up the hunting knife to show to his fellows.

4. The Light of Knowledge

EARLY ONE morning, Tarzan set forth alone to revisit the cabin. It took him only a short time to open again the latch. He then found that he could close and lock the door from within, and this he did so that there would be no chance of his being surprised. He went again to the books. There were some children's readers, picture books and a dictionary. All of these he examined, but the pictures caught his fancy most. Squatting upon his haunches on the tabletop in the cabin—his smooth little body bent over the book, his long black hair falling about his head and over his bright eyes—Tarzan of the Apes was making his way out of ignorance and into the light of learning.

His little face was tense, for he had begun to grasp the solution to the problem of the little marks on the pages. In his hands was a primer opened at a picture of a little ape similar to himself, but covered, except for the hands and face, with strange, colored fur, for such he thought the pants and shirt to be. Beneath the picture were three marks—B-O-Y.

And now he had discovered in the text upon the page that these three marks were repeated many times. Another fact he learned—that there were not very many different marks. Slowly he turned the pages, scanning the pictures and the text for the same series of marks. Soon he found it beneath a picture of another little ape and a strange animal which went upon four

Slowly he turned the pages.

legs like the jackal. Beneath this picture the marks appeared as: A BOY AND HIS DOG.

There they were, the three little marks which always went with the little ape. And so he progressed very, very slowly, for it was a hard task which he unknowingly had set himself—a task which might seem to you or me impossible—learning to read without having the slightest knowledge of letters.

He did not succeed in a day, or in a week, or in a month, or even in a year; but slowly, very slowly, he learned, so that by the time he was fifteen he knew the various combinations of letters which stood for every pictured figure in the little primer and in one or two of the picture books.

One day when he was about twelve, he found a number of pencils in a drawer beneath the table, and, scratching upon the table with one of them, he was delighted to discover the black line it left behind it. He worked so hard with this new toy that the table was soon a mass of scrawly loops and lines. Then he tried to copy some of the little marks that scrambled over the pages of his books. It was difficult, for he held the pencil as one would grasp the hilt of a dagger. But he went on for months, at such times as he was able to come to the cabin, until at last he could roughly copy any of the little marks.

Thus Tarzan made a beginning at writing.

His education progressed; his greatest finds were in the illustrated dictionary, for he learned more through pictures than through words. By the time he was seventeen, he had learned to read the simple child's primer and had realized the true purpose of the little marks.

No longer did he feel shame for his hairless body or his human features, for now his reason told him that he was of a different species from his wild and hairy companions. He was a M-A-N, they were A-P-E-S, and the little apes which scurried through the forest top were M-O-N-K-E-Y-S. He knew, too, that old Sabor was a L-I-O-N-E-S-S, and Histah a S-N-A-K-E, and Tantor an E-L-E-P-H-A-N-T. And so he learned to read.

From then on his progress was rapid.

And soon, his little English heart began to beat with the desire to cover his nakedness with *clothes,* for he had learned from his picture books that all *men* were so covered, while *monkeys* and *apes* and every other living thing went naked.

Many moons ago, when he had been much smaller, he had desired the skin of Sabor, the lioness, or Numa, the lion, or Sheeta, the leopard, to cover his hairless body, that he might no longer look like hideous Histah, the snake. One day, as the tribe continued their slow way through the forest after seeing Sabor, Tarzan's head was filled with his great scheme for slaying his enemy, and for many days he thought of little else. After a terrible rainstorm, in which his tribe was drenched with cold rain, it came to Tarzan that clothes would have kept him warm!

For several months the tribe lingered near the beach where stood Tarzan's cabin, and his studies in the books took up more and more of his time. He did not neglect his body altogether, however; for instance he always, when journeying through the forest, kept a rope ready, with which he practiced until he could throw it as well as a cowboy could a lasso.

Tarzan of the Apes lived on in his wild jungle with little change for several years, except that he grew stronger and wiser, and learned more and more from his books of the strange worlds which lay somewhere outside the forest.

To him, life was never dull. There was always Pisah, the fish, to be caught in the many streams and little lakes, and Sabor, with her ferocious cousins, to keep one ever on the alert. Often they hunted him, and often he hunted them, and though they never quite reached him with those sharp claws, yet there were times when one could scarce have passed a leaf between their talons and his smooth hide. Quick was Sabor, the lioness, and quick were Numa and Sheeta, but Tarzan was lightning.

Only with Tantor, the elephant, did he make friends. On many moonlit nights Tarzan and Tantor walked together, and when the way was clear Tarzan rode, perched high upon Tantor's mighty back. All others in the jungle were his enemies, except his own tribe.

He spent many days during these years in the cabin of his father, where there still lay, untouched, the bones of his parents and the little skeleton of Kala's baby. At eighteen, Tarzan could read and understood nearly everything in the books on the shelves. Also, he could write, with printed letters, but script he had not mastered; he could read it, but with great trouble. Thus, at eighteen, we find him, an English lordling, who could speak no English, and yet who could read and write his native language. Never had he seen a human being other than himself.

High hills shut off the little home of his tribe on three sides, the ocean on the fourth. Though alive with lions and leopards and snakes, the jungle was isolated and undisturbed. But as Tarzan of the Apes sat one day in the cabin reading, the old safety of his jungle was broken forever.

At the far eastern edge, along a hilltop, was a line of fifty warriors, armed with spears and long bows and poisoned arrows. On their backs were oval shields, in their noses huge rings, while on their heads they wore colorful feathers. Across their foreheads were tattooed three lines of color, and on each chest three circles. Their teeth were filed to sharp points.

Following them were several hundred women and children, the women carrying upon their heads cooking pots and ivory. In the rear were a hundred warriors, similar in all respects to the advance guard.

For three days the line of men and their families marched slowly through the heart of this unknown and untracked forest, until finally, early on the fourth day, they came upon a little spot, near the banks of a small river, which seemed less overgrown than any ground they had yet seen. Here they set to work to build a new village, and in a month a great clearing had been made, huts and fences built, plantains, yams and corn planted, and they had taken up their old life in a new home.

Several moons passed by before they ventured far into the territory surrounding their village. But one day, Kulonga, a son of the old king, Mbonga, wandered far into the dense jungle of the west. Carefully he stepped, his spear ever ready, his long oval shield grasped in his left hand close to his body. At his back was his bow, and in the quiver many arrows, well smeared with poison.

Night found Kulonga far from the safety of his village, so he climbed into the fork of a tree and curled himself up to sleep. Three miles to the west of him slept the tribe of Kerchak.

Early the next morning the apes began searching for food. Tarzan made his way to the cabin, picking up his breakfast along the way. The apes scattered by ones, twos and threes in all directions. Kala had moved along an elephant track toward the east, and was busily searching under fallen trees for tasty bugs, when a strange noise caught her attention.

Down the trail, fifty yards away, she saw a strange and fearful creature—Kulonga. Kala turned and went rapidly away along the trail. Close after her came Kulonga. Here was meat! He could make a killing and feast well this day. On he hurried, his spear ready for the throw. At a turning of the trail he cast his spear, and it grazed Kala's side.

With rage and pain, the ape turned upon the man. As she charged, Kulonga shot an arrow at her, and this cut straight into her heart. He heard the other apes approaching, and he turned and ran, fleeing like an antelope.

On the far beach, by the little cabin, Tarzan heard the faint cries and sad moanings of his tribe. He hurried toward the scene, and when he arrived he found the entire tribe gathered jabbering around the dead body of his mother.

Tarzan's grief and anger roared out. He beat upon his chest with his clenched fists, and then he fell upon Kala and sobbed. So what if Kala was a fierce and hairy ape! To Tarzan she had been kind, she had been beautiful. After his grief Tarzan controlled himself, and, questioning the members of the tribe who had witnessed the escape of the murderer, he learned all that their words and signs could tell him.

They told of a strange, hairless ape with feathers growing upon its head, who shot a death-dealing stick from a slim branch, and then ran away. Tarzan now leapt into the trees and swung rapidly through the forest. All day Tarzan followed Kulonga, catching up to him, but not dropping upon him, for the ape-man saw the magical death the warrior was able to produce by flicking the string of his bow and sending a short straight stick into the skin of even a wild boar, not to mention a hyena or a monkey.

Tarzan thought much on this wondrous method of slaying as he swung slowly along at a safe distance behind his enemy. That night Kulonga slept in the fork of a huge tree, and far above him crouched Tarzan of the Apes.

When Kulonga awoke, he found that his bow and arrows had disappeared. The warrior was furious and frightened. He searched the ground below the tree, and he searched the tree, but there was no sign of them. He was defenseless now, except for a knife. His only hope

He took the headdress and placed it on his head.

for life lay in reaching the village as quickly as possible. As soon as he began running, Tarzan swung quietly after him. Kulonga's bow and arrows were tied high in the top of a tree, where Tarzan could find them later.

As Kulonga continued his journey Tarzan traveled almost over the warrior's head. He was anxious to discover where the warrior was going. Just as they came in view of the great clearing where the new village lay, Tarzan dropped his lasso around Kulonga's neck and pulled him to a stop. Tarzan leapt down and plunged his knife into Kulonga's heart.

Kala, Tarzan's foster mother, was avenged.

The ape-man examined the warrior closely, for never had he seen any other human being. The warrior's knife and belt attracted him, and so he took them. A copper anklet also took his fancy, and he took it and put it on his own leg. Finally, he took the feathered headdress and placed it on his own head.

Then he removed his rope from the warrior's neck and dashed up a lofty tree, where he sat on a perch from which he could view the village of thatched huts. Along the tree tops he then made his way for a closer look. He came to rest, finally, in a tree within the village. Below him he observed a new, strange life.

There were naked children running and playing in the village street. There were women grinding dried plantain in stone mortars, while others made little cakes from the flour. Out in the fields he could see still other women gardening. All wore grass skirts, and many were loaded with brass and copper anklets, armlets and bracelets. Tarzan of the Apes looked with wonder at these creatures. He saw several men dozing in the shade, while at the outskirts of the clearing he caught glimpses of armed warriors.

Finally his eyes settled on the woman directly beneath him. Before her was a pot standing over a low fire, and in it bubbled a thick, reddish, tarry substance. On one side of her lay a number of wooden arrows, the points of which she dipped into the liquid, before setting them upon a narrow rack which stood at her other side.

Tarzan knew nothing of poison, but his reasoning told him that it was this liquid on the arrows that killed, and not the arrows themselves. How he should like to have more of those little sticks! If the woman would only leave her work, he could drop down, gather up a handful and be back in the tree again. As he was trying to think of some plan to distract her, he heard a wild cry from across the clearing. A warrior was shouting and waving his spear.

The village was in an uproar instantly. Armed men rushed from their huts and raced toward the warrior. After them trooped the old men, and the women and children too, until, in a moment, the village was deserted.

Quickly Tarzan dropped to the ground beside the pot of poison, gathered up all the arrows he could carry under one arm, and disappeared back up the tree. The sun was high in the heavens. Tarzan had not eaten this day, and it was many miles back to the place where his tribe was gathered. So he turned his back on the village and melted away into the leafy darkness of the forest.

5. "King of the Apes"

THE NEXT day, Tarzan was practicing with his bow and arrows at the first gleam of dawn. Before a month had passed he was a good shot.

The tribe continued to find the hunting good near the beach, and so Tarzan of the Apes varied his archery practice with further reading of his father's books. It was during this period that the young English lord found hidden in the back of the cabin's cupboards a small metal box. In it he found a faded photograph of a smooth-faced young man, a golden locket on a small gold chain, a few letters and a small book.

The photograph he liked most of all, for the eyes of the man were smiling. Though he could not have known, it was of his father. The locket, too, took his fancy, and he placed the chain about his neck in imitation of the men he had seen. The handwritten letters he could hardly read, so he put them back in the box with the photograph and turned his attention to the book. This was filled with handwriting, but while the little marks were all familiar to him, their combinations were strange, and he could not understand them.

It was the diary—kept in French—of John Clayton, Lord Greystoke. Tarzan replaced the box in the cupboard, but always remembered the smiling face in the photograph.

That night he slept in the forest not far from the village, and early the next morning set out slowly on his

35

homeward march, hunting as he traveled. Suddenly he saw Sabor, the lioness, standing in the center of the trail not twenty paces from him. The great yellow eyes were fixed upon him, and the red tongue licked its lips as Sabor crouched, worming her way with belly flattened against the earth.

Tarzan unslung his bow and fitted a poisoned arrow, and as Sabor sprang, he let loose his shot to meet her in midair. At the same instant Tarzan of the Apes jumped to one side, and as the great cat struck the ground beyond him another death-tipped arrow sunk deep into her. With a roar the beast turned and charged once more, only to be met with a third arrow; this time, however, she was too close for the ape-man to avoid, and Tarzan went down beneath the great body of his enemy, his knife drawn and thrust into her. For a moment they lay there, and then Tarzan realized that she was dead.

He got up and placed a foot upon the body of his powerful enemy, and roared out the awful challenge of a victorious ape. The forest echoed with the roar, and birds fell still, and the larger animals and beasts of prey slunk away.

Before Tarzan set out for his tribe he skinned the animal; then he hurried along to show his fellows the trophy. "Look!" he cried. "See what Tarzan, the mighty killer, has done. Who else among you has ever killed one of Numa's people? Tarzan is mightiest amongst you."

These remarks angered Kerchak, and he erupted in a fury, challenging the smooth-skinned ape to fight. The tribe rushed into the trees to avoid the coming violence, and from high above they watched.

Kerchak stood nearly seven feet on his short legs. He

He faced Kerchak now with only his hunting knife.

had enormous shoulders and a snarling face, with fearsome fangs.

Awaiting him stood Tarzan, only six feet in height. His bow and arrows lay some distance away, where he had dropped them while showing Sabor's hide to his fellow apes; he faced Kerchak now with only his hunting knife. As his foe came roaring toward him, he held out his knife and rushed swiftly to meet the attack. Just as their bodies were about to crash together, Tarzan of the Apes grasped one of Kerchak's wrists, and then drove his knife into the chief's body, below the heart.

Kerchak was dead!

Withdrawing the knife, Tarzan placed his foot upon the neck of his enemy, and once again, loud through the forest rang the fierce, wild cry of the winner. And this is how the young Lord Greystoke became King of the Apes.

For a short time the tribe of Tarzan lingered near the beach, for their new chief hated the thought of leaving the little cabin. But when, one day, a member of the tribe discovered great numbers of men from the village clearing a space in the jungle and putting up huts on the banks of the little stream that served as the apes' watering hole, the apes would remain no longer, and so Tarzan led them inland.

Once every moon Tarzan would go swinging back through the branches to have a day with his books, and to replenish his supply of poisoned arrows from the men's village.

The villagers had not as yet discovered Tarzan's cabin on the distant beach, but the ape-man lived in constant dread that, while he was away with the tribe, they would loot his treasures. So it came that he spent more and more time near the cabin, and less and less with the tribe. Soon the apes began to quarrel constantly.

At last some of the older apes spoke to Tarzan on the subject of his frequent absences and the resulting disruptions while he was gone. After giving some thought to the matter, the ape-man told his tribe that he was leaving them. "Tarzan," he explained, "is not an ape. He is not like his people. His ways are not their ways, and so Tarzan is going back to his home by the waters. You must choose another to rule you, for Tarzan will not return."

The following morning, Tarzan set out toward the west and the sea coast. Once there, he decided to steal what few clothes he could from one of the villagers, for nothing seemed to him more of a sign of manhood than clothes and jewelry. He collected various arm and leg bands, and wore them the way he had seen them worn. About his neck hung the golden chain from which hung the locket of his mother. At his back was a quiver of arrows slung from a leather shoulder belt. About his waist was a belt for his knife. Around his waist was a handsome deerskin breechcloth. The long bow which had been Kulonga's hung over his left shoulder.

The young Lord Greystoke, however, worried that he might turn back into an ape, for was not hair beginning to grow on his face? All the apes had hair upon theirs, and so Tarzan was afraid. Almost daily he sharpened his knife and scraped at his young beard.

6. The Strangers

ONE MORNING, from where Tarzan stood by his cabin, a strange sight came to his eyes. On the calm waters of the harbor floated a great ship, and on the beach two small boats were drawn up. A number of white men were moving about between the beach and his cabin. Tarzan saw that in many ways they were like the men in his picture books. He crept closer through the trees until he was quite close to them.

There were many people, unloading boxes and bundles. Tarzan returned to his cabin then, snatched up a piece of paper, and printed on it several lines with a pencil. This notice he stuck upon the cabin door with a splinter. Then, gathering up his precious tin box, his arrows and as many bows and spears as he could carry, he hurried through the door and disappeared into the forest.

Several minutes later, one of the two boats returned to the ship, the *Arrow*, rowed there by burly sailors. Meanwhile, a party of five, including a young, beautiful girl of about nineteen and her heavyset maid, approached the cabin.

One of the five, an older man, a professor, came to the door and read the sign aloud:

THIS IS THE HOUSE OF TARZAN OF THE APES, THE KILLER OF BEASTS AND MANY MEN. DO NOT HARM THE THINGS WHICH ARE TARZAN'S. HE WATCHES.

"Who the devil is Tarzan?" wondered a young man.

"What does 'Tarzan of the Apes' mean?" cried the girl.

"I do not know, Miss Porter," replied the young man. "What do you make of it, Professor Porter?" he added, turning to the old man.

"I have no idea," said the professor.

Two keen eyes had watched every move of the party from behind the leaves of a nearby tree. Tarzan had seen the surprise caused by his notice, and while he could understand nothing of the spoken language of these strange people, their gestures and facial expressions told him much.

After a time, the professor and his assistant, Samuel T. Philander, became interested in the vegetation and wandered off into the jungle, out of sight. Some minutes later, Clayton, the young man, handed the girl his revolver and told her and her maid to go within the cabin and lock themselves in, if possible, while he went and searched for her absentminded father and his assistant.

A few moments later, the maid, Esmeralda, opened the door of the cabin and, entering, let out a shriek of terror.

Jane Porter rushed in and saw the cause of the maid's cry. Upon the floor before them lay the whitened skeleton of a man. A further glance revealed a second skeleton upon the bed.

"What horrible place are we in?" murmured the girl. She crossed the room to look in the little cradle, and saw there a third, smaller skeleton. The girl shuddered, but turned to her shrieking maid and said, "Stop, Esmeralda; stop it this minute! You are only making it worse."

She barred the door from within as Clayton had told

The man leapt upon the lion, choking it with his arm.

her to do, and then she and Esmeralda sat down upon a bench with their arms around one another, and waited.

When Tarzan saw the sailors row away toward the ship, and knew that the girl and her companion were safe in his cabin, he decided to follow the young man into the jungle and learn what his errand might be. He swung off rapidly in the direction taken by Clayton, and in a short time heard in the distance the faint calls of the Englishman to his friends. Tarzan soon caught up to the young man, and he hid himself behind a tree to watch this member of his own species. The fierce jungle would make short work of this stranger if he were not guided in his return to the beach cabin.

Yes; there was Numa, the lion, even now stalking the young man a dozen paces to the right. Clayton heard the great beast nearby, and now there rose the animal's thunderous roar. The man stopped and faced the bushes from which came the awful sound. For a moment all was still. Clayton stood rigid. At last he saw it, not twenty feet away—the long, strong body of a huge, black-maned lion! The beast was upon its belly, moving forward very slowly. Then Clayton heard a noise in the trees above him. There was a twang, and at the same instant an arrow lodged in the yellow hide of the crouching lion.

With lightning speed a man leapt out of the trees upon the lion, choking it with his muscular right arm, while with his left he plunged a knife time and again into the lion's shoulder. In a few moments, the lion sank lifeless to the ground.

Then the strange man, naked except for a loincloth and a few bracelets and necklaces, stood upon the dead body, and, throwing back his head, gave out a fearsome cry.

In the silence that followed the jungle-man's call, Clayton spoke to the man in English, thanking him for his brave rescue, but the only answer was a stare and a shrug. When the bow and quiver had been slung on his back, the wild man once more drew his knife and carved a dozen large strips of meat from the lion. Then, squatting, he began to eat, motioning to Clayton to join him.

But Clayton could not bring himself to share the uncooked meat with his host; instead he watched him, and there dawned upon him the belief that this was Tarzan of the Apes, whose notice he had seen posted upon the cabin door. If so, he must speak English.

Again Clayton tried to speak to the ape-man, but the replies were in a strange language, which resembled the chattering of monkeys and the growling of some wild beast. No, this could not be Tarzan of the Apes, for it was very evident that he did not know English. When the ape-man completed his meal, he rose and, pointing in a different direction from that in which Clayton had been going, started off through the jungle. Clayton followed.

Suddenly Clayton heard a faint gunshot—and then silence.

We must go back a few moments in time to explain that in the cabin by the beach, the two terrified women still clung to each other as they crouched upon a low bench in the gathering darkness. The maid sobbed, while the girl sat dry-eyed and outwardly calm. There came to them the sound of a heavy body brushing against the side of the cabin. A gentle scratching sound was heard on the door.

Moments later, the head of a huge lioness showed in the tiny square of the barred window. Her gleaming eyes were fixed upon them. Then the head disappeared, and for the next twenty minutes the brute sniffed and tore at the door, occasionally giving out a wild cry of rage. At length, however, the lioness abandoned the door, and Jane heard the beast return to the window, where she paused, and then launched herself against the time-worn bars.

The girl heard the wooden rods groan, and a few moments later, on the second attempt, one great paw and the head of the animal thrust within the room. Slowly the powerful neck and shoulders spread the bars apart, and the beast protruded further and further into the room.

Jane drew out the revolver Clayton had left, pointed it at the lioness, and pulled the trigger. There was a flash, a loud crack and an answering roar of pain from the beast. Jane saw the beast fall back from the window, and then she and Esmeralda fainted.

But the lioness was not killed. The bullet had but given her a painful wound in one of her shoulders. In another instant she was back at the window. She saw her prey—the two women—lying senseless upon the floor. Slowly she forced her great bulk, inch by inch, through the window. Now her head was through, now one forepaw and shoulder.

It was on this sight that Jane again opened her eyes.

Meanwhile, Tarzan had heard the strange sounds of the lioness' efforts to force her way through the window, and he swung Clayton up over his shoulders, and began his quick way through the trees, gliding from one vine to the next until they reached the cabin.

The ape-man seized the long tail of the lioness in both hands, and, bracing himself with his feet against the side of the cabin, threw all his mighty strength into the effort to draw the beast out. In a few moments the lioness came tumbling out of the window and onto the ground.

With the quickness of a striking rattlesnake, Tarzan launched himself full upon her back, his strong arms wrapping around the beast. With a shriek, the lioness turned completely over, falling full upon her enemy. Pawing and tearing at the earth and air, she rolled and threw herself this way and that, in an effort to unloose this strange foe.

Higher crept the forearms of the ape-man along her back and around her throat. At last Tarzan snapped the lioness' neck.

In an instant he was on his feet, and for the second time that day Clayton heard the ape-man's savage roar of victory.

In an instant he was on his feet with a roar of victory.

Then he heard Jane's cry:

"Cecil—Mr. Clayton! Oh, what was that?"

Running quickly to the cabin door, Clayton called out that all was safe. She raised the bar on the door, and said, "What was that awful noise?"

"It was the cry of victory from the throat of the man who has just saved your life, Miss Porter. Wait, I will fetch him and you may thank him."

She went with Clayton to the side of the cabin, where lay the dead body of the lioness. Tarzan of the Apes was gone.

Clayton called several times, but there was no reply, and so the two returned to the inside of the cabin. "What a frightful sound!" said Jane.

Then Clayton told her of his experiences with the strange creature—of how the wild man had saved his life. "I cannot make it out at all," he remarked. "At first I thought he might be Tarzan of the Apes, but he neither speaks nor understands English, so he cannot be."

"Well, whatever he may be," said the girl, "we owe him our lives."

Several miles south of the cabin, upon a strip of sandy beach, there stood two old men, arguing. Before them stretched the Atlantic Ocean, at their backs the continent of Africa; close around them loomed the jungle. They had wandered for miles in search of their camp, but always in the wrong direction. They were hopelessly lost.

"Bless me! Professor," said the nearsighted Mr. Philander, "there seems to be someone approaching."

Professor Porter turned and said, "Yes, indeed, though your someone appears to be a lion!"

They speeded up their steps before looking over their shoulders again.

"He is following us!" gasped Mr. Philander. The two old men broke into a dash. From the shadows of the jungle peered two keen eyes, watching this race.

It was Tarzan, of course, and he immediately swung quickly through the vines, drawing first one of the gentlemen up by his collar into a tree, and then the other. The three of them watched from that height until the lion, disgusted with waiting for a meal to drop out of the tree to him, wandered off.

Now for the first time, the professor and Mr. Philander acknowledged Tarzan.

"Good evening, sir!" said the professor.

For reply the man motioned them to follow him, and setting them down upon the jungle floor, set off.

"I think we might continue in his company," said Mr. Philander.

In silence they proceeded for what seemed like hours to the two tired and hopeless old men, but at last they passed over a little rise of ground and were overjoyed to see the cabin lying beneath them, not a hundred yards distant.

Here Tarzan pointed toward the little building and then vanished into the jungle.

"Most remarkable!" gasped the professor, and he and his assistant marched on to the cabin. It was a happy party that found itself once more united. Dawn discovered them still telling of their various adventures, and wondering who the strange hero was.

Esmeralda was positive it was none other than an angel, sent down especially to watch over them.

7. Burials

THE NEWCOMERS' next task was to make the cabin livable, and to this end it was decided to remove the skeletons, although Professor Porter and Mr. Philander were interested in first examining them. The two larger, they said, had belonged to an adult male and female. The smallest skeleton was given but passing attention, as its location, in the crib, left no doubt of its having been the infant of this couple. Even so, Mr. Philander made a startling observation about it, which, however, he refrained from sharing with the others.

As they were preparing the skeleton of the man for burial, Clayton discovered a ring on the man's finger. Examining it, he gave a cry, for the ring bore the crest of Greystoke. At the same time, Jane discovered the books in the cupboard, and on opening to the flyleaf of one of them saw the name *John Clayton, London.*

"Why, Mr. Clayton," she cried, "what does this mean? Here are the names of your relatives in these books!"

"And here," he replied, "is the ring belonging to my uncle, John Clayton, Lord Greystoke."

"But how do you account for these things being here?"

"There is but one way to account for it," said Clayton. "The late Lord Greystoke was not drowned, as was presumed. He died here in this cabin, and this skeleton is all that is left of him."

"Then this must have been poor Lady Greystoke," said Jane.

The bodies of the late Lord and Lady Greystoke were buried beside their little African cabin, and between them was placed the tiny skeleton of the baby of Kala, the ape.

Tarzan watched the ceremony from the trees, but most of all he watched the sweet face and figure of Jane Porter. In his savage soul new emotions were stirring. He could not understand them. He wondered why he felt such great interest in these people—why he had gone to such pains to save the three men. But he did not wonder why he had rescued the girl. She was beautiful!

When the grave was filled with earth, the little party turned back toward the cabin, and Esmeralda, still weeping, chanced to glance toward the harbor.

"Look at those brutes out there!" she cried. "They're deserting us, right here in this jungle!"

And, sure enough, the *Arrow* was making for the open sea, slowly, through the harbor's entrance.

"They promised to leave us guns and ammunition," said Clayton. "The merciless beasts!"

"I regret that they did not visit us before sailing," said Professor Porter. "I had requested them to leave the treasure with us."

Jane looked at her father sadly. "Never mind, daddy," she said. "It is solely for the treasure that the men killed their officers and landed us upon this awful shore."

"Indeed?" wondered the professor, who was all too innocent.

"Yes, sir," confirmed Clayton and Mr. Philander.

Tarzan noted the confusion on the faces of the little group as they witnessed the departure of the *Arrow,* and so, following the course of the ship, he hurried out to the point of land at the north of the harbor's mouth to obtain a nearer view.

Swinging through the trees, he reached the point just as the ship was passing out of the harbor, so that he had an excellent view of this strange, floating house, the like of which he had never seen before. There were some twenty men running here and there about the deck, pulling and hauling on ropes. Suddenly the ship slowed to a crawl, and the anchor was lowered; down came the sails. A few moments later a rowboat was lowered over the side, and in it a large chest was placed. Then a dozen sailors rowed toward the point where Tarzan crouched in the branches of a tree.

In a few minutes, the boat had reached the beach. The men jumped out and lifted the great chest to the sand. They were on the north side of the point, so that their presence was hidden from those at the cabin.

One sailor, pointing at a spot beneath Tarzan's tree, said, "Here's a good place." The soil was soft, and soon they had dug a large hole in which to bury the chest. Then they covered it. Their work done, the sailors returned to the small boat and pulled off rapidly toward the *Arrow*. The ship got under full sail immediately, and bore away toward the southwest.

Tarzan sat wondering about the strange actions of these men, and about the contents of the chest they had buried. He dropped to the ground and began to uncover the earth from atop the chest. When this was done, he dragged the chest from the hole. Four sailors had sweated beneath the burden of its weight—Tarzan of the Apes picked it up as though it had been an empty packing case, and carried it off into the densest part of the jungle.

He could not swing through the trees with it, and so he kept to the trails, and made good time. For several hours he traveled northeast, until he came to the meeting place of the apes. Near the center of the clearing, he began to dig. After much labor he buried the locked chest.

By the time Tarzan had hunted his way back toward the cabin, feeding as he went, it was quite dark.

Within the little building a light was burning, for Clayton had found an unopened tin of oil. The lamps were still usable, and so the interior of the cabin appeared bright as day to the astonished Tarzan. He had often wondered about the purpose of the lamps. As he approached the window nearest the door, he saw that the cabin had been divided into two rooms by a sailcloth. In the front room were the three men, the two older ones deep in conversation, while the youngest read one of Tarzan's books.

Tarzan was not interested in the men, however, so he went to the other window. There was the girl. How beautiful! She was writing at Tarzan's own table beneath the window. Upon a pile of grasses at the far side of the room lay the maid, asleep.

For an hour Tarzan feasted his eyes upon Jane while she wrote. How he longed to speak to her, but he feared that he might frighten her away. Soon she got up, leaving her letter upon the table. She went to the bed, upon which had been spread several layers of soft grasses. Then she loosened her hair, and put out the lamp.

Still Tarzan watched from outside. Cautiously he put his hand through the window to feel upon the desk. At last he grasped the papers upon which Jane had been writing, and pulled them out. He folded the sheets and tucked them into the quiver with his arrows. Then he melted away into the jungle, as softly as a shadow.

Early the next morning Tarzan awoke, and hurriedly brought forth the letter hidden in his quiver. Here is what he read:

To Hazel Strong, Baltimore, Maryland

> *West Coast of Africa,*
> *About 10 Degrees South Latitude*

> February 3, 1909

Dearest Hazel:

It seems foolish to write you a letter that you may never see, but I must tell somebody of our awful experiences since we sailed from Europe on the *Arrow.* If we never return to civilization, as now seems likely, this will at least be a brief record of the events which led up to our final fate.

As you know, Papa discovered a long-lost treasure map from 1550, drawn by a Spanish sailor. To make a long story short, we found the treasure—a great iron-bound oak chest. It was simply filled with gold coin, and was so heavy that four men bent beneath its weight. The horrid thing seems to bring nothing but murder and misfortune to those who have anything to do with it, for, three days after we sailed from the Cape Verde Islands, our own crew mutinied and killed every one of their officers.

They were going to kill us, too, but one of them, the leader, would not let them, and so they sailed south along the coast to a lonely spot where they found a good harbor, and there they landed and have left us. They sailed away with the treasure today.

We have had the most extraordinary experiences since we landed here. Papa and Mr. Philander got lost in the jungle, and were chased by a real lion. Mr. Clayton got lost, and was attacked by a wild beast. Esmeralda and I were cornered in an old cabin by a lioness. But the strangest part of it all is the wonder-

The following morning, Jane found her missing letter.

ful creature who rescued us. I have not seen him, but Mr. Clayton and Papa and Mr. Philander have, and they say he is a god-like, dusky-tanned man, with the strength of an elephant and the bravery of a lion. He speaks no English, and vanishes quickly after he has performed some valorous deed.

Then we have another unusual neighbor, who printed a beautiful sign in English and tacked it on the door of his cabin—which we have moved into—warning us to destroy none of his belongings, and signing himself "Tarzan of the Apes." We have never seen him, though we think he is about.

The sailors left us but a meager supply of food, so, as we have only a single revolver with but three bullets left in it, we do not know how we will get meat, though Mr. Philander says we can live on the wild fruit and nuts which abound in this jungle.

I am very tired now, so I shall go to my bed of grasses.

Lovingly,
JANE PORTER

Tarzan sat, after he had finished reading the letter, his brain in a whirl. So they did not know he was Tarzan of the Apes! He would tell them. He had constructed in his tree a rude shelter of leaves and boughs, beneath which, protected from the rain, he kept the few treasures he had brought from the cabin: among these were some pencils.

He took one, and beneath Jane Porter's signature he wrote:

I am Tarzan of the Apes.

He thought that would be enough. Later he would return the letter to the cabin. In the matter of food, thought Tarzan, they had no need to worry—he would provide that.

The following morning, Jane found her missing letter in the exact spot from which it had disappeared two nights before. When she saw the printed words beneath her signature, she felt a chill run up her spine. She showed it to Clayton.

"But he must be friendly," said Clayton, "for he has returned your letter, and he has left the carcass of a wild boar outside the cabin door."

From then on, scarcely a day went by that did not bring its offering of meat. Sometimes it was a young deer, or strange, cooked food—stolen from the Mbonga's village—or a boar, a leopard, and once a lion. Tarzan got great pleasure in hunting for meat for these strangers.

A month passed, and Tarzan finally determined to visit the camp by daylight. It was early afternoon. Clayton had wandered to the point at the harbor's mouth to look for passing ships. Professor Porter was strolling along the beach, with Mr. Philander at his elbow. Jane and Esmeralda had ventured into the jungle to gather fruit.

Tarzan waited in silence before the door of the little cabin for their return. His thoughts were of the beautiful girl; they were always of her now. He wondered if she would fear him. While he waited, he passed the time writing a message to her:

> I am Tarzan of the Apes. I am yours. You are mine. We will live here together always in my house. I will bring you the best fruits, the tenderest deer, the finest meats that the jungle provides. I will hunt for you. I am the greatest of the jungle hunters. I will fight for you. I am the mightiest of the jungle fighters. You are Jane Porter, I saw it in your letter. When you see this you will know that it is for you and that Tarzan of the Apes loves you.

As he stood by the door, waiting after he had finished the message, there came to his keen ears a familiar sound. It was the passing of a great ape through the lower branches of the forest. Then from the jungle came the scream of a woman, and Tarzan, dropping his letter upon the ground, shot like a panther into the forest.

Clayton also heard the scream, as did Professor

Porter and Mr. Philander, and in a few minutes they all arrived at the cabin; Jane and Esmeralda were not there. Instantly, Clayton, followed by the two old men, plunged into the jungle, calling the girl's name aloud. For half an hour they stumbled on, until Clayton came upon the fainted form of Esmeralda.

"Esmeralda," he shouted. "Esmeralda! For God's sake, where is Miss Porter?"

"Isn't Miss Jane here?" cried Esmeralda, sitting up. "Oh, Lord, now I remember! It must have taken her away." And she began to sob.

"What took her away?" said Professor Porter.

"A great big giant all covered with hair."

"A gorilla, Esmeralda?" questioned Mr. Philander.

"I thought it was the devil, but I guess it must have been one of them gorillas. Oh, my poor baby, my poor little honey," and again Esmeralda broke into sobbing.

Clayton began to look about for tracks, but he could find nothing. For the rest of the day they looked for Jane through the jungle, but as night drew on they were forced to give up, for they did not even know in what direction the ape had taken Jane.

It was long after dark before this very sad group reached the cabin.

8. The Call of the Wild

THE NEW KING of the apes, Terkoz, who had taken over when Tarzan left, had been right above Esmeralda and Jane when he first saw them. The first moment Jane became aware of him was when the hairy beast dropped to the earth beside her. One piercing scream escaped her lips as the brute clutched her arm.

This hairless white ape, thought Terkoz, would be one of his wives, and so he threw her across his shoulders and leaped back into the trees, bearing Jane away farther and farther into the jungle.

The scream that had brought Clayton and the two older men stumbling through the undergrowth had led Tarzan straight to where Esmeralda lay, but it was not Esmeralda in whom his interest centered, though he paused over her to see that she was unhurt.

For a moment he studied the ground below and the trees above, until the ape in him, combined with his human intelligence, understood the whole story as plainly as though he had seen the thing happen with his own eyes.

And then he was gone again into the swaying trees, following the trail no other human eye could have noticed. Here, on this branch, a caterpillar had been crushed by the ape's great foot, and Tarzan knew where that same foot would touch in the next stride. Here he looked to find a tiny particle of debris, and there he saw a bit of bark that had been upturned by the scraping hand.

But Tarzan's strongest sense was scent, for his trained nostrils were as sensitive as a hound's. From early infancy his survival had depended on keen eye-sight, hearing, smell, touch and taste.

Almost silently the ape-man sped on in the track of Terkoz and Jane, but the sound of his approach reached the ears of the fleeing beast and spurred it on to greater speed. Three miles were covered before Tarzan overtook them, and then Terkoz, seeing that fur-ther flight would do him no good, dropped to the ground in a small open glade, that he might turn and fight for his prize, or be free to escape unharmed if he saw that Tarzan was too much for him.

He still grasped Jane in one arm as Tarzan bounded like a leopard into the arena which nature had provid-ed for this battle. From the description which Clayton and her father had given her, Jane knew that the new-comer must be the same wonderful creature who had saved them. But when Terkoz pushed her roughly aside to meet Tarzan's charge, and she saw the size of the ape and its mighty muscles and fierce fangs, she was fright-ened.

Like two charging bulls the man and beast came together, and like two wolves went for each other's throat. To oppose the long, sharp teeth of the ape was Tarzan's thin-bladed knife.

Jane—backed up against a tree, her hands pressed against her chest, her eyes wide—watched the battle. Before long, Tarzan had stabbed the huge ape a dozen times, and the beast rolled over, dead. Jane then sprang forward with outstretched arms toward the ape-man who had fought for her.

Tarzan took the woman in his arms and kissed her, then swept her up and carried her into the jungle.

Early the following morning, the four within the little cabin by the beach were awakened by the booming of a cannon. Clayton was the first to rush out, and there, beyond the harbor's mouth, he saw two ships lying at anchor.

One was the *Arrow,* the ship which had abandoned them there, and the other a small French cruiser. The sides of the French ship were crowded with men gazing shoreward. Both vessels lay at a great distance from shore, and it was doubtful whether they could see the waving hats of the little group. Esmeralda removed her red apron and waved it frantically above her head, and Clayton hurried off toward the northern point where lay his pile of wood, heaped up for just this occasion. Quickly lighting the pile in a dozen places, he hurried to the point of the land, where he stripped off his shirt, and, tying it to a branch, stood waving it back and forth above him.

Soon Clayton saw the two ships begin to steam slowly back toward shore. At some distance away they stopped, and a boat was lowered and rowed toward the beach. As it drew up onto the sand, a young French officer stepped out.

"Monsieur Clayton, I presume?" he asked.

"Thank God, you have come!" was Clayton's reply. "And it may be that it is not too late, even now."

"What do you mean?"

Clayton then told of how the ape had stolen away Jane Porter.

"Mon Dieu!" exclaimed the officer.

Soon the entire party had come ashore, where stood Professor Porter, Mr. Philander and the weeping

Esmeralda waved her apron frantically above her head.

Esmeralda. Among the officers in the last of the boats to put off from the French ship was the commander, and when he had heard the story of Jane's kidnapping, he called for volunteers to go with Professor Porter and Clayton in their search.

Not an officer or a man was there who did not quickly volunteer. The commander then selected twenty men and two officers, Lieutenant D'Arnot and Lieutenant Charpentier. Within a few minutes the group of sailors and the two French officers, together with Professor Porter and Clayton, set off upon their quest into the jungle.

When Jane realized she was being carried away a captive by the strange forest creature who had rescued her, she lay quietly in his strong arms, looking through half-closed eyes at the face of this man who strode so easily through the tangled undergrowth with her. He seemed to her extraordinarily beautiful.

Soon Tarzan took to the trees, and Jane, wondering that she felt no fear, began to realize that she had never felt more safe in her life than now, lying in the arms of this strong, wild creature, being carried, God alone knew where, deeper and deeper into the savage jungle.

When they had come to their destination, Tarzan of the Apes, with Jane in his grasp, swung lightly to the turf of the open space where the great apes held their meetings.

Though they had come many miles, it was still but midafternoon. The green turf looked soft and cool. The many noises of the jungle seemed far away and hushed, like surf upon a distant shore. A feeling of dreaminess stole over Jane as she sank down upon the grass where Tarzan had placed her. As she watched him, Tarzan crossed the clearing toward the trees upon the further side. She thought what a perfect creature he looked! Never had such a man walked the earth since God created Adam.

With a bound Tarzan sprang into the trees and disappeared. Jane wondered where he had gone. Had he left her there to her fate in the lonely jungle? She glanced nervously about. Every vine and bush seemed to be the lurking place of some huge and horrible beast. Every sound terrified her.

For a few minutes, which seemed hours to the frightened girl, she sat with tense nerves. She heard a sudden, slight sound behind her. With a shriek she sprang to her feet and turned to face her end. Instead, there stood Tarzan, his arms filled with ripe fruit.

Jane became dizzy and would have fallen, had not Tarzan, dropping the fruit, caught her in his arms. Tarzan stroked her soft hair, and tried to comfort and quiet her as Kala had him, when, as a little ape, he had been frightened by Sabor, the lioness, or Histah, the snake. He pressed his lips upon her forehead, and she sighed.

Then she pointed to the fruit upon the ground, and seated herself, for she was hungry. Tarzan quickly gathered up the fruit, and, bringing it, laid it at her feet; then he, too, sat, and with his knife prepared the fruits for her meal. Together and in silence they ate, until finally Jane said, "I wish you spoke English."

Tarzan shook his head. Then Jane tried speaking to him in French and in German. Again Tarzan shook his head.

Finally, he got up and went into the trees, though not without first trying to explain, by signs, that he would return shortly; he signaled so well that Jane understood and was not afraid when he had gone. Only a feeling of loneliness came over her, and she watched with longing eyes the point where he had disappeared, awaiting his return. As before, she knew he had returned when she heard a soft sound behind her, and she turned to see him coming across the turf with an armful of branches.

He then went back again into the jungle, and in a few minutes he reappeared, his arms filled with soft grasses and ferns. Two more trips he made, until he had gathered quite a pile of material. Then he spread the ferns and grasses upon the ground in a soft flat bed, and above it he leaned many branches together so that they met a few feet over its center. Upon these he spread layers of huge leaves, and with more branches and more leaves he closed one end of the little shelter he had built.

Then they sat down together and tried to talk by signs. The magnificent diamond locket which hung about Tarzan's neck had been a source of much wonder to Jane. She pointed to it now, and Tarzan removed it and handed it to her.

She noticed that the locket opened, and, pressing the hidden clasp, she saw the two halves spring apart to reveal in either section a miniature portrait. One was of a beautiful woman, and the other might have been a likeness of the man who sat beside her. She looked up at Tarzan to find him leaning toward her, gazing on the miniatures with astonishment. His manner showed her that he had never before seen them, nor even guessed that the locket opened. Jane now wondered how this necklace had come to a wild and savage creature of the jungle. She also wondered how it could be that the image of the man in the locket resembled this forest god.

Tarzan gazed at the two faces for a moment. Soon he removed the quiver of arrows from his shoulder, and, emptying its contents upon the ground, he reached into the bottom of the quiver and drew out a flat object wrapped in many soft leaves and tied with bits of long grass. Carefully he unwrapped it, removing layer after layer of leaves, until at length he held a photograph in his hand.

Pointing to the miniature of the man within the locket, he handed the photograph to Jane, holding the open locket beside it. The photograph only served to puzzle the girl still more, for it was evidently another likeness of the same man whose picture rested in the locket beside that of the beautiful young woman.

Jane pointed to the photograph and then to the miniature and then to him, as though to show that she thought the likenesses were of him, but he only shook his head, and then, shrugging his shoulders, he took the photograph from her and rewrapped it before placing it again in the bottom of his quiver.

Jane held the little locket in her hand, turning it over and over until a simple explanation occurred to her. The locket had belonged to Lord Greystoke, and the likenesses were of himself and Lady Alice. This wild creature had simply found it in the cabin by the beach. How stupid of her not to have thought of that before. But to account for the likeness between Lord Greystoke and this forest god—that was quite beyond her, and it is not strange that she did not imagine that this half-naked savage was indeed an English nobleman.

It was growing dark now, and so they ate again of the fruit which was both food and drink for them, and then Tarzan rose and leading Jane to the little bower he had built, motioned her to go within.

The girl entered and lay down upon the soft grasses, while Tarzan of the Apes stretched himself upon the ground across the entrance.

When Jane awoke, she did not at first recall the strange events of the day before, and so she wondered at her odd surroundings—the little leafy bower, the soft grasses of her bed, the unusual view from the opening at her feet. After she remembered why she was there, she moved to the entrance of the shelter to look for Tarzan. He was gone; but this time she was not frightened, for she knew that he would return.

In the grass at the entrance to her bower she saw the

imprint of his body where he had lain all night to guard her. With him near, who could be afraid? She wondered if there was any other man on earth with whom a girl could feel so safe in the middle of this jungle. Why, even the lions no longer scared her now! She looked up to see him drop softly from a nearby tree. As he caught her eyes upon him, his face lit up with a bright smile.

He had again been gathering fruit, and this he laid at the entrance of her bower. Once more they sat down together to eat. When they had finished their breakfast, Tarzan motioned to her to follow. He walked toward the trees at the edge of the clearing, and took her in one strong arm and swung to the branches above.

The girl knew that he was taking her back to her people, so she could not understand the sudden feeling of sorrow which crept over her.

For hours they swung slowly along. Tarzan did not hurry. Several times they halted for a brief rest, which he did not need, and at noon they stopped for an hour at a little stream, where they quenched their thirst and ate. It was nearly sunset when they came to the cabin, and Tarzan, dropping to the ground beside a great tree, parted the tall jungle grass and pointed out the little cabin to her. She took him by the hand to lead him to it, that she might tell her father that this man had saved her from death, and that he had watched over her as carefully as a mother might have done. But Tarzan drew back, shaking his head.

The girl came close to him, looking up with pleading eyes. Somehow she could not bear the thought of his going back into the jungle alone. Still he shook his head, and finally he drew her to him very gently and stooped to kiss her. She threw her arms around his neck and kissed him back.

"I love you," she said. "I love you."

From far in the distance came the faint sound of many guns. Tarzan and Jane stopped and listened; the noise brought Esmeralda and Mr. Philander out of the cabin as well. From where Tarzan and the girl stood, they could not see the two ships lying at anchor in the harbor. Tarzan pointed toward the sounds, touched his chest, and pointed again. She understood. He was going, and something told her that it was because he thought her people were in danger.

"Come back to me," she whispered. "I shall wait for you—always."

Then he was gone—and Jane turned to walk across the clearing to the cabin.

Mr. Philander was the first to see her. "Jane!" he cried. "Jane Porter! Bless me! Where did you come from? Where in the world have you been? How—"

"Mercy, Mr. Philander," interrupted the girl. "I never can remember so many questions."

"Well, well," said Mr. Philander. "Bless me! I am so filled with surprise and delight at seeing you safe and well again that I scarcely know what I am saying, really. But come, tell me all that has happened to you."

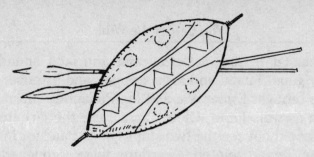

9. French Lessons

A s THE little expedition of sailors toiled through the dense jungle, searching for signs of Jane Porter, the hopelessness of their venture became more and more clear, but the grief of the old man and the heartsick eyes of the young Englishman prevented the kindhearted D'Arnot from turning back. He sent out his men in formation from where Esmeralda had been found, and they sweated their way through the tangled vines.

It was slow work. Noon found them but a few miles inland. They halted for a brief rest then, and after pushing on for a short distance, one of the men discovered a well marked trail. It was an old elephant track, and D'Arnot decided that they all should follow it. He was in the lead and moving at a quick pace when a half dozen tribal warriors suddenly arose about him.

D'Arnot gave a warning shout to his men as the warriors closed in on him, but before he could draw his revolver he found himself gripped by his arms and dragged into the jungle.

His cry had alarmed the sailors, and a dozen of them ran up the trail to their officer's aid. A spear struck one man, and then a volley of arrows fell among them. Raising their rifles, they fired into the underbrush in the direction from which the arrows had come. It was these shots that Tarzan and Jane had heard.

Lieutenant Charpentier, who had been bringing up the rear of the line of men, now came running to the

scene, and, on hearing the details of the ambush, he
ordered the men to follow him. In an instant they were
in a hand-to-hand fight with some fifty warriors of
Mbonga's village. Arrows and bullets flew thick and
fast.

Minutes later, the warriors backtracked, but the
Frenchmen did not follow, as four of their twenty were
dead, a dozen others were wounded and Lieutenant
D'Arnot was missing. Night was falling, and so they
made camp where they were.

The warriors who seized D'Arnot had in the meantime hurried him along, and they now brought him to a
good-sized clearing, at one end of which stood their
thatched and gated village. It was now dusk, but the
gatekeepers saw the approaching prisoner, and a cry
went up. A great throng of women and children rushed
out to meet the group.

Then began for the French officer the most terrifying
experience a man can encounter upon earth—the
reception of a prisoner into a village of cannibals.

They fell upon D'Arnot tooth and nail, beating him
with sticks and stones and tearing at him, but not once
did the Frenchman cry out in pain. They soon arrived
at the center of the village, where D'Arnot was tied up
to a post from which no live man had ever been
released. A number of women scattered to their several huts to fetch pots and water, while others built a row
of fires on which portions of the feast were to be boiled.

Half fainting from pain, D'Arnot watched what
seemed to be a nightmare.

Tarzan of the Apes knew what those sounds had
meant. With Jane's kisses still warm upon his lips, he
swung with incredible swiftness through the forest,
straight toward Mbonga's village. He was not interested

in the location of the battle, for he judged that that would soon be over. Those who were killed he could not help; those who escaped would not need his help. It was to those who had neither been killed nor had escaped that he hurried. And he knew that he would find them by the post in Mbonga's village.

Many times had Tarzan seen Mbonga's raiding parties return from the north with prisoners, and always were the same scenes carried out about that stake, beneath the light of many fires.

He knew, too, that the villagers seldom lost much time before eating their captives. On he sped. Night had fallen and he traveled high along the trees, where the tropic moon lighted the confusing pathway through the gently waving treetops. In a few minutes Tarzan swung into the trees above Mbonga's village. Ah, he was not too late! Or was he? He could not tell. The figure at the stake was very still, yet the warriors continued to prick it with their spears.

Tarzan knew their customs. The death blow had not been struck. The stake stood forty feet from the nearest tree. Tarzan coiled his rope. Then there rose suddenly above the singing of the villagers Tarzan's terrible, apelike cry.

The dancers halted as though turned to stone.

Tarzan flung the rope high above the villagers. It was unseen in the flaring lights of the campfires.

D'Arnot opened his eyes. A huge tribesman, standing directly before him, lunged backward as though struck by an invisible hand. Struggling and shrieking, the tribesman, rolling from side to side, was jerked quickly toward the shadows beneath the trees. Once beneath the trees, the body rose straight into the air, and as it disappeared into the leaves above, the terrified vil-

The figure at the stake was very still.

lagers, screaming with fright, broke into a mad race for the gates.

D'Arnot was left alone. As he watched the spot where the body had entered the tree, he heard the sounds of movement there. The branches swayed—there was a crash and the warrior came sprawling to earth again.

Immediately after him came a young giant, who moved quickly toward him from the shadows into the firelight. What could it mean? Who could it be?

Without a word Tarzan of the Apes cut the bonds which held the Frenchman. Weak from suffering and loss of blood, D'Arnot would have fallen but for the strong arms that caught him.

The French officer felt himself lifted from the ground. There was a sensation as of flying, and then he fainted.

It was not until late the next afternoon that the patrol reached the clearing by the beach. For Professor Porter and Cecil Clayton, the return brought such great happiness that all their sufferings were forgotten. As the little party emerged from the jungle, the first person that the professor and Clayton saw was Jane, standing by the cabin door.

With a little cry of joy she ran forward to greet them, throwing her arms around her father's neck and bursting into tears. Professor Porter sobbed as well. Clayton's heart was filled with happiness to see that the woman he loved was safe. "Jane!" he cried. "God has been good to us, indeed. Tell me how you escaped."

"Mr. Clayton," she said, offering her hand to shake, "let me thank you for your loyalty to my father. He told me how good you were to accompany him in his search for me. How can we ever repay you?"

"I am already repaid," he said, "just to see you and the professor both safe, well and together again."

"But tell me," said Jane, "where is the forest man who went to rescue you? Why did he not return?"

"I do not understand," said Clayton. "Whom do you mean?"

"He who has saved each of us—who saved me from the gorilla."

"Oh?" said Clayton in surprise. "It was he who rescued you? You have not told me anything of your adventure. Please tell me."

"But, no—haven't you seen him? When we heard the shots in the jungle, he left me. We had just reached the clearing, and he hurried off in the direction of the shots. I know he went to help you."

"We did not see him," said Clayton. "He did not join us. Possibly he joined his own tribe—the men who attacked us."

"No!" said Jane. "It could not be. They were savages—he is a gentleman."

Clayton looked puzzled, and remarked of the man he did not know was his cousin, "He is a strange, half-savage creature of the jungle, Miss Porter. We know nothing of him. He neither speaks nor understands any European language—and his jewelry and weapons are those of the savages." He saw she was made unhappy by these words, but he continued. "There are no other human beings than savages within hundreds of miles. He must belong to the tribes which attacked us—he may even be a cannibal, a man-eater."

"No, I will not believe it," said Jane. "It's not true. You do not know him as I do."

"Possibly you are right, Jane," said Clayton, "but the chances are that he is some half-crazed castaway who will forget us quickly. He is only a beast of the jungle."

The girl did not answer. Slowly she turned and walked back to the cabin, murmuring to herself, "Beast? Then God make me a beast; for, man or beast, I am his!"

The next morning Clayton left early with the expedition in search of Lieutenant D'Arnot, for they did not know that Tarzan had already rescued the officer.

When D'Arnot came out of his faint, he found himself lying upon a bed of soft ferns and grasses beneath a little A-shaped shelter of boughs. At his feet, an opening

D'Arnot tried to talk with the man, but it was useless.

looked out upon a green clearing, and at a little distance beyond was a wall of jungle. He was very lame and sore and weak.

After some time he remembered the whole terrifying scene at the stake of the natives, and he finally recalled the strange figure in whose arms he had fainted away. He wondered what would happen now. He could not see or hear any signs of life. The hum of the jungle—the rustling of millions of leaves—the buzz of insects—the voices of birds and monkeys—seemed blended into a purr. Suddenly, through the opening at his feet, he saw the figure of Tarzan.

The ape-man came toward the shelter. Stooping, he crawled into the shelter beside the wounded officer, and placed a cool hand upon his forehead.

D'Arnot spoke to him in French, but the man only shook his head. Then D'Arnot tried English, but still the man shook his head. Then he tried Italian, Spanish and German, but with the same response from Tarzan.

After he had examined D'Arnot's wounds, Tarzan left the shelter and disappeared. In half an hour he was back with fruit and a hollow gourd filled with water. D'Arnot drank and ate a little. Again he tried to talk with the strange man, but it was useless.

Suddenly Tarzan hurried from the shelter, only to return a few minutes later with several pieces of bark and—wonder of wonders—a lead pencil. Squatting beside D'Arnot, Tarzan wrote for a minute on the smooth inner surface of the bark, then handed it to the Frenchman. D'Arnot was astonished to see, in plain print, a message in English:

"I am Tarzan of the Apes. Who are you? Can you read this language?"

"Yes!" cried out D'Arnot, "I read English. I speak it also. Now we may talk. First let me thank you for all that you have done."

The man only shook his head and pointed to the pencil.

"Mon Dieu!" cried D'Arnot. "If you are English, why is it then that you cannot speak English? You must be a deaf mute!" So he wrote to Tarzan a message on the bark, in English:

"I am Paul D'Arnot, lieutenant in the navy of France. I thank you for what you have done for me. You have saved my life, and all that I have is yours. May I ask how it is that one who writes in English does not speak it?"

Tarzan's neatly printed reply filled D'Arnot with wonder:

"I speak only the language of my tribe—the great apes who were Kerchak's, and a little of the languages of Tantor, the elephant, and Numa, the lion. With a human being I have never spoken, except once with Jane, by signs. This is the first time I have spoken with another of my kind through written words."

D'Arnot was amazed. It seemed incredible that there lived upon earth a full-grown man who had never spoken with a fellow man. He looked again at Tarzan's message, and wrote, "Where is Jane?"

And Tarzan replied: "Back with her people in the cabin of Tarzan of the Apes."

"She is not dead then?" wrote D'Arnot. "What happened to her?"

Tarzan took the pencil now and wrote: "She is not dead. She was taken by Terkoz to be his wife, but Tarzan took her away from Terkoz and killed him before he could harm her. None in all the jungle may face Tarzan of the Apes in battle, and live."

For many days D'Arnot lay upon his bed of soft ferns. The second day a fever had come and D'Arnot thought that it meant he would die. An idea came to him. He called Tarzan and wrote to him: "Can you go to my people and lead them here? I will write a message that you may take to them, and they will follow you."

Tarzan shook his head and wrote: "I had thought of that the first day, but I dared not. The great apes come often to this spot, and if they found you here, wounded and alone, they would kill you."

D'Arnot lay in a fever for three more days, and Tarzan

sat beside him, and bathed his head and hands and washed his wounds. Two days after the fever had passed, D'Arnot was able to stand with Tarzan's help, but he was still as weak as a baby.

D'Arnot wrote his rescuer a message: "What can I do to repay you for all that you have done for me?"

"Teach me to speak the language of men," wrote Tarzan.

And so D'Arnot began at once, pointing out the familiar objects and repeating their names in French, for he thought it would be easier to teach this man his own language.

So when Tarzan pointed to the word *man* which he had printed upon a piece of bark, he learned from D'Arnot that it was pronounced "homme," and in the same way he was taught to pronounce *ape* as "singe" and *tree* as "arbre."

He was an eager student, and in two more days he had mastered so much French that he could speak little sentences such as: "That is a tree"; "This is grass"; "I am hungry." The Frenchman wrote little lessons for Tarzan in English, and had Tarzan repeat them in French, but this was often confusing for them both. D'Arnot realized now he had made a mistake of crossing the languages, but it seemed too late to go back and do it all over again.

On the third day of lessons Tarzan wrote D'Arnot a message asking if he felt strong enough to be carried back to the cabin.

"But you cannot carry me all the distance through this jungle," wrote D'Arnot.

"Mais oui!" Tarzan said, and D'Arnot laughed aloud to hear the phrase from the ape-man's mouth.

So they set out, D'Arnot marveling as had Clayton and Jane at the wondrous strength of the ape-man.

Midafternoon brought them to the clearing.

Midafternoon brought them to the clearing, and as Tarzan dropped to earth from the branches of the last tree, his heart leaped in expectation of seeing Jane. But no one was in sight near the cabin, and D'Arnot was surprised to notice that the two ships were no longer at anchor in the bay outside the harbor.

Neither spoke, but both knew before they opened the closed cabin door what they would find within. Tarzan lifted the latch and pushed open the door. It was as they feared; the cabin was deserted. The men turned and looked at one another.

D'Arnot knew that his men thought him dead, but

Tarzan thought only of the woman who had kissed him and now had fled from him. But as Tarzan stood in the doorway brooding, D'Arnot noticed that many supplies had been left from the ship: a camping stove, some forks and knives, a rifle and ammunition, canned foods, blankets, two chairs and a cot.

"They must intend to return," said D'Arnot. He walked over to the table that John Clayton had built so many years before to serve as a desk, and on it he saw two notes addressed to Tarzan. He handed them to the ape-man, and Tarzan sat down on a stool and read them.

To Tarzan of the Apes:
    We thank you for the use of your cabin, and are sorry that we could not thank you in person. We have harmed nothing of your goods, but have left many things for you which may add to your comfort. If you know the strange jungle-man who saved our lives and brought us food, thank him for his kindness.
    We sail in an hour, never to return.
                                        Very gratefully,
                                        CECIL CLAYTON

Tarzan had a look of sorrow as he read through this letter, which he then handed to D'Arnot. The second, as Tarzan feared, was from Jane:

To Tarzan of the Apes:
    Before I leave, let me add my thanks to those of Mr. Clayton for the kindness you have shown in permitting us the use of your cabin. That you never came to make friends with us has been a regret to us.
    There is another I should like to thank also, but he did not come back, though I cannot believe that he is dead. I do not know his name. He is the great giant

who wore the diamond locket upon his chest. If you know him and can speak his language, carry my thanks to him, and tell him that I waited seven days for him to return.

Tell him, also, that in my home in America, in the city of Baltimore, there will always be a welcome for him.

I found a note you wrote me lying among the leaves beneath a tree near the cabin. I do not know how you learned to love me, but I must tell you that I already love another.

I shall always be your friend,
JANE PORTER

It was evident to him from the notes that they did not know that he and Tarzan of the Apes were one and the same. *"I already love another!"* he sighed to himself again and again. Then she did not love *him!* How could she have pretended to love him? Maybe her kisses were only signs of friendship. How was he to know, who knew nothing of the customs of human beings?

Suddenly, he turned to D'Arnot and asked, "Where is America?"

D'Arnot pointed toward the northwest, and said, "Many thousands of miles across the ocean. Why?"

"I am going there."

D'Arnot shook his head. "It is impossible, my friend." D'Arnot pulled an atlas from the bookshelf, showing the ape-man that the blue represented all the water on the earth, and the bits of other colors the continents and islands. Tarzan asked him to point out the spot where they now were.

D'Arnot did so.

"Now point out America," said Tarzan.

And as D'Arnot placed his finger upon North America, Tarzan smiled and laid his palm upon the page, spanning the great ocean that lay between Africa and the Americas.

"You see, it is not so very far," said Tarzan.

D'Arnot laughed. Then he took a pencil and made a tiny point upon the shore of Africa. "This little mark is many times larger upon this map than your cabin is upon the earth. Do you see now how very far it is?"

Tarzan thought for a long time. "Do any Frenchmen live in Africa?"

"Yes."

"And where are the nearest?"

D'Arnot pointed out a spot on the shore just north of them.

"Have they big boats to cross the ocean?" asked Tarzan.

"Yes."

"We shall go there tomorrow," announced Tarzan.

So on the following day they started north along the shore. For a month they traveled north, sometimes finding food in plenty, and again going hungry for days.

Tarzan asked questions and learned rapidly. D'Arnot taught him many of the refinements of civilization— even the use of knife and fork.

On the journey Tarzan told D'Arnot about the great chest he had dug up and carried to the gathering place of the apes, where it now lay buried.

"It must be the treasure chest of Professor Porter!" exclaimed D'Arnot. Then Tarzan remembered the letter written by Jane to her friend—the one he had stolen when they first came to his cabin, and now he knew what was in the chest and what it meant to Jane.

"Tomorrow we shall go back after it," he announced to D'Arnot.

"Go back?" wondered D'Arnot. "But, my dear fellow, we have now been three weeks upon the march. It

For a month they traveled north.

would require three more to return to the treasure, and then, with that enormous weight, it would be months before we made it this far again. I have a better plan, my friend. We shall go on together to the nearest settlement, and there we will charter a boat and sail back down the coast for the treasure, and so transport it easily."

"Very well," said Tarzan.

At last they reached the settlement. For a week they remained there, and the ape-man, keenly observant, learned much of the ways of men. Tarzan saw many boats, and gradually he became used to the strange noises and odd ways of civilization. D'Arnot purchased clothes for him, and so no one knew that this handsome young Frenchman had been, only weeks before, swinging half-naked through the jungle.

D'Arnot succeeded in chartering an old boat for the coastal trip to Tarzan's harbor. The trip was uneventful, and the morning after they dropped anchor before the cabin, Tarzan, once more dressed in his jungle costume, set out for the meeting place of the apes. Late the next day he returned, bearing the great chest upon his shoulder, and at sunrise the little boat made its northward journey.

Three weeks later Tarzan and D'Arnot were on board a French steamer bound for Marseilles, and after a few days in that city D'Arnot took Tarzan to Paris. During the journey, Tarzan showed his friend the diary which John Clayton, Lord Greystoke, had written in French, and which the ape-man had carried as a keepsake within his quiver of arrows; once he had read the journal, D'Arnot was almost able to convince his friend that his mother had been not Kala, the kind ape, but Lady Alice, and that he, Tarzan, was rightfully the new Lord Greystoke.

"Then how is it that a baby's skeleton was found within the cabin, mon ami?" asked Tarzan. "Was that not the child of the Greystokes?"

"I do not know how to account for the skeleton, Tarzan, but as sure as I am D'Arnot, I am sure you are Greystoke."

10. Tarzan to the Rescue

UPON THEIR return to America, Jane Porter, her father, Mr. Philander, Esmeralda and Clayton visited the little farm Jane's mother had left her in Wisconsin. Jane had not been there since childhood.

The farmhouse stood on a little hill. It had been filled recently with every modern convenience—a gift from Clayton. Jane understood that Clayton loved her and wished her to be his bride.

"You know we can't repay you," cried Jane. "Why do you want me to be under such obligations?"

"It's not just for you, Jane," said Clayton. "It's for your dear old father. I could not bear to see him staying in the place as I and Philander found it."

"Oh, Cecil, then I thank you."

The next morning found a cloud of smoke lying low over the nearby forest, but it was not seen by the visitors to the farm, and Jane did not notice it as she set off unaccompanied on a walk. She would not let her admirer Clayton go with her; she wanted to be alone, she said, and he respected her wishes.

As Jane walked, Professor Porter and Mr. Philander remained in the house, discussing a weighty scientific problem. Esmeralda dozed in the kitchen and Clayton lay napping on the couch in the living room.

To the east, black smoke clouds rose high into the heavens, and then began to blow west. On and on the black clouds came, the wind carrying the forest fire in the direction in which Jane was walking. For many minutes she did not notice the smoke, for it blew along the treetops.

A French automobile approached the house Jane had left, coming from the northeast. With a jolt it stopped in front of the cottage, and a black-haired giant leaped out to run up onto the porch. Without a pause he rushed into the house. On the couch lay Clayton. The newcomer was at the side of the sleeping man with a bound. Shaking him roughly by the shoulder, he cried: "My God, Clayton, are you all crazy? Don't you know a fire is nearing? Where is Miss Jane Porter?"

Clayton sprang to his feet. He did not recognize the man, but he understood the words and was up and outside on the veranda in a moment. "Great Scott!" he cried, and then, dashing back into the house, "Jane! Jane! Where are you?"

"She's gone for a walk," said Esmeralda.

"Which way did she go?" demanded the black-haired man of Esmeralda.

"Down that road," cried the frightened maid, pointing to where a wall of roaring flames shut out the view.

The muscular figure sprinted away across the clearing toward the fire.

"Who *was* that?" asked Professor Porter.

"I do not know," replied Clayton. "He called me by name and knew Jane, for he asked for her. And he called Esmeralda by name."

"There was something familiar about him," exclaimed Mr. Philander, "and yet I know I never saw him before."

When Jane had turned to retrace her steps homeward, she was alarmed to note how near the smoke of the forest fire seemed, and she hurried onward. A short run down the road brought her to a halt, for there before her was another wall of flame. She realized it would be but a matter of minutes before she was met by fire on all sides.

Suddenly she heard her name being called aloud through the forest:

"Jane! Jane Porter!" It rang strong and clear, but in an unfamiliar voice.

"Here!" she called in reply. "Here! In the roadway!"

They had passed beyond the fire now.

Then through the branches of the trees she saw a figure swinging with the speed of a squirrel. The wind blew a cloud of smoke about them, and she could no longer see the man who was speeding toward her, but suddenly she felt an arm around her. Then she was lifted up, and she felt the rushing of the wind as she was carried along.

She opened her eyes. Far below her lay the undergrowth and the hard earth. About her were the waving branches and leaves of the forest. From tree to tree swung the giant figure who carried her, and it seemed to Jane that she was living over in a dream the time she had spent in the African jungle. And, of course, it was the same man who was carrying her!

"My jungle-man!" she said.

"Yes," smiled Tarzan, "your jungle-man, Jane; I am that savage who has come out of his jungle to claim his mate—the woman who ran away from him."

"I did not run away," said Jane. "We waited a week for you to return, and they would not allow me to stay."

They had passed beyond the fire now, and they now returned to earth. Side by side they began walking toward the cottage. The wind had changed once more and the fire was burning back upon itself—another hour and it would be burned out.

"Why did you not return?" she asked.

"I was nursing D'Arnot. He was badly wounded."

"I knew it!" she cried. "They said you had gone to join the savage tribe—that they were your people."

He laughed. "But you did not believe them, Jane?"

"No!" She smiled. "What shall I call you?"

"I was Tarzan of the Apes when you first knew me," he said.

"Tarzan!" she exclaimed. "Then that was your note! I was sure it wasn't yours, for Tarzan of the Apes had

written to us in English, and you could not understand
a word of it."

Tarzan laughed. "It is a long story, but it was I who
wrote what I could not speak—and now D'Arnot has
made matters worse by teaching me to speak French
instead of English. But these words I do know: Jane
Porter, will you marry me?"

She did not reply. What did she know of this strange
creature? What did he know of himself? Who was he?
Who were his parents? Why, his very name showed his
strange and savage life. Could she be happy with this
jungle orphan? Could she find anything in common
with a husband whose life had been spent in the treetops of a jungle, frolicking and fighting with fierce apes,
tearing his food from fresh-killed prey, while his fellows
growled and fought for their share?

"You do not answer," he said.

"I do not know what answer to make," said Jane.

"You do not love me?"

"Don't ask me that—not that. You will be happier
without me. You were never meant for civilization, and
in a little while you would miss the freedom of your old
life."

"I see now that you could not be happy with—an
ape."

"Don't say that," said Jane. "You don't understand."

She remembered the spell that had been upon her in
the depths of that far-off jungle, but there was no spell
of enchantment now in Wisconsin. Did she love him?
She did not know—now.

She thought of Clayton. Did not her best judgment
point to this young English nobleman, whose love she
knew to be of the sort a woman should want? Could she
love Clayton? She could see no reason why she could
not.

Before long they were with her father and friends. At the sight of Jane, cries of relief and delight came from all, and Professor Porter took his daughter in his arms.

Clayton held out his hand to Tarzan. "How can we ever thank you? You have saved Jane.—You called me by name in the cottage, but I do not seem to remember yours, though there is something very familiar about you."

Tarzan smiled and he took Clayton's hand. "You are quite right, Monsieur Clayton," he said, in French. "You will pardon me if I do not speak to you in English. I am just learning it, and while I understand it fairly well, I speak it very poorly."

"But who are you?"

"Tarzan of the Apes."

"By Jove!" Clayton exclaimed. "It is true!"

And Professor Porter and Mr. Philander came forward now to express their thanks to Tarzan, and to voice their surprise and pleasure at seeing their jungle friend so far from his savage home.

Tarzan, on his part, was pleased to say to Jane's father: "Your treasure has been found."

"What—what is that you are saying? It cannot be."

"It is, though. I saw the sailors bury it, and, ape-like, I had to dig it up and bury it again elsewhere. When D'Arnot told me what it was—and what it meant to you—I returned to the jungle and recovered it. Mr. D'Arnot is holding it for you."

"To the already tremendous thanks we owe you, sir," said Professor Porter, "we now add more."

"Bless me!" exclaimed Mr. Philander. "Who would ever have thought it possible! The last time we saw you you were a wild-man, leaping about among the branches of a jungle, and now you are in Wisconsin, having arrived in a French automobile! It is remarkable."

"Yes," agreed Tarzan, asking then for a private word with the man. "Mr. Philander, do you recall any of the details of the finding and burying of three skeletons found in my jungle cabin?"

"I remember everything," said Mr. Philander.

"I want you to answer my question to the best of your knowledge—were the three skeletons you buried all human skeletons?"

"No," said Mr. Philander, "the smallest one, the one found in the crib, was the skeleton of an ape."

"Thank you," said Tarzan. He now knew with certainty that he was the son of Lord and Lady Greystoke, rather than that of Kala and a white-skinned ape.

As the two men talked, Clayton took Jane off to one side, out of hearing of Tarzan. The English lord asked, "Won't you say yes to my proposal now, Jane? I will devote my life to making you very happy."

"Yes," she whispered.

That evening, in the cottage, Tarzan found the chance to be alone with Jane. He said, "For your sake I have become a civilized man—for your sake I have crossed oceans and continents—for your sake I will be whatever you want me to be. I can make you happy, Jane, in the life you know and love best. Will you marry me?"

For the first time Jane realized the depths of the man's love—all that he had done in so short a time solely out of love for her. Turning her head, she sobbed. What had she done? Because she had been afraid she might agree to Tarzan's proposal she had accepted Clayton's. She confessed this to the jungle-man.

"What can we do?" he asked. "You have admitted that you love me. You know that I love you. But I do not

"I could never face you if I broke my promise to Mr. Clayton."

know the rules of your society. I shall leave the decision
to you."

"I cannot tell Clayton now, Tarzan," she said. "He, too,
loves me, and he is a good man. I could never face you
nor any other honest person if I broke my promise to
Mr. Clayton."

Tarzan turned his face away. By Mr. Philander's con-
firmation, Tarzan now knew that he—not Clayton—was
in fact the rightful Lord Greystoke, and yet Clayton was

going to marry the woman whom Tarzan loved—the woman who loved Tarzan. If Tarzan told them who he truly was, what a great difference it would make! It would take away Clayton's title and land and his castles, and—it would take them away from Jane also.

The happy Clayton approached the silent Tarzan and Jane. "I say, old man," said Clayton, patting the jungleman on the shoulder. "I haven't had a chance to thank you for all you've done for us. It seems as though you've had your hands full, saving our lives in Africa and here. I'm awfully glad you came on here. I often thought about you, you know, and the amazing life you led. If it's any of my business, how the devil did you ever get into that jungle?"

Tarzan replied, "I was born there, and my mother was an ape. I never knew who my father was." For Jane's sake, Tarzan had renounced his title of Lord Greystoke.

CHILDREN'S THRIFT CLASSICS
DOVER

The Three Musketeers

ALEXANDRE DUMAS *père*

English Adaptation by Alan Weissman
Illustrated by John Green

DOVER PUBLICATIONS, INC.
New York

DOVER CHILDREN'S THRIFT CLASSICS

EDITOR OF THIS VOLUME: THOMAS CROFTS

Note

ALEXANDRE DUMAS *père* (so called because his son—Alexandre Dumas *fils*—was also a famous author) published *The Three Musketeers* in 1844.

Specializing in plays and novels with historical settings (including a play about Napoleon), Dumas *père* was known for his thrilling, rambunctious and passionate tales. *The Three Musketeers*, one of his best, is set in seventeenth-century France. The historical background, such as the siege of La Rochelle, is basically accurate, but the chief action, completely fictitious, is concerned with a heroic group of Musketeers (members of the King's private army) and a young gentleman swashbuckler named D'Artagnan.

Bibliographical Note

This Dover edition, first published in 1994, is a new English adaptation of *Les Trois Mousquetaires* (1844). The illustrations and introductory Note have been specially prepared for the present edition.

Library of Congress Cataloging-in-Publication Data

Weissman, Alan, 1947–
    The three musketeers / Alexandre Dumas ; English adaptation by Alan Weissman ; illustrated by John Green.
        p.   cm. — (Dover children's thrift classics)
    In seventeenth-century France, young D'Artagnan initially quarrels with, then befriends, three musketeers and joins them in trying to outwit the enemies of the king and queen.
    ISBN 0-486-28326-7
    1. France—History—Louis XIII, 1610–1643—Juvenile fiction. [1. France—History—Louis XIII, 1610–1643—Fiction. 2. Adventure and adventurers—Fiction.] I. Dumas, Alexandre, 1802–1870. Trois mousquetaires. English. II. Green, John, 1948– ill. III. Title. IV. Title: 3 musketeers. V. Series.
PZ7.W448165Th   1994
[Fic]—dc20   94–34998
                                                                   CIP
                                                                    AC

Manufactured in the United States of America
Dover Publications, Inc., 31 East 2nd Street, Mineola, N.Y. 11501

Contents

List of Illustrations

1

D'Artagnan Meets the Musketeers

LONG AGO in France, on a bright spring morning—in April of 1626, to be exact—a young man from the country, of noble but somewhat awkward bearing, walked firmly down a lonely road outside Paris with the near-certain belief that within the hour he would be dead.

This eighteen-year-old gentleman, whose name was D'Artagnan, was newly arrived from Gascony, from which distant province he had come, as proud as he was poor, to pledge his service to the King, the Queen and the Cardinal. Yet he had not been in Paris for more than a few hours before he had somehow committed himself to fighting no fewer than three duels!

Now, this Cardinal, who was also a duke—the Duc de Richelieu—was almost as powerful as the King—some said even more powerful. He was always creating trouble, it seemed, even within the royal household. He had recently managed to raise suspicions in the King's mind against the Queen herself, accusing her of an unlawful relationship with the English Duke of

Buckingham. Alas, there was some truth to this charge. Both the Queen and the Cardinal had powerful networks of spies who helped them in their bitter rivalry.

The entire nation of France was the scene of great troubles then, there being violent hatred between the Catholics, led by Cardinal Richelieu, and a sect of French Protestants called the Huguenots, whose main stronghold was the coastal city of La Rochelle.

As D'Artagnan had plunged into this atmosphere of conflict, he was forced to take sides. Though as yet unable to join the elite band of the King's Musketeers, he had been allowed to join the lesser force of the King's Guards (who, with the Musketeers, were rivals of the Cardinal's Guards). He also had dared hope that perhaps he would become the valiant knight of some beautiful damsel in distress.

D'Artagnan had other problems. On his way to Paris, in the town of Meung, he had been mocked by a mysterious, evil-looking blackguard, evidently of high rank, with an ugly scar on his temple, who had set his servants to thrash him. Then, before D'Artagnan could deal with him properly, in gentlemanly sword-to-sword combat, the man, after exchanging mysterious words with an even more mysterious lady in a coach, had sped off on his horse like a coward.

Now came the greatest trouble of all. The three men with whom D'Artagnan was about to fight duels were all Musketeers! It had all come about because of some silly words of anger exchanged between D'Artagnan and the Musketeers in the mansion of Monsieur de Tréville, their leader.

By now, walking along under the hot sun, his sword flapping against his leg at his left hand, D'Artagnan had approached a grim windowless building surrounded by bare fields, part of a convent on the outskirts of Paris. Just then a clock in a nearby tower struck twelve and D'Artagnan, aware that he was about to meet his fate and very likely leave this earth, saw before him the noble figure of Athos, one of the Musketeers.

Athos, though in pain, the result of a wound he had received in another duel, stepped forward to meet his adversary. D'Artagnan, on his part, took off his hat and bowed deeply.

"Monsieur," said Athos, "I have engaged two of my friends as seconds; I do not know why they are late, as it is not their habit."

"I have no seconds, Monsieur," replied D'Artagnan, "as I have just arrived in Paris. But I see you are suffering terribly. I have a balsam for wounds, which I freely offer you. Within three days you will be cured, and then—well, sir, it would then still do me great honor to be your man."

"I am afraid that in three days word of our plans would be certain to leak out and our combat would be prevented. But," said Athos, "your words are those of a true gentleman. There is one of my seconds, I believe."

Walking down the road the gigantic Porthos appeared.

"What!" cried D'Artagnan. "Is your first witness M. Porthos?"

"Does that disturb you?"

"Not at all—and is the second M. Aramis?" Aramis was just then coming up behind Porthos.

"Of course. Are you not aware that we are never seen one without the others, and that we are called, among the Musketeers and the guards, at court and in the city, Athos, Porthos and Aramis—or the Three Inseparables? But then, you would not know that since you are from—"

"Tarbes," said D'Artagnan.

"Porthos, this is the gentleman I am going to fight," said Athos, gesturing toward D'Artagnan and greeting his friend at the same time.

"Ah! What does this mean? It is with him that I also am going to fight!" said Porthos.

"But not before one o'clock," said D'Artagnan.

"And I also am going to fight this gentleman," said Aramis as he walked up.

"But not before two o'clock," said D'Artagnan.

"But what are you going to fight about, Athos?" asked Aramis.

"Faith! I don't well know. He hurt my shoulder. And you, Porthos?"

"We are going to fight because—we are going to fight!"

"We had a little discussion about dress," explained D'Artagnan tactfully.

"And you, Aramis?"

"Oh, ours is a theological quarrel."

"Yes, there is a passage in St. Augustine upon which we could not agree," said D'Artagnan.

At this sign of courteous evasion Athos smiled slightly, thinking, "Decidedly this is a clever fellow."

"And now, gentlemen," announced D'Artagnan, "should M. Athos succeed in dispatching me, I offer my apologies that I will be unable to fight as agreed. But for now—on guard!" With the most gallant air imaginable, D'Artagnan drew his sword.

"As you please, Monsieur," replied Athos, likewise drawing his weapon.

Thus the two stood, with swords crossed, when, from the other side of the nearby convent, a troop of five of the Cardinal's Guards marched into sight.

"The Cardinal's Guards!" cried Aramis and Porthos. "Sheathe your swords, gentlemen, sheathe your swords!"

But it was too late. The Guards' commander, a M. Jussac, advanced toward D'Artagnan and the Musketeers, followed by his men.

"So! Despite the Cardinal's edicts against dueling, I see you are fighting here! Sheathe your swords, if you please, and follow us. We will charge upon you if you disobey."

"There are five of them," said Athos quietly, as if to himself, "and we are but three. We shall be beaten and must die on the spot, for, on my part, I declare I will never again appear before our captain as a conquered man."

"Monsieur," said D'Artagnan, "allow me to correct your words, if you please! You said you were but three, but it appears to me we are four."

"But you are not one of us," said Porthos.

"That is true," replied D'Artagnan, "I have not the uniform but I have the heart of a Musketeer. I am with you. Try me, gentlemen, and I swear to you, by the honor of the name D'Artagnan, that I will not abandon you whether we prevail or are conquered."

"You are a brave fellow," said Athos.

"Well—have you decided?" asked Jussac.

"Yes," replied Athos. "We are to have the honor of charging you! Athos, Porthos, Aramis and D'Artagnan, forward!"

At this the nine combatants joined in a furious battle. While the Musketeers were fighting certain of the Cardinal's men, it fell to D'Artagnan to fight Jussac himself!

The heart of the young Gascon beat wildly—not from fear, which emotion he scarcely knew, but from the thought that here at last was the opportunity to prove his worth by fighting on the side of the King's Musketeers.

Jussac was a fine swordsman who had had much practice. Nevertheless, with far less experience, D'Artagnan combined the hot blood of youth with both sound theory and extreme agility. When, angered that his skill should be so thwarted by a mere youth, Jussac thrust out in hot haste, lowering his guard, D'Artagnan glided like a serpent beneath his weapon and passed his sword through his body. Jussac fell like a stone. He was seriously wounded, though still breathing.

The rest passed quickly. The Musketeers and D'Artagnan soon overcame the three Guardsmen who were still on their feet, disarming them and forcing a surrender. The wounded were carried under the porch of the convent, and the convent bell was rung.

As the victors returned to Paris, D'Artagnan was intoxicated with joy. The four walked down the street arm in arm.

"If I am not yet a Musketeer," said D'Artagnan to his new friends as he passed through the gateway of M. de Tréville's mansion, "at least I have entered upon my apprenticeship, haven't I?"

After this trial, D'Artagnan became a part of the circle of the three Musketeers, who grew much attached to their young comrade. The friendship that united these four men and the need they felt of seeing one another three or four times a day, whether for dueling, business or pleasure, caused them to be continually running after one another like shadows. Now they were "the Four Inseparables"!

2

An Errand for the Queen

A T THIS TIME, with the financial help of his
friends, D'Artagnan rented lodgings from a
wealthy merchant, one M. Bonacieux, and secured the services of a manservant named
Planchet. In D'Artagnan's lodgings, especially
when his duties perforce separated him from the
Musketeers, they would all meet in the evenings.
By candlelight and over wine, all would recount
their adventures of the day, or, occasionally, of
days gone by. When it came to the past, however, D'Artagnan noticed frequent gaps, especially
in the discourse of Athos. Aramis often dis-
cussed his ambitions to leave the military life
altogether and commence a career in the church.
But, apart from this, in his case it was mainly the
present he avoided discussing, especially the
mysterious letters his manservant Bazin frequently
brought him, the contents of which could instantly transform his face to an image of joy or of
gloom. To his annoyance, Athos and Porthos
sometimes joked about his having a secret mistress among the high nobility.

Porthos was the least secretive about his life, often boastful of the attention paid him by a woman he referred to as his "duchess." As Athos and Aramis had reason to believe, however—and failed not to chide him about—this "duchess" was a woman some years older, not very good-looking, and the wife of a minor government official. Besides returning Porthos's cavalier attitude with admiration, this woman provided him with something perhaps even more important to him: money, with which he would feed his vanity by attiring himself in splendor.

Athos's past was the most mysterious, although sometimes when he had taken too much wine—which was often enough—he would begin to tell some bizarre story, seemingly unconnected with anything else in his life, but which would suggest that something extremely unfortunate had happened to him years earlier.

And so the days passed. Despite the turmoil and all the half-secret dueling going on at this time, however, the ordinary life of a soldier when not on the battlefield could grow dreary, and D'Artagnan began to pine for excitement. It was not long before he was satisfied.

One evening, before the customary arrival of his friends, he heard a clatter and commotion in the rooms downstairs, the residence of the merchant M. Bonacieux and his young wife. Now, as D'Artagnan was aware, the merchant had gone away for a few days, leaving his wife alone under the protection of a few old servants.

"Help! Help!" came a cry from below. At this, D'Artagnan strapped on his sword and leaped down the stairs into the street where two men were attempting to carry off the merchant's wife. D'Artagnan made quick work of her two assailants, only one of whom was armed anyway, and sent them running, leaving the gasping, terrified Mme. Bonacieux in D'Artagnan's arms.

"Quick, Monsieur, take me away from here, I beg you. These men were trying to kidnap me."

D'Artagnan helped her up the stairs to his own apartment, where he sat her in a chair.

"Planchet! Some water for the young lady, if you please!" he cried. This necessary item having been brought, D'Artagnan signaled for his man to withdraw discreetly.

When the beautiful young lady had recovered some of her calm, she began to show some embarrassment. She only half looked D'Artagnan in the eye, saying,

"Monsieur, please forgive my imposition on your kindness, but I must impose upon it once more by inquiring if you know of any place I can stay to be safe."

"It seems, Madame, that you are involved in matters that grow too large for you to handle, is it not true?" D'Artagnan ventured somewhat daringly.

She was silent. D'Artagnan knew from gossip at M. de Tréville's that the Queen herself, who

D'Artagnan made quick work of her two assailants.

had her own circle of spies and informers, made frequent use of Mme. Bonacieux (who was a high-ranking personal servant of the Queen's) in her intrigues.

"Of course, I know you must be bound to secrecy," said D'Artagnan more gallantly, "but if you confide in me, I swear upon my honor as a gentleman and a loyal member of the King's Guards that your secret shall not pass my lips to any but a chosen few who can be trusted. I ask this only because I have become acquainted with those who might be in a position to assist you if only they knew the nature of your difficulty."

Now, D'Artagnan, if the truth were told, did not make this offer out of entirely disinterested motives. From the first he had been attracted to his beguiling young neighbor. He had even felt what might be termed love for this ravishing young woman. Though the morals of the period were somewhat loose, this feeling was sustained in him by a degree of genuine idealism. He justified to himself the idea that he might be her rescuer, even her lover, by the thought that her marriage to M. Bonacieux, a man twice her age, had been arranged by her family out of convenience only; it was evident that little love passed between the woman and her staid, stingy merchant of a husband. So here was a situation that afforded D'Artagnan the excitement that he had been craving, the opportunity to save the royalty of

France—and even the opportunity to be the knight of a lady in distress.

She hesitated, then said, in a soft, sweet voice, "You appear to be a brave young man who can be trusted . . . ."

Fired up by these words, D'Artagnan grew animated.

"By my honor, by the faith of a gentleman, I will do all that I can to serve the King and be agreeable to the Queen!"

"Well . . . I know of no one else I can trust. And . . . there is one . . . in a very high place who is in grave danger. If you could find the time for a mission of great importance, you will be well rewarded, so long as that is in my power. I dare not show myself near the Louvre now." (The Louvre was in those days still the palace of the French royal family.) "But—can I trust you with a password so you may gain admittance by a door I will tell you of?"

"I swear to you I will forget that password as soon as it has served its purpose!"

Mme. Bonacieux then gave D'Artagnan involved instructions for obtaining a letter from one of the Queen's servants. With this letter would be provided further instructions for its delivery. Here was a mission worthy of the greatest trust and courage!

"Now, Madame," said D'Artagnan, moving closer, sorely tempted to forget his restraint and plant a kiss on her youthful lips, "we must meanwhile decide where you might stay."

"Well, Monsieur," said she, much relieved by the hope of accomplishing a mission that would serve the Queen, yet also a bit frightened at the unanticipated sudden physical proximity of a man who was almost a stranger, "perhaps I may safely remain in my house one more night. Tomorrow my husband returns."

Suddenly she rose and walked quickly toward the stairway.

Feeling that it was just as well that he was thus able to avoid further temptation, D'Artagnan said,

"Very well. But should you require assistance, do not hesitate to call on me. Or if I am away on this most sacred mission, my servant Planchet will see to your safety."

Mme. Bonacieux turned once, nodded in gratitude, and disappeared down the stairs.

For half an hour, D'Artagnan sat, pondering the situation. Then, although it was already quite late, he seized his hat and cloak, and stole off toward the Louvre.

About midnight, with a low fire flickering in the fireplace, Planchet was dozing in a chair when the door burst open and in strode D'Artagnan, a satisfied look on his face.

"Planchet, my man! Up! There will be no sleeping until late tonight—tomorrow I ask for emergency leave—which I have no doubt M. de Tréville will assist me in obtaining—and by nightfall we will be off on a mission of great importance!—Oh, one other thing: has there been any further disturbance downstairs?"

"No, Monsieur, it has been very quiet."

"Very good! Now let us have some nourishment. And then you must pack necessaries for a week and see about our horses in the morning."

"Certainly, Monsieur."

The night passed without further incident.

The following day D'Artagnan spent in scurrying about Paris, first to M. de Tréville, then to M. d'Essart, the commander of the King's Guards, and to the three Musketeers as well. M. de Tréville, assured of the urgency of this mission and its value to the Queen, inquired no further and granted the Musketeers leave as well as his intercession with M. d'Essart on D'Artagnan's behalf.

The three Musketeers of course pledged their full support. They all gathered in the evening at their usual meeting place—D'Artagnan's lodgings—but their usual gaiety was tempered by a sense of the importance of the mission on which they were about to embark.

"Now," said Porthos, "let us lay down the plan of campaign. Where do we go first?" There was some disagreement and bickering, but soon they worked out a scheme, suggested by Athos. D'Artagnan carried a precious letter (no doubt from the Queen herself!) to be delivered in England to the Duke of Buckingham, but it was decided that, in case D'Artagnan were to be killed or wounded, only one Musketeer was necessary to take the letter and deliver it.

Some further details were determined, and then, "Well," said D'Artagnan, "I decide that we should adopt Athos's plan, and that we should set off before sunrise. And remember our motto: All for one and one for all!"

"Agreed!" shouted the three Musketeers in chorus.

3

D'Artagnan in England

A T TWO O'CLOCK in the morning, our four adventurers and their servants left Paris by the Barrière St. Denis. Not many would have attempted to interfere with their passage, as the appearance of the caravan was formidable.

They stopped for breakfast in Chantilly. So far, so good. Yet, they began to feel that they were being watched with suspicion. But they rode on without incident. An inn in Beauvais provided shelter that night. Again, nothing out of the ordinary occurred, except that on their departure the following morning, once more it seemed that the innkeeper was watching them too closely. When Athos sharply returned the stare, the man abruptly turned away.

On they went. In the early afternoon they had to go through a narrow pass between two embankments where some workers were filling in potholes in the unpaved road. Incredibly, the workers seemed scarcely to acknowledge the presence of the travelers. The horses, slipping in the mud, had a difficult time of it. Aramis, his

17

patience exhausted, let loose a few choice words at the workmen. He received only an insolent remark in return.

"Whoa! Stop!" cried Aramis. "I am going to teach this fellow some manners!" At this, the entire party stopped and dismounted to confront the workmen. Suddenly from over the embankment several more men appeared, armed with muskets! Athos leaned over to D'Artagnan and quietly said in his ear, "I knew there was something odd about these workmen. This is an ambush. When the gunfire begins, you escape with Planchet and we will carry on as best we can."

D'Artagnan needed to hear no more. A volley of shots was already being exchanged between the false workers and the Musketeers' servants. D'Artagnan motioned to Planchet and they leaped on their horses and galloped off, managing to skirt the mud-filled holes. As they escaped with the precious letter, D'Artagnan had the utmost confidence that his companions would overcome their assailants. It was only a matter of time—time that D'Artagnan could not now afford to lose.

D'Artagnan and Planchet galloped on through woods and meadows. Late in the afternoon they came abreast of another who like D'Artagnan was obviously a gentleman. With his own servant he was galloping in a rush, apparently also toward the harbor at Calais. As it happened,

D'Artagnan and this stranger both stopped at the same inn on the margin of a wood outside the town. After having briefly refreshed themselves, they and their servants both left their horses in the care of the innkeeper, and soon they found themselves walking at a brisk pace through the wood toward the harbor.

"Monsieur," said the strange gentleman, "I see you are in a hurry. If I may be so bold as to inquire, is it your intention to sail for England?"

"It is," replied D'Artagnan, without saying more.

"Then I might save you the trouble. All ports have been placed under restriction. Unless you have express written permission from the King or Cardinal, it is impossible to get on board for any money."

At this interesting bit of news, D'Artagnan began to think.

"Monsieur!" said he, "urgent personal business makes it essential that I be in London by tomorrow morning. It would appear, from what you say, that you possess the necessary letter of permission. How much do you ask for it?"

The man stopped and faced D'Artagnan, at which the entire party halted. By now they were in a little wood outside of the town.

"I am very sorry, Monsieur," said the man, "but that is impossible. I have traveled sixty leagues in forty-four hours, and I must be in London by midday. Business of the King, you know!"

"I am sorry too, Monsieur. I have traveled the

same distance in forty hours and I must be in London by ten o'clock—on even more urgent business."

"That is indeed your business, Monsieur, certainly, but—"

D'Artagnan, desperate and convinced of the priority of his mission, abruptly drew his sword and motioned to Planchet.

"I am sorry, but I must have that letter. Hand it over instantly!"

"This is outrageous!" cried the stranger. "Lubin! My pistols!"

"Quick, Planchet, you take care of the lackey; I will manage the master!" Planchet, young, strong and vigorous, sprang upon the servant, got him in a stranglehold and wrenched his pistol free. Meanwhile D'Artagnan and the strange gentleman were lunging at each other with drawn swords. The stranger was young and agile but no match for D'Artagnan. After receiving a slight wound, D'Artagnan thrust his sword home and the man fell—not dead, but seriously wounded.

D'Artagnan helped Planchet subdue the servant, whom they gagged and tied to a tree. They propped his master next to him, D'Artagnan searched for and found the letter of permission, and in twenty minutes they had shown it to the governor of the port and were on board the vessel.

As the ship began to sail out of Calais harbor, D'Artagnan leaned on the rail and contemplated his situation. It was a very risky one indeed. Here he had stabbed and nearly killed a man, a high-ranking nobleman no less, for it turned out that this was one Comte de Wardes. Now D'Artagnan had to compound the felony by impersonating the man to gain admittance on board the ship. This was a very serious matter. But so was the well-being of the Queen!

Soon it was proved that his desperate haste and extreme actions had been justified. For they had been swaying over the briny waves for only a few minutes or so when D'Artagnan saw a flash and heard a detonation. That cannon shot meant that the port had now been entirely closed by the Cardinal's orders!

Night fell. The winds were poor and for some time D'Artagnan thought he would never make it to Dover. About ten o'clock, however, the boat docked. Then came the next problem: how to get to London. This was not easy for one who, like D'Artagnan, knew little English. Finally, a pair of post horses took them to London. Then, with difficulty, they discovered that the Duke of Buckingham was at Windsor with the King of England. At last D'Artagnan was admitted to the august presence of the French Cardinal's counterpart—the most powerful man in England, next to the King himself. D'Artagnan was awed by the splendor of the room into which he was admitted: high-ceilinged, hung with artistic treasures, worthy of a prince of the realm.

D'Artagnan bowed upon entering to face the
Duke, still a young man, handsome, splendidly
attired, truly worthy of the connection with the
Queen of France. This connection was doubtless
a reality, no matter the cost in international
tension, even war, that such a simple personal
alliance brought in its train. Fortunately for
D'Artagnan, the Duke spoke fluent French.

D'Artagnan, bidden to sit before the Duke,
knew immediately that he was in the presence of
greatness. Firm as he was in his own purpose,
assured as he was of his own courage and
loyalty, he could not but be impressed by one
who obviously possessed more nobility of heart
and more power—combined with more reckless-
ness—than almost any courtier in Europe. The
King of England's favorite and one of the wealthi-
est and handsomest men in the world, George
Villiers, Duke of Buckingham, set the world in
disarray at his fancy, and then calmed it according to his whimsy. Whatever his object, he
stopped at no means to achieve it. Thus he had
succeeded in obtaining the affection of the
equally proud and noble Anne of Austria, Queen
of France, flouting all the dangers of such a
position—a position that was at this very moment
bringing D'Artagnan before him. Who could pre-
dict the consequences of this meeting?

D'Artagnan looked up and, even to his surprise,
saw a magnificent portrait of the Queen of France
herself—whom he just barely recognized, having

seen her on only one occasion, and then imperfectly.

"So!" the Duke interrupted D'Artagnan's thoughts. "Where is this letter of utmost importance you have brought me, no doubt at the risk of your life?"

D'Artagnan glanced around them and saw that the servants had retired. "Yes. The letter," he murmured, and he reached into a hidden pocket, withdrawing a creased envelope.

"Good Heavens!" exclaimed the Duke. "This *is* serious!"

D'Artagnan, puzzled by this utterance, looked down and saw that the envelope was stained with blood and was partly cut through.

"Oh yes," said he, "there was a little problem at Calais. But," he said as he handed it over, "you observe that the seal remains unbroken."

The Duke, uncharacteristically betraying nervous agitation, quickly tore open the envelope and scrutinized its contents. After sitting in thought for a few minutes, his face growing redder, he carefully locked away the letter in a drawer. Suddenly he jumped up.

"You will excuse me for a moment."

The Duke left the room briefly. When he returned, he sat down again. He paused a moment, looked D'Artagnan in the eye, and spoke:

"Sir. You have already done enough to earn my eternal gratitude. If I may impose upon your kindness further by requesting that you remain in England two more days . . . ."

The Duke spoke these words courteously but with an undertone of one more accustomed to giving orders than requesting favors. Nevertheless D'Artagnan replied, "I think I have already made it perfectly clear that I will do anything to aid the Queen. I am at your service!"

"Well spoken!" The Duke paused and thoughtfully fingered his elegant mustache. "Given the strange circumstances that bring us together and, more important, your unquestioned loyalty to your Queen, I think I may confide in you. Besides, you may be able to do your Queen a further service."

"I am listening."

"It has become clear," the Duke went on, "that Anne . . . that is, your Queen, has enemies, very powerful enemies. Do you know that a very personal token of her esteem that I had the honor of wearing at a ball a week or so ago— two of a set of a dozen diamond studs—well, these two (the rest remain in her own hands), as I have just confirmed, are missing. And all the evidence points to one conclusion: they have been stolen, stolen by one in whom I had placed great trust—the Comtesse de Winter, lately returned from a soujourn in your country. I see now that she must be one of the Cardinal's spies—that is, your Cardinal Richelieu's."

"I was aware of his power and have learned of his spies, but here in England . . . ."

"Yes, the Cardinal is a very powerful man indeed." The Duke went on for some minutes more. In the course of his explanation, he described this Comtesse de Winter at greater length. Suddenly D'Artagnan started.

"You say this Comtesse—she goes by the name, in my country, of the English word 'Milady'?"

"Yes—why, do you know her?"

"I begin to think I have met her." D'Artagnan thought back to his unfortunate stop in Meung on the way to Paris, the mysterious gentleman there and the even more mysterious lady in the coach, headed, as it now seemed clear, for the Channel and England.

"My Lord Duke!" said D'Artagnan warmly, "You may be sure that if ever I should have the fortune to encounter this lady again, I will do all in my power to see that she is brought to justice. Not, you understand, for your sake, and not for mine— for the Queen!"

The Duke rose, D'Artagnan following him to his feet. Extending his hand to D'Artagnan, the Duke said, "Again, well spoken! I see we are in complete sympathy! For the Queen!"

He explained further to D'Artagnan what his accommodations would be for the next two days, and what D'Artagnan would then be expected to take back with him to France.

4

Mme. Bonacieux Is Kidnapped

TWO MORNINGS later, D'Artagnan found himself and Planchet leaving a small fishing boat in a secret cove near Boulogne-sur-Mer on the French side of the Channel. The Duke's power had helped him overcome every obstacle imposed by the Cardinal. He approached with some trepidation a tiny inn down an obscure path, his hand by his sword, expecting to be set upon by a gang in service of the Cardinal. He approached the innkeeper—indeed, the gloomy-looking bearded man was practically the only soul in the remote spot, save for a few grooms in the stable and some other servants—and, assured he was facing the right man, according to the Duke's description, softly mouthed the word—in English, though he was on French soil—"Forward." The man immediately showed he understood, nodded, welcomed him, and showed him to a pair of fine horses well stocked with provisions for a long journey, including a pair of pistols. The man carefully gave directions to the next resting place where again the password was to be spoken and the horses changed, and wished him a good journey.

As D'Artagnan and Planchet galloped down a network of little-used roads, getting ever close to Paris, the wind whistling in their faces, D'Artagnan from time to time fingered a little pouch at his side and felt satisfied. This was the means for saving the honor of the Queen, and it seemed that his goal would be reached. (Although he was ignorant of all of the Duke's arrangements he correctly suspected that the pouch held a pair of clever counterfeit replacements for the stolen diamond studs.) As he went along he also had time to wonder about his companions—whether Athos, Porthos and Aramis really had survived the encounter with that party of rogues in the Cardinal's service posing as road laborers. In this way they galloped on, raising clouds of dust behind them and drawing rivers of sweat from the flanks of their overworked horses. By dark they were on the outskirts of Paris, having covered an astounding sixty leagues in twelve hours. Determined to waste no time, D'Artagnan sent Planchet ahead of him and proceeded directly to the secret gate in the Louvre that he had been shown before. Knowing just the right words and the persons to see, he was admitted by the back stairs to a small private chamber. There he sat and waited impatiently for some time.

At length a young girl, well dressed but evidently still a servant, though of a higher order, explained to him that he must wait in semidarkness for a while, and then he would see what to do. After she had departed, D'Artagnan noticed that there was a curtain on one side of the room, behind which evidently was a door through which some light seeped. He fancied the light getting stronger. Then, to his surprise, a female arm and hand, of exquisite loveliness, emerged from behind the curtain. At once he knew what to do. He grasped a little packet in which was enclosed the results of his mission, and placed it in the hand, which disappeared behind the curtain. He was about to withdraw, but the hand returned and beckoned him to remain. In another few moments the hand again appeared holding a small object. Had an outside observer been present, that observer would have witnessed at that moment a scene that might have occurred in a church. In the half-light, D'Artagnan knelt by the hand, in which could be seen something that glittered with an extraordinary radiance like an exquisite gem, which in fact it was. D'Artagnan, after receiving the gem, planted a light, respectful kiss on the marble-like fingers as they withdrew.

It was the crowning moment of his life thus far. D'Artagnan well knew the Queen herself had personally bestowed upon him this precious reward. Evidently he had returned with exactly what was necessary to assure her happiness.

At last he stood up straight and examined the gift; it was a ring, which he at once reverently

*D'Artagnan, after receiving the gem, planted a light,
respectful kiss on the marble-like fingers.*

placed on his finger. He paused for another moment in uncertainty, but just then the young girl from before reentered and quietly conducted him out of the Louvre by a back way.

As D'Artagnan strode home through the dark streets of Paris, he reflected on what had occurred. But he also thought back to his friends the Musketeers and began to think of how he might determine what had been their collective fate. He also wondered about the fair Mme. Bonacieux. Would he soon be seeing her as well? Would she demonstrate her gratitude for his having aided her royal mistress? As he mused upon all this, D'Artagnan began to be increasingly aware of his great weariness. He had endured much, and he longed for rest, which he would soon have at last.

Yet rest was not to come so easily. Expecting to arrive at his lodgings, tumble into his bed, and sleep for twenty-four hours—at least that is how severe his need for rest seemed to him—he forced himself to stride in his dust-caked boots ever faster through the dark streets of Paris.

Scarcely had he arrived at his doorstep when Planchet emerged.

"Monsieur, I thought you would never return," said he in a loud, agitated whisper. "First, I must inform you that all three Musketeers are alive—"

"Really? That is wonderful!" exclaimed D'Artagnan, his heart at once lightened by this good news.

"—Monsieur Athos has arranged to visit you this evening. There is much to be told."

"I am sure. But, tell me, Planchet, how is it that you will not let me into my apartment? Why all this down here? Could it not wait a few seconds?"

"You have, I am afraid, a visitor!"

"At this hour?"

"He did not come far—he had only to walk up the stairs."

"Bonacieux? What does he want from me at this time? His rent has been paid!"

"I thought I would prepare you, Monsieur, but now perhaps it is best to let the man himself explain."

D'Artagnan followed his servant up the stairs.

At the top of the stairs D'Artagnan encountered a short, balding, slightly plump man of about fifty, bowing and trembling at the same time. This man, though D'Artagnan rarely saw him, he recognized as his landlord, the merchant Jacques-Michel Bonacieux.

"Monsieur, Monsieur, forgive this intrusion, but they have done it again! I am beside myself! What to do? What to do?"

"Done what?" said D'Artagnan impatiently. "Speak!"

"My wife! They have taken her away again! It happened only this evening, before your servant here arrived. Don't think I am not grateful to you for having saved her the last time! Yes! But if you can help me find my wife again, you will not have to worry about the rent here for a long time."

There was no help for it. D'Artagnan had to listen to this man's pitiful wailing. But as we know, he had his own motives for finding Mme. Bonacieux, and he was, in his outwardly calm way, himself disturbed about this new turn of events. He urged the merchant, who continued to complain, to enter his apartment and sit down. When the latter had quieted down somewhat, D'Artagnan said, somewhat testily:

"All this groaning and wailing is of no use. Do you have any idea who was responsible for this abduction?"

"It is all political! My wife, as you know, is a servant of her Majesty the Queen, and I am sure that this is the work of the Cardinal. Alas! that I ever let her get involved . . . . But then again, my wife is a very headstrong woman. She never listens to anything I say! I knew this would happen! I knew it!"

"Come, come! We are getting nowhere. Can you describe any of the men who are responsible for this? Cease your whining and think!"

There was silence for a moment as the merchant was obviously struggling to contain himself. Then he said: "Well, I think I did notice that there was one who seemed in command. He had black hair, a dark complexion. A man of very lofty carriage, you see . . . . Ah, yes! I remember now! The man had a scar on his temple . . . ."

At this, D'Artagnan started. The description fitted that of the mysterious man of Meung, his nemesis! At first it was only a suspicion, but then the matter seemed confirmed when Bonacieux went on:

"In fact, Monsieur, I think I have seen the man before. Yes, I believe he is the same man my wife once pointed out to me as a man to beware of, a man who does the evil bidding of the Cardinal!"

"Well!" said D'Artagnan. "Now we are getting somewhere. I believe I know the man myself. You may rest assured, M. Bonacieux," said he, rising, "that I will not be satisfied myself until I have found this man and restored your wife to safety. But for now, you must leave me and be patient. There is much to be done, but it is too late to act immediately." At last the landlord rose and retreated down the stairs.

D'Artagnan sat for a while. Thoroughly exhausted after all his recent traveling, he did not remain awake much longer, but was resolved to ask the advice of Athos when he saw him later and to get to work finding the unfortunate Mme. Bonacieux as soon as he could. It would not, however, be simple. He knew he was swimming in dangerous waters.

5
Athos's Terrible Story

THE NEXT morning, or, rather, afternoon, when Planchet had finally roused him, provided him with nourishment and fitted him to return to his ordinary existence, D'Artagnan called upon M. d'Essart to resume his duty with the King's Guards. Before he arrived there, he was several times tempted to change his course and immediately run off to find Mme. Bonacieux—only he had not the slightest idea where to begin the search. He must ask Athos's advice in this matter.

Among his old companions in the Guards, as well as the Musketeers he met in the street, he fended off all inquiries about where he had been. But attention was distracted from such a minor matter as his unexplained leave of absence. Practically all talk that day was of the grand ball that the King was to give that very evening for the Queen. A grander affair had never been seen in Paris, it was said, and preparations had long been underway near and in the Louvre to provide the spectacles, the decorations, the music and the food for all the nobility of Paris.

Most of D'Artagnan's compatriots in the Guards had extra duty that night; it was only M. d'Essart's understanding indulgence of one of his favorite men that permitted D'Artagnan to be excused, as he had only just returned from his exhausting mission abroad.

That evening D'Artagnan was pleased to receive as his guest Athos, as planned, only there was a surprise visitor as well: Porthos. The latter had a bandage around his shoulder and limped in, helped by a cane. After they had been seated awhile and had expressed their mutual delight that they were still capable of meeting like this, they began to enlighten each other about their adventures after the time they were separated in the battle with the false road workers.

"You would not believe how bad the food can be at a country inn!" bellowed Porthos, who, wounded in the encounter on the road, had to spend time at one such place.

"Porthos complains of the food at country inns," said Athos. "However that may be, you may be certain that the wine is truly abominable. Aramis and I had to spend the night at one on our return to Paris after we dispatched those devils on the road, and there is never anything to drink at those places worth bothering about."

At this hint from a man who, as D'Artagnan knew, loved his wine, D'Artagnan had Planchet go downstairs and procure some bottles of a very fine vintage from Bonacieux. Athos, tasting the first glass of many, observed, "This is very good wine. How is it that your landlord is so quick to provide it? I thought you were on bad terms with him ever since you had so much difficulty paying the rent on time."

"I do not think that Bonacieux, tight-fisted as he is, will stint us this pleasure. I am sure he will be kind to me now, for reasons that I will explain shortly.

"But where is our friend Aramis? I am glad that he has remained with us, but have you not heard from him?"

"Aramis has aspirations to sainthood!" exclaimed Porthos.

"Or at least to holiness of some kind," continued Athos. "He was wounded, but has recovered. I do not think he has recovered from the wound to his spirit, however. After he killed two of those treacherous workers—"

"And a quick job it was, let me tell you! Aramis always was a good swordsman!" added Porthos.

"—he began to repent all the bloodshed, or so he says, and he has resumed his studies under some abbé in order that he may take holy orders himself."

"This will not last," said Porthos. "Listen to me! One word from his secret mistress—whoever the devil she is—and the four of us will be together again, let me tell you!"

"Be that as it may, at the moment he has, in his words, renounced worldly affairs. We scarcely see him."

Soon Porthos took his leave, remarking on his departure, "You know, gentlemen, we had best be looking after ourselves. For soon we may have the chance for great distinction in battle. I hear word at M. de Tréville's that M. the Cardinal remains dissatisfied with the rebelliousness of the Huguenots at La Rochelle. I think it likely he will persuade His Majesty to gather his forces and put down the troublemakers once and for all."

"Then let us indeed prepare ourselves," said D'Artagnan. "I only hope that Aramis will once again feel the spirit of a warrior and join us on the field of glory."

When Porthos had left, Athos opened another bottle of wine, and he and D'Artagnan sat down again.

"Do you know," said Athos, who even before he had begun to drink had been more talkative than was his custom, "that the Cardinal has suffered a blow?"

"What do you mean?" asked D'Artagnan, though he sensed what was coming.

"As you know, this was the day of the ball for the Queen. No doubt at this moment the nobles of the kingdom are enjoying a late supper. Well," continued Athos, pouring another glass, "I had the opportunity to look in during the grand ballet in which the King and Queen performed. Her Majesty looked stunning, by the way, and His Majesty looked absolutely his finest. Well, just before the ballet began, something passed between the two and the Cardinal. It seemed to be about some jewelry the Queen was wearing. Nobody could hear what was said but the face of the Cardinal bore signs of mischievous glee. The King at first seemed very angry, but something happened in which he counted some diamonds the Queen was wearing. He then seemed confused and turned to his Eminence the Cardinal. Then the Cardinal seemed angry and the Queen appeared to radiate joy. Finally the King and Queen appeared reconciled, while the Cardinal wore a face of gloom afterwards."

All the while Athos was relating this, D'Artagnan showed a gleam in his eye.

"Just as I thought, my friend," said Athos, looking directly at D'Artagnan. "You know more than I do, and you were not there. This incident would not, by any chance, have anything to do with your recent mission to England?"

"I think, Athos," replied D'Artagnan, "that you know the answer to that question. Although it is true that there are details of this affair with which I am unacquainted—and would not be at liberty to divulge even to you if I *did* know them—I think we may all rest assured that the trouble we took in that matter, all the risk of our lives on the road to Calais, has not been in vain. Behold!"

D'Artagnan raised his hand, displaying the ring that he had received only the day before.

"My God!" exclaimed Athos. "You did not get

that magnificent gem from anyone of a station lower than—"

"Exactly, Athos. The Queen. Of course this must be known to none but us four. Although this ring was given to me alone, the donor could not have known of the invaluable assistance I received in helping her. Naturally, you may be sure that if ever you or any of us is in need of money, I will sell this ring for what it will bring and—well, what is mine is yours."

"I am grateful for the thought, D'Artagnan, but if I were you I would not part with that gem for anything. It must be worth a King's—or rather a Queen's ransom!" Suddenly, Athos raised his glass and almost shouted, "A toast! A toast to her Majesty the Queen!"

The suddenness of this vociferation made D'Artagnan aware of two things: first, that Athos, having already dispatched the contents of almost two full bottles of wine, was beginning to show their effects; and, secondly, that although he had imbibed much less than his friend, he was beginning to feel slightly intoxicated himself. Then he felt sad.

"Something is troubling you, my friend?" asked Athos.

"I am afraid, Athos, that I cannot hide my concern. In fact I had wished to speak to you about this. Mme. Bonacieux, the wife of my landlord, has been kidnapped once again."

"And why should you be so concerned about

the wife of your landlord, D'Artagnan? What is she to you?" When D'Artagnan offered no reply to this and his face showed signs of darkening in anger, Athos continued, "I knew it! Beware, my friend. Danger lies ahead. He is old compared to her, she appears to favor you . . . . I know, but, as I say, beware!"

"I am afraid that this is love, Athos, and there is no helping it."

"And I suppose you believe that she returns your love? That she would willingly be your mistress? You child! Why, there is not a man who has not believed, as you do, that his mistress loved him, and there lives not a man who has not been deceived by his mistress."

"Except you, Athos, who never had one."

"That's true," said Athos, after a moment's silence, "That's true! I never had one! Let us drink!"

"But then, philosopher that you are," said D'Artagnan, "instruct me, support me. I stand in need of being taught and consoled."

"Ah! You wish to be consoled, do you? Taught, yes; consoled, I think not. I will tell you a tale, D'Artagnan, a tale that will make your blood curdle. But first, drink!"

As D'Artagnan hesitatingly raised his glass, he stared at Athos and wished that he had not ordered the wine, that he were someplace else, anything but this. For the lateness of the hour, the amount that Athos had drunk and something that evidently was weighing on Athos's mind connected with the story he was about to relate combined to lend a devilish cast to Athos's countenance. Athos was at a period of intoxication in which most ordinary drinkers begin to doze off. In a sense he *was* asleep, and yet wide awake at the same time. In what followed he spoke as if describing in vivid, horrible detail the contents of a nightmare that was at that moment passing through his feverish brain.

"This is a story, D'Artagnan, that happened to a good friend of mine, a count of the highest order. Not to me, you understand . . . to a friend of mine."

D'Artagnan hesitated to interrupt and Athos continued.

"This man was of the best of families. Unfortunately, he was also a man of honor. Why 'unfortunately,' you shall see. Well, at the age of twenty-five he fell in love with a girl of sixteen living in a cottage on his land. This girl was as beautiful as fancy can paint and had the mind of a poet. No one knew where she came from but since her one known relative—her brother with whom she shared the cottage—was a priest, and since it was rumored that she was of good family, her character seemed unimpeachable.

"Now, you understand, as so high-ranking a nobleman, my friend was also magistrate of his district as well as this girl's landlord. In effect, he was the law, and had he been unscrupulous he might easily have taken advantage of this nearly solitary girl with only her brother to defend her.

"But, no, he was an honorable man." An almost demonic undertone could be heard in Athos's voice as he softly repeated these words. "He married her." D'Artagnan sat transfixed, with a growing sense of horror, not knowing exactly what was coming but knowing it would be bad. Athos poured himself another glass of wine and downed it almost in one gulp.

"Well," continued Athos, "Not long afterwards, the newly married couple were out hunting. The young bride had an accident and fell from her horse. My friend, alarmed that she could hardly breathe, cut her restrictive clothing free at the neck. When a strip of cloth fell below her shoulder, what he beheld was the most horrifying sight he had ever seen. What had been concealed by the darkness of the marital bedroom was now clearly visible in broad daylight: the brand of the *fleur-de-lis!*"

Athos paused and looked into D'Artagnan's eyes. D'Artagnan just stared straight ahead, mesmerized. As he uttered not a word, Athos went on.

"The *fleur-de-lis*, as you know, is the brand of the Catholic Chruch for having committed one of the most horrible sins: stealing the sacred vessels from a church. It was immediately obvious that I—that is, my friend—had been deceived by a pair of the worst criminals in France. Well, at this revelation, he lost control over his calmer nature and immediately became judge, jury and executioner: in a fit of outrage, he tore part of her clothing from her, twisted it into a rope, tied it around her neck and hanged her from the nearest tree."

"But Athos," said D'Artagnan finally, in a scarcely audible voice. "That was murder!"

"No less. But if ever murder was justified—" Athos paused to down another glass of wine. "Her scoundrel of a 'brother,' who no doubt was really her lover and accomplice and plotted with her to secure her a position in the highest society, soon vanished. But it may be hoped that by now he too has been discovered and brought to justice."

"Then—then, the girl at least is really dead?"

"It would appear so. Although I—my friend— didn't have the heart to witness her last gasp, it doesn't seem very likely that she would have survived a hanging, does it?"

"My God, my God!" murmured D'Artagnan, genuinely horrified.

"Well, this incident—hearing about this incident—has cured me of all beautiful, poetical and loving women. God grant that you will take this to heart and forget all about 'love'! Come! Have another glass of wine."

A Conversation with the Cardinal

THE NEXT morning, D'Artagnan's head was spinning like a top. He knew not how the morning came, or how Athos had left; indeed, he scarcely remembered where he was, so affected was he by what he had heard the night before.

To steady himself, he forced himself to focus on one purpose: the impending battle at La Rochelle, for which he spent the next couple of days preparing. Of one thing he had no doubt: that he was honor-bound to serve his King, who, when he was not distracted by his favorite pastime of hunting, was exhibiting surprising enthusiasm for the battle. Of the part in all this played by the Cardinal, who no doubt had his own far-reaching schemes, D'Artagnan tried to think as little as possible.

At last the chilly morning dawned when D'Artagnan joined his troop of the King's Guards who, in a noble procession, began to make their way out to La Rochelle, where the stubborn Huguenots awaited the siege of their walled city. The noblest part of the procession, of course, was that in which the three Musketeers took their places in advance of the Guards, where D'Artagnan could not see them.

Just as Porthos had predicted, Aramis was among them, no doubt because he had indeed received the aforementioned word from his mysterious mistress. The Musketeers had all recovered from their recently acquired wounds and thought of the ordeal that lay ahead of them and the honors they might acquire.

As daylight broke on the troubled and tumultuous soil of France, D'Artagnan's heart was lightened when he saw before him the glittering arms and waving plumes of column upon column of His Majesty's soldiers. Over several days, with several stops at encampments and, for the officers, inns along the way, this mass of warriors gradually encroached upon La Rochelle.

Absorbed in his thoughts as he was leaving Paris, D'Artagnan had failed to notice three figures on horseback at the side of the road, one a lady, the other two men of obviously far lower station. Had D'Artagnan then looked to the side as he was moving along the crowded boulevard, he might have seen that the lady bore a striking resemblance to the woman he had briefly seen on a fateful occasion and with whose life his had become fatefully entwined: the woman called "Milady." Even then he could not have heard the whispers of the three, but, as the woman discerned D'Artagnan in the procession and indicated him to the two men beside her, and as the two nodded with a grim look, D'Artagnan might have been certain that their looks meant no good. In fact, as he had known when he risked his life for the Queen, he was indeed swimming in dangerous waters.

As he was quite unaware, however, of what was being planned for him, D'Artagnan's mood now actually lightened. At times he became quite confident that he would distinguish himself on the battlefield, eventually be reunited with the Musketeers, and even rescue Mme. Bonacieux.

At one point during some deployment of troops, D'Artagnan spotted attire and plumes that looked familiar to him.

"Aramis!"

The noble warrior on horseback turned at this exclamation. "So, D'Artagnan, it is you. I trust we shall meet on the glorious field of battle," said Aramis, for indeed it was he.

"Aramis, how glad I am to see you here, for another reason as well." D'Artagnan's mind had never ceased to dwell on the whereabouts of Mme. Bonacieux, in whom, despite Athos's cautionary tale, D'Artagnan had never once lost faith. At this fortunate meeting, D'Artagnan explained to his friend, who, it appeared, had secret connections in very high circles, the mystery of the abduction of Mme. Bonacieux.

"Alas, my friend," said the pious Musketeer, "I cannot work miracles. However, should God spare our lives a few weeks longer, I may be able to discover something that would be of help to you."

"You would earn my eternal gratitude," said D'Artagnan.

At this heartfelt utterance, before a word more could be spoken, the flowing river of soldiers parted in two and the noble friends had once again each to flow with his own stream.

At La Rochelle, the encampments were abuzz with a mixture of news and rumors. The Huguenots had been surrounded, but, though few in number, they were resisting fiercely. More of the King's and the Cardinal's troops kept pouring in, but the Rochellais maintained their resistance.

Through all this, D'Artagnan kept busy instructing his own troops and receiving commands from his superior officers. Thus far, all that had happened was generally expected. But then, one evening, as D'Artagnan was striding down an isolated road, the unexpected occurred. He saw three shadowy figures on horseback ahead of him.

"Who goes there?" came a shout from this group.

"Nay," returned D'Artagnan, who abruptly stopped, "it is for me to inquire of you, 'Who goes there?'"

The middle figure emerged from the shadows. Dressed regally, this was obviously no ordinary guardsman. Then he spoke:

"I perceive," said he, "that either you are a fool or you are unaware of the presence you are in. But I now see who you are, and I know, M. D'Artagnan, that you are no fool."

D'Artagnan stood in perplexity as to who this could be. Then moonlight glinted off a large cross on the man's chest, and suddenly, though he had never met the man, D'Artagnan knew whose presence he was in: that of the Cardinal himself!

Somewhat afraid—who wouldn't have been in such a circumstance?—D'Artagnan nonetheless mustered up his usual courage. His mind racing, he knew that his behavior in the next few minutes could affect his entire life. He removed his hat and made a low bow.

"Your Eminence," he said, "I did not recognize you in the dark. As you know, however, guarding this area is my responsibility."

The Cardinal did not answer immediately. When he did, his voice suggested a combination of nobility, shrewdness, nervousness and, as would be no surprise to his intimates, illness. Like the King, the Cardinal was perpetually wracked by a number of painful ailments.

"No doubt, M. D'Artagnan, no doubt. Indeed, I depend on your valor to guarantee my safe conduct through dangerous territory. Before we proceed, however, a word with you." He signaled his men to retire some distance and to D'Artagnan to approach him.

"What is it I can do for you, Monseigneur?"

"It is not, M. D'Artagnan, what you can do for me, but what you can do for yourself. I have just said that you are not a fool. I stand by that judgment. Nevertheless, it needs some qualification. You are, as one might say, somewhat impetuous and idealistic."

D'Artagnan was conscious of the intense scrutiny of the Cardinal, for no one had a more searching eye than the Duc de Richelieu. But he only nodded his head slightly and allowed the Cardinal to continue.

"That, at any rate," said the Cardinal, a trace of anger entering his voice, "is the only way I can explain your behavior when you meddle in affairs that do not concern you."

D'Artagnan restrained himself and still said nothing. He could not help reflecting, however, that what was said about the Cardinal's network of spies must in fact have a good deal of truth to it.

"Nevertheless, M. D'Artagnan," —now his voice softened— "you are evidently no ordinary young man from the provinces. Indeed, I admire your courage and your loyalty. Therefore, I am willing to make you an offer, which, from the nature of the circumstances, I strongly suggest you take: the commission of an ensign in my own private troop of Guards. I should be very pleased to have the protection of so capable and courageous a soldier."

D'Artagnan was hereby placed in a very un-comfortable situation. The Cardinal of course made this offer not so much to enable D'Artagnan to keep guard over him but so that he could watch over D'Artagnan. Nevertheless, to refuse the Cardinal's offer might be taken as an insult. He thought for a moment.

"I am indeed flattered and honored, Monseigneur. Nevertheless, as you yourself have said, I am loyal. I am already in His Majesty's Guards. All of my friends are in His Majesty's Guards or Musketeers. There is not—I say this since your Eminence appears to allow me to speak freely—the best of good will between the forces of the King and the Cardinal, and I should be ill received in one place and ill regarded in the other if I accept. I must therefore respectfully decline to accept your offer."

"I fully understand your decision, M. D'Artagnan. I will not press the matter. Nevertheless I will make an observation. You are young. Now, perhaps you shine in all your glory and you attribute it to your actions alone. Someday, you will come to realize the importance in life of your friends—and enemies. If you had accepted my offer, you would, I dare say, have had the benefit of the guidance of one older and wiser than you. As things stand now, I cannot answer for your safety." With these cautionary, indeed threatening words, the Cardinal motioned to his men, turned

D'Artagnan was placed in a very uncomfortable situation.

and rode off. Naturally, D'Artagnan was somewhat disturbed by this vague threat, yet he was satisfied that he had held his ground and, indeed, remained loyal to his King and his principles.

7

An Important Discovery

THE FOLLOWING day, D'Artagnan, though he certainly had not forgotten his encounter with the man who was at that moment perhaps the most powerful in France, had enough to occupy his attention. Already, as he was drilling his troops, he noticed that he was being observed by M. d'Essart. But not only M. d'Essart—behind him stood Monsieur himself. Monsieur—that is, the younger brother of the King—was overseeing his brother's forces at this location and now sought urgently a cadre of some of the finest men for a mission of particular importance. It seems that some of the most obstinate of the Rochellais may have remained to defend a fortified position that was originally thought to have been evacuated. The bastion in which they were believed to remain was in a dangerous position, and anyone approaching it might receive a bullet in his head for his curiosity.

Monsieur walked behind M. d'Essart, up and down among the troops. As they stopped next to D'Artagnan's men, Monsieur was heard to say to

M. d'Essart, "I want for this mission three or four volunteers, led by a man who can be depended upon."

"As to the man to be depended upon, you see him before you now, Monsieur," responded M. d'Essart, "and as to the three or four volunteers, Monsieur has but to make his intentions known, and the men will not be wanting."

The moment had come for D'Artagnan to distinguish himself, and he did not hesitate for an instant.

"Four courageous men who will risk being killed with me!" said D'Artagnan, raising his sword.

Two of his comrades of the Guards immediately sprang forward. Somewhat to his surprise, two other soldiers of a lower rank then appeared from he knew not where and eagerly volunteered to risk their lives with his. After some moments, a few other soldiers offered to add themselves to the company, but D'Artagnan, thinking he could best oversee the mission with the original four volunteers, thanked the others and declared to M. d'Essart that he was ready to depart on command.

As the five set out down the line of a trench, D'Artagnan tried to suppress an uneasy feeling. He was worried less about the danger of the objective than about something strange in the two unknown volunteers—exactly what, he could not tell. Perhaps it was his having to trust his life to men he knew nothing about, whereas his companions from the Guards he had drilled and mounted guard with for months.

The five marched on in silence. At a turning of a corner in the trench, the bastion loomed ahead. Nothing indicated whether it was indeed occupied. Then D'Artagnan heard a whisper at his side. It was one of his companions directing his attention, not to the bastion, but to the rear: the two soldiers had disappeared! Aha! thought D'Artagnan, so their cowardly hearts have betrayed them after all. Their hasty volunteering was merely a show of bravado. Well, perhaps undertaking the mission with only two trusted companions would ultimately be best. Not losing a moment, the stouthearted three continued to advance.

Suddenly the giant stone fortress was enveloped in smoke, loud crackling rang out, and a dozen bullets whistled around the heads of the three men. That was all they needed to know; the bastion was guarded after all. To remain longer in this spot would have been imprudence, not courage. The three turned in unison and commenced a rapid retreat.

Just as they had turned the angle of the trench that would shield them from further attack, one of the Guardsmen fell. He had been hit by a bullet after all! The other continued around the corner of the trench, safe and sound, headed for the camp. D'Artagnan, however, did not have the heart to abandon his comrade. He stopped abruptly and stooped to raise him and assist him in regaining the lines. At that moment, however, two more shots were fired, one almost grazing his head. D'Artagnan's first impulse was to duck. As he paused to think what to do next, however, a strange feeling came over him. Those bullets had not come from the bastion but rather from the rear! He glanced over the trench behind him and all at once knew what was wrong with those two soldiers who had turned back and whose heads he now discerned looking out from an abandoned pit. They were hired assassins whose sole purpose was to kill him!

Two more shots rang out. His thoughts moving as quickly as the bullets, D'Artagnan dropped, falling upon the body of his comrade as if dead.

In a few moments the assassins approached D'Artagnan to be sure he was in fact dead; after all, he might only be wounded and live to denounce their crime. Fortunately, deceived by D'Artagnan's trick, they had neglected to reload their guns.

When they were within a few paces, D'Artagnan, who in falling had taken care not to let go of his sword, sprang up. The assassins, too, thought quickly. If they were to flee back to their own camp—which was also D'Artagnan's—without having killed their man, they should be accused by him; therefore, it was to the enemy that they decided to run. One of them, flailing at D'Artagnan with the barrel of his musket, by this means managed to throw D'Artagnan off balance and make his escape. The other bandit was not so lucky. D'Artagnan managed to wound him in the thigh and he fell.

On the other hand, the luck of the first bandit ran out very quickly. The Rochellais, ignorant of his intentions, fired upon him, and he fell with a bullet lodged in his shoulder.

Meanwhile, D'Artagnan had the point of his sword at the throat of the second man.

"Do not kill me!" cried the bandit. "Have mercy! I will tell all."

"Wretch!" cried D'Artagnan. "Speak quickly! Who employed you to assassinate me?"

"A woman whom I do not know, but who is called 'Milady.' "

Stunned at this revelation, D'Artagnan almost dropped his sword. His situation was becoming all too clear to him.

"But," he continued, "if you do not know this woman, how do you know her name?"

"My comrade knows her, and called her so. It was with him she agreed; he even has in his pocket a letter from her. I have heard him say that she attaches great importance to you."

"But how did you become concerned in this villainous affair?"

"He proposed that I undertake it with him, and I agreed."

"Simply proposed it? Come, how much money were you offered for this enterprise?"

"Well, a hundred livres."

"A hundred livres!" D'Artagnan almost laughed out loud. "Well! She thinks I am worth something. That would be temptation indeed for a pair of wretches like you; I am almost inclined to pardon you."

At these words, something like a flicker of hope flashed across the countenance of the bandit, and he appeared about to rise. Immediately the point of D'Artagnan's sword was again at his throat.

"Not so fast! Perhaps I shall pardon you. But only on one condition."

"What is that?" asked the soldier, uneasy at perceiving that all was not over.

"That you go and fetch me the letter your comrade has in his pocket."

"But," cried the desperate bandit, "that is only another way of killing me. How can I go and fetch that letter under the fire of the bastion?"

"All right," cried D'Artagnan. "I will show you the difference between a man of courage and such a coward as you. Wait here. I will go myself."

This maneuver required considerable agility, as well as planning, to avoid the most exposed areas. As D'Artagnan darted in zigzag fashion along the trench, bullets again came flying. But once again, he had an inspiration. When he reached the dying man, he immediately hoisted him onto his shoulders, making of the man's body a shield. As they returned, the crackle of a bullet, the feeling of a jolt, and the final cry of agony from the man wrapped around him made D'Artagnan certain that this scoundrel, who would have killed him, had now, in perishing himself, saved his life!

Once around the bend of the trench, D'Artagnan could wait no longer. He lowered the man, now a lifeless corpse, searched him and came up with a wallet in which was the following note:

Since you have lost sight of that woman, and she is now safely in the convent, which you should never have allowed her to reach, try, at least, not to miss the man. If you do, you know that my hand stretches far, and that you shall pay very dearly for the hundred livres you have from me.

There was no signature. Nevertheless the origin of this villainous writing was very plain. As he made his way back to the wounded survivor of the two would-be assassins, he mused on its implications. This Milady understandably bore him ill will for having foiled her scheme to aid the Cardinal against the Queen. But the length to which she would go in her vengeance was obviously extreme. She was no opponent to trifle with, and his life continued to be in real danger.

On the other hand, there was good news in this note that lightened his spirits considerably: "that woman" whom the note referred to was almost certainly Mme. Bonacieux! She was now

The origin of this villainous writing was very plain.

"safely in the convent." Surely Aramis, with his connections in the church, would now better be able to assist him in rescuing her.

When D'Artagnan reached the man who was waiting for him he made up his mind to say nothing about the attempted assassination. More than his dead companion who had arranged the matter, this man seemed misguided by temptation rather than truly evil.

When they arrived at the camp, they were at first greeted with astonishment, since the first man to escape the Rochellais' bullets had honestly thought that his companions had all been killed. Then D'Artagnan was acclaimed a hero, and for a day the whole army talked of nothing but this expedition. Monsieur himself personally paid his compliments to D'Artagnan, who once again basked in glory. Through it all, however, his thoughts kept turning to how he could rescue Mme. Bonacieux.

8

A Perilous Breakfast

SEVERAL DAYS passed. The flurry and scurry of war kept D'Artagnan busy, and the flying bullets and flailing swords of the Rochellais kept him from brooding about the threat to his life from a less predictable and more sinister quarter. Several positions of the Rochellais had been overcome, and the number of their dead continued to increase. Though a few strongholds continued to be occupied, signifying that the war was not over, a lull came.

One evening at this time Planchet brought a note. It was from Athos and it read:

> Must see you soon to relate glorious exploits of war. Tomorrow morning you will find us at the Parpaillot.
>
> ATHOS

This was a curious sort of note coming from Athos, who was not one to boast of his accomplishments. Something else was certainly on Athos's mind, something that he dared not put in a letter. But this was opportune. D'Artagnan himself had for a long while been bursting with things to discuss with his friends.

Therefore, early the next morning, D'Artagnan, who was fortunately now able to get away from his troops for a short time as a result of the lull in the fighting, headed to the Parpaillot, an inn near the camp that officers of all sorts were known to frequent.

Little did he imagine the result of his meeting with the Musketeers, who were indeed all there. Before he knew what was happening, Athos had them agree to a bet with a rival group of four officers that they could spend an hour at the recently taken but still dangerous Bastion St. Gervais.

"All right," said Athos at the inn. "We four shall shortly proceed to the bastion and consume our breakfast there, remaining for a full hour. If we emerge a minute before then, we buy the four of you breakfast tomorrow. If we stay, provided that we survive, it is for you to provide us with the breakfast. Agreed?"

"Agreed!" said the leader of the rival officers. He and Athos then shook hands.

Athos silently motioned to his lackey Grimaud, who was standing in a corner frequented by the servants. In his usual quiet manner, Athos let Grimaud know what he was to do, and thus it was that in fifteen minutes the four were to be seen, armed to the teeth, walking down the path to the bastion St. Gervais. Grimaud followed with a large basket containing breakfast.

Porthos and Aramis seemed a bit uneasy. As for D'Artagnan, his head was spinning. When they were out of earshot of the curious group of soldiers who watched them depart, Aramis leaned over to Athos and said, "Do you know what you are doing? If it is really as the man says, even we are foolish to go up against a hundred Rochellais!"

"My dear Aramis, do you think I would risk our lives for nothing? All will go well, I promise you." Athos paused for a moment. They were approaching the bastion where, for now at least, all was quiet. "Now, can you think of a better way for the four of us to discuss our private affairs without risk of being overheard?"

No one could contradict this. There seemed, indeed, no other way to accomplish their purpose.

Their feet crunched over loose pebbles as they filed into the half-ruined fortress, and an odor of gunpowder lingered in the air.

"Aha! So, my friend, you knew!" said Aramis with a smile when they were inside. He referred not so much to the sight—ghastly to be sure—of more than a dozen dead men, but rather to the fact that these unfortunate soldiers were heavily armed. What with the muskets and powder and bullets, which Grimaud began collecting as soon as he had spread out the breakfast upon a stone bench, they had ammunition enough to fend off a hundred Rochellais.

After they had been eating their breakfast for a few minutes, D'Artagnan looked at Athos and said, "Well, I don't suppose you really sent that note to provide an opportunity to brag of your exploits. However, what I have been unable to tell you until now I think you will find most interesting. There has been an attempt on my life—"

"—No doubt that accursed woman had something to do with it," interjected Athos.

"What! How do you—"

"Hush!" said Aramis. There had been a noise. Now there could be heard in the distance the tramping of feet on gravel. All laid down their breakfast, picked up their muskets, and scrambled to the front wall. Sure enough, a troop of half a dozen soldiers was advancing upon the bastion, expecting to find it empty. All of a sudden one of them looked up and let out a cry, and they all opened fire upon the fort. But the Musketeers and D'Artagnan, as well as the faithful Grimaud, were ready. After a few minutes of crossfire, three of the soldiers lay dead and the others had beaten a hasty retreat.

"Gentlemen," said Athos, "our breakfast is unfortunately cold by now. Nevertheless, let us make the best of it.

"Yes," Athos continued when they were seated, "D'Artagnan, my friend, all our lives are in danger so long as this demon of a woman is alive—Yes, D'Artagnan, I know more than you think." As he said this, a grim look came over his face and he swallowed a glass of wine. Immediately this brought D'Artagnan back to that horrible night and Athos's nightmarish tale.

"You no doubt remember a tale I told you about a 'friend' of mine. Well, as you must have realized, that friend was myself. And that woman, whom I thought was safely in her grave, is alive."

D'Artagnan's glance immediately darted from one to the other of the Musketeers.

"Yes, all of us now know the truth. If I can trust any of God's creatures in this world they are with me now. And by this time I think you will agree that Grimaud has proved his loyalty. Now, I think you will also agree that it is our duty to search out and bring this fiend in human shape to justice.

"It will not be an easy task. Somehow, she has become involved in the Cardinal's schemes. Moreover, she is slippery as an eel. I thought that she could not leave this area without my learning of it, yet she has vanished as suddenly as she has appeared. I first suspected her presence in these parts several weeks ago, when she was evidently up to no good."

"As I should know," interjected D'Artagnan.

"Yes, but then she vanished, only to return as mysteriously a few days ago."

"But," said D'Artagnan once again, "can you

be sure that we are talking about the same woman? Not that this woman called 'Milady' is not—"

"I can absolutely attest to her identity," replied Athos. "For I have seen her. You see," he continued, glancing Heavenward, "there is some justice left in this world. I was placed in a position to overhear a conversation between her and the Cardinal at the inn a few nights ago. Then I surprised her when she was alone before she could escape."

He paused a moment, a grim look on his face.

"I would have strangled her right there but— where would be the proof of my justification in doing so? This is not so easy a matter. Meanwhile, however, I had a good look at her and she at me. From her reaction, I know she recognized me. And, moreover, I did force from her, at the point of my sword, this."

He drew from a hidden pocket a piece of paper—wrinkled, but obviously of fine quality and with the seal of nobility. On it D'Artagnan read:

It is by my order and for the good of the State that the bearer of this has done what he has done.
RICHELIEU

D'Artagnan looked up. "This is incredible! Could it be . . . ?"

"Yes, it is a *carte blanche* from the Cardinal

himself. I do not know what story she concocted to obtain such a document from him. I do know that with it she would be able to claim the lives of almost anyone. No local magistrate or officer of the law would dare go against the written word of the Cardinal."

"In fact," said Aramis, "it is an absolution according to rule."

"The first thing to do," said D'Artagnan, who saw in Athos's hands his sentence of death, "is to tear that paper to pieces."

"On the contrary," said Athos, "it must be preserved carefully. I would not give up this paper if covered with gold. You see, this is a two-edged sword that now may be used to our purpose. Meanwhile, I must build a more certain case against this woman. She has, at all events, vanished again from these precincts, in part probably because I know too much of her past. Yet the time must come soon when we bring her to justice, or else there is no doubt that she will act first. As you see, she has already made an attempt on your life. If she meanwhile contrives a plot against any of the rest of us . . . ."

Athos broke off, turning to Aramis.

"There is something else for our young friend here, is there not?"

Now it was Aramis's turn to bring forth a piece of paper. This was a letter, and far neater in appearance than what Athos had just displayed. The writing was a woman's, and D'Artagnan read as follows:

My Dear Cousin,

   I think I shall make up my mind to set out for Béthune, where my sister has placed our little servant in the convent of the Carmelites. This poor child is quite resigned, as she knows she cannot live elsewhere without the salvation of her soul being in danger . . . .

And more of the same. It was signed by one "Marie Michon." D'Artagnan looked up at Aramis. A ray of hope shone within his heart. "Then this is about . . . ?" Aramis simply smiled slightly and nodded as he hid the paper.

The message to D'Artagnan was clear: Mme. Bonacieux, who was obviously referred to by a sort of code, had been located by Aramis's religious associates, and was now living under some kind of protection at the above-mentioned convent.

"Gentlemen, I would be honored," said D'Artagnan, "if, when you possibly can leave your duties for a time, you would assist me. For many reasons I believe that Milady may cause grave harm to be done to my beloved Constance." This was Mme. Bonacieux's first name. D'Artagnan recalled vividly the words he had read in the letter he had retrieved from the dead man who had made an attempt on his life.

"Yes, D'Artagnan," said Athos quietly, "we must act as quickly as we can. Once this fiend of a woman discovers Mme. Bonacieux's hiding place, if she has not already, one may not give two sous for the young woman's existence. Shortly I shall try to communicate with some friends of mine near the convent who may help us in bringing the consequences of the acts of a she-devil onto her own head. —What is it, Grimaud? Yes, you may speak!" His servant, whom he had trained to be silent in all but the most exceptional circumstances, was motioning vigorously from his position near the wall of the bastion that faced the town.

"Monsieur, it appears that an enormous army is advancing upon us. Let us get out of here while we may!"

All of the Musketeers but Athos jumped to their feet. Athos rose more slowly, saying, "Fear not, my friends. I have an idea." He glanced at his watch. "Fortunately we have been here over an hour." He pointed to the corpses of Rochellais strewn about the floor of the bastion. "I believe we have here a fine troop of soldiers, do we not?" He hoisted one of the bodies over his shoulder and propped it in an upright position overlooking the outlook in the wall.

"By George, that's the way!" shouted Porthos, as he and the others scrambled to arrange their massive bluff.

"Now let us take our belongings and depart without undue haste," said Athos, as a shot rang out at the lifeless figure now taken for a living soldier. "This puppet show will give us the time to depart this place like men!" Methodically, after having fired a few shots of their own out of the fortress, the four filed out of the rear entrance, Grimaud following with the remains of their breakfast.

As they neared the lines of their own side, Athos said quietly to his companions, "By now the Rochellais have discovered our ruse and retaken the bastion. It is a desperate move that cannot ultimately gain them much. But, as for ourselves, I think we are now in a position to look forward to a fine breakfast tomorrow morning! Gentlemen, in about two or three days I hope to have some news and some plans worked out. Meanwhile . . . ."

"Athos, Aramis, Porthos, how can I thank you?" exclaimed D'Artagnan. "For now I shall be silent and patient, with hope in my heart."

The four then rejoined their compatriots, a certain four of whom, in a state of amazement that the Musketeers and D'Artagnan had returned unscathed, were almost uncaring that they had lost their wager.

9

A Devilish Adversary

D'ARTAGNAN WAS now perforce separated from the Musketeers for a while, but the opportunity to rejoin his friends soon came in an unexpected way. One morning a summons came from M. d'Essart, who with a strange look in his eye gave D'Artagnan leave to see M. de Tréville. Though M. de Tréville was always like a benevolent uncle to him, D'Artagnan could not imagine the reason for this summons. He was careful to be on his best behavior as he entered the inn where M. de Tréville was headquartered, as this was also the wartime residence of the King.

D'Artagnan was asked to step into an inner chamber that was more lavishly decorated than anything he had been used to. Before he knew what he was about, he realized that seated before him on a cushioned chair was the King himself. Somewhat abashed, he started to withdraw, but M. de Tréville, who was standing next to the King, motioned him to step forward.

D'Artagnan made a low bow. Although Louis

XIII was still a relatively young man, he had a somewhat drawn look upon his face. As ever, this sign of frequent illness was mingled with impatience and boredom.

"Yes, step forward, young man. Tréville," he continued, turning his head to one side, "I suppose we must do what we must do. I am heartily sick of hearing nothing but tales of this D'Artagnan's acts of bravery. Now that the Cardinal has mentioned him as well, I suppose that we must do something to put an end to all the chatter."

The Cardinal! Could it be that a man whom D'Artagnan had come to regard as his enemy had spoken favorably of him to the King?

"Young man, you will henceforth report to M. de Tréville here, with whom I believe you are already well acquainted."

"Your Majesty, how can I ever express my gratitude—"

"Yes, yes, enough of this. Tréville, you will go with him now and make the necessary arrangements. Yes, go now. Ah, I am exceedingly sick of this place. Soon, soon I think we depart for Paris . . . ."

D'Artagnan's ears were ringing as Tréville led him out of the royal presence. It was almost too good to be true. Scarcely fully able to comprehend what was happening, D'Artagnan had suddenly been made a member of that elite group that had long been the embodiment of his highest ideals: the King's Musketeers.

Tréville had already spoken to M. d'Essart about D'Artagnan's departure. Later that day D'Artagnan bade farewell to his comrades of the Guards, wound up his affairs there, and transferred his belongings to the very inn at which his bosom companions Athos, Porthos and Aramis were quartered!

The Three Musketeers had now become the Four Musketeers!

His elation soon subsided, however, for a dangerous situation remained. Milady was still at large, and Mme. Bonacieux was still awaiting rescue. While this was so, D'Artagnan could not entirely be at ease.

Nevertheless, now that he was a Musketeer, it seemed to him that his goals, shared by his sympathizing companions, would be easier to realize. This was true; however, another occurrence that was out of their control—along with the actions of the perennially cooperative M. de Tréville—made these tasks much easier. The King, who was ever restless and easily bored, even by the noble call to war, decided to return to Paris, planning also to indulge in his favorite sport of falconry on the way. His personal guard of Musketeers was thus called away from La Rochelle before the Rochellais had been quite defeated. Since the band in its entirety was now superfluous, as even His Majesty had to admit, M. de Tréville managed to obtain permission to

The Three Musketeers had now become the Four Musketeers!

grant a portion of them leave. Naturally, the favored four were the first to be granted this leave. A pretext was easily found.

As the four rode, with their trusty servants, toward the town of Béthune, some forty leagues north of Paris, they had something new to talk about. The Duke of Buckingham had been assassinated!

"But why," asked D'Artagnan of Athos with a feeling of dread in his heart, "do you believe that Milady had anything to do with *this?*"

"That woman is a pure incarnation of evil. But, more than that, she had every reason to bear him ill will for having thwarted her scheme to discredit the Queen."

"Or the Cardinal's scheme."

"Yes, most certainly, but you may be sure that she entered into such a devilish plan as eagerly as if it had been of her own devising. And remember something else. Supposing that she *was* involved in this, she is now free to cook up more deviltry."

"And therefore, as you continue to insist, I should not attempt the rescue of Mme. Bonacieux alone."

"You are the very soul of courage and loyalty," said Aramis, "but I agree with our friend Athos. We have to do here with a woman whose propensity to evil is almost more than human. Your success in achieving your goal is, more than is ordinarily the case, in the hands of a Higher

Power. But it is just as much our duty to assist you as best we can."

These observations struck a chill into D'Artagnan's heart. D'Artagnan was afraid of no mortal; but an adversary who was a devil in human form . . . .

About four o'clock in the afternoon, a few hours before the four expected to reach Béthune, another incident occurred in the courtyard of an inn, where they were preparing for the final stage of their journey. Another gentleman emerged from another part of the same inn and mounted his horse. D'Artagnan caught a flashing glance of this man's countenance and froze: it was his nemesis, the man from Meung, the blackguard who had more recently been involved in the abduction of Mme. Bonacieux. It was for but an instant that D'Artagnan's blood froze in his veins. In an instant more, his sword was drawn and he was inches from the horse on which the man had mounted.

"You scoundrel! Draw your sword and fight like a man!" shouted D'Artagnan.

The man, startled by this outcry, turned in his saddle and, when he perceived D'Artagnan, did, in fact, draw his sword to ward off the impending attack. But at almost the same moment he dug his spurs into the flanks of his horse, seized his hat, which had almost flown off his head, and charged out of the courtyard.

D'Artagnan ran back to mount his own horse,

to the astonishment of his companions. But then he stopped, for in his better judgment he understood the futility of his efforts. The man had gotten a head start on a fresh horse, and, moreover, was headed in a different direction. To pursue him now would mean the indefinite postponement of his present mission.

As D'Artagnan and the other Musketeers stood in a circle discussing this new development, Planchet approached them.

"Excuse me, Monsieur, for interrupting," said he, "but I think this will interest you," handing over a folded piece of paper. "It fell out of the hat of the departing gentleman."

D'Artagnan read what was on the paper and then passed it around to his friends. Written on the paper was only a single word: "Armentières."

"What can this mean?" D'Artagnan was perplexed.

"Armentières," said Aramis, "is the name of a town, not very far from Béthune."

"The devil if anyone knows what these puzzles mean," said Porthos, "but hadn't we best be on our way? Béthune is still a ride of a few hours from this place."

"My friends," said Athos, retrieving the paper, "I think that it has been our great fortune to have this paper. I cannot say for sure, but I do believe that, if this man is he whom D'Artagnan thinks he is, as I have no doubt, this paper may soon prove to be worth more than its weight in gold.

"But, yes, for now we must continue on our mission. It is all the more urgent if such a man as this has been seen so close to our destination. As things are, we can only pray that we are not too late."

As the sun was setting, they had arrived at last in Béthune, and the four were now riding down the winding path from the gate of the Carmelite convent to the main building. The Mother Superior proved to be a well-bred, cultivated woman and seemed glad to receive visitors in that lonely spot.

"Well," said she, "this most pleasant young lady whom you wish to see has been the cause of our receiving more visitors here than we are accustomed to. Why, just yesterday a most distinguished guest arrived, a Comtesse de Winter, who professed a great interest in the young lady. They may be together as we speak."

At this revelation all four Musketeers jumped slightly and exchanged meaningful looks. D'Artagnan immediately inquired as to where they might visit Mme. Bonacieux and, once directed to the correct path, ran rather than walked to the building, his companions lagging behind.

D'Artagnan called out Mme. Bonacieux's name. Receiving no response, he opened the door, which had been left slightly ajar.

"M. D'Artagnan, is that you?" came a faint woman's voice from the other end of the room.

She was still there! Indeed, there she sat in an

armchair. And no one else was in the room. D'Artagnan was not too late!

In a wave of passion, he ran to her and partly lifted her from the chair.

"You need fear no more! You are under my protection now! But—what is the matter?"

Something was in fact wrong. Mme. Bonacieux wore a look of ghastly paleness and seemed hardly able to move or speak.

She stared into his eyes and murmured faintly, "D'Artagnan! D'Artagnan! Do you know? I have loved you all along!"

Could this truly be? D'Artagnan impulsively drew her to him and planted a lingering kiss on her precious lips.

But suddenly he felt her body grow limp in his arms.

"She . . . she's dead!" he murmured, as a sense of horror froze his blood in his veins. Kneeling beside the lifeless figure, he lifted his hands in prayer. "Oh, just Heavens! Can this be?"

"I'm afraid it can," came a familiar voice from behind him. He turned his head and saw that his friends had arrived. Athos, who had spoken, stood by a table examining a glass that had been there. "Poison!"

"Poison! But why?"

"I have said we are dealing not with a creature of God but rather of the devil." A grim look passed over his face as he murmured through clenched teeth, "There will nevertheless be an end to this. There must be an end." He put his arms around the still trembling D'Artagnan. "My friend, I must ask you to have patience. Bear up like a man. We will see that Mme. Bonacieux receives a decent burial." D'Artagnan began to shake uncontrollably. "Then, though it is little comfort to you now, I think finally we may see to it that justice is done."

"With the help of the Lord," said Aramis, crossing himself.

There was a guest house where the four remained for a few days. Meanwhile, Athos was strangely absent for a good part of the time.

"Our friend," said Porthos quietly to Aramis, "knows more about this than he lets on."

"Is that not always the way with Athos?" replied Aramis.

10
Milady

ALL IN ALL, the next few days were like none other that D'Artagnan ever spent. He passed hours transfixed before the coffin of his beloved Constance Bonacieux, racked by waves of weeping. Athos was frequently absent but when he returned from his mysterious outings he lost some of his typical reserve and was like a father or elder brother to D'Artagnan.

"Weep now, my boy. Have your fill of weeping," he said one time, secretly wishing he could experience such relief himself. "Soon it will be time to have your vengeance like a man."

It was indeed a strange time. After a while D'Artagnan noticed that not only was Athos absent, none of the four servants was to be seen either.

"Yes," said Porthos, "my Mousqueton is away as well. But it is necessary. Our friend Athos must have his little schemes, eh?"

Finally, having bid his last heart-wrenching good-bye to the spirit of his beloved, D'Artagnan followed the others, like an automaton, he knew

82

not where. Athos had rejoined them and they set off. They spent a morning at an inn a few leagues from Béthune.

"If we may now be permitted to know, exactly where are we headed?" asked Porthos.

"Do you remember," said Athos, "it now seems ages ago, when the faithful Planchet discovered this paper" —he now held it before them— "with the one word 'Armentières'? Well, there is a God in Heaven, for it is by this paper that justice will be done."

"Is . . . she in Armentières, then?" asked D'Artagnan.

"Yes, and under close surveillance. She will not escape us now. But, as far as I can tell, she has no suspicion that she is watched. Remember that, although she knows very well who we are, she is not likely to recognize our servants."

With this remark, some of the clouds of mystery began to clear, and D'Artagnan thought he could begin to understand something of what was going on.

In a moment, however, D'Artagnan again felt himself surrounded by mystery. A man walked in the door, unfamiliar to D'Artagnan but obviously with the dress and behavior of a man of rank. Yet no one seemed to know him.

"Gentlemen," said he, with a slight English accent, "since I am obviously not known to any of you, I must inquire—does one of you go by the name of M. Athos?"

At this inquiry, Athos's face showed a sign of recognition. "Ah, yes, I was expecting you, my lord." "My lord"—so he was a nobleman!

"Allow me," continued Athos, "to introduce my fellow Musketeers, Porthos, Aramis and D'Artagnan. My friends, this is Lord de Winter, who at my behest has come here from England."

De Winter! D'Artagnan had reason to know that name: the Duke of Buckingham had remarked to him that that was the real name of the woman often called "Milady"! D'Artagnan thought that now he could comprehend a little more of the mystery. But the relationship of this man to Milady yet remained unclear.

Lord de Winter, for reasons still known only to Athos, became a member of the party that soon set out for Armentières.

D'Artagnan still felt a chill at his heart, but Athos, whom he thought of as an older brother, inspired confidence in him like no other man, and D'Artagnan followed him without hesitation.

Indeed, Athos himself had every reason to be emotionally distraught at the recent turn of events, given especially the recently revealed connection with his own past. Yet now were his noble qualities, his self-control, his gift of command over others and over every detail of a complicated operation, in evidence as never before.

Before arrival at their final destination, which was still known only to Athos, two stops had to be made. The first was yet another small inn on the outskirts of Armentières.

"What is it that we have to do here?" inquired Aramis.

"Wait," replied Athos, consulting his watch. And they did little but that for two or three hours more. Had D'Artagnan not still been in a state of shock, the suspense would have been unbearable. As it was, Porthos did nothing but pace back and forth the whole time.

Then, when darkness had fallen, the five rode to a deserted spot on the other side of town, where there stood a dilapidated cottage just off the road. Here Athos bid them wait a moment more, and shortly he returned from the cottage with yet another member of the party.

The newcomer was an elderly man with a long beard, wearing a black hood that partially concealed his face. He said not a word. Yet another mystery! The group—now six—rode on.

Ultimately they arrived at their final destination, an even lonelier cottage in the middle of a remote field. It seemed that the cottage, visible in the moonlight, was deserted. Then D'Artagnan thought he could see a flicker of light behind a curtain in a window.

Suddenly a figure emerged from the shadows and approached Athos. It was Bazin, Aramis's manservant!

"She is there," he said softly to Athos.

"Very good," replied Athos in a whisper. "And the back door?"

"Mousqueton is posted there. Grimaud and Planchet will now join us."

"Excellent. Gentlemen, let us go."

Athos knocked several times at the front door, but there was only silence in response.

"We shall have to break down the door, I'm afraid," said Athos.

This was not too difficult, as the little wooden door was old and the latch weak.

When they entered, a young woman with ruby-red lips and a pale face surrounded by black hair jumped up from a table on which stood a flickering candle. Her beauty sharply contrasted with the squalor of her surroundings.

"Who are you? What do you want from me?" she gasped.

D'Artagnan was astonished by what he saw and by the entire situation. Could it be that they were making a grave mistake? He was not even certain he recognized this woman as Milady.

"We want justice," proclaimed Athos in a stern voice. "And you know very well who we are. You also know the crimes for which you have to answer."

Though Milady was a consummate actress, alarm showed in the flickering of her eyes around the room. Still, an innocent woman surprised by a strange band of men would show alarm as well as a guilty one.

"It has been many years," continued Athos, "and perhaps you don't recognize me. But you know your brother-in-law, Lord de Winter, and—"

With a little gasp, she turned and attempted to bolt out of the back door, only to come face to face with Mousqueton. Grimaud and Planchet, who had entered behind the Musketeers, seized her arms. Soon she was again seated, Bazin pointing a loaded pistol at her head.

"If you have come for vengeance," she cried, "how can you be certain you are not mistaken? Your—"

"It is not vengeance we desire but justice. We have sufficient proof." He pointed to the mysterious man who had recently joined them. "This man has the ultimate proof of your identity. You may remember him as the Executioner of Lille."

Milady let out a stifled gasp but otherwise remained silent.

"Let us begin," continued Athos, "and have done with this hideous business. I shall start the proceedings.

"Charlotte Backson, *alias* Lady de Winter, *alias* Milady, you are hereby accused of the following crimes. First, you married me under false pretenses while living in sin with a man you falsely claimed was your brother and while you were in secret a branded criminal. D'Artagnan, you next."

D'Artagnan, transfixed by the horror of all this, nevertheless mustered his courage, stepped up and, drawing out the paper he had taken from his would-be assassins, said:

"And I accuse you, first, of having murdered Constance Bonacieux in cold blood. Second, I accuse you of having attempted to have me murdered, as this paper proves."

"Good," said Athos. "Now, Lord de Winter . . . ."

De Winter stepped forward, rage written across his face. "I accuse you, first, of having falsely married my brother, the late Lord de Winter, although you were already married, and, then, of having murdered him for his money. Second, I accuse you of having inspired a crazed fanatic to assassinate the Duke of Buckingham. This murderer, a man I had entrusted to keep watch over you, had been in my employ, and I shall regret that the rest of my life. Nevertheless the guilt remains on your shoulders. I believe you are next, sir." He looked at the strange man who had last joined them.

"Charlotte Backson," he began in a cracked voice, "or shall I still call you the Comtesse de Fère?" The Comtesse de Fère? Here at last was the missing link. Although Athos had revealed much of his past to his friends, implying that he was of high birth, he had never actually told them his real name. The Comte de Fère! That meant that he represented one of the noblest families in France. When the Musketeers began to realize the significance of this, they darted inquiring looks at him. D'Artagnan thought he perceived only a faint nod in response.

"I accuse you, first, of having murdered Constance Bonacieux in cold blood."

Meanwhile, the former Executioner of Lille continued, "You may or may not remember me, although I think you do. For it was I who branded you in punishment for your sacrilegious act against the Church. And it was my brother who was the priest whom you seduced into living with you in sin. And then, when you thought he would turn against you for having murdered Lord de Winter, you poisoned him." He turned to Athos. "Is that all?"

"Yes. It is more than enough to justify what we are about to do." He looked at the servants. "Seize her and bring her outside."

This they did. At first she began to struggle like a trapped animal but soon saw that it was no use.

"Wait!" cried D'Artagnan, touched by her relative youth and, if truth be told, her beauty. "Can it not be that we are making a terrible mistake? Death is final. If given another chance she may repent . . . ."

Athos stepped between Milady and D'Artagnan, facing the latter, his hand on the hilt of his sword.

"D'Artagnan! You are to me like a brother. Yet were you my blood brother, my own son, I would sooner run this sword through you than let this fiend go unpunished." D'Artagnan knew that Athos was right, and said nothing more. In a softer tone, Athos then said, "Perhaps you will want to wait here with Porthos and Aramis. The rest of us will not be gone long."

Porthos put his arm around D'Artagnan and led him to a chair as the others marched out the door.

About five minutes later a muffled cry came from the distance.

In another few minutes Athos returned alone. "The others will attend to the disposal of the body. We may now depart."

Slowly, the other Musketeers rose and filed out of the door to retrieve their horses.

"Gentlemen," said Athos, "soon, I assure you, we will feel relief as we realize that the world is now rid of a demon. This has not been a pleasant task, but at last justice has been done. We may now return to Paris."

Of my story, little remains to be told. D'Artagnan had been afraid that when the execution of Milady became known to the Cardinal, he and his companions might end up in the Bastille for their audacity. Instead, the Cardinal was relieved to be rid of an accomplice whom even he had had difficulty keeping under control. The Musketeers were allowed to go their own way. D'Artagnan in fact soon was surprised to receive a commission as a lieutenant.

Alas, this was at first of little comfort, for he soon had to say farewell to his friends. Athos returned to his old life as the Comte de Fère, living on a distant estate. Porthos, on finding that the husband of his "duchess" had died, proved his loyalty by marrying the woman, and soon he departed the Musketeers to live on her inheritance. Aramis kept his faith with the Church and retired to a monastery. D'Artagnan eventually became captain of the Musketeers, an ever-courageous but older and wiser man.

Of the King, the Queen, the Cardinal and the nation of France—their fate is history.

THE END